PRAISE F[illegible]S

ENC[illegible]

"[Tina Wainscott's] current nov[illegible]AT augments her growing reputation for some of the finest off-beat tales on the market today . . . Anyone who wants to read a believable enactment of the unbelievable needs to peruse a Wainscott novel because she makes the impossible possible."
—Harriet Klausner

"Tina Wainscott has her finger firmly on the pulse of the romance genre, and with IN A HEARTBEAT she catapults to the top of her peers . . . A unique plot complements characters of depth and perception that fold in and around a story as fresh and exhilarating as a spring breeze. Run, don't walk, to the nearest bookstore to buy this novel, which could possibly be the best contemporary of the year."
—Kathee Card, *Under the Covers*

Second Time Around

WON BEST SUPERNATURAL ROMANCE IN
AFFAIRE DE COEUR'S READER/WRITER POLL

"Ms. Wainscott has a talent for making unusual situations believable . . . Bravo!"
—*Rendezvous*

"A fabulous romantic suspense drama that melts readers' hearts . . . SECOND TIME AROUND is worth reading the first time around, the second time around, and the *n*th time around."
—*Affaire de Coeur*

"This highly satisfying paranormal romance is a must read . . . SECOND TIME AROUND is a well-written, romantic, feel-good story."
—*Gothic Journal*

More . . .

Dreams of You

"A delightful and compelling romance with two memorable protagonists and an assortment of true-to-life street people. A tenderly beautiful fairy tale. Readers will be enthralled!"
—*Affaire de Coeur*

"A fast-paced contemporary, hot and spicy with a hero to die for. Enjoy!"
—Kat Martin, bestselling author of *Silk and Steel*

On the Way to Heaven

"Talented newcomer Tina Wainscott makes a smashing debut . . . An exciting blend of page-turning suspense and sensual romance with a heavenly twist."
—Marilyn Campbell, author of *Pretty Maids in a Row*

"Contemporary romance with an intriguing twist. A pleasure for fans of romantic suspense and the paranormal."
—Deborah Smith, author of *Silk and Stone*

"A winner . . . Tina Wainscott's fantastic debut provides the audience with an enjoyable reading experience."
—*Paperback Forum*

"A fantastic debut novel that promises to enthrall, entertain and leave readers believing in the miracle of true love."
—*The Talisman*

Shades of Heaven

"Tina Wainscott is a promising author with her star on the rise. *Shades of Heaven* is a touching and memorable tale of second chances and the love and courage it takes to accept them."
—*Romantic Times*

"A fantastic romance . . . Readers will be enchanted and clamor for more from terrific Tina Wainscott."
—*Affaire de Coeur*

St. Martin's Paperbacks Titles
by Tina Wainscott

ON THE WAY TO HEAVEN

SHADES OF HEAVEN

DREAMS OF YOU

SECOND TIME AROUND

IN A HEARTBEAT

A TRICK OF THE LIGHT

A Trick of the Light

Tina Wainscott

St. Martin's Paperbacks

A TRICK OF THE LIGHT

Author photograph on inside back cover by Bob's Photos.

ISBN: 0-312-97403-5

Printed in the United States of America

St. Martin's Paperbacks edition / March 2000

St. Martin's Paperbacks are published by St. Martin's Press, 175 Fifth Avenue, New York, N.Y. 10010.

10 9 8 7 6 5 4 3 2 1

This book is dedicated to my mom, Christine Ritter.
Thanks for everything that you do, who you are,
and all the love you have given me my whole life.
I love you, Mom.

This book is also for Craig, Laurie, Kayla and Kyle.
For dreams lost and new dreams found . . .

Acknowledgment

My sincere appreciation to Arnie Gruskin and Terry G. for advice on family law.

A Trick of the Light

Chapter One

THE VOICES IN HER HEAD WERE MAKING WANDA McKain's brain hurt. Urgent whispers, too many of them and louder than usual:

Hide your son.

Don't let anyone know he's different.

Dylan doesn't understand different people. You know how he is; everything has to look so freakin' normal.

She knew why, and she'd thought she could fit into his life anyway. When she'd fallen in love with Dylan, the voices had stopped. She thought their love had cured her. He was taller than a superhero, gorgeous like a movie star, with dreams of living a successful, normal life. It sounded like Heaven. All she'd had to do was keep her own past a secret.

Then the voices came back, on her wedding day, no less. She backed away from him whenever the murmur of voices kicked in. Luckily he started working a lot after that first year.

He'll find out you've got crazy in your blood, maybe even put you back in the hospital.

Just that terrifying thought reinforced her mission. Her dad had called her crazy. Mommy was too timid to defend her. The voices said her parents were the crazy ones, but those people in the hospital believed them, not her. She knew other people heard voices. They put bumper stickers on their cars that read, I DO WHAT THE VOICES IN MY HEAD TELL ME. Why was she considered crazy when they weren't?

She'd gotten good at pretending she was normal, giving the responses the doctors—and the world—expected. She'd even fooled Dylan. But the voices were getting more insistent. They told her she couldn't fool Dylan much longer. Just the other day she'd answered out loud, and he'd looked at her funny. Three times now Camilla, their housekeeper, had caught her talking to them. It was only a matter of time, the voices said, until they'd take Teddy from her and put her away.

Once she and Teddy and Mommy were hidden away, Wanda wouldn't have to pretend. She could get fat, luxuriously fat, and not worry what people thought of her, because no one else would be around. The voices had worked out all the details. She'd been consumed with "the plan" for two months now. It was finally time to act.

Get moving!

But don't drive too fast.

Use your signals.

"Shhh!" She waved away the voices. "I hate when you all talk at the same time." She glanced back at her son. He was strapped in the back seat, lost in his own world. The doctor had confirmed her fears that Teddy was different. Wanda knew the doctor would ignore her pleas not to tell Dylan.

"I'll protect you," she said to Teddy in a strangled voice she barely recognized as her own. "We're going to go away together so no one will ever know."

She pulled into the nursing home complex where her mother lived. Ironic, wasn't it, that Mommy was now in a home all these years later. Anne Dodson had Alzheimer's, or that's what they told Wanda. The voices said it wasn't true, that the nurses were trying to trick them. Maybe they were performing experiments on the people who resided there. Anne was all right. She just forgot things once in a while.

Wanda went through the procedure to sign out her mother, keeping the voices at bay. People looked at her strangely if she let the voices distract her. Sometimes she'd forget and tell them to shut up, only to find a startled cashier or waitress staring at her.

"Have a nice vacation," the desk clerk said as Wanda hurried her mother out of the cheery lobby. That's what Wanda had told them, that she was taking her mother on a week-long trip to North Carolina.

"Are you new?" Anne asked, blinking as Wanda pulled her out into the sunlight. "They keep hiring new people all the time, how's a girl supposed to keep up with all those faces when they keep changing?"

"Mommy, it's me, Wanda. Your daughter. Remember how I told you I needed you? You gotta take care of Teddy for a couple of hours." Once she had Anne strapped into the passenger seat, she said, "We're going to the safe place now. No more nurses, nobody looking at you like you're crazy, no more having to pretend you're just like everyone else. I'm going to take you and Teddy to the safe place first, then I have to go home for a few minutes. It's all part of 'the plan.' Camilla won't even know me and Teddy are missing until she leaves for the day, and maybe not even then. We'll have plenty of time to get into place. You have to take care of Teddy while I'm gone."

Anne nodded. "That's important, isn't it? You said it with an important tone in your voice."

"Yes, it's important."

"Take care of Teddy," Anne repeated. "I can remember that."

As Wanda pulled away from the nursing home, the

voices got louder. She shook her head, but that only made her dizzy. "Stop it! I'm taking care of Teddy. You hear? Nobody's going to get to him now."

CHLOE SAMMS was led in to see Mr. Barnes, the senior partner of the Fifth Avenue law firm. She had to remind herself to shake his hand. Having grown up in a community of women, she usually greeted people with a hug.

No way was she going to hug Mr. Barnes. He had bulging eyes in a wide, speckled face and reminded her of those fat little pacman frogs she'd seen in Petland. His chin didn't pulse with his breathing . . . only when he swallowed. She pasted on an optimistic smile, but before she could say anything, he said, "You've come to see if I'm hiring your accounting firm."

"You said you'd have a decision by today."

A respectable law firm in the heart of Naples, Florida, would be a nice way to lend credibility to C. S. Accounting. Lord knew she needed all the credibility she could get.

"I'm afraid I've decided to go elsewhere." He held up his hand, as though expecting a rebuttal. "It's nothing personal." His gaze slid over her, lingering on a chest she did everything to downplay. "You're a cute thing and all—"

Don't let him see your disappointment. Be tough, be strong. "I'm not all that cute, really." She grimaced. "I can be downright ugly if I put my mind to it. You should see me in the morning." She rolled her eyes. "What I mean is . . ." She hated when she got this way, jabbering and making it more than obvious that she was desperate for this account. She gestured toward her shoulder-length blond hair. "Beneath these curls is a brain, Mr. Barnes." She picked up a ledger on his desk and glanced down the list. "The total is forty-two thousand five hundred and fifteen dollars. Go ahead and check it."

He took the ledger back. "I'm sure you are smart, Ms. Samms. I like your spunk, and that's why I even considered hiring your firm."

"But?" She'd tried to inject strength into that word, but it came out like a drizzle.

"My partners felt that having someone associated with Lilithdale wouldn't be a wise public relations move."

She took a deep breath, not sure if she wanted to scream or cry. "Fourteen hundred twenty-two divided by twelve equals one-eighteen and a half. Seventy-eight times twelve equals nine thirty-six."

"Now, Ms. Samms, don't embarrass us both by grovel— What did you say?"

"Some people count to ten. I do calculations." It was a habit that had started when she was six. Usually she did it in her head, but sometimes she was so mad, she had to say it aloud to keep anything else from spouting out. She nodded curtly and turned to the door.

"Oh, Ms. Samms? I gotta know, is it true what they say? That you girls have drunken orgies out there?"

"I hate to crush your lurid fantasies, but there are no orgies. On New Year's Eve the residents take a skinny-dip in the bay. It's a symbolic way of shedding last year's baggage, bad memories . . . and negative feelings toward pigheaded, demoralized men who have nothing but sex on their minds."

His expression didn't change at all. "So . . . are you all lesbians or what?"

It wasn't a new question; heck, Chloe had had to answer this one hundreds of times. This creep wanted it to be true. "The women who live in Lilithdale are as heterosexual as you." Her gaze slid over what she could see of the man. "Probably more so. They just don't have any need for"—*let's see if it sinks in this time*—"pigheaded, demoralized men who have nothing but sex on their minds."

He sat back in his chair. His leering smile faded, but his smugness remained in place. "If I didn't know better, I'd think you meant that as a slanderous insult against me personally."

Not only him. It also applied to another man who had done more than make her angry; he'd shattered her heart into a hundred and twenty-one pieces. She gave Barnes her sweetest smile. "If I implied that you were a blunt-minded, frog-faced, depraved, sorry excuse for a man, I'm sure I meant it in the nicest possible way."

She walked out, leaving the door swinging open. Outside, she leaned against the wall and closed her eyes. *I can't believe I said that to him.* She didn't know whether she should feel ashamed, proud, or angry. At the moment, all three fought for dominance. She felt the slightest smile break free, then a choked laugh. Then the snorting kind of laughter that brought tears to her eyes.

She pushed away from the wall and caught her reflection in a jewelry store window. Definitely she wore her hand-in-the-cookie-jar face. Her smile faded. Maybe she could hack off her curls, deepen her voice. She didn't dress cute, though her yen for pastels probably didn't help. Cute was tiny, and she was too full-figured to be considered tiny. But cute wasn't her biggest problem; Lilithdale was. The bane of her existence. The place she'd called home since her mother died of breast cancer and left her in her aunts' care when she was five.

Lilithdale started out as a refuge for a handful of repressed women back in the fifties. The newly independent women took over a small undeveloped part of east Marco Island. They built a large house and lived by selling seashells to tourist shops. More women came and settled in, but not because they were repressed. They were oddities in their own worlds. Many were psychic in nature, seeing visions, auras, or, in the case of one woman, a person's last moments on earth. One woman talked to dead people, and there was her Aunt Stella, who communicated with animals.

Belle had so much energy in her body she could light up a bulb by just holding it in her hand. Irina had once been billed "the strongest woman in the world." She could pull a car with her teeth. And then there were women who believed they had some kind of gift, but nobody could say for sure whether they really did or not. No matter what ability you believed you had—whether it was real or not—you belonged in Lilithdale.

Unless you had no special ability, like Chloe. Besides her gift with numbers (which didn't count, since it was left-brained and too ordinary), she had nothing, not even good instincts. Her ordinariness made her an anomaly in Lilithdale; her connection to Lilithdale made her an odd-ball to the rest of the world. The only person Chloe could intimately relate to was Marilyn of the Addams family, who was pitied for her normality.

"Can I . . . help you?" An attractive blonde dressed in silk and linen was leaning out of the doorway. She didn't want to help, not by the way her gaze disdainfully took in Chloe's pantsuit or the way her lip lifted at the sight of Chloe's green Keds. There was nothing wrong with her Keds. Thanks to her grandma, the dyeing guru, her shoes were a perfect match to her outfit. What the blonde was really saying was, *Stop blocking our first-class window with your second-class self.*

Just like she'd done for years, Chloe swept her gaze

down the woman's attire, pretending to find something amiss. "I can't imagine a thing you could help me with." Head and shoulders high, she spun around and walked away. It didn't hurt. Not even a tiny bit.

The sun sparkled on the Porsches and BMWs parked along Fifth Avenue. Her green '66 T-Bird didn't stand out like a bruised knuckle. It didn't.

A gorgeous guy was eating a sandwich on the whale's tail of his Porsche. She smiled at his cleverness in finding a table, but he looked right through her. Men in suits and women in outfits that probably cost more than Chloe's whole wardrobe passed her on the sidewalk. She heard snatches of conversations, this stock going up, the Heart Association's gala that weekend, look, new Ferragamos in the window, I'm going to try them on. Not even a mention of going fishing that afternoon, good vibes, or getting their chakras cleared. What was she even doing there?

Forget the Porsches, the snooty blonde, and the frogman, she told herself. *Enjoy the perfect winter day.*

In Naples, Florida, winter meant the temperature barely had the decency to dip into sweater-wearing weather. It was too warm, but the snowbirds that migrated from the north to take up residence in their condos weren't complaining.

She pulled out the list Aunt Stella had given her. Buy a bacon-scented chew toy for her session with the troubled Great Dane. Pick up plum foot cream from the Day Spa for Gisella. Then Sangeeta needed Chloe's help at the tea house for a few hours while she went to regress to her previous lives at Aunt Lena's Total Balance Women's Center. Oh, and she was supposed to pick up Nita's books so she could work on the monthly accounting.

Two hundred and fifty women now lived in Lilithdale,

most having moved down once they'd packed their kids off to college. Chloe had been the only child to grow up there. Over the years the surrounding communities had taken notice of their psychic neighbors and started going for readings. While they were there, they had tea and tofu and sometimes stayed for dinner. Slowly it had become a mecca for women seeking anything from a psychic reading to advice, from animal counseling to a bookstore specializing in women's tomes.

While the residents welcomed visitors, they abhorred leaving town, so they always loaded Chloe with errands whenever she drove into Naples. Since their requests were accompanied by hugs, how could she resist?

Chloe's smile faded when she remembered Gisella's warning: "Be extra careful today. I feel something bad's gonna happen."

DYLAN MCKAIN met with Judge Neely late that morning. When a judge asked for a meeting in her chambers, Dylan thought it unwise to tell her that most of his clients came to his office.

Neely told him to make himself comfortable in the wood-paneled office. "We almost met two months ago. The mayor's open house party. You did a fabulous job designing his house."

"Thank you." The mayor had made him the official guest of honor. Not only did Dylan hate being the center of attention—although for his firm's sake, he'd suffer it—Wanda had manufactured her usual crisis before every important social event. People were beginning to wonder if he'd made up a wife, since she never made any appearances.

"I understand you're doing the Kraft Theater on Third

Street. *N* magazine said you were the sole architect. The kind of project to elevate your firm to national status."

"It's an exciting project. The exposure is just a bonus."

"My husband and I are planning to build a home in Pelican Bay and we want you personally to design it for us."

Dylan usually had a hard time saying no to opportunities like this. But he'd made himself a promise that morning and he was going to stick with it. "I'm afraid I can't. I've already had to delegate my projects to my associates because of the theater. But I have talented people who do great work."

The judge surprised him with her pout. "But we want you."

He smiled. "I appreciate that, but the theater is going to take all of my professional time for the next several months. If you're not in a hurry, I'd be glad to schedule an appointment as soon as the theater requires less time."

"Sure you can't put in some evening hours if I pay you a bonus?"

"Afraid not. I already work too many weekends and evenings. Frankly, I need to spend more time at home." This morning he'd eaten his bagel at the empty table and realized the sacrifice he was making. He never saw his son anymore. Teddy was still asleep when Dylan woke, and Wanda usually had him put to bed by the time he got home. Whenever he made a point to spend time with his son, Teddy was either sick or tired from playing.

Neely's pout disappeared. "All right, I can understand that. Family should always come first. Put me on your schedule." She gave him a wink. "I want to be first on your list."

Dylan shook her hand. "Count on it."

It was strange, the ache he'd gotten that morning as

he'd looked at his son's booster seat and realized he never saw Teddy sitting there. He had to make time for his son. He glanced at his Movado watch as he walked to his Mercedes. It was early, but maybe he'd stop by the house on his way back to work and have lunch with his son. He had to go right by Royal Harbor anyway.

He felt good about seeing Teddy on the spur of the moment until he saw Wanda's car in the garage. Odd that the garage door was open. He looked at her BMW and for a moment didn't want to go inside.

She never complained about his long hours and never accused him of neglecting his family. In fact, she seemed agitated when he did decide to take a weekend morning off or come home early. He just figured he threw off her schedule—like he was doing today.

Lately she'd been acting odd, like disappearing for a few hours and not telling him where she'd been. He would have suspected an affair, but she didn't look . . . satisfied. Then again, what did satisfaction look like exactly?

He pushed himself out of the car. He nearly collided with her as she barreled out the door that separated the garage and the laundry room.

Her eyes went wide with panic. "Dylan! What are you doing home? You're not supposed to be here."

She looked guilty, and he rethought the affair idea. "I had an appointment down at the courthouse and thought I'd stop by and see Teddy."

"Courthouse?" She wrapped one arm around her waist and chewed the tips of her fingers.

"A judge wants me to design her house," he said absently, taking in Wanda's disheveled appearance and dowdy clothing. Maybe not an affair, then. "What's wrong? Where were you going in such a hurry?"

"Nothing. Nowhere. What's with all the questions? I was going out for a walk, that's all. And you can't see Teddy. I just put him down for a nap."

He checked his watch. "Already? He's only been up a few hours."

"He was tired."

"You said you were going to take him to the doctor—"

"I did and there's nothing wrong with him. He's perfectly normal. Why don't you go on to work? I know you're busy with that new project. Come on, I'll walk you to your car."

Every nerve ending went on alert. He glanced at the door behind her, then at her hand as she tugged on his arm. The only time she ever touched him lately was when she was trying to get rid of him. And no doubt that's what she was after now.

He didn't budge. "Is Camilla working today?"

"Of course. Her car's right there, and isn't she always here, right on time every weekday from seven to three? She's cleaning the pool right now. Dylan, you really should get going. I don't want you to lose this project. I know how important it is to you."

Her face was flushed and splotchy now. Wanda wouldn't have a lover hidden away inside, not with Camilla and Teddy there. He realized she played this game a lot, keeping him from his son. But she'd never been desperate before. He jerked his arm free and walked inside.

Instead of following him, she grabbed her car keys and walked back out to the garage. Something wasn't right. Why was Wanda running from him? He glanced to the hallway where Teddy's room was. A car engine started. He had to make a decision. He bolted out to the garage in time to see her back up, then gun the car around the drive. She nearly hit the fountain. Her tires squealed as she maneuvered the circle and turned onto the street. He didn't have to think about it; he jumped into his Mercedes and followed her.

When she reached U.S. 41, she paused at the light. Her eyes widened in the rearview mirror when she saw him. She gestured as though she were talking to someone in the car. The light turned green, and she punched the gas and made a left. Traffic was jammed up because of construction, but she managed to maneuver around the lanes. He wasn't about to let her get away. He knew Teddy wasn't at the house. Dylan sure as hell hoped he wasn't in the car.

He managed to catch up to her at the Goodlette Road light. He waved her over, but she kept going. She ran the red at the Four Corners intersection, causing a ruckus of brake squeals and blaring horns. He followed her. She wouldn't hurt Teddy. But at the moment she was acting crazy.

Wanda charged down Fifth Avenue, going way too fast for a busy shopping area filled with tourists and businesspeople. If she was stupid enough to endanger her life, there wasn't much he could do about that. But to endanger others . . . and what if Teddy *was* in the car?

Dylan had to drive just as crazily to keep up with her. He beeped his horn to warn people to get out of the way. Others beeped too, and pedestrians waved their arms at her recklessness. Traffic slowed her down as someone made a right turn—but only for a second. She swerved into the oncoming lane to go around.

Dylan's heart stopped when he saw the woman herding a Muscovy duck across the street. She looked like an angel, with the sun lighting up her blond curls. She checked for traffic to the left, not even looking in their direction. The duck reached the sidewalk. Wanda wasn't slowing down; she was looking at Dylan.

Dylan slammed on his horn. Everything went into slow motion, including his heartbeat. The woman looked up. The expression on her face changed from disbelief to terror. A car wasn't supposed to be coming from that direction, that's what she was thinking. Wanda hit her brakes and swerved, but it was too late. Dylan's body shook as the car made impact. The woman flew several yards through the air and landed on the sidewalk.

The sound of shattering glass filled the air. Everything froze, except for the sick feeling in his stomach. People on the sidewalk stared with horror on their faces. It felt like hours passed in that frozen state. Then, as though someone had released the pause button, everyone broke out of their trances. The woman was surrounded by a crowd, and only when he couldn't see her anymore could he focus on Wanda.

Her car had gone through a plate-glass window and been stopped by an interior wall. The horn wailed. He felt a sickening chill in his stomach. Then the paralysis dropped away as he pulled down a side street and propelled himself from the car. His first thought was Teddy. If he'd been in the car . . .

Relief washed over him when he saw the empty car seat. Wanda was drooped against the steering wheel, and her head was twisted at an angle. Her eyes stared at nothing. He started to reach in through the shattered window.

"Don't move her!" a man behind the counter shouted, dropping the phone with a thud. "Something might be broken. I just called for help. We'd better wait."

Something probably *was* broken, and beyond repair. The chill spread slowly through him. "I'm going to check her pulse." She was still warm. She had to be alive. His finger slid against the blood on her neck. He felt nothing, not even a shallow beat. Where were the ambulances already?

"Keep an eye on her," he told the guy in the store, and walked outside. His brain was on automatic now. As he walked around to the trunk of Wanda's car, he called Camilla on his cell phone. "Is Teddy there?"

"What's wrong?" she asked.

"Is Teddy there?" he asked more urgently, jamming his key into the lock of the trunk.

"No, sir, he's not. Mrs. McKain took him out early this morning, right after you left."

"Where did she take him?" He wrenched the lid open and breathed in relief. No Teddy. He didn't think Wanda would put her son in the trunk, but nothing made sense right now.

"I don't know, sir. Is something the matter?"

Dylan headed across the street. "She didn't bring him back when she returned?"

"This will sound strange, but she pretended to have him with her. I mean, she was talking to him real loud, like she wanted me to hear. But I didn't see him."

"Make sure he's not in the house. I'll call you back."

He approached the crowd of people surrounding the woman Wanda had hit. His heart felt leaden. This was his fault. If he hadn't been chasing Wanda, none of this would have happened.

He could only see glimpses of her through the crowd, the beautiful woman who'd just seconds before been trying to save a duck's life. Blood reddened those golden curls and stained her pale green pantsuit.

And then he heard someone say, "Oh, my God, she's dead."

Chapter Two

MISPLACING YOUR PURSE OR KEYS WAS ONE THING. MISplacing your body . . . well, that could be a real problem. And yet, Chloe felt the most incredible peace and light, as though she'd floated into a cloud. Warm, fuzzy sunlight surrounded her and seemed to penetrate her being, whatever that was at the moment. It was different than any other light she had ever seen, from clear sunrise-filled mornings to a crisp moonlit winter night. It was almost . . . solid, or maybe more like a liquid.

She started to close her eyes and absorb the essence of this wondrous place . . . then she realized it. She belonged here. For the first time in her life, she fit in. Even though she wasn't sure she actually had a mouth, she knew she was smiling.

But things started to change. The misty clouds began swirling, slowly at first, then faster. They formed a vortex of shimmering white light. Chloe could still feel the peace, joy, and acceptance, but as she looked down the circular walkway that spiraled out of view, she knew it was time to move on. No chance to say farewell to her aunts or grandma or her pets. Sadness filled her soul at the thought of never seeing them again. Time to step into Heaven. Embracing that thought, and the light that beckoned her forward, she took her first step.

Shadowy silhouettes advanced from the far end of the tunnel. She wasn't afraid. She could hardly remember what fear was like. Even the grief was fading.

There were maybe eight people—she guessed they

were people—all walking forward to greet her. Chloe waited for them. They would guide her, she knew this.

Another silhouette emerged from behind and walked around the others with hurried movements. Her mother, maybe? Chloe's spirit lifted at the thought.

It was a woman, but Chloe didn't recognize her face. It had been twenty-five years since she'd last seen Mom. Still, she expected some flash of recognition.

She wondered if she looked the way this woman did, ethereal like a holograph, moving without actually walking, clothing blurred to indistinct lines.

"I'm so sorry," the woman said, pain etched in her face. "You must understand, I thought I was doing the right thing . . . at the time. I believed those voices, though now I realize it was crazy. Everything is so clear here, and . . . I'm so sorry. What have I done?"

Chloe wasn't sure what the woman was sorry about. "It's all right. I'm here now, where I belong."

"No, you can't stay! You've got to go back and save my son. Teddy needs you."

"But . . ." Chloe gestured toward herself. "I can't go back, not now."

"They said you could. I can't go back; it was my fault. But you can, because you're innocent."

Chloe looked ahead. "But they're waiting for me. And I want to stay here."

The woman's desperation was a tangible thing, like the light. "I've done a terrible thing, and only you can make it right. My son is special . . . different. He needs your help. I hid him away, thinking I was protecting him . . . and myself. I need you to get him and take him to his father."

Chloe was pretty sure she couldn't go back, but this

woman's desperation touched her so deeply, she said, "All right, I'll go back and find Teddy. Where is he?"

Other voices intruded. Just murmurs at first, then urgent words from a distant plane: "Come on, come on." She searched for the source, but saw nothing. The silhouettes that had been coming toward her were fading into the distance. She turned back to the woman, who was also fading. "Where's Teddy?"

The woman opened her mouth. Instead of words, a siren blared.

In that instant, the pure, joyous light transformed to harsh sunlight. Electricity rocketed through her body. She was engulfed with a sense of pain and heaviness. The air around her had changed too, and breathing became an effort. She smelled a woodsy cologne. Her cheek ached. Her chest hurt. And then a mouth came down over hers, and a gust of warm breath filled her lungs. She felt the pressure of a hand pushing in rhythm on her chest, then of a finger pressed against her throat. A hoarse male voice said, "She's back."

"We've got her, thanks," a woman said.

Chloe tried to open her eyes, but they were too heavy. Who had her? She'd started the journey to Heaven. Now she was back where she didn't belong. She wanted to cry.

"Can you hear me?" the woman said.

Chloe tried opening her eyes, squinting in the sun. The first person she saw wasn't a medic. It was a man standing nearby. He was tall, with dark hair and eyes, and he was looking at her as though he'd seen a ghost.

"Can you tell us your name?" another medic said, drawing her attention away from the man. "What day is it?"

It took her a minute, but she remembered everything. She wanted to replay those earlier moments, back in the vortex, but the medic kept interrupting her thoughts. Had it even been real?

As they strapped her onto a gurney, the medic asked, "Who's Teddy?"

"What?"

"You asked where Teddy was when you came back. Is he your son? Is he here somewhere?"

She looked at the crowd of people gawking as though she were part of some macabre show. "I said that?"

"Yeah. We figured it must have meant something."

Her eyes met the man's again. "It did. I just don't know what."

DYLAN WATCHED the medics slide Chloe Samms into the ambulance. He'd heard her faint voice recite her name and birth date, just thirty years old. More importantly, he'd heard her say his son's name.

This had to be a nightmare, despite the glaring sun and crowd. Everything was revolving around him like a carnival ride. The scenes flashed around and around in his mind. The last several minutes were a haze.

"Excuse me, sir, we need to clear the area," a policeman said, ushering him to the sidewalk.

The ambulance holding Chloe came to life, sirens whooping as it inched forward through the crowd. He hurried back to Wanda in time to see the medics loading a sheet-covered gurney into another ambulance.

"That's my wife," he said.

"I'm sorry, sir. She broke her neck. There was nothing we could do for her."

Dylan watched the ambulance drive away without benefit of sirens. He'd known deep inside that she was dead the moment he'd seen her, but he still couldn't believe it. No matter how distant they'd become to each other, she was still his wife and the mother of his child. She was still a person, and now she was gone. The pain welled up in his throat and stole his breath away.

Then he saw the light green sneaker lying on the sidewalk. Chloe's sneaker. His insides caved in, and he had to choke back a sound of anguish.

Both women had died; but one had come back.

And that woman had come back with his son's name on her lips. It was a coincidence, surely. Teddy was probably her husband or lover. Maybe even her own son. Still, it was eerie.

"Mr. McKain!" one of the police officers called out. "We need to talk with you. We understand you were following your wife, and she hit the young lady who was crossing the street."

Dylan winced. It was his fault. No matter that it was Wanda's car that hit Chloe Samms, Dylan had caused her flight. "I can't talk right now. I have to find my son."

HIS SON was gone, really gone. Dylan and Camilla had checked the house twice, their voices echoing in the tile and glass rooms as they called Teddy's name. Everything was in its place, just so, everything except for Teddy. What he wouldn't give to find his son hiding behind one of the huge pots filled with silk flowers. He'd been methodical in his search, covering every place a three-year-old could find as refuge. He checked the garage, the shed, the attic, and even their hardly used boat. Then he tackled the yard, his shoes sinking into the thick St. Augustine grass.

Royal Harbor, an older, upscale neighborhood that skirted Naples Bay, was undergoing a resurgence. Although his firm had done remodeling plans for some of the homes in his area, he didn't know any of the people living nearby. He got to meet several of them as the search grew more frantic. He was surprised to find that no one knew Wanda.

"She kept to herself," the woman next door said with a shrug. "I invited her over for lunch a couple of times. My husband works a lot too, and I thought it'd be nice to have company. But she was busy every time I asked her, so I stopped asking."

"She wouldn't even wave at you," another neighbor said. "She'd look at you like you were trying to pull something, suspicious-like."

Dylan kept walking alone. A sharp pang lanced him whenever he saw a boy near Teddy's age laughing, playing with other children, doing things Teddy didn't do, at least in Dylan's presence. Wanda told him that Teddy laughed and talked all the time, but only when he was around her. What she'd meant was, *you're a lousy father, your kid's not comfortable with you.*

After a couple of hours, Dylan realized that he wasn't getting anywhere. The few people who had ever seen Wanda hadn't seen her that day. No one along the route out of Royal Harbor had spotted her leaving that morning.

It was time to call for help.

DETECTIVE YOCHEM looked like one of those 1970s TV detectives: short and paunchy with a perpetual analytical squint. Tucked into one of the small offices off the main hallway, he took down information and asked what had to be a hundred questions.

"Where were *you* this morning?"

"Me?" Dylan asked. "I went to the office, then had an appointment with Judge Neely—about house plans—and then stopped by my house to have lunch with Teddy.

That was at eleven this morning." It seemed like years ago, when his world was under control.

"You always stop by the house like that?"

"No." Dylan lowered his head. "Never."

"Why this morning?"

"I . . . I realized I need to spend more time with my son."

"Ah-huh." Yochem jotted something down. "Did you see him before you left for work?"

"No. I head to work before anyone else is up."

"You don't have breakfast with your family?"

"No. It's . . . awkward."

"You and your wife fight a lot?"

"No, nothing like that. We just don't . . . talk much."

It was too hard to keep a conversation going.

What do you have planned for the day, Wanda?

Nothing.

Why don't you take Teddy to the park? He'd probably enjoy being around kids, and maybe you could meet other stay-at-home mothers.

Maybe.

You could get some sun; you look like you never leave the house.

Why, so I can look pampered and spoiled? So people think you're so good to me, all I have to do is lie around in the sun?

I am good to you. And you could lie in the sun all day if you wanted.

She'd push her chair away with a screeching sound across the tile and stomp off, muttering to herself. He hated when she got like that. He did take care of his family.

Had he ever really loved her? Or had his feelings turned cold over the years? Hell, maybe he'd always been cold. He'd never looked at her and known he'd die for her. He'd never held her and not wanted to let go. Even when they had shared a bed, he'd never spent the night wrapped around her.

Sometimes the thought of going home had made his throat feel tight. He kept doing one more thing before leaving. Or he'd pull out the Lego set he'd ostensibly bought for Teddy and start building something. He'd escaped in Legos as a child. But it hadn't been an escape now. Or had it?

"Too messy for you?" Yochem asked, making Dylan realize he'd started rearranging the array of pencils and pens lying on the cluttered desk.

"Sorry." Didn't they say bad habits returned under stress? When he was a kid, he'd kept his room in perfect order because it was the only aspect of his life he had any control over.

"You ever abuse the kid? Am I going to find anything when I run a check on you?"

Dylan shot to his feet. "Why the hell are you running a check on *me* when my son is out there somewhere? Why aren't you calling in every cop you have in this station to find him? What about the FBI? CIA?"

"Sit down, Mr. McKain. First of all, I'm running this operation, not you. Second, we're going to be checking on you, your housekeeper, and everyone who has anything to do with the kid. Most missing children are taken by a parent or someone close to them. That's the fact, like it or not."

Dylan remained standing. "That means you're looking at me as a suspect."

"We're looking at everyone until they're eliminated. It's nothing personal, it's just the way it is. Something terrible happens, and we gotta walk the line between feeling sorry for the person closest to the victim and suspecting him. If you think it's tough, put yourself in my place. Now, if we can continue . . ." He waited until Dylan slowly dropped back into his chair.

"Do you really think you're in a worse position than a parent who can't find his child?" Dylan asked.

Yochem seemed to run Dylan's words through his mind. "It's a saying, and not the right one for the situation." That was as close as the man could get to an apology. "All right, Mrs. McKain left the house at seven, and she was back by eleven. That's four hours she had. If she was planning to run with him, she probably just tucked him away somewhere safe until she could get back to him. She couldn't have gotten far unless she had help. Who could have helped her? Friends? Family? Could she have been seeing anyone?"

"Was she having an affair, no, I doubt it. She doesn't have any friends, and her only family is her mother, who's in a nursing home with Alzheimer's."

"Which one?"

"Woodsworth. I'll talk to her—"

"We'll talk with her. We'll circulate Teddy's picture, canvass the area. Somebody had to see something. I know you want to help, but the best thing you can do is sit tight and think about any place she might have stashed him. You probably know the place, somewhere she mentioned in passing."

Dylan pulled a business card from his gold case and wrote his cell number on it. "I want news of anything, even a rumor."

"You'll go nuts if we call you with every lead. We're going to get maybe hundreds, and most, if not all of them are going to be zippo. We're going to need to search your house, see if we can find anything that'll point us in the right direction."

"Fine. I'll let my housekeeper know you have free rein." He started to rise, then halted. "The woman Wanda hit . . ."

"Chloe Samms?"

"Yeah. When she . . . came back, she said, 'Where's Teddy?' It probably doesn't mean anything . . ."

"We'll check into it, see if there's any connection."

Dylan walked out into the sunny afternoon and stopped. For the first time in his life, he didn't know what to do. Wanda was dead. It was unreal that she was gone, that he'd never see her again. He loosened his tie; the damned thing was choking him. He walked to his black Mercedes, pausing to look at his reflection in the tinted window. On the outside he still looked together, successful, and in control. Inside he'd cracked into a hundred pieces.

He couldn't go to work. Everyone would be asking questions. Jodie would start crying, and he wasn't good at handling tears. As sweet and generous as his assistant was, she had a tendency to mother him. He didn't need a mother; one had been more than enough.

He got into his car and drove. Inside he felt hollow. Something would click. He'd remember a comment Wanda had made or someplace she liked to go.

The hospital was the last place she would have hidden Teddy. Yet there Dylan was, pulling into the parking lot and walking to the emergency room waiting area.

Four women were huddled together crying. A part of him wanted to cry too, but guilt, sorrow, and fear had him too tangled up inside. He walked to the check-in desk.

"I need to know how Chloe Samms is doing."

All four women got up as one and walked over to him. A blond woman with a leopard-spotted bow in her hair said through a teary voice, "You know our Chloe?" A miniature dachshund popped out of the zebra-striped bag slung over her shoulder.

"My wife was the one who hit her. I wanted to see how she was doing."

"I'm Chloe's aunt, Stella. This is my sister, that would make her Chloe's other aunt, Lena," she said, gesturing to a tall woman with upswept red hair.

"I'm her grandma, Marilee," a petite old . . . older . . . lady said, nudging her way up front. "You're always forgetting me."

"I didn't forget you, Mama, I just hadn't gotten to you yet. You always jump in before I can."

"Well, maybe you should introduce me first, then. Show some respect for an old lady. Yeah," she said to Dylan, "you can call me an old lady—I've outgrown 'older.' "

Had the woman read his mind? "About Chloe . . ." Dylan said.

Stella said, "Chloe! Our sweet Chloe. We raised her from a little girl, didn't we, Lena? Nothing ever happened to her. When we sensed something, we warned her. We promised her mama's spirit we'd take care of her, love her as our own."

"And we did," Marilee said.

Lena said, "Remember how she used to cry whenever we pulled up the crab traps or caught fish? And that first time we caught her taking the bait fish out of the well and setting them free? We explained they were meant for bait, and she nodded like she understood and all, and then she set the buggers free on the sly."

"I raised her too, don't forget," said Marilee. "Made her favorite get-well soup whenever she ailed."

"She hates pickle soup, Mama," Stella whispered.

"Does not! She smiles and thanks me every time I bring some over."

"About Chloe . . ." Dylan said again.

"It's all my fault," a petite lady in a black jumpsuit said. "I should have warned her better."

"Aw, Gisella, how could you have known? You had a feeling, nothing specific."

Gisella nodded, dabbing her eyes. "You know how they can be sometimes? Nothing concrete."

"Excuse me," Dylan said. "But how is she?"

"They brought her back from the dead," Lena said in a deep, throaty voice. "Did you know that?"

"Yes. I . . . I was there." It was all a blur of sounds and images now.

Before he could get any of his questions answered, they all moved in on him and demanded answers of their own.

"How did it happen?"

The dachshund yipped and Stella said, "Rascal wants to know whose fault it was."

"You know how our Chloe can get lost in her own world, she gets that la-tee-da face of hers. Maybe she didn't see the car coming."

"She was probably trying to save some lizard from getting run over."

"Did the police make any arrests?"

Dylan couldn't even tell who was asking which question. He reined in his impatience and answered them, explaining without getting into too much detail.

They wanted details.

"How fast was your wife going?"

"Why was she running from you?"

"Have you found your son?"

Dylan took a breath. "Listen, I just came to find out—"

"Ladies, you can see Chloe now," a nurse said. "Two at a time, please, and just for a few minutes."

All four crowded forward, a tangle of colors and arms, until the two aunts took control and walked forward. Marilee snagged Lena's arm and pulled her back, stepping forward with surprising agility. Not to be bested, Lena slipped back up beside the others. The nurse simply shook her head and led them away. Wise woman.

Gisella had dark curly hair and one of those little-girl faces. She walked right up to him, and even though she was at least a foot and a half shorter, her studied perusal made him uneasy.

"You know, Dylan McKain, you have a lot of repressed emotions inside. You need to free them. In doing so, you'll free yourself." She waved her hand in front of his stomach, *tsk-tsk*ing. "Your second chakra is a mess."

He caught himself glancing down. "I don't have a . . . chakra. Or repressed emotions. I just want to know how Chloe is doing."

She stared into his eyes, and he felt the urge to close them and keep her out. "You got plenty of repressed emotions: anger, guilt—that's a biggie. Some sexual anxiety as well. That's where the second chakra comes in. Our seven chakras are centers of force where we receive and transmit life energies, you know."

He leaned closer to her, gritting his teeth. "Can you see frustration?"

"Oh, yes," she said, not backing away an inch. "If you'd like, I can read your feet. They'll tell me more. Maybe we can get to the root of the problem."

"I don't have a problem with my root." He blinked,

realizing what he'd said. "I just want to know how Chloe is."

Loud sobbing preceded the two aunts and the grandmother as they returned. The knot in his stomach doubled.

"How is she?" Gisella asked, already crying.

"She's so banged up," Marilee wailed. "Bruised, a gash on her lip, a scrape on her cheek, those beautiful curls all matted with blood. Girls, she has her boo-boo face on."

"Oh, no, the boo-boo face!" Gisella said.

"What's a boo-boo face?" Dylan asked.

Stella said, "Ever since she was a girl, we named her faces. Her expressions," she clarified at Dylan's puzzled look. "The cookie-jar face, when she's been caught doing something. The bulldozer face, when she's stubborn and determined."

Lena said, "They won't let anyone else see her now. The nurse said we were too much, making her cry and all. We'll have to wait until tomorrow when they release her."

Dylan couldn't wait until tomorrow. He had to find out if she knew anything about Teddy and to see for himself that she was all right.

"She's okay . . . well, as much as can be expected," Lena said, finally answering Dylan's original question. "Shaken up, of course. The impact shocked her heart into stopping, poor thing. The man who gave her CPR saved her life. She didn't have any internal injuries, thank you, God. They're gonna keep her here for the night, they said, to make sure she's all right and all."

"Who saved her life?" Marilee asked. "We ought to do something for him."

Lena looked over at Dylan, then away. "The medics didn't get his name in all the confusion."

Dylan said, "I want to help out with the medical bills, give her some money to get by while she recovers."

Lena wrapped long, leathery fingers around his arm. Her deep blue eyes crinkled with warmth. "That's just so sweet of you, hon, but it's not necessary 'tall. Chloe's got medical coverage, and we're here to help her get by." She looked at the rest of the women. "Somebody's got to get good with figures around here, though."

"Figures?"

"She's an accountant. The only left-brained one in the bunch, but we love her anyway. Got her own little business on 951, full of plants, you can hardly look anywhere without seeing green. Our girl's going to be all right. Give me your name and number, hon, and we'll give you a little jingle and let you know how she's doing. Ooh, an architect." Lena fingered his business card, then tucked it into her bra. "That unusual mix of logic and creativity. We'll tell Chloe you stopped by. She'll appreciate that, I'm sure."

Without giving himself time to think about it, he walked through the doorway that led to the emergency room. The many cubicles were separated by blue cloth curtains.

"We're going to move you into a regular room for the night," a woman's voice said. "Just rest for a while; we'll come back and get you settled in."

"Thank you," a soft female voice said.

Somehow he knew it was Chloe. His chest tightened as he stepped back while the nurse passed.

Chloe looked pale, and her mouth was drawn tight in what he hoped wasn't pain. The scrape across her cheek and cut on her lip were shiny with salve. She opened eyes still damp from tears and looked at him.

"You," she said.

He turned around to see if she meant someone standing behind him. Nobody was there. He took a step closer, feeling less certain than he had a few seconds earlier.

"Who are you?" she asked.

"Dylan McKain."

"I'm Chloe Samms—" She rolled her eyes. "Well, you must know that." She lifted her nose and inhaled. "You're the one, aren't you?"

"The one?" The one who'd nearly gotten her killed.

The smile that lit those light blue eyes jump-started his heart. "You saved my life."

Chapter Three

CHLOE SAT UP IN HER BED. *OW, OW, OW. DON'T GIVE AWAY the pain and screw up the moment.* The man standing next to her reached out to steady the tubes and wires attached to her body. He had a long face, with a strong jawline and wide-set eyes. She never went for classically handsome, and classically handsome never went for her either. Maybe it was because he'd saved her life, but she felt an enormous pull toward him anyway. That woodsy cologne she remembered blended with faded sweat.

His intense brown eyes were troubled. She couldn't understand why, not when he'd done something wonderful. She'd come back to life and seen him standing nearby. She'd known that his mouth had been on hers, that his breath had brought her back, and that his hands had pumped her heart into action again.

"Don't you remember?" she asked, watching him trying to put some puzzle together.

His focus shifted inward. "It all happened so fast. My wife . . . you lying there . . . someone said you were dead. Then I walked over and . . ." He looked at her, his expression dumbstruck. "I did. I wasn't thinking, wasn't even aware. I took a CPR class when my son was born, but I've never used it. Until now."

Wife. Well, of course he'd be married, a guy like him. And what did it matter anyway? She leaned forward and took his hands. "Thank you. I mean, that seems so inadequate, you saved my life." She shook her head. "Can I hug you?"

"There's something you should know . . ." he was

saying, but leaned forward and let her slip her arms around him.

His body was strong and hard. She closed her eyes and savored the singular pleasure of being held by a man. Her ribs ached, her body felt bruised, but the way he held her was better than any medicine. She felt his large hands splayed across her back, holding her close against him. Despite that, she sensed his awkwardness at the situation. Before she was ready to let him go, he backed away.

"Can I do something for you?" she asked, knowing there was nothing she could do to repay him. "I'll take care of your accounting needs for the rest of your life. I'll tutor your children in math. Anything."

He rubbed his jaw, not meeting her gaze. "You should know that it was my wife Wanda who hit you."

"Oh. I didn't see what happened to the driver. It all happened so fast." She fiddled with the edge of the thin sheet, feeling the terror all over again. Her hands were black from the asphalt, knuckles scraped, and nails broken. "Is your wife all right?"

He looked away, pain and disbelief on his features. "She died at the scene."

"Oh . . . I am so sorry."

He swallowed hard before meeting her gaze. "I am too." He cocked his head. "You mean that, don't you? About being sorry?"

"Of course I do."

"But she nearly killed you."

"She didn't hit me on purpose."

He looked at her as though she were some strange specimen. She mentally replayed the conversation. Nope, nothing strange.

"No, she didn't," he said. "It was my fault."

She rubbed her forehead. It was sore, and she winced. "I'm not sure what you mean."

She caught a spark of tenderness as his eyes took in her expression of pain. "I was following my wife and panicked her. She was acting strange, crazy." Several emotions crossed his face, but he quickly masked them. "I wanted to see if you needed anything. I feel like I should help somehow."

"But you saved my life." Her voice was getting thick. "That's all I could ever ask for." Or was it? Another hug would be nice, even if it was a little painful. Dylan wasn't a man who dispensed hugs easily, that much she could tell. In any case, she'd better not indulge.

"I gave your aunt my card. Call me if you need anything. Anything at all, okay?"

She nodded, thinking again of being held in his arms. His gaze swept over her, making her realize what a mess she must look. She thought of fluffing her hair, but didn't have the energy.

"Was the duck all right?" she asked.

"Duck?"

"I was trying to get a duck out of the street just before . . . I just wondered if it was all right."

He started to shrug, but then said, "The duck made it."

She wasn't positive that he'd even noticed the duck, but she didn't have the energy to probe further.

"I'd better go," he said. "You look tired."

She nodded, pulling the blanket up to her chin. "Thanks for coming by."

He paused at the doorway. "Did you find Teddy?"

Exhaustion was pulling her down now, making her eyelids feel like clay. They'd given her something to sleep, but she didn't want to sleep yet. "Hmmm?"

"When you came back, you asked where Teddy was. Did you find him?"

She closed her eyes, sliding into oblivion. "I don't know anyone named Teddy."

DYLAN'S NEXT stop was the nursing home. If Anne was going to talk to anyone, it'd be him. If she remembered who he was today. Anne had always been cool toward him, but if he could convince her that her grandson's life was at stake, she would help him.

Usually when he drove through Naples, he noticed the burgeoning subdivisions filled with high-end homes and guarded by elaborate gatehouses. He wondered how many of the homes within were of his firm's design. Now he looked for anyplace Wanda could have hidden his son on the way to the Woodsworth Nursing Home.

He approached the woman at the marble desk in the lobby. "I need to speak with Anne Dodson. I'm Dylan McKain, her son-in-law."

"Didn't you know?" the lady said after looking in her paperwork. "Your wife took her for a vacation this morning."

A HALF hour later, Dylan had talked to Jackie, the nurse in charge of Anne. Jackie Gardener was an attractive redhead who looked warm and soft but had an efficient gleam in her eyes. They'd checked Anne's room, Jackie methodically going through each drawer while Dylan checked the bed and beneath the furniture. She then led him to their security room, where they viewed the videotape. Wanda had waltzed in looking pleasant and under control and signed out her mother for a supposed trip to

North Carolina. Teddy hadn't been with her, but he could have been in the car. No one could say for sure.

Lastly, Jackie queried her staff. All her efficiency came down to nothing. "I'm sorry, Mr. McKain," she said, that authoritative tone leaking away to compassion. "I didn't know there was a problem."

"I didn't either," he had to admit. If Wanda had taken her mother out of the nursing home the same day she'd taken off with Teddy, then he must be with Anne.

"If they're together, alone . . . is my son all right with her?"

"She won't hurt the boy, of course. But she may not know who he is or that she's supposed to take care of him. It comes and goes with her."

He nodded. "Did Anne say anything about the upcoming trip?"

Jackie shook her head, but her expression turned thoughtful. "I don't know if this will help, and I probably shouldn't tell you. Then again, I don't know if it's even true. Anne felt a great deal of remorse over putting Wanda in a hospital when she was a teenager. The shock treatments were the hardest thing for Anne to talk about."

Dylan went cold. "A mental hospital?"

"That's the impression I got. Apparently Wanda heard voices in her head, and her father thought she was crazy. He made Wanda go into the hospital, and Anne felt terrible that she didn't fight harder to keep her out. Wanda never forgave her for it."

Wanda in a mental hospital? He remembered back in college when they'd gotten to that sharing stage of the relationship. He'd told her about his manic-depressive mother, the pity and humiliation that shadowed him, and worse, singled him out as different. *Poor Dylan. His mom's crazy.* Some mothers wouldn't even let their sons play with him, and no one ever went to his house. That was fine; Dylan didn't want anyone to see his mother running around the house pulling all the phones out of the jacks because the FBI was tapping them. Or making them live in the dark so the hidden cameras wouldn't pick up their movements.

He'd told Wanda all that out of some sense of duty, and she'd listened thoughtfully. If she'd had her own unbalanced past, would she have hidden it from him? Is that why she'd never wanted to go back to her Detroit hometown? And why her mother had always been cold and quiet, maybe afraid to say the wrong thing?

As crazy as it sounded, it was starting to make sense. If Wanda wasn't in her right mind, finding Teddy was going to be even harder.

YOCHEM CALLED Dylan's cell phone that night. "Nothing has panned out on the North Carolina story yet, though I figured that was a ruse. We have Mrs. Dodson's picture circulating up there and here in town. We think the best thing for you to do at this point is to take it to the media. When the news programs show their pictures, somebody'll remember."

"Whatever I need to do to get Teddy back." He hated publicity, hating making his problems public. He pulled at his collar, feeling the noose tightening. He'd had enough of people probing his personal life. *But this isn't about you. It's about Teddy.*

Yochem set up a press conference to be aired on the evening news and then rerun at eleven. All they needed was a direction.

Afterward Dylan stayed at the police station waiting for calls. And they came, all funneled to Yochem and five other officers waiting for the deluge. It was all Dylan could do not to grab one of the ringing phones. Instead, he kept rearranging the notepads and pens, anything to stay calm.

They repeated each lead as they took notes. "You saw them at a convenience store on Immokalee Road at ten in the morning?" one man said.

"You saw Wanda and her mother heading to Miami at ten-fifteen," another confirmed.

How could Wanda be everywhere at once? Dylan scrubbed his fingers through his hair in frustration.

"Don't worry, this is normal," one female officer said, handing him another cup of coffee. "Wait till the psychics start calling in. It really gets interesting then."

"Does this work? Do any of these leads ever pan out?"

"Sure. The problem is, we never know which ones. We have to investigate them all, no matter how crazy they sound."

"Give me some. I'll start checking them out."

"You just hang tight, Mr. McKain. That's our job."

By eight the next morning, the police were still investigating telephone leads. Dylan felt ragged, exhausted and wired all at the same time. They finally sent him home, or, more precisely, out of their hair.

Camilla was staying at the house in case Teddy showed up. Even in a state of crisis, she wore her standard white industrial shirt and black pants, filling both with her stocky figure.

"Why don't you take a nap, Mr. McKain? You gotta refill your energy tanks."

"No way could I sleep right now. I'm going to jump in the shower. Bang on the door if you hear any news."

She narrowed her eyes, as though Dylan were some recalcitrant charge. "I'll fix you something to eat while you're in the shower, then."

"I can't eat. My throat's too tight for anything more than coffee."

"You have to take care of yourself, Mr. McKain. Food and sleep are more important than showers!"

Her words drifted to him as he walked into his room. All he knew about Camilla was what Wanda had told him when she'd hired her. Camilla was originally from Spain but knew English well. She had recently divorced her husband and was taking night courses at a local college toward getting a teaching degree. Since she'd been a housewife her whole life, taking care of a house was her greatest skill. From the pristine floors and windows to the lack of dust in the most out-of-the-way places, she evidently did a good job.

When he joined Camilla in the kitchen fifteen minutes later, he asked, "Any calls?"

"Several people from your office want to know what's going on. The hospital morgue called and want to know what arrangements we're making for Mrs. McKain. I'll handle it if you'd like. I've taken care of this kind of thing before."

He couldn't even think about it. "Handle it, then. Please."

When she pushed a plate of club sandwiches in front of him, he shook his head. "I've got to go. Thanks for holding down the fort."

"Who's going to hold down the fort inside you?" she called as he walked out.

DYLAN SPENT the day driving north on I-75. Wanda could have taken any exit, east or west. She could have gone anywhere. He gripped the steering wheel so tight, he was afraid he'd wrench the thing out of the dash.

"I held out as long as I could," he told Yochem on the

phone. "Have any of those leads from last night panned out?"

"Not yet. But we're still getting leads, don't worry."

How could he not worry? "What about Chloe Samms?"

"One of our officers talked to her at the hospital before she checked out."

"Checked out? Oh, jeez, you don't mean . . ."

"No, no," Yochem said. "She left the hospital very much alive. Did your wife ever go down to Lilithdale?"

"I doubt it."

"Other than that possibility, there's no tangible connection between the women."

That should have been enough to put Chloe out of his mind. But it wasn't. Dylan didn't believe in gut instincts; facts were facts. But something in his gut was pointing to Chloe Samms.

LATE THAT afternoon, Dylan drove to the office. South Florida Architectural Associates took up the top floor of a contemporary office building on U.S. 41. This was the first time his three-story building didn't bring him any comfort or satisfaction. All he could think about was how quickly he'd give it up to get his son back.

Just as he'd suspected, the moment he walked through the oak door, Jodie rushed into his arms.

"You poor thing, what you must be going through!" Jodie was an attractive blonde with a lush figure and a heart big enough to encompass anyone's troubles. When he'd helped her buy a car after her divorce, she'd thanked him no less than fifty times, with hugs, words, and even flowers.

"We've been calling since last night when we saw the

news. What are the police doing? They wouldn't tell us anything when they came by this morning."

"They came by . . . here?"

"Yes, asking questions about you. Have they found anything? We want to help. This is crazy!"

Several other employees came out of their offices and inundated him with questions, suggestions, or just plain concern.

He rubbed his chin, feeling the stubble. "He's going to be all right. I just have to figure out where Wanda hid him. She wouldn't have left him anywhere dangerous, I know that much." But had she been in her right mind?

"I'm sorry about Wanda," Steve Ritter, his senior architect said, clapping Dylan on his shoulder. "I'm sure it was some misunderstanding."

The image of Wanda in the car flashed through his mind and made his throat go dry. "Thank you." No one knew that his marriage was nothing more than a legal technicality, and he wasn't about to enlighten them. He was grateful that they didn't ask why she'd suddenly taken off with their son.

"Oh, I forgot! There's someone here to see you," Jodie said, nodding toward one of the plush chairs in the lobby.

When he saw Chloe, his heart jumped for a moment. In surprise, that's all. Or maybe because of the bruises on her face. She was wearing a pale blue jumpsuit, a matching headband to hold back her curls, and a bandage on her cheek. The sneakers matched her outfit, making him think of the heart-wrenching sight of that one lone sneaker on the sidewalk. He swallowed hard, tugging at his collar.

"Hi," she said in a whisper, then cleared her throat and

slowly stood. She clutched a large, colorful canvas bag. "I need to talk to you."

Did she want something? Well, hadn't he offered her anything? He didn't care what she wanted; he'd write a check, whatever. Maybe that would ease his mind and eradicate the persistent thought of her.

He led her to the grouping of chairs in the corner of his office. "I'd rather stand," she said. "Kinda hurts to move up and down." She put her hand to her throat and fiddled with a small owl pendant on a gold chain. On her index finger she wore an intricate butterfly ring.

Her stiff movements made him wince in sympathy. He didn't like the effect she had on him. "Are you . . . all right?"

"The aches I can live with. The nightmares are the worst. I keep seeing the car coming at me." She blinked away the haunted shadow in her beautiful blue eyes and met his gaze. It made him think of the boo-boo face her aunts had mentioned. "I'm all right. And very lucky." She looked away for a moment. "Or maybe I should say blessed."

He was blessed too. The first close look at her face could have been on the evening news with a reporter telling how a freak accident had snuffed out her life.

"Can I get you anything? Coffee? Soda? Money?"

She choked, placing her hand to her chest. "Do you always offer visitors those choices?"

He caught himself smiling for a moment, realizing how his words had come out. "Not usually. Then again, we don't have any visitors quite like . . . you."

"Yeah, I'm different," she said in a soft, resigned voice.

He bet she had a great mouth when it wasn't marred by the gash on her lower lip. "I didn't mean it like that," he said, pushing away a disturbing memory of how that mouth felt beneath his. "I meant . . ."

"I know what you meant. No, I don't want anything, thank you."

If she didn't want money, what could she possibly want? Another hug?

"Why did I come here? That's what you want to know." She laughed, a thin kind of laugh. "When I should be home in bed instead of out scaring people. I tried that, believe me. The last thing I need is to be standing here with you"—she swallowed—"about to tell you what I'm going to tell you. I saw you on the news. You have to understand, I thought it was a dream."

"You've lost me."

"I may be able to help you find Teddy," she said, visibly tensing in anticipation of his reaction.

"You knew Wanda?"

"Not exactly. Not in a knowing kind of sense."

"In what sense did you know her, then?"

"I met her right after she died."

Chapter Four

"YOU WANT TO RUN THAT BY ME AGAIN?"

Her words weren't coming out right. He was throwing her off by watching her too intensely. As soon as she told him, he was going to get that look on his face, the same one she got whenever she mentioned her association with Lilithdale.

"Let me see if I can think of a better way to say this."

She bought time by looking around his office. Behind his desk hung a framed cover of *Architectural Digest,* presumably with a mansion he'd designed on the cover. Pictures of other majestic homes covered the slate-colored walls. Dark blue carpet, polished wood furniture, all the signs of success. Well, except for the two yellow Legos in the candy dish. There were two framed pictures of a smiling Teddy, and one picture of Teddy and Wanda. And there was Dylan, tall, handsome, if fatigued. He fit into this world of thick carpet and rich wood.

Which meant he was going to think she was one Froot Loop shy of a full bowl.

Fifteen times two-hundred fifty is thirty-seven hundred fifty.

She turned back to him, mentally reciting another calculation. All right, it was her crutch, but she wasn't about to let go of it now.

"Don't laugh, just please don't laugh. Something happened when I died. Believe me, nothing like this has ever happened to me before."

His expression remained blank. She walked over to the large window; she found herself seeking the light now, though it would never be as wondrous as the light in the tunnel.

She started plucking dead leaves off a staked philodendron plant. "Have you ever heard of near-death experiences?"

He walked up beside her. "Where people who die supposedly see a tunnel and their dearly departed loved ones?"

Ah, now she could see the skepticism, but she forged ahead. "It was the most incredible thing I have ever experienced. It was the first time I felt like I belonged somewhere, really belonged." *Let's not go there.* "It was incredibly peaceful, and there was the light they talk about, but I could feel it as much as I could see it. And I know now . . . there's nothing to be afraid of when we die." She could feel it all over again as the memory came alive inside her.

He'd been watching her, and she wondered what her face had looked like. She pinched another dead leaf off the plant.

"Go on," he said, masking what he thought of her story so far.

"You've heard of people who feel they've been given a second chance for a reason? But they don't know what that reason is? Well, I know. Wanda was in that tunnel. She told me I couldn't die yet because I had to find Teddy. She was about to tell me where he was when you revived me. She said the voices told her to hide him, but now she knew they were wrong."

At that, his expression hardened. "You know about the voices?"

She nodded, focusing on a new section of the plant now. "She said Teddy was special. Different. That I had to find him."

Dylan released a breath and leaned against the glass. She dared a glance at him.

"You knew her, didn't you? Maybe you were helping her, maybe you were supposed to meet her there. And now you're worried because she's dead and you know my son is hidden somewhere. The question is, why didn't she tell you where?"

Chloe crushed the collection of dead leaves in her hand. She'd expected disbelief, certainly, but not accusations. "I never met Wanda before that day. When I saw her picture on the news last night, that's when I knew it wasn't a dream." She caught herself pulling another yellow leaf from the plant and stopped. "What about my asking for Teddy when I came back?" Her eyes narrowed. "You came to the hospital to ask me about it."

"I came to see how you were doing."

"That was your cover story. You asked if I'd found Teddy, pretended it was an afterthought."

"At the time, I thought it was a coincidence, that Teddy was a husband or someone you were with."

She crossed her arms over her chest, but found the movement too painful. "I don't have a husband, I wasn't with anyone, and I don't know any Teddys."

Dylan moved closer, placing a palm against the glass to the left of her head. "Near-death experiences are nothing more than the mind's way of easing a person into death. I read about it on a plane once."

"I suppose you're an expert, then. Explain why we're allowed to come back sometimes. Explain why some people have scary experiences where they go to hell."

"I don't have all the answers. What I do know is . . ." His gaze dropped down over her face, then up to her hair.

She knew she looked terrible, beaten and bruised, but disgust wasn't what she saw in his eyes. Wonder, maybe.

"What?" she asked, finding her voice only a whisper. Afternoon sunlight was spilling in through the glass, washing his face in radiant light. She realized that she wasn't breathing; she was holding her breath, waiting for . . . what?

He remained there, transfixed. Then he pushed away from the window, turning his back to her and running his hand through his thick hair. When he turned back to her, he was wearing that impassive mask again. "Great, another nutcase."

"Don't disparage me. I came here to help you."

He nodded toward her hand. "It looks like you came here to groom my plant."

She slid her hand behind her back. "Do you want my help or not?"

"What are you going to do, pull out your crystal ball? Lay out tarot cards? Consult a genie?"

"No, no, no. I don't do any of that. I'm just . . . ordinary."

He actually laughed as his gaze took her in. "Yeah, right. Do you know how crazy that sounds, meeting my wife in a tunnel? You're even nuttier than I think you are if you expect me to believe that nonsense."

She scrubbed her fingers through her curls. "I am not nutty. All I know is that God gave me a second chance because I need to help find your son. Does my story sound crazy? Probably. Is there anything I can do about it? No." She leaned toward him. "I hope the police—or you—find Teddy today, in the next hour, right now. Then I can go back to my cat and dog and my little life and take advantage of my second chance. But until he's found, I can't do that. I can't turn my back on a desperate woman and a boy in trouble. If you don't want to listen to me, I can damn well look myself." She grabbed up her bag, then shoved the crushed leaves into his hands. "Here."

Then, with as much dignity as her battered body would allow, she walked out of his office. Employees were still milling around the lobby, probably curious about the woman who'd come to see their boss. Well, give them a few minutes, and they'd think she was as crazy as Dylan did. He'd probably laugh as he told them her story. It didn't matter. It didn't. As long as she didn't hear it.

When she opened the ornate wood door, she came face-to-face with Ross Allen. Tall and lean, with dark hair and a hook nose—the man who had broken her heart ten months ago. Great. Now she was sure she was wearing her finger-in-a-socket face. She'd read that his construction company had won the Kraft Theater job; marrying a commissioner's daughter probably hadn't hurt.

"Chloe, what happened to you?" he asked, then looked beyond her. "Dylan, hey, bud! You designing my little Chloe here a house? Or did you just go a few rounds with her?"

She braced herself for the usual knifelike pain that accompanied seeing Ross. It was more like a hammer in her chest, dull and pounding.

Dylan shook Ross's hand, but his eyes were on her. "Neither."

She waited for some kind of editorial comment, but he left it at that. *Thank you for that, at least.*

She expected to feel unnerved by Ross. Instead she was more unnerved by Dylan. If she'd ever entertained thoughts of a man in her life, he wasn't what she wanted.

She walked to her T-Bird and flung her bag on the passenger's seat. Not that she'd ever admit to anyone that she wanted a man in her life. She'd grown up in a society of women who didn't need men other than for an occasional date or physical release. It was one more thing that set her apart from them, but this one was her secret. She did want a man in her life. She wanted a man to love her beyond bounds, to hold her throughout the night, to know life would be incomplete without her in it. She wanted a poet or an artist, someone sensitive and romantic.

Dylan wasn't even close to that man. Then why did her heart speed up at the thought of him?

Because she was a nutcase, that's why.

DYLAN STOOD at the window and watched Chloe Samms drive off in an iridescent green Thunderbird. He'd figured her for something pink with painted daisies.

"So I thought I could embrace this search and give myself a little PR in the process," Ross was saying as Dylan tuned back in. "We both win. What do you think?"

"You want to use my son's disappearance to get publicity?"

"And help find your son. That's where the win-win comes in. I'll sponsor the search."

Dylan held back angry words about opportunism. Help was help. "Sure, whatever you can do."

"Great. While I'm here, I'd like to take a look at the theater plans, see where we are. I want that early completion bonus. Big kudos for us. They're trying to book Barry Manilow if it's done in time. I know this whole missing kid thing has been a strain . . . if you think you can't deliver—"

"I said I'd deliver with my signature on the contract."

He clenched his hands so he wouldn't be tempted to throttle Ross.

"Good. Because they want you to do the project, only you. Hey, I'm sure you'll find your kid."

"Thanks for your support," Dylan said through gritted teeth.

"Hey, I'm here for you, bud. So, you know Chloe Samms?"

"Sort of. I take it you know her."

"Oh, yeah." Ross's chuckle grated on Dylan's nerves. "We had a thing going last year. She's cute. And a pill, no doubt about that. Our most memorable argument happened when we were on our way to a dinner engagement and she spotted a lizard hanging onto the hood. She was all worried it was going to fall off and get run over. We were running late, but she made me stop so she could relocate it to a bush." When Dylan waited for more, he added, "It didn't work out. For me and her, I mean. The lizard survived. I needed someone like Melonie to move me into the right circles. She knows the money people."

"You broke up with Chloe for professional reasons?" Dylan didn't know why irritation slipped into his voice. He could understand what someone like Chloe would do to a man's reputation.

"Hey, I felt bad, believe me. I wanted to marry that woman, have kids with her. She's the kind of girl you want to hold and protect from the world." His voice went low. "She's that kind of girl."

"She's definitely that." Dylan had to agree with that last part, curious about the way Ross's eyes were getting all soft.

Ross blinked. "Don't get me wrong. Melonie's a great gal. She and I are going places; I'd never have gotten the Kraft job without her."

Dylan narrowed his eyes. "Don't worry, Ross. I'd never get you wrong."

AFTER ROSS left, Dylan spread out a map of Naples on his drafting table, securing the corners with tape dots. How far could Wanda have gone? He calculated distance based on speed, roads, and time.

A soft knock preceded Jodie opening the door. "Hi, sweetie. Just wondered if you needed anything."

"Just some time alone, thanks."

She hesitated in the doorway. "You know, hon, we're here if you need us. It's okay to reach out."

"I appreciate that."

He could see disappointment on her pretty face as she left him to his silence. As a boy, he'd needed his mother, and she hadn't been there mentally for him. He'd needed his father, but he hadn't been there physically for him. So he'd stopped needing people.

A minute later, he was on the phone with Detective Yochem, relaying Chloe's story.

Yochem laughed, a low, gritty sound. "Let me tell you something about Chloe Samms. She not only lives in Lilithdale, she grew up there. You know that place, right? A town of all women."

"I've heard about it. They seem to keep to themselves."

"Thank goodness for small favors, too. That place seems to draw the oddballs, like the woman who can light up a bulb with her fingers. Most of them are so-called psychics, with all kinds of twists: new-age nonsense, astrology, biorhythms. My wife got this harebrained idea that our dog had a motive for pooping on the carpet and took him to a dog psychic. The fruitcake claimed the dog just wanted a little one-on-one time before we left him alone."

"Did it work?"

"Well . . . yeah, but the dog was ready to be housebroken, that's all."

Dylan thought of Chloe's sensual mouth and had to ask, "Are these women gay?"

"Supposedly they're just independent. They don't hate men or anything, least that's what the wife says. She's nosy, got to ask all sorts of questions. Said she didn't see any hanky panky going on. Bottom line is, they believe in more mumbo-jumbo than you can fit in a spaceship. She's one of them. Chloe Samms, not my wife. Next thing you know, she'll be channeling your wife's spirit à la Shirley MacLaine. I think she's just shook up. Chloe, not Shirley MacLaine. You know, getting hit, dying, and all. That little cookie is nothing but trouble."

Wasn't that the truth. Dylan hung up and went back to the map. Chloe might be a kook in her own right, but he'd seen something in her eyes that spoke of being alone in a crowd. Hadn't the aunt said Chloe was the only left-brained one in the bunch, but they loved her anyway?

He knew about being singled out. Maybe that was why he was drawn to her. The only reason. Other than the memory of his mouth on hers and of her body coming back to life in his arms. Any psychiatrist could explain it away. They had shared a traumatic moment.

A knock on the door preceded the arrival of the entire top-level staff of South Florida Architectural Associates. Jody and Steve headed the group of ten. They all wore sober, determined looks on their faces.

Jodie jumped in first. "Dylan, we know you're a private person, that you like to handle things yourself. But you need us, whether you like it or not."

Steve approached next. "We want to help you find

Teddy. You're the boss; you tell us what you need us to do. Everything except butt out."

"Look, it's not necessary—"

"Yes, it is," Jodie said, her hands on her hips.

Dylan surveyed his team. They weren't going to butt out. He ran his hand over his mouth and smiled. "Well, maybe there are a couple things you could help with. . . ."

TEDDY DIDN'T like this place. His things were not here. There were only two people in the outside world that he sometimes allowed into his world: Mom and Camel. He called her Camel, because her real name was hard to say. She laughed whenever he said it, a light, tinkly sound that he liked. So he kept saying it over and over, focusing on the word and the sound of laughter and nothing else. He wished he could laugh.

Mom and Camel weren't here in this place he did not like. Another woman was, an old woman who sat in the tiny room and seemed lost in her own world. She talked a lot, almost as much as Mom, but at least she didn't want a response from him like everyone else did. She didn't wait, didn't get that grimace like Mom did when he repeated the phrase because he knew he had to say something, but he didn't know what.

But Mom wasn't here. He'd looked for her, space by space. It didn't take long.

Like he did whenever he went to a new place, he focused on an item. He could focus so hard, everything else would go away. Mom used to take him to a place with other people, kids like him. No, not like him. They played together and talked and laughed. He couldn't understand what they were doing. Sometimes they would take his hand and try to drag him over to their game, and he cried until they let go. Then they looked at him funny and watched when he played alone, lining up letters and blocking out everything but those colorful cubes.

He kept hearing a sound now, and he focused on it. It came from outside, but he was too afraid to go out there. So he sat on the carpet and imagined. First it was a tapping at the door. Then it was Camel's mop bucket when the water sloshed around inside. He put himself in a familiar place. His dad was there, throwing a ball to him. Dad kept saying, "Throw the ball back," and Teddy would repeat it over and over.

Another sound invaded his world. The old lady sat on the couch, talking and talking. Mostly it was just a babble of noise. It took too much work to understand people, especially when they talked on and on like that. But he needed something. He wasn't sure what it was, but he had a hole feeling in his tummy. So he sat down in front of her and tried really, really hard to listen to what she was saying.

"Wanda, why are you so quiet all of a sudden? Usually you're talking all the time, talking to people who don't exist, answering them. Your father thinks you're plain crazy, and I know it hurts your feelings when he calls you that. I wish I could make him stop, but you know how he gets when I tell him what to do. And I know it scares you when he talks about putting you in a hospital—it scares me too. This quiet is good, except you got to stop repeating stuff. That sounds crazy too. We'll fool your father, you hear? We'll make him think everything's just fine. All you got to do is act normal."

It was too many words for Teddy to understand. Stop repeating, he knew.

"What happened to your hair, child?" The woman

touched his curls. "It's a tangled mess. Where's your brush?"

Teddy hated having his hair brushed. He put his hands over his hair so she wouldn't see it. She walked to the kitchen and started opening drawers.

"It's gotta be here somewhere. Ah, this'll work even better."

She held up a pair of scissors. Scissors cut things. He remembered that, cutting, cutting, until Mom saw and got mad.

He touched the curls on his head, pulling one until he could see it in the corner of his eye. He liked the feel of his hair. It was attached to him. He didn't like people to touch what was his. Everything that was his was part of his world—part of him. Touching those things meant touching him, and he hated being touched. It made him feel funny.

"All right, Wanda," that other voice said, and he felt a tug on his hair.

He pulled away from the violation. He tried to reach for the scissors; he liked to cut things. But she tugged them away and grabbed some of his hair again. And then she snipped, and his hair fell to the floor.

He opened his mouth to scream. But as usual, no sound came out.

Chapter Five

"WHY IN HEAVEN'S NAME DIDN'T YOU TELL US FIRST, HON?" Lena's fingers dug deeper as she massaged cypress/lemon oil into Chloe's muscles.

"Ow, ow, ow!" Chloe resettled her face in the headrest on the massage table. They were using one of the small massage rooms under the light of flickering vanilla candles. Massage rooms were only part of the Total Balance Women's Center. Lena started the center with one massage room in the back of the tea house. She had recently built a two-thousand-square-foot building to accommodate the many spiritual healing services she now offered. Lena had created a successful business that was patronized by women in Naples and even Ft. Myers and Bonita Springs. Women came here to express their emotions, explore their higher selves, and sometimes just to have someone listen without judging.

"I hadn't intended to tell him first. I wanted more time to figure it out, to see if it was real. Next thing I knew, I was at his office."

"And he thought you were a nutcase," Stella said.

"Exactly."

"They all do," she said on a sigh. "Until they need us."

Chloe started to sit up. "That man doesn't need anyone."

Lena pushed her back down again. "The architect. That strange combination of creativity and logic. Let me tell you, logic wins every time. I dated one once. 'Member him, Stell?"

All Chloe could see was the carpeted floor of the dim

massage room, and occasionally Lena's sandal-clad feet and painted toenails. Then Rascal came around and tried to jump up and lick Chloe's nose.

"Well, I don't want to date this guy," Chloe said firmly. "I just want to help find his son. Go 'way, Rascal!"

"Oh, I sense some interest there, hon," Lena said. "Not that kind of sense," she said to Stella.

Chloe started to get up again and deny it.

Lena pushed her back down. "Look, there's both a logical and spiritual reason why you're drawn to him. He did save your life, Chloe. There's certainly something bonding in a person saving your life and all."

"And the logical part?" There was nothing logical about her attraction to the man.

"He's as sexy as a tiger," Stella added with a laugh.

"He is that," Chloe muttered before catching herself. "And nothing but trou—ouch—trouble." Lena had rubbed a particularly sore spot.

"Well," Stella said, "if you want a fling, that's fine. Nothing wrong with some recreational sex once in a while. It's the getting attached that's the problem, always the problem. Use them the way they use us, then walk away if they want something permanent."

"And never, never fall in love," Chloe said. Living in Lilithdale meant a woman had asserted her independence. They played the game like men. Like her father. Walk away when it got too serious, when real responsibility tugged. When her mother had gotten pregnant, he pretended to be responsible by immersing himself in his trucking job. He sent a check once in a while, stopped in to say hello, and then he was gone again. Hi ya, Dad. 'Bye, Dad.

What Chloe never told anyone was how much she'd wanted him to stay. She'd learned young that needing a man was unacceptable. A strong woman took care of herself. She wanted to be strong. She'd been taught well, had the best role models. But deep in her soul, she feared she wasn't strong at all.

Rascal popped up and licked Chloe on the nose.

"Augh!"

"Dylan's not the right type even for a fling. He's too part of the mainstream," Stella said. "And Rascal just reminded you about your bad instincts where men are concerned."

From anyone else, that statement would have seemed odd. But Stella did indeed have a knack for communicating with animals.

"How can I forget?"

Oh, she knew when a man was wrong for her. Unfortunately, it was only either just before or during lovemaking. Then everything would clarify for her. Mostly she'd had the epiphany before doing the deed. She'd wanted it to work so badly with Ross, she'd ignored the instinct.

"I'm not going to get into that kind of situation with Dylan," Chloe promised, more to herself. "I just want to help find his son."

She sensed the heavy silence and managed to sit up before Lena could push her back down. She twisted the sheet around her and took in the looks being exchanged between the two women.

"What?" Chloe asked.

"I just don't want to see your life ruined, hon," Lena said softly. She closed the bottle of oil and set it on the shelf.

"You mean like what happened in Sarasota?"

Another look passed between them, a communication Chloe could never interpret. Probably she needed some kind of psychic ability.

"That's exactly what I'm talking about," Lena said at last. "I thought I was doing the right thing, going to the police with my information."

Chloe crossed her legs on the table. "But you did help them find the missing girl. Even if it was too late to save her, at least her parents had a body to bury."

The color drained from Lena's smooth, tanned skin, and her blue eyes darkened. "Still, the family blamed me for not coming forward in time. The girl's mother came to my house and screamed that it was my fault her daughter had died. Then she had a breakdown on my front porch. It was on the news for a week, playing over and over, that woman crying and pointing her finger at me. The media hounded me, the police denied working with me . . . and worse, my friends turned their backs on me."

That was the most Chloe had ever heard about the events that brought Lena to Lilithdale.

Stella put her arms around her sister. "It was one of the most painful experiences we've gone through, 'cept for losing your mother. We don't want you to go through that, especially since . . ."

"I don't have any real powers," Chloe finished. They never said it, but it always hung between them. Poor Chloe, no powers, no abilities.

They exchanged another look, Stella asking, Lena saying no.

"What? Tell me."

"I know you don't remember any of what happened; you were too young. And then your mother died, and . . ." Stella let the words fade, meeting Lena's gaze again. "I'm telling you, you don't want to go through it. The ridicule, the accusations. It was ugly."

Chloe slid to her feet, sheet wrapped around her. "You're not telling me everything."

It was Lena who most reminded Chloe of her mom: the soft, rounded lines of her face and a shadow of vulnerability in her eyes. Lena usually tried to hide that vulnerability with a grimace. This time she simply walked out of the room. Stella put her hand on Chloe's bare shoulder. "It's just that this whole thing is bringing back unpleasant memories. Your mother had no special abilities, you know."

"What does this have to do with my mother?"

Stella fell quiet, looking at Rascal. "Nothing."

"Is Lena afraid that the publicity will touch her again?" Chloe asked.

"She values her peace here, yes. Mostly she's worried about you."

Chloe gave Stella a hug before she left, remembering how close she'd come to never hugging her again. Then she got dressed and made her way to the entrance.

The sound of screaming filtered through one of the closed doors she passed. The Primal Scream Room. The one-day seminar taught women how to release their pent-up emotions. Chloe hurried outside; she always found herself wanting to scream if she listened too long.

She glanced over at the park as she made her way to her car. She couldn't help but pause and watch the women prepare for their sunset games. Every night they chose a different game: bridge, Pictionary, or mah-jongg, all played on pink picnic tables.

Conversations were a-hum on the salty breeze, punctuated by laughter. Marilee, her grandmother, was already there, setting up the punch bowl; it was her turn to bring the rum runners. With her typical flair, she'd colored them purple.

Chloe was sure there was nowhere on earth like Lilithdale. In nearby Naples and Marco Island, the trend was toward high-end housing developments and the tourist trade. Every time Chloe drove into Naples, she discovered a new traffic light or more land cleared for a subdivision or shopping center.

But Lilithdale was timeless. Most residents weren't bothered by outsiders coming for an afternoon, but nobody was interested in attracting hoards of tourists. No one tried to outdo her neighbor with a bigger, better house. Most of the homes were nothing more than cottages built back in the fifties and sixties. There were a few mobile homes that were built on stilts because of flood zones. One tiny motel, a few restaurants, and the various small businesses were all these women needed in their lives.

People had their routines and no desire for change. The only change they wanted was a new flavor of coffee or one of Marilee's colorful concoctions at the Blue Moon Supper Club. Anything more and they started getting uneasy.

Even though Chloe didn't feel as though she really belonged, she was fiercely protective of her hometown. Though Lilithdale was viewed as an oddity, it didn't go unnoticed that they had some beautiful views. As one sleazy developer had asked their mayor several years ago, why waste million-dollar views on two-bit cottages? Imagine tearing them down, building beautiful homes that would give the island prestige.

All the residents could imagine were outsiders and high property taxes. That night they all met in the park and made a pact: No one would sell to an outsider. Everyone was asked to stipulate in their wills that their homes be sold to the township of Lilithdale at a reasonable price, with the profits going to any outside beneficiary. Chloe was pretty sure that's why Irina had left her home to Chloe when she died. She'd had no other beneficiaries.

Chloe stopped to admire a pair of cardinals flitting through patches of sun, and with the toe of her pink sneaker pushed a shiny black beetle away from a swarm of ants. She couldn't bear to see anything suffer. How many times had she saved a hapless lizard or ladybug from her cat's clutches? She shook her head. It had nothing to do with being tender.

SITTING ON her upstairs deck, Chloe let her dog, Shakespeare, and cat, Gypsy, lavish affection on her. She'd adopted Shakespeare, a black and white border collie, from the animal shelter. She'd found Gypsy wandering along the side of the road leading to Naples.

"I almost didn't get to see you guys again."

She pulled her stuffed frog from where she kept it buried in the cushions on her chaise lounge. It was an impulse buy a few years ago, a long-legged frog wearing a crown and velvet robe, bearing a sign that read, KISS ME. After settling on the lounge, she cradled him to her chest with a sigh. A prince was her fairy tale. Frogs were her reality.

She slid into dreams before the sun had even set. Sunshine glinted off something metallic, water lapped rhythmically. A little boy sat in a canoe watching her. *Teddy.* He opened his mouth to say something . . . but no sound came out.

She woke with a start, her heart pounding. Gypsy jumped off her lap, meowing indignantly at the disruption. "Sorry, sweetie," Chloe said absently, staring into the darkness.

She'd always been a vivid dreamer, but this wasn't a regular dream. It was as real as the tinkling sound of the wind chimes above her. She made her sore, achy way down the wooden stairs to the dock where she kept her canoe. Shakespeare jumped in beside her, always eager for a ride. The water was smooth, and the air was cool. She heard a large fish churning nearby, maybe a tarpon. Water gently lapped against the sides of the canoe. The sound in her dreams was something like that, but not exactly.

She let the canoe glide and listened to the sounds around her: the rustle of a raccoon searching for dinner and the eerie call of a bird. In the dim moonlight, the mangrove islands made her feel as though she were lost in a cave system.

The woman in the tunnel . . . she was real, wasn't she? Chloe could still feel the urgency of her words.

"Teddy," she whispered to the night. "Where are you?"

"CHLOE, WHAT in Heaven's name are you doing out here?"

Chloe blinked awake, wondering what Lena was doing in her bedroom. And Stella. And Marilee. When Shakespeare jumped to his feet, her head hit the bottom of the canoe with a thud. She pulled herself up, rubbing the back of her head. Shakespeare had evidently been her pillow.

Chloe's sleepy eyes took in three concerned faces. "I went for a late-night paddle."

Stella's purple caftan shimmered in the morning breeze. "We got worried when you didn't answer your phone. Gypsy showed me the way."

"Yeah, we were worried," Marilee said.

Chloe fixed her animals their breakfasts, mixing up fresh ingredients, then holding Shakespeare's dish while he gobbled it down. That was a quirk he'd come to her with; he wouldn't eat unless she held the bowl. Stella said Chloe's vibes were essential to her dog's digestion.

They were all watching her, including Rascal.

"I'm fine," she said. Even exaggerating the truth didn't work around them. "I've been having dreams since the accident. I'm pretty sure they're about Teddy."

"What kind of dreams?" Lena asked, that shadow in her eyes.

"Psychic dreams?" Marilee asked.

"Not psychic; Chloe's disabled," Stella said.

"We really shouldn't call her disabled. It's so politically incorrect," Marilee said.

"But it's her word."

"What are your dreams about?" Lena asked over their conversation.

"Teddy in a canoe looking at me. Okay, it doesn't sound earth-shattering, but I felt this urgency to look for him. Out there." She nodded toward the mangroves. "I think it has to do with meeting Wanda in the tunnel."

Lena sat down with a thud.

Chloe dropped to her knees in front of her aunt. "What's wrong?"

"Lena's been having visions again," Marilee said.

"She's been trying not to," Stella put in.

Lena's voice sounded strained. "But since your accident, with that boy missing and you feeling so strong about it and all . . . they've started to come back."

Chloe laid her cheek on Lena's lap. She could feel her pain and reluctance. "Lena, I need your help. I can't find this boy on my own." Chloe had seen that grimace on Lena's face all her life. Lena had been fighting visions while claiming she no longer had them.

Marilee surprised Chloe by saying, "Think about what Chloe does for you, me . . . for all of us. Nobody will know the information came from you. We'll keep it to ourselves."

"But what about . . ." Lena let her words drift off, staring at her mother with pleading eyes.

"Chloe's stronger. She'll handle it."

Chloe got to her feet. "Would someone please tell me—"

"All right," Lena said. "I'll help."

Chloe let her questions go, too grateful for Lena's help to press for answers.

AN HOUR later they had eaten the pink pancakes Marilee had whipped up, then gathered in a circle on the back deck. Sunlight filtered through the mangroves and danced on the faded wood planks. Wind rustled through the leaves, and a seagull cried plaintively as it hovered over the glistening water of the bay.

Lena sat with her eyes squeezed shut. Every few minutes she trembled like an earthquake tremor. When she swayed, Chloe started to catch her, but Stella and Marilee quelled the action with a shake of their heads.

Lena sucked in a breath, then released it with an agonized groan. She shuddered, then collapsed against Chloe. They carried Lena to the chaise lounge, and Chloe inconspicuously tucked her frog back into the cushions. No need to raise eyebrows with her silly dreams of finding a prince. *Poor Chloe, a lost romantic soul. We thought we raised her better than that.*

We sure did, Marilee would agree.

"Is she all right?" Chloe asked.

Lena opened her eyes. "I saw the boy. He's somewhere near the water. Either on a boat or in a small house right on the water. And someone is with him."

"His grandmother."

"No, a man. And birds. Teddy's okay. I felt hunger and fear, but he's alive." Her voice had grown faint on the last few words. "I'll have to try again later."

Chloe was elated by the clue, but nervous about what it meant: She was going to have to see Dylan again.

Chapter Six

By Wednesday afternoon, Teddy had been missing almost three days. Dylan had mapped out every possible route Wanda could have taken. He'd organized search teams, and for an entire day, he'd felt in control again. Then night fell, and Teddy was still gone.

Three television stations were waiting to capture the grieving father when he pulled up in front of his house. *Same act as before, don't show emotion. They'll just suck it up and replay it as a sound bite.* He gave them the only words that meant anything: "If anyone has seen my son, please contact the police. Look at his picture and think: Have you seen him?"

Camilla opened the door as soon as he reached it. Her shoulder-length salt-and-pepper hair was disheveled. "It's been like this all day, Mr. McKain."

"I'm sorry you have to go through this. Do you need help?" He rubbed the back of his neck. "And call me Dylan, please."

She lifted her chin. "I can handle them."

He took in her strong shoulders and the determined gleam in her brown eyes. "I don't doubt that," he said, wishing he felt that strong just then. "Do I pay you enough?"

"Eh."

"I'm doubling your salary until we get Teddy back. We'll talk about your permanent raise later."

"Thank you, sir."

"Anything I should know about?"

She picked a legal pad off the counter. "We've had

plenty of calls, people wanting to help, one guy actually wanting money—*money!*—to help. I told him where he could stuff his generous offer. I hope I wasn't out of line. Oh, and your father called."

He stiffened, a natural reaction whenever Will was mentioned.

Recently Will McKain had been trying to contact the son he'd never had time for. Dylan remembered too many years of waiting for even a smile or a minute of his time. "What did he want now? You didn't tell him . . ."

"There goes my raise. I figured, him being your father and all, you'd want him to know. I did bad, didn't I?"

"Don't worry about it."

"He asked if there was anything he could do. Did we need money, did we want him to come down, that kind of thing. I said you would contact him if you needed him."

Fat chance of that.

He set the cell phone on the dining room table. "Go home and get some rest. I'm in for the evening."

She straightened, military-style. "I can put in the hours, sir. Dylan, I mean. If you need me, I'm here."

"No, you go. I appreciate your help."

"There's something else. That detective came by today."

"Again?"

"He asked more questions about you. I don't like him or his implications."

The hairs on Dylan's neck stood. "What implications?" This wasn't about him; it was about Teddy.

"He asked what kind of father you are. What kind of life you live."

"Let him ask what he wants." After a moment, he asked, "What kind of father did you tell him I was?"

"Hardworking, good provider."

Dylan found himself rearranging the napkin holder and crystal salt and pepper shakers. Camilla couldn't say he was a good father because she'd never seen him in action. He loved his son, from that first moment the doctor had put the little guy in his hands. He couldn't believe how perfect life was.

"Oh, and one more thing, Dylan, sir. You're going to have a visitor tonight," Camilla said, gathering her purse. "That woman Mrs. McKain hit. She called earlier, said she had to talk to you."

He covered his face with his hands and heard a groan, then realized it had come from him.

"I did bad again, didn't I? Since your wife hit her, and you went to see her at the hospital, I figured it was all right to tell her to come over. She said she might be able to help find Teddy. You don't think she's planning to sue, do you?"

"I wish she was." That would be a sane reason for her coming over. He had to stop her. "Did she leave a number?"

"I always get a number. But it doesn't matter, because she left twenty minutes ago."

He heard a car door slam shut and voices rise. "Oh, great. Just what I need."

I MUST be crazy to come here. She was sure, positively sure, the only reason was to help find Teddy.

She ignored the reporters' questions as she walked toward the front doors. He was waiting in the doorway, watching her gather her courage along with her canvas bag. She took the flight of steps leading to the front door like a woman going to the dentist. Dylan's tall frame filled the opening, and she wondered if he would make her speak her piece there in the grand front entry. He looked tired, and the shadow of his beard lent a rather dangerous-looking countenance. He was ready for a fight.

Be strong, Chloe. Don't let him bully you; this is too important.

He moved aside reluctantly, as though he'd just then decided to let her in. She had to brush by him as she walked inside, meeting his eyes as she did so. She walked into a living room straight out of an interior design magazine, with white leather furniture, beige carpet, and everything in its place. He led her around a corner to a kitchen the size of her living room. She could *live* in this kitchen. The ceilings were vaulted, tall enough to accommodate a pot-covered rack over the center island. Everything was white except for the black granite countertops. He poured a glass of scotch, then lifted the bottle toward her.

"No, thank you. I don't drink."

He took a long sip, keeping his gaze on hers. She didn't like the way it made her feel, those dark eyes surveying her, heating her from tippy-toe to head. Her cowardice won out, and she shifted her gaze to the family room. The last dying rays of the sun filtered through the wall of French doors that overlooked a terraced deck and pool area, and beyond that, Naples Bay. Even the ceilings were spectacular, a criss-cross pattern inlaid with wood and lights. He had designed this house, she was sure of it. The lighted niches, arched doorways, and rounded corners, everything was perfect. Including the man standing in front of her, arranging a pair of glass salt and pepper shakers on the counter. And rearranging them.

"What are you doing exactly?"

He caught himself shifting the shakers as though he

weren't aware he was doing it. "It's an old habit when I'm tense."

She couldn't help her smile. "A quirk."

"No, it isn't."

"Yes, it is. I saw you doing it in your office. Admit it, it's a nutty little quirk."

"Is not." He pushed the shakers out of range.

He wore a white linen shirt and black dress pants. With one finger, he loosened his tie and unbuttoned the top two buttons of his shirt. Recessed lights above them reflected off the copper pots and filled the kitchen with a warm glow.

"A glass of water would be nice. Please." Her throat suddenly felt tight and dry.

He pushed away from the counter and walked toward the bank of cabinets. He opened one, then another before finding the glasses. He wasn't home enough to know where the glasses were kept.

She didn't know what to do—sit, lean, stand. She felt dumb just watching him pouring water from a cobalt-blue bottle. She supposed she could focus on his long fingers and neat hands. Maybe that wasn't a good idea either.

As soon as she'd drained half her glass, he asked, "What do you want?"

"I want to help you find Teddy."

"For?"

"My own peace of mind. Because deep inside I have to."

"I mean, what do you want for your help?"

"Don't be a jerk. You think I want money?"

"I'm not sure what you want. I can't figure you out."

She walked right up to him before she could think better of it. "You already offered me money, coffee, anything. All I want is a hu—" She stopped herself. She didn't want a hug, she didn't. "All I want is to find Teddy. Isn't that what you want?"

"Of course that's what I want. What I don't need is a pretty little waif with out-of-this-world ideas to distract me."

"Waif?" Jeez, was she going to have to adopt a butch look for anyone to take her seriously? And pretty? She wasn't even going to think about that. "All right, I admit that my story is a bit . . . out there. Like I asked for this? Believe me, I don't want to be here. I don't need you as a distraction either—I mean, this whole thing, finding Teddy. I wish I could put it behind me." She knew the driving force behind her desire was finding Teddy, but Dylan was part of it too.

Something about the man drew her, and she wished she knew what it was. That he was gorgeous couldn't be the reason; looks had never factored into any decision she'd ever made concerning a man. But it sure didn't help matters either. "I can't go on, not until we find Teddy."

"We?"

She crossed her arms in front of her. "Well, I'm looking for him, you're looking for him . . . that sort of makes us a team."

He finished off his scotch and set his glass on the counter with a thud. "We are not a team."

She had to convince him, somehow, some way. "You need me. You don't know it yet, but you need me."

"I don't need anyone. Especially you."

Beneath his icy facade, she sensed something vulnerable. It seemed preposterous that this hard man would be vulnerable in any way. But he let it slip once in a while, a brief flash in his eyes before the shutters fell back into place. He did need someone, but he wasn't ever going to admit it, not even to himself.

"I know where Teddy is."

"What?"

She walked over to a large framed picture of Teddy over the massive stone fireplace. On the mantel were other pictures, of Teddy, Dylan, and Wanda. The perfect family, to fit into the perfect house. Everything looked good on the surface, but something was missing. Everyone in the family portrait was in his or her separate world. The pictures were staged.

She picked up a smaller picture of Teddy and ran her finger along the edge of the silver frame. "Teddy is near the water."

"I guess you can tell that by touching his picture?"

She had seen that mocking glint before. Somehow, coming from him, it stabbed her in the stomach.

"No, I've been dreaming about him. Ever since the accident, it's like I'm connected to him somehow. The dreams are vague, but I can see this kid and he's near water. I thought maybe it would help, that clue. I hoped you might know somewhere Wanda may have hidden him that was near the water. He might be on a boat. With a man."

For a moment, as he looked at his son's picture, she saw a flash of pain and fear. Just as quickly, it vanished. Dylan was adept at masking his feelings.

"Do you realize that in Florida there is water everywhere? Pools, canals, the Gulf of Mexico, ditches. So no, that clue doesn't help."

"I . . . well, I didn't think of that. But it's not pool water or a ditch. It's bigger than that, like the Gulf of Mexico or maybe the bay."

"And," he continued, "she didn't take our boat because it's still out there by the dock. In case you haven't been paying attention to the news reports, Teddy's with a woman, not a man. Anything else, Miss Crystal Ball?"

She twisted her mouth. "I don't have a crystal ball. Nobody in Lilithdale does, Mister Smarty Pants."

"Do you, by chance, communicate with animals?"

"No, that's my Aunt Stella. Why, is there a dog we can ask?" He rolled his eyes, and she guessed not. "Look, I'm not even psychic, okay? I'm disabled."

His gaze surveyed her body. "Pardon?"

"In Lilithdale, everyone has gifts or abilities; I don't, so I'm disabled. I don't even have good instincts." How true that was, she realized. She wanted to touch him, to reach him. As usual, her instincts were leading her down the wrong road. "But I know this: Teddy is out there on or near the water. You've got to trust me."

"I will never trust a woman again. Between the police and the press, the last thing I need is to be associated with you."

She blinked. *Don't let him see. His words don't matter anyway. They don't.*

She found herself gripping his forearm. "Forget what the press thinks. Forget what anyone thinks. Think only about Teddy."

Dylan looked at her in the same intense way he had at his office. *Look away, Chloe. Don't let him see right into your soul.* Her heart was hammering in her chest. His other hand came up to catch her chin. She tried to shake her head, but she couldn't move. Her instincts should have been screaming for her to get away from him, this man who was nothing like a poet and who thought she was a nutcase. Those instincts locked her in place and stole away her words.

"You like men, Chloe?"

"What?"

"You heard me."

She tried to pull free of his grip, but he wouldn't let go. She tried to remember what she'd told that frog-faced attorney. But Dylan wasn't froggy. "Of course I like men. Just not overbearing, unemotional, close-minded men." That made him loosen his grip, and she pulled her chin free. "Why are you doing this?"

"Because I want you to leave. Because I don't need you distracting me from finding my son. Because I hate that you *are* distracting me, and it's not your crazy story or even that my wife put those bruises on your face." He ran the tips of his fingers across her scraped cheek, and she shivered. "Maybe I was hoping you preferred women so you wouldn't be so damned distracting. I'm all those things you mentioned; so why when I look at you do I want to . . ."

Chloe couldn't breathe; she was sure her heart had stopped beating in anticipation of his next words. Finally she said, "What?" giving away her anxious state in that desperately whispered word.

His expression shuttered again. "I need to be looking for my son, not thinking about you."

"You've been thinking about me?"

He turned toward the French doors. "What kind of man thinks about a woman while his son is lost?"

Obviously a tortured one. She didn't know what to say other than to ask him what he was thinking. But that hardly seemed appropriate, and it probably wasn't a good kind of thinking anyway.

"Especially," he continued, "a woman who's probably as crazy as his wife was." He pressed his palms to the glass.

She blinked, knocked out of the spell by those words. Logic. She needed logic. She ran some numbers through her mind. Numbers always made sense; feelings never did. She opened her mouth and out came, "Twenty-two hundred fifty eight."

"Pardon?"

She waved her hand. "It's a thing I do. When I get discombobulated, I run numbers, calculations. Sometimes they slip out. Okay, let's approach this logically."

"Logically?"

She might as well have said, *Let's take a bath in mint chocolate chip ice cream.*

"We both want to find Teddy," she said.

"I'm with you so far."

"Okay, next: We have no business being . . . distracted by one another. I can't be anywhere near the type of woman you like, and you're not a romantic poet with tender sensibilities, so—"

He tilted his head. "You want a romantic poet with—"

"Forget that." He had a knowing smile on his face as though he'd caught her with her hand in the cookie jar. "All right, so what? I want a romantic poet type. A *guy*. Back to the logical part: We shouldn't be distracting each other one iota. This is strictly business."

"What's strictly business?"

"Us finding Teddy."

He shook his head. "There is no us!"

She let out a sound of exasperation. She definitely had no business being distracted by this man. "You may not need anyone to help you find your son, but I need to help. Can you understand that?" She didn't give him a chance to answer. "How can you? I can hardly explain it to myself. All I know is that deep inside, I need to be involved in the search." She'd grabbed hold of his arms. "I'll try not to distract you, I promise. How *do* I distract you, anyway? Maybe if you tell me, I can fix the problem. Will it help if I go butch? I mean, in looks only."

"No, don't do that." He looked down where her fingers were wrapped around his linen shirtsleeves. "I don't want to think about how you distract me. I just know I don't like it."

She looked up at those narrowed brown eyes of his. "It's not a good kind of distraction, is it?"

His gaze swept over her face, her mouth, then back to her eyes. She couldn't swallow for a moment; his eyes looked as liquid as melted chocolate. He touched the cut on her lower lip with his thumb, so gently it almost tickled.

"No, it's not a good kind of distraction," he said in a voice that sounded lower. He regarded her with a hard expression, though she suspected the hardness was aimed at himself and not her. "Chloe, you need to go away. Now."

"I can't."

"Why the hell not?"

"You need me."

He ran his fingers over his shadowed jaw. "And what gave you that idea?"

"I'm the only link you have to your son. Maybe it's a mother's instinct I picked up from Wanda. I can't explain it, but I can feel your son when I dream."

A shrill noise interrupted. Dylan pulled away and answered his cell phone. She took a deep breath, wondering what the heck he'd meant. A not-good kind of distraction could be her being so ugly he couldn't stand the sight of her.

She focused in on the call, praying it was the police with good news. Dylan's slumping shoulders didn't make that a hopeful prospect. He leaned on the counter, rubbing his forehead.

"Like what? . . . All right, I'll see you in a few minutes."

He set the phone back on the counter. Without realizing it, she'd come closer to him, but fought an instinct urging her to put her arms around him.

"Is everything all right?"

"Don't know. That was Teddy's doctor. He's got some information that's going to change the entire search."

Chapter Seven

DYLAN HADN'T ASKED CHLOE TO LEAVE BEFORE DR. Jacobs arrived, so she'd stayed, feeling somehow as though she needed to be there. Dylan paced in front of the French doors, and she sat on the leather couch and tried not to watch him. That's when she spotted a brown lizard on the inside of one of the glass door panes.

"You have a lizard in the house," she said.

He absently glanced down to where she pointed. "It won't hurt you."

"I know that. But it'll die in here."

He paused in his pacing and looked at her. "Are you compulsive about saving things?"

"I just don't like things to die."

"Saving that duck could have cost you your life, you know."

She shrugged. "I guess I'm compulsive about saving things."

"Is that why you're so insistent on saving Teddy?"

She shook her head. "Teddy's different."

When the doorbell rang, Dylan launched himself toward the entry. Chloe opened the door and shooed the lizard out before Dylan and the doctor walked into the living room. Dr. Jacobs looked like a professor, with small glasses, a tall frame, and a tired brown sweater.

"Dr. Jacobs, this is Chloe Samms," Dylan said.

For a moment, she got distracted by the way her name sounded coming from Dylan's mouth. She shook the doctor's hand. "Nice to meet you."

Dylan invited him to sit down, then took a seat in one

of the plush chairs with the fringed pillows. The room, overlooking the terraces and pool, was set up for entertaining. Chloe could imagine Wanda in an elegant gown playing hostess to her husband's prestigious clients, parties spilling out onto the lit terrace. She felt an odd prick of jealousy that Wanda had shared his life, his house . . . his bed.

Twenty-four hundred fifty divided by forty-five is fifty-four point forty-four.

Enough of those thoughts! This isn't my world; I'd never belong here with him.

She pushed herself into a corner of the couch with her legs tucked beneath her. Now she knew what her frog prince felt like.

"First, I want to say how sorry I am to hear about Mrs. McKain's accident and Teddy's disappearance."

"Thank you," Dylan said.

"A police detective came to see me today, asking if Teddy had ever come in with questionable injuries."

Dylan surged to his feet.

Dr. Jacob waved him to calm down. "He wasn't accusing, just asking."

Dylan slowly sank down on his chair, but stayed on the edge. "Was it Detective Yochem?"

"Yes, and he wouldn't say why he was asking. I told him that Teddy's records indicate no more than the usual boy's scrapes and bruises. But there was something that concerned me. The police didn't know about Teddy's condition. I find that disturbing considering how important it is that everyone searching for the boy know what they're dealing with."

Chloe scooted closer to Dylan.

"I don't understand," Dylan said. "What condition?"

"That's what I was afraid of, that your wife hadn't told

you. She was very upset, of course, but she was also preternaturally concerned about your reaction. She kept saying you'd put her away. I told her that was ridiculous, no one would be put away. I wanted her to bring you in so we could discuss what needed to be done, but she said you'd never tolerate your son being different. She begged me not to tell you. I called her several times, but she wouldn't take my calls. My assistant notified me that your wife was having Teddy's records transferred to another doctor. I suspect she always did that as soon as she heard something she didn't like; your son had been to several doctors before I saw him."

"What's wrong with Teddy?"

Chloe could hear the careful control in Dylan's voice. He wanted to throttle the words out of the doctor. She watched him rein in his feelings. Before she realized what she was doing, she'd dropped down on the carpet next to Dylan's feet. She saw his long fingers gripping the arm of the chair, and those crazy instincts wanted to pry his fingers away and hold them in her hands. She pressed her palms together instead.

"Teddy is autistic."

Dylan had prepared himself since the moment the doctor had entered the house, putting on the layers like he had as a boy. Fully prepared to hear anything, the word "autistic" bounced against the padding. What was it?

He glanced down at Chloe. Something inside him wanted to reach out to her. She was right there, within touching distance. Something bigger wanted her to leave. Why hadn't he asked her to go when the doctor arrived?

He started shifting round ceramic things—he didn't even know what they were—in the large bowl on the coffee table. His voice sounded thick as he envisioned the worst when he asked, "What is it?"

"Autism is a neurological disorder of the brain that causes lifelong developmental disabilities. I'm not a specialist, but I have an autistic nephew, so I'm familiar with it. Teddy needs to be tested to determine how severely he's affected."

Dylan's mind stopped on the words "disorder of the brain." He had done this to his son through his mother's mad genes. He had inadvertently destroyed Teddy's life by causing Wanda's death, and now this.

"Is he . . . crazy?" Dylan asked.

"It's not that kind of disorder. It's caused by a neurological dysfunction, though no one knows for sure what causes the dysfunction. It largely manifests itself in social impairment. You had him tested for deafness when he was a baby because he didn't always respond to your voices or loud, sudden noises."

"That's right. But he was fine. Other than that, his development was normal. He started walking on schedule, saying words. When he was two, he stopped talking as much. We took him to a speech therapist who said every child has to learn to talk at their own pace. We took him to his regular doctor and had some tests run. He said the same thing, that every child develops at a different rate and not to worry. He started talking again a few months later, though he was mostly repeating words."

Dr. Jacobs was nodding. "All of that's typical with autism."

"Did Wanda know? Is that why she brought Teddy to see you?"

"No, he was only in for a routine checkup. Perhaps I would have overlooked the symptoms if autism wasn't a personal issue in my life. It's easy to overlook or misdiagnose; only four or five out of every ten thousand births will result in full-blown autism. As I worked with Teddy during the exam, I saw several symptoms. He didn't greet me, didn't seem to know where he was or why he was there. He immersed himself in the knob that lowers my chair. Children are curious about a doctor's examination room, but they don't usually focus on one item for long periods of time, particularly an uninteresting item. But it was the look in his eyes that struck me. Have you noticed that your son is often in his own little world?"

"Yes, I have. Wanda kept telling me it was normal, that he was just imaginative." That he was too focused and unemotional, like his father. "He did seem to be creative. He painted pictures of houses like any kid. Sometimes I painted with him."

"Autistic children turn their focus inward. They might very well be creative, but they remain withdrawn, using their imaginations to entertain themselves. Did he notice your paintings?"

Dylan had to think. "No, he was pretty immersed in his own. I figured that was normal. When Teddy began talking again, we thought the doctor had been right, that he was just developing at his own pace. At about that time, things got hectic at work, and I put in a lot of long hours. Wanda told me Teddy talked, laughed, and played games. She said the reason he never did any of that around me was because . . ." He shook his head. "She made up all kinds of reasons, that Teddy wasn't feeling well or that he was tired." That his father was never around.

Dylan looked at the pictures on the mantel. Teddy rarely looked at the camera. His gaze was always to the right or left. And his eyes weren't focused on anything. "But he smiles." He felt an ache inside. What he wouldn't do to see that smile again.

"Autistic people can and do enjoy life. They're often

very intelligent. They're able to lead independent, successful lives. The good news is I suspect Teddy may have Asperger's disorder. That's a collection of symptoms or characteristics at what they call the 'higher-functioning' end of the autism spectrum. I brought some books on the subject so you'd understand." He handed Dylan three books. "To communicate with your son, you must learn to see his world. Then, perhaps, you can help him see ours."

"I'll do whatever I need to do."

For another half hour, the doctor patiently answered Dylan's questions. When his pager went off, he read the small panel and got to his feet. "I must be off. It's our thirtieth anniversary, and if I miss another one, I believe I'll be shot." The smile on his face waned. "You need to alert the media and educate everyone who's looking for Teddy. I'd be glad to assist you if you'd like. He may not realize he's in trouble. Most likely he's reverted to his own world because he isn't comfortable where he is. Autistic children don't handle change well. He probably won't call for help and won't respond when someone calls his name. It makes the search harder. You could walk right by him and never know it. When Teddy comes back—and he will come back, we've got to believe that—we'll schedule the tests. Then we can work with a specialist and get Teddy pointed in the right direction."

Dylan shook his hand. "Thank you for coming here. For helping me understand." He walked Dr. Jacobs to the door. "One more question," he said quietly. "Could autism be caused by . . . mental illness in a parent's background?"

"It's possible. As I said, no one really knows what causes it." He started to leave, but stopped. "Oh, and one other thing. You might want to donate some blood . . . in case your son has injuries when he's found."

Dylan didn't want to think about injuries. "I'll do it first thing in the morning."

"Just stop by my office, and we'll take care of it. Good night, Mr. McKain."

Guilt weighed down hard on him. He'd been so focused on the firm, he hadn't noticed that his wife was crazy. He'd chased her to her death. And he might, through his genes, be responsible for Teddy's affliction.

Dylan returned to find Chloe looking at one of Teddy's pictures. She looked like an angel in a yellow jumpsuit and matching sneakers, golden curls catching the last of the day's light streaming through the windows. He half expected to find disgust on her face, but he saw nothing but tenderness.

And then he remembered something. "You knew."

She started, obviously lost in her thoughts. "What?"

"You knew he was different."

She put the picture back on the mantel. "Wanda told me."

"Yeah, right. You knew Wanda before the accident."

"I didn't know her." She shifted her feet. "I don't exactly hang out in your circles."

She said those words without bitterness or envy. Whatever this woman was, she wasn't deceitful. Not on purpose, anyway. Most likely she was off balance, like Wanda. For that reason alone, he should have nothing more to do with her. He certainly shouldn't want to pull her close and rest his cheek on top of her head. Or wonder why she smelled so sweet and flowery.

She backed away as though she could read his thoughts. "For a few moments Wanda and I were both dead. Our souls were in the same place. She knew she'd hidden her son and mother away and probably knew they couldn't survive long on their own. Think logically. Who else could she tell?"

He laughed. "Logically. Right."

She tilted her head. "Don't you believe in Heaven?"

He didn't like the thickness of his voice when he said, "I don't know what I believe anymore." He could remember his mother dragging him to church every Sunday when he was a boy. Every Sunday he prayed for a different mother. A mother who didn't take circuitous routes everywhere because she thought she was being followed by the bad guys, whoever they were.

"Why?" she asked, studying him so intently that for a moment he was sure she could see into his soul. The compassion and tenderness in her voice touched him in a place no one had touched in a long time. Maybe ever. It made him feel small and young and vulnerable, and he shut himself away like he'd been doing since he was young. It kept people out, people who asked too many questions, kids who teased him.

"Maybe I'm just too focused on everything else in my life. I've got enough to deal with here on earth to think about Heaven."

"I can tell you, it exists," she said. "I can't explain it, but I can remember how it was. I never wanted to come back."

She sighed, and a palpable peace settled over her expression. Her brief smile stirred him the way a shot of tequila did: a momentary jolt, then a warm, burning sensation in the pit of his stomach. He had a feeling that if she stayed any longer, he'd soon feel that intoxicating buzz . . . and, invariably, the resulting hangover.

She wasn't looking at him, but at some distant place. Her fingers caressed her owl pendant as she spoke.

"And the light was incredible. It wasn't like any light I've ever seen. It was everywhere, even flowing through me—"

He gave in and kissed her. Truth was, he couldn't stop himself. Her lips were warm and soft beneath his. Slowly they started moving, responding. She shifted to the left and tilted her head. A soft, breathy sigh escaped her throat, and he deepened the kiss. Her mouth opened, and their tongues connected, hers tentatively to his. Forget tentative, he wanted to taste her, to feel her warm, wet tongue slide against his. She was sweet, drugging his senses. He'd forgotten what it was like to kiss a woman, to really kiss a woman, but Chloe didn't feel like just any woman. She was sweeter, softer, her mint taste overcoming his scotch. He wanted to devour her, to inhale that second sigh that came from deep within her.

Her silky curls twined around his fingers. Her skin felt soft beneath his thumbs as they grazed her jawline. He wasn't sure he could stop, he was like an alcoholic who'd found the ultimate drink, just one more, then another, he was drowning, sinking fast and not caring.

He could feel that light she described flowing through his veins like an electric drug. It lit up the dark corners of his soul and made him feel more alive than he'd ever felt. This was where she belonged, right here, nowhere else.

He had to stop, to reach for the surface before he was a goner. He wrenched himself away. The light faded, but he didn't care. He could breathe again, could think . . . logically.

"You'd better leave."

Her eyes were liquid blue, her mouth slack and pink.

She covered her mouth with her hand. "Why did you do that?"

She sounded breathless; he'd taken her breath away, it was an intoxicating idea, breathless Chloe, and he wanted to keep her that way. *Stop it, she's making you crazy.* He rubbed his hand over his eyes. "Maybe I'm crazier than you are."

"Don't disparage me. I'm not crazy."

"Why do you use that word, 'disparage'? Why are you here, why am I here?" He was crazy. Had to be. Because he wanted to kiss her again, he was hooked on her. It wasn't logical, and everything in his life was logical. Everything had to add up to something, and he and Chloe weren't going to add up to anything.

Her movements became more hurried as she searched for that monstrosity of a purse. "I'm going."

When she passed him, he took hold of her arm. He stared at his hand, willing it not to pull her close. "I know," she said before he could speak. "That kiss didn't mean anything. It was a mistake. There's no way a man like you could get involved with a woman like me because you've got your reputation to think about. You can let go of me now."

His fingers were locked around her arm, and for a moment they wouldn't obey his command to let go. What part of him didn't want to let her leave? He had inherited his mother's insanity, at least a speck of it. And Chloe brought it out. Finally his fingers sprung open, and she walked away. She didn't look at him as she slung her purse over her shoulder and walked to the door. He couldn't stop looking at her, an angel in yellow, an angel he'd brought back to life. Had she been talking to his wife about Teddy when he'd put his mouth over hers and breathed life into her? His touched his lips, remembering the illusory feel of the moment.

She'd heard that speech before, that one she'd made for him. He could see it in her eyes, hear it in her voice. Somebody had kissed her and told her it meant nothing. Dylan was pretty sure that person had lied.

He walked to the front door and watched the green Thunderbird back out of the driveway. The press had tried to talk to her again, but she ignored them. He felt a strange tug inside as he watched her fade into the distance. He'd probably gotten rid of her for good this time. Relief surged through him. That was relief, wasn't it, that bittersweet ache?

He walked to Teddy's room. The boy had always put his things away in perfect order. Most of the toys he'd bought for his son sat neatly on the shelves of the massive built-in bookcase. The toys in the oak chest sat waiting for a boy who wasn't there to play with them. Dylan picked up a See n' Say, a large stuffed rabbit, typical kids' toys. Not typical were the collection of buttons arranged just so on the chest. Wasn't Wanda forever sewing on buttons, making excuses that they came off in the dryer? Had she been covering for Teddy?

And what about the alphabet blocks? Dylan had been proud at how fast Teddy learned the alphabet, lining up the blocks over and over . . . and over again. Now Dylan could see the obsessive way Teddy played with those blocks, to the exclusion of everyone around him.

How could he have missed that his son was different? Because he'd seen what he wanted to see.

The problem was, Dylan didn't know what a normal child was like. It had all looked so normal on the outside.

He'd been so busy putting the exterior together, he hadn't noticed the cracks in the foundation.

IT USED to be that when the morning sun came up, his mom would pull him out of bed and make him get dressed. Teddy used to hate that, because that meant he had to leave his room. That was the best place in the world.

Now he wished Mom would come wake him up. Anything to be regular again. He wanted his room back. His life. His things. It was starting to scare him, being here, no Mom or Dad or room. Something was wrong. He was afraid to think about it.

The woman talked to him. He'd learned to try to listen to what people said; it was always an effort, but he really, really tried. He didn't try with the old woman. For one thing, she always called him Wanda. He didn't know any Wandas, and he was sure he wasn't one. It was a girl's name, and he didn't know hardly any girls.

Teddy walked to the little kitchen and ate some Cocoa Puffs. The woman always left her bowl, the milk, and the cereal box out, so he just helped himself. She had cereal all the time, even for dinner. Teddy didn't mind. He liked Cocoa Puffs.

A while later, the woman started moving very fast. He sensed something was wrong, so he tried to understand what she was saying.

"Where are we? Why is there water all around us? I have to get into town. The sale on strawberries is over on Saturday. How am I going to make strawberry shortcake without strawberries? Tell me that. Tell me . . ." She looked at him, and he looked away. "Have you seen my purse? My gosh, look at the time! I've got to get my afternoon nap. The nurses will be after me if I don't get my nap."

When the woman was asleep, he crept up to her like a kitty cat and pulled the buttons off her sweater. These were familiar, at least. He also pulled the buttons off his own shirt. They weren't pretty like the woman's. Hers were pink and swirly.

He set the buttons in the beam of sunshine that poured in through the glass door. One, two, three, four, five, six, seven, eight, nine, ten. He arranged them in lines, counting up, down, and from side to side. He counted them in twos and fives. He liked numbers, liked the way they added up every time.

But there weren't enough buttons, not enough variety. He went into the room he and the woman slept in. It wasn't quite like his room, but he recognized drawers. He went to work setting out his clothes in stacks by color. Blue here, red here. Stripes got tricky, because there were two colors. Sometimes more.

He went to work removing each button, sometimes biting the strings. He lined them up along the edge of the dresser. Now he had more colors to add to the rest.

Movement caught his eye, and he looked up. A little boy stared back at him. Who was in his room? His heart started pounding at the thought of a stranger. He scooped up his buttons so the other boy wouldn't take them.

Then he remembered: That boy was himself. Teddy reached up, and so did the boy. He blinked; so did the boy. He looked at the boy's eyes. His mom was always saying, "Look at me." He repeated it, because that's what he thought she wanted. It wasn't. She got that ugly look on her face and grabbed his chin. "Look at me!"

It seemed important to everyone that he look at their

eyes. He didn't like to look in people's eyes. It made him feel funny inside. But he wanted to make his mom happy, so he practiced with the boy who was him. He stared at the boy's eyes. They looked like buttons. Blue buttons. If he imagined them as buttons, it didn't bother him to look into his eyes.

But something was different. He frowned. He didn't like change, but everything had changed lately. His mom wasn't here. Or his dad. Or Camel. Nobody familiar but the boy, and even he looked different.

Teddy reached up to his hair—and screamed. A squeak emerged from his mouth, but in his head he could hear a big roar. His hair was gone. The curls he liked coiling around his fingers had been killed.

That woman was bad. She'd taken his curls. She called him Wanda when he knew his name was Teddy. He had to get away from her.

He scooped up his buttons and tucked them in his pockets. He walked back to the place where the woman slept. At least she hadn't taken his buttons. But they had moved, because they weren't in the sunlight anymore.

He put those buttons in his pocket too. Then he looked at the door. He would have to go out there to get away from the bad woman. He started to reach for the door lever.

"Wanda! Where are you going?" the woman's voice screeched.

She pushed herself up and reached for the tiny table in front of her. That's how she got to her feet.

"You have to stay inside. Your father will be home soon, and you know how angry he gets when we're not here for him."

He pulled at the lever, fingers gripping it so hard it hurt.

She got to her feet, then took a step. He pulled the lever all the way, and the door opened. White birds scattered from the trees. The air was cool and smelled salty. It was a big place out there. He didn't like big places. But the woman was coming closer. In his fear, her voice had become a garble of noise. Her hand was stretched out toward him. He looked outside again. And then he ran.

Chapter Eight

CHLOE HAD GONE TO BED DETERMINED TO FORGET ABOUT both Dylan and Teddy. She'd woken up thinking about Dylan and Teddy. The more she tried to put them out of her mind, the more they demanded her attention.

Especially Teddy. The dreams she'd had last night were so real, she could smell his little-boy sweat. He needed her, even if his stubborn father didn't. Frustration knotted her insides. She threw on cotton pants and a tank top and went down to the workshop beneath her house. She had spent many days as a youngster watching Irina create things out of clay. Chloe loved the way just a gentle touch of her finger created a groove as the wheel spun. It was almost hypnotic, watching her hands mold the clay, creating a pot or vase out of a lump of wet clay. Too bad she was miserable at it.

An hour later, she threw the fourth failure against the door. Her twisted flower lamps and warped face pots were all a testament to her lack of creative skill.

She spotted a butterfly duck in through the doorway. Another lost soul trapped where she shouldn't be. It took fifteen minutes to get her out, fifteen minutes of jumping, shooing, climbing on barrels and stools, only to have the fragile butterfly land on her hand. "You're way too tender to be stuck in here," she said, lifting her hand outside and watching it take flight.

She closed up her workshop and looked for something more productive to spend her energy on. Grabbing the hedge shears, she went to work on the thorny bougainvillea plants with the papery purple flowers. As the long blades were about to sever another branch, she stopped in time to save a moth from being sheared in half. Chloe wondered why the moth hadn't moved, then saw the cocoon it was protecting. A mother going to any length to protect her own. Chloe left the branch alone. She realized she'd nearly butchered the bushes and still hadn't quelled her restlessness. So she did the next best thing: She cut her hair.

Now she stared at her reflection, devoid of curls. She ran her fingers down the shorn locks that fell to just a few inches below her ears. She'd moussed it so the curls would straighten. No more cute Chloe.

"Wonder what Dylan would think. Not that he'll see it. The man is the biggest pain in my tushy." And he'd kissed her silly.

Not that the kiss was silly; her reaction to it was. Her heart had jumped around in her chest like a sprung rubber ball. She had never, *never* been kissed like that before, as though she were the only thing that mattered in the world. For those beautiful moments, she'd thought of that long-forgotten romantic poet she'd dreamed about, before she'd become cynical.

She smirked at her frog prince sitting on the bathroom counter. *Yeah, right.* "That's the problem. I'm not cynical enough. You'd think I'd learn. First I fall head over for a builder with political aspirations. Now I fall head over—" She slapped her face, then winced because she'd slapped her scraped cheek. "I am not falling for him." She stared again at her reflection, at the dreamy sparkle in her blue eyes. A new face; maybe she'd call it her marshmallow face. "Just what you need, Chloe Samms. A man who doesn't believe in miracles, who thinks you're a fraud or a loony, take your pick, and is probably married to his work."

She sighed and moved away from the mirror. She definitely needed to ground herself.

Chloe walked outside, enjoying the feel of the cool earth beneath her bare feet. Lena had taught her at a young age that grounding herself meant occupying her own space. It meant flushing out other people's vibes and energy and focusing only on her own. She sat on the white bench in her back yard, inhaling the temperate air and pushing her toes into the soil. The rustle of leaves soothed her almost as much as Gypsy's purring. The world smelled of earth and flowers and salty breezes. The ground was a kaleidoscope of changing patterns as sunlight danced through the moving leaves.

A flock of snowy egrets took sudden flight from one of the mangrove islands in the distance. Something had startled them. She walked to the water's edge and listened. The ever-present sound of boat engines filled the air with their hum. Water lapped against land. Sunshine glittered on the ripples of the water. All of the beautiful things she never took for granted. Nothing out of the ordinary.

Then why did she feel restless?

She decided to go into "downtown Lilithdale," as it was affectionately called. She headed to the Happy Haven Tea House for a cup of Oregon Chai latté to go.

"Chloe! You cut those beautiful curls," Sangeeta said before even greeting her.

"It was time for a new look."

"But I loved those curls!"

Chloe grinned. "You want them? Maybe we can glue them to your head."

"Silly girl." A few minutes later Sangeeta brought her a recycled, earth-friendly container of latté. "You want me to read the leaves? Oh, shoot, there are no leaves with this stuff. It comes in a mix."

Chloe inhaled the heavenly blend of spices, honey, and vanilla, getting a dab of foam on her nose. "Maybe next time."

"Oh, Chloe, am I happy to see you!" Nita said when Chloe walked in the doorway of the little bookstore. Nita was a petite woman with blond curls of her own. "I've got to peepee so bad, and there are three customers in here. Two are tourists," she said on a whisper. "Thanks, sweetie!" After a kiss on the cheek, Nita disappeared behind the purple curtain in the back.

Chloe settled behind the counter and searched for the account books she was supposed to have picked up the day of the accident. Maybe work would distract her.

Warm natural light spilled in through the high windows. Curling up in one of the worn chairs in a corner, breathing in the scent of incense and books, sounded heavenly.

"Ma'am," one of the tourists said, approaching the counter, "do you have any books on neurocranial restructuring? My holistic doctor suggested coming here."

Chloe blinked. Whatever it was, it sounded way painful. "Your head looks all right to me." When the woman gave her a strange look, Chloe added, "Nita will be right back, and she'll be able to tell you offhand. I think the woman has every title in here memorized."

"Against the back wall in the right corner," Stella said, sailing through the door in a flowing leopard-print dress. "Dr. Schlatzy, great book. Chloe, you have such a peaceful aura about you this morning. And you look a lot better, doesn't she, Rascal?" Her dachshund popped out of the big tote bag and made a slurping sound. "Maybe a little pale, yes. Oh, my, you're right! Chloe, you cut off your curls!" She kissed Rascal on the head and set him on the floor.

"I needed a change." Chloe gave her a hug and held on for a moment.

"What's that for?" Stella asked, though she didn't hesitate to squeeze her back.

"Because I'm here and I can."

Stella set a cup of pungent lemon tea on the counter. "Any more dreams about the boy?"

"Another one last night. I don't know what to do about them. I don't have any abilities; how am I going to find him?"

"Pay attention to those dreams. They'll tell you something."

"I've been writing them down, but so far nothing has clicked. And every day that passes . . ." She didn't want to think about that little boy alone out there. "I went to see Dylan yesterday. He still thinks I'm a flake. And get this—"

"He kissed you!"

"How do you *do* that?"

Stella shrugged. "It was the way you said his name. Definitely had a kiss sound to it."

"Well, he did kiss me, but that's not what I was going to say. We found out Teddy is autistic. Remember how Wanda told me he was different? He *is* different. And it makes it all the more urgent that we find him."

"You'll find him. I know you'll find him."

"Has Lena had any . . ."

Stella shook her head, dislodging her matching bow. "She's feeling as down as a dog in the summer heat. I think it's all coming back to her, the visions, the fear, and the mess it all became. It's not that she's a hard-hearted woman—"

"I know that. She's just afraid. I understand afraid."

Stella pinched Chloe's chin. "Better get going. I've got a manic-depressive dalmatian at ten and a German shepherd with an inferiority complex at eleven. Rascal, honey!"

Rascal's nails click-clicked on the tile floor as his little legs carried him to Stella. That dog was her baby, without a doubt. He slept in his own cherrywood sleigh bed, and every night she covered him up with a quilt she'd made for him. She got up in the middle of the night to make sure he was still covered. And she even warmed up his dog food.

That wasn't anything like Chloe holding Shakespeare's dog bowl. And she only made their food from scratch because it was healthier; no preservatives and all that. But she drew the line at warming it up. Except on very cold mornings.

"Oh, a word of warning. Mom's in dire need of help at the Blue Moon tonight. Pepper's got mono, poor pup, and Lena's not up to it."

"Thanks for the warning, but—"

"Yeah, I know," Stella said with a wave. "You can't turn your back on someone in need. You're a love. I've got a skunk having stink withdrawals at seven-thirty, but I'll try to swing by and relieve you for the second seating. Hey, Nita! Just stopped in to let you know Lena got the shipment of juniper berry skin cream. There are three bottles behind the counter for you."

Nita joined Chloe at the counter. "I'll stop by and get them this afternoon. Thanks, Chloe. My bladder is very grateful."

"No problem. I found your books, so I'll get started on them today."

"Oh, your hair!"

"It'll grow out."

As soon as Chloe walked out of the bookstore, she spotted Marilee coming from the Pink Motel's office. She and Gerri, the owner, always had their morning prayer session and coffee together on the patio.

"Sure, I can help," Chloe said before Marilee could ask. "What time do you need me?"

"What, you get psychic on me?"

"Stella warned me."

"Ah, you're a sweetheart. Never let me down, you haven't. Six'll be great. I've got seven tables going so far."

When Chloe passed the white cottage Stella and Lena shared on the edge of the bay, her shred of peacefulness slipped away. She didn't want to hurt her aunt, but she needed her help. Before she could decide whether to approach Lena now or wait a few hours, Lena opened the door. She was wearing the pink fuzzy robe that looked like a bedspread. She took in Chloe's chopped tresses, but didn't comment. Neither that nor the grave look on her face boded well.

"Oh, boy, Chloe. You're not going to like this, not one bit."

Chloe's heart kicked into gear. "A bad feeling? It's Teddy, isn't it?"

"No, nothing more metaphysical than the daily paper."

DYLAN, DETECTIVE Yochem, and Dr. Jacobs scheduled another press conference announcing Teddy's autism. It was too late to make the six o'clock news, but they'd make the eleven o'clock news and the morning broadcasts. Afterward, Dylan went home alone and told himself to get some sleep.

He couldn't sleep, so he got up and started reading the books Dr. Jacobs had given him.

The house was too quiet, too empty. In a way he couldn't quite understand, it *felt* empty. He kept walking to Teddy's room, as though expecting him to miraculously appear. Only he didn't believe in miracles.

Finally his body and mind overloaded, and he fell asleep. He dragged himself awake a few minutes later, only to discover it was ten o'clock in the morning. In the living room, he could hear the television and the sound of water running. Camilla. He hadn't realized what a wonderful sound . . . sound was. Just knowing someone else was in the house. When had it become important to him?

Since you've been alone.

He felt a pang at the realization that Wanda would never make another sound in the house again. He was so focused on finding Teddy he hadn't had a chance to mourn her death.

Groggy and disoriented, he wasn't ready to face those thoughts yet. Or Camilla. He took a shower and got dressed. Then he called the office and told Jodie to reschedule his morning appointments and apologize for any he missed. She had a funny tone in her voice. Probably pity.

He should be used to it by now, but he wasn't. He sure hadn't gotten immune to it as a kid. The worst was when his mother had picketed town hall with a blank sign. She claimed only the bad guys could read it. The cameras had already been there when someone called him. Dylan had raced his bike downtown to bring her home. That night on the news everyone in town watched him plead and cajole his determined mother into leaving. That's when they knew what they'd only suspected—his mom was crazy. That's when the looks of pity became unbearable. Last night when he'd gone on the air about Teddy, it felt the same . . . and again he'd had no choice.

As soon as Dylan walked into the family room, Camilla poured him a cup of strong coffee. It felt odd, sitting there at this hour in the morning. "Camilla, did you notice anything strange about Teddy's behavior?"

"Strange?"

"Is he a . . . normal kid?"

"All children are different, sir—Dylan. They develop at their own pace."

"Be straight with me. I know I wasn't around a lot. I should have been, but I wasn't. Maybe I missed it, maybe I didn't know what to look for." Maybe he hadn't wanted to see. "Tell me what Teddy did around here all day."

"He is a little different, for a boy of his age. I asked Mrs. McKain about it, but she said he was normal and for me to mind my own business. She said don't ever mention it to you, or she'd accuse me of stealing and fire me."

"Wanda said that?" Camilla nodded. Dylan would have believed Wanda. In the same way he could see the truth in Chloe's eyes, he could see it in Camilla's. "I'm not going to fire you. Talk to me."

"I wasn't around him much. He spent a lot of time in his room. I would hear her in there with him, talking for hours. The woman could talk. I always thought it was strange that Teddy never said hello or good-bye. He never came in and asked for anything. Never told me about anything. He would spend hours playing with those letter blocks, stacking and unstacking. If I tried to divert him, even to feed him lunch, he would throw a temper tantrum. He wouldn't scream, mind you, but he tried. And then there was the doors."

"Doors?"

"He would spend hours opening and closing every door in the house. And God forbid if I had to go into a room where he'd closed the door."

"I've never seen him throw a tantrum. He's always so . . . well behaved."

"Most of the time he is, but sometimes . . ." She shook her head, eyes wide. "And the goldfish. That was unusual."

How much didn't he know about his son? His chest ached with the answer. "What about the goldfish?"

"Do you ever notice how the fish keep changing in the aquarium?"

"No," he had to admit. He hardly noticed the fish at all. That was Wanda's hobby..

"Teddy liked . . . well, he liked to eat them. He'd climb up and pull off the lid. Then he'd catch them and pop them into his mouth. Quick little bugger too. I had to keep buying new fish. But Mrs. McKain told me never to tell you, that you'd get upset."

Dylan leaned on the counter, rubbing his forehead. "There's a reason for his behavior."

"I saw it on the news. I'm sorry."

He shook his head. "Don't be sorry. Whatever you do, don't be sorry." He wouldn't have Teddy pitied. "Any calls while I was in the shower?"

"I've been fielding calls all morning." She picked up the yellow legal from the counter. "Two from families with autistic children who'd like to help you understand your child. And a strange thing."

His ears perked. "What?"

"Well, first we had the call from a Selma. Just Selma, no last name. Like Cher, I suppose. She said that Teddy is with a tall man with blue eyes, and they're driving toward Vero Beach. Another woman . . . let's see, Lulu Craven, said she saw Teddy on a roller coaster somewhere warm. And then—"

"*Saw* Teddy?"

"In a vision. A man called from Miami and said he had a dream that Teddy was in a small room somewhere near a lot of people but hidden from sight. There was a large structure nearby. He said he's had many pre . . . precognitive dreams and has helped the police in the past."

When the phone rang again, he picked it up. "This is Dylan McKain," he answered in reply to the woman's query.

"My name is Lourda Monroe. I'm a renowned psychic in Palm Beach, and I'd like to work with you on finding your son. I see that you're working with a Chloe Samms, and I have to tell you, I've never heard of her. Work with someone who's well-known in regard to missing persons cases, someone the press recognizes. The only thing I ask is that we allow the press to publish that I'm now working on the case. I've already had several visions about Teddy. If I can touch something of his, it'll help immensely. I've already contacted—"

"I don't know who you are or where you got the information that I'm working with Chloe, but I'm not interested in any of your psychic tricks. Don't contact anyone, understand?"

He hung up before she could respond. "That's what you've been dealing with all morning?"

"Afraid so, sir."

"But why . . ." The apprehensive look on Camilla's face killed his words. "What?"

"It could be because of this." She unfolded the *Naples Daily News* and slid it toward him.

"Oh, no," he said as he read the headline: SEARCH FOR MISSING SON LEADS NAPLES MAN TO LILITHDALE PSYCHIC. He skimmed the article, in which Chloe's involvement got more space than Teddy's autism. His son was still in the news, but Dylan appeared to be a desperate man who believed in nonsense.

"How did they . . ." He ran his fingers down his jaw. "They saw her here last night, probably traced her tag."

"You also had a call from a reporter wanting to know if Chloe had any leads yet."

"Give me that number."

"You want me to handle it, sir?"

"No, thanks. I'll take care of this." He snatched the pad and started dialing. His cellular phone rang before he could complete the first call. "McKain."

"Didn't I tell you to stay away from the Lilithdale woman?" Yochem's voice said on the line, and he sounded cranky. "Someone just handed me the paper. We usually get a load of crackpot calls on these kinds of cases, but now they're really coming in fast."

"First of all, she came to me. I'm going to clear this up with the press, and that should take care of the calls." He hung up and continued his call to the reporter. When he got the man on the line, he said, "I am not working with Chloe Samms on anything. I don't believe in any of her nonsense."

"So you're saying she came to you with information, you didn't solicit it?"

"Exactly." Dylan opened a cabinet and found a rack

full of spices. "She's a nutcase, I'm not interested in anything but concrete clues, and that's all I have to say." He repeated the conversation three more times with reporters from the other area papers. By the time he'd hung up, he'd alphabetized the spice jars in the rack. He knew it was a way to feel in control of his life, but he couldn't seem to stop himself. By damn, the woman *was* driving him crazy.

"Now I'm going to talk to Chloe," he said to himself. "She's going to call these reporters and corroborate that she's not involved in any way. That should be the end of it. And her."

Chapter Nine

DYLAN HAD NEVER BEEN TO LILITHDALE BEFORE, NEVER thought much about it until Chloe barged into his life.

What a mess that woman had created. All day he'd had to fend off reporters, friends, and acquaintances who'd thought he'd lost it. He'd been obligated to go to the office and straighten their suspicions too. Dave Wahlberg, his friendly rival, had called to extend his sympathy and offer his help. But even he couldn't resist asking what the psychic had said.

It was nearly dark by the time he reached the portion of Marco Island called Lilithdale. During the entire drive he searched for Teddy. He was pretty sure his son wasn't hidden away in the swampy land surrounding the road to Lilithdale, but he looked anyway. He even tried to peer inside the cars as they came toward him on the two-lane road.

Fliers. That's what he needed, fliers. As soon as he got this errand taken care of, he was going to design one and have a thousand, a million, of them printed and distributed. The more people who saw Teddy's picture, the better chance they'd find where Wanda had hidden him. Someone had to have seen them—with their eyes, not in their visions.

He crossed the bridge and took a left on the road that wound back to the small community. Wildflowers lined the road before it became mangroves and water. Did men ever come here? he wondered.

It looked cozy and quaint. There was a small shanty restaurant called the Crabby Lady that filled the car with the aroma of fried seafood. A pink motel that was called . . . the Pink Motel. Some of the little houses had pink driveways. Cottages were well kept, gardens filled with flowers and plants, all the signs of love and attention a woman could bestow on something she loved. If she wanted to.

Lanterns gave the small, winding roads a festive glow. Women wandered down the sidewalk, sat at café tables, or gathered in small groups. In a park on the water were several tables where women played card games.

He had Chloe's address, but hadn't a clue as to how to find Gumbo Limbo Lane. It was a small place, though; it wouldn't take him long. He knew he was being typically male by not asking directions, but being male was very important to him at the moment.

Her house was at the end of the lane, all by itself and right on the bay. Her yard was overgrown with trees, bushes, and a riot of flowers everywhere. The bougainvillea bushes were trimmed almost too much—except for one long branch and contrasted with the untamed look of the rest of the yard. Her mailbox was covered with hand-painted birds and flowers. The sound of wind chimes played on the night air. The house also looked loved, like a home, and that thought gave him a strange, warm feeling in the pit of his stomach.

Until he saw the plastic bat hanging from the highest pitch of the house in front of a large glass window. Didn't that prove the woman was batty?

He took the mossy flagstones to the stairs leading up to the front door. A black and white dog came running down the pathway from the back yard. The dog danced around him, maybe its way of greeting. Dylan decided he'd get Teddy a dog. Every boy should have a dog.

A painted wood sign on the door read, MAY ALL GOD'S

CREATURES FIND REFUGE HERE. Again that strange feeling alighted in his stomach. It was an ache, a gnawing hunger for something. But didn't he have refuge at work? Hadn't that always been the place where he found peace of mind? There was another nagging question invading the edge of his mind. Where did he find love? Not at work, and not at home either.

He'd convinced himself long ago that he didn't need love to make his life complete. He needed acceptance and success and financial security. He had all of those. Then why did Chloe's home—even the silly clay lovebug doorstop—touch something deep inside him?

He forced those thoughts away and knocked on the door. The only sounds he could hear were the breeze fluttering through the leaves and wind chimes, and beyond that the distant lapping of water. Lights dimly illuminated the interior of the house. Deciding that she just couldn't hear him, he peered through the mullioned glass window.

Architecturally speaking, it was an intriguing house. Not unlike its owner. The whole house was open, separated only by partial walls and varying floor levels. The highest point toward the back of the house must be her bedroom. He could barely see swags of fabric that made up a headboard, though he couldn't see a bed. She had candles and plants everywhere. The sink was half filled with dishes; no surprise that those dishes were covered with flower designs.

The half-octagonal living area that faced the large windows was filled with more pillows than furniture. Ceramic lamps were in the form of plants with goofy faces. The couch was a futon covered in beige cushions. A cat was curled up on one of the flowered pillows. Warm tones, with creature comforts—and creatures. Chloe's place was definitely a refuge.

He drove back into town and parked the car, then walked along the brick sidewalk that paralleled the stores fronting the bay. Interesting stores such as the Good Vibes Art Shop; the Island Lady Clothier; and Women's Ecstasy, a Chocolate Boutique. All the shops had tables or benches outside, and every few yards was a ceramic urn with a smiley face asking to pretty please keep Lilithdale clean.

He had never felt so out of place in his life. Women stared at him with curiosity. Those stares brought back memories of his youth, when everyone in his small town stared. *There goes Dylan. His mama's crazy, you know.* But these women didn't know about his mother. All they knew was he was a man, and here, that's all it took to be an oddity.

"I haven't seen a man looking so lost in a long time," an attractive woman said from one of the tables outside the Happy Haven Tea House. "Of course, I haven't seen a man in a long time either. Come to think of it, they always looked lost. Can I help you find something?" She giggled. "Your feminine side, maybe?"

He tried to force a smile. "I'm looking for Chloe Samms."

"Our little Chloe? Now, what do you want with—oh, you're the guy whose son is missing?"

"How did you know?"

"Call it a lucky guess partly inspired by the fact that Chloe's been tacking up posters all day about a man's missing son, and here you are."

"Posters?"

"Well, take a look around." She gestured toward a post. Then to a telephone pole across the street.

Dylan couldn't read the pink posters in the dim light, so he walked across the street. Teddy's face smiled at him and made his insides twist. Chloe must have gotten the picture from the article in the paper and made posters. Now that he knew what he was looking at, he could see them everywhere: MISSING! THREE YEAR OLD BOY WITH AUTISM. IF YOU HAVE ANY VISIONS, PSYCHIC DREAMS, OR GUT FEELINGS, PLEASE SEE CHLOE.

The words punched him in the gut. He pushed his way past the warm, cloudy feeling and reminded himself that this was probably why he and the police were getting calls from kooks.

He walked back to the woman at the table. "Do you know where she is?"

"She's helping Marilee at the Blue Moon. Don't know what we'd do without her, the dear. It's right over there."

He thanked the woman and walked toward a half-moon-shaped building washed in blue lights. Strange instrumental music floated from hidden speakers. The pathway leading to the entrance was flanked by lush gardens dotted with small tables and chairs. Scattered in the courtyard were plants in the strangest pots: They looked like warped heads with plants growing out of the top.

As he was taking it all in, and considering waiting outside until Chloe was done with whatever it was she was doing, a woman said, "You don't have to be afraid to go in. It's harmless, really." Her voice was filled with laughter.

He turned to two women having coffee at one of the tables. "I'm looking for Chloe Samms. Do you know when she'll be done [illegible] in there?"

"She just started." She looked at her watch. "We should be getting in ourselves. It's about to start."

"What's about to start?"

Both women grabbed up their purses and coffee cups and walked toward him. "The dinner show, silly," the other woman said.

Wearing long, flowing dresses, they looked happy and at peace with the world. They each took an arm and led him down the walkway. "We'll show you the way, hon."

Dylan had a feeling he wasn't going to like this. But he sure wasn't going to back down like a coward. He'd find Chloe, tell her what he had to tell her, and leave. Oh, and thank her for putting up the posters.

A spry older woman greeted them at the door wearing a bright pink sarong. "Good to see you again, ladies. And what do we have here? Wait a minute, I know you. You're the fellow from the hospital, the one whose son is missing."

He remembered her too. Chloe's grandma.

"Wait till Chloe sees you. She's gonna have her finger-in-a-socket face for sure."

"Look, all I need—"

"Is some relaxation, don't I know it. You've had a tough time of it and you need to unwind for an hour. Is he with you, Gerri?"

"He is now," the woman said, looping her arm through his again. "You poor thing, what you must be going through. You must be tenser than concrete."

Marilee led them into an open room scattered with tall tabletops. Around those tabletops were dozens of women, laughing and talking and drinking wine, and every one of them stopped midstream when they spotted him.

"Once in a while couples come in, but we don't usually get a man by himself," Marilee said, gesturing to a table. "Don't worry, they'll get used to you. And dinner's on the house. It's the least we can do for the man who saved Chloe's life."

"You're the one who saved her life?" Gerri asked, and Dylan had to explain what had happened.

Lights resembling bubbles floated through the room,

giving Dylan the distinct impression he'd landed on another planet. One waitress appeared to be wearing a white nightgown.

Big band music started, then grew louder until the "wall" on the far side parted to reveal the kitchen. The chef, a tall German-looking woman, stepped forward and bowed to the applause. Then she lifted what looked like a blowtorch and brought flames to life. The staff in the kitchen started bringing her plates, and she browned whatever was on each plate with the blowtorch. Fireworks shot forth, spraying white sparks everywhere.

He leaned toward the woman named Gerri. "Look, all I want is to talk—"

"Shhh! I love this part."

In perfect coordination, the waitresses, all dressed in white nightgowns and barefoot, took their browned plates and flowed into the room to deliver the first course.

That's when he spotted Chloe. At least he thought it was her. He'd recognize those dreamy blue eyes anywhere, and yet, she looked different. Her hair. Her curls, specifically. Oh, hell. She'd gone butch. Not that it mattered. He didn't plan to twine his fingers through those curls again. He caught himself lining up the pewter salt and pepper shakers.

Chloe balanced three plates as she made her way into the dim room filled with the bubble lights. She delivered the plates to the first table, then sailed back into the kitchen for more.

Dylan blinked. Had he actually thought . . . *dreamy* blue eyes?

He couldn't interrupt her now, so he sat back and watched. Gerri leaned close. "Wait till after dessert, which is always absolutely to die for. They go around giving massages." She squeezed his shoulder. "Yep, hard as concrete."

"Er, I don't want a massage," he said, shifting away. "I just want Chloe. I mean, to talk to Chloe."

"Hey, hon!" Gerri waved at Chloe, who nodded in response. And then her eyes went right to him and she nearly dropped the tray of plates. Not that he could blame her. He couldn't believe he was there either.

Chloe walked over, plates still in hand. "What are you doing here?" She glanced down at her filmy nightgown, naked toes peeking out from beneath the folds.

"I need to talk to you." He looked around. "In private."

"I'm working right now."

"I can see that."

Her chest filled out the nightgown splendidly, and he caught himself noticing just that. He met her gaze again and realized by the flush on her cheeks that she'd caught him looking.

"I thought you were an accountant."

"I am, and I can't talk now," she said, taking the plates to another table.

"It'll only take a minute," he said after her, wondering if it was Chloe who smelled so good or the food.

"Are you courting our Chloe?" the other woman asked, a coy smile on her face.

"They don't court women anymore," Gerri said. "I think they call it propositioning now. Besides, he's got other things on his mind."

"Looks like propositioning our Chloe," she said, and Dylan realized he'd been watching her every move.

"I'm sorry about your son," Gerri said. "If there's anything we can do to help . . ."

"Thank you, but Chloe's done enough." He wasn't

sure if he meant the posters or her causing the media circus. Maybe both.

Chloe brought their plates, meeting his eyes with a questioning look: What the heck was he doing there? Good question.

"What would you like to drink?" she asked instead, perching on the empty chair. She forced her gaze to include the table. "Gerri, Trish?"

"Why don't we all share a bottle of Kunde Viognier?"

"Chloe, can I see you for just a minute?"

"I can't. Everything's timed just so."

He started to protest again, but realized it was fruitless. "I'll have a beer."

"Sorry, no beer."

"Johnny Walker on the rocks?"

"No hard liquor either."

"Then whatever they said."

"The appetizer tonight is conch bollos with mango mustard aioli. The entrees are either Bahamian hummus with yucca toast points, served with mango, jicama and red pepper salad, or sesame tuna with fried spinach and ginger remoulade. Gerri, the hummus?" After Trish ordered, Chloe turned to Dylan. "And you?"

For the past three days people had tried to get him to eat. At least they'd offered him something appetizing. Something he knew. "I'm not hungry."

She touched his arm, and that simple contact shot heat right up his arm and into his chest. "You need to eat. Try the tuna. I'll have them hold the spinach and ginger."

The way she was looking at him, he would have granted her the world. He blinked. Where had that insane thought come from? This place was getting to him in a big way. And those dreamy blue eyes, looking at him like she cared, really cared about him. All he could do was nod, and she smiled, coming to her feet. Possibly the cutest feet he'd ever seen. All he'd seen before were her color-coordinated Keds.

I'll be right back with your wine." And then off she flitted to the kitchen.

"One warning: Everything drink-wise may be colored. It's Marilee's trademark. Sometimes the food is too. Remember the green chicken last St. Patrick's day, Trish?"

Dylan was watching Chloe, who kept glancing over at him and then quickly looking away. "Does she do this a lot?"

"Chloe helps everyone out. We're all like that, really, but Chloe, she's our champ."

"And never complains," Trish put in.

"Considering . . ." Gerri said, pity on her face.

"Considering what?"

"She has no abilities. Takes it like a soldier."

AN HOUR later, Chloe brought out the final act: dessert. It was all he could do to eat the tuna. He particularly couldn't stomach either the grilled banana split or the chocolate fudge truffle, the one dessert the women had been moaning in ecstasy about. He did not need to hear moaning. It was time to leave.

He wasn't even sure why he'd let himself get talked into staying through the whole dinner act. Then Chloe walked out of the kitchen again, and somewhere deep inside he knew why he'd stayed.

To tell her to stop interfering with his life. Yeah, that was why.

That was why he felt that strange gnawing feeling inside him. He was sure of it. Positive.

The massages came after dessert. More moaning ensued, more than Dylan's psyche or libido could stand. Everyone in the kitchen came out to rub shoulders and necks.

"Where are you going?" Gerri said, tugging his arm. "You haven't gotten the best part yet."

"You'd better do him first," Gerri said to someone standing behind him. "He's gettin' antsy."

Dylan turned to find Chloe standing behind him, something akin to a startled deer's look on her face. "You don't have to—"

"It's part of the dinner," she said softly, then laid her hands on his shoulders.

"But I didn't come—"

Then she started stroking, slowly at first, then harder, kneading his muscles. He could feel her breath on the back of his head, long, deep breaths growing deeper. Throughout dinner and dessert, the music had returned to that strange new-age mix, and Chloe massaged him to the rhythm, light for the flutes, deeper for the bass. Her fingers were surprisingly strong for their delicate appearance. His muscles melted beneath her touch, and he resisted the urge to lean back and feel her softness against him. He could feel the heat from her hands right through his shirt. God, had anyone ever touched him like this, to solely give pleasure?

The essence of Chloe wrapped around his senses, her sweet perfume, spices, and the soft puff of her breath against his neck. Her fingers worked right up to the base of his skull with hypnotically slow strokes. He hadn't realized he'd closed his eyes until they snapped open again. Gerri and Trish were smiling, enjoying their own mini-show. Oh, brother.

He turned to look at Chloe. Her head was tilted to the

side, eyes closed, mouth turned slightly upward. He had the strangest urge to pull her down onto his lap and bury his tongue in her mouth.

Which was not what he'd come here to do.

He shook his head, trying to dispel the crazy thought. Chloe blinked, opening her eyes as though she'd drifted off. Now her eyes were definitely dreamy, the way they'd been after their kiss. Which stirred his insides and made him want to kiss her again. She looked away as though that would keep him from seeing the smoke in her eyes or the flush on her creamy complexion. She cleared her throat and moved on to Gerri.

The front door opened, and the aunt he recognized as Stella came sneaking in. She waved at Chloe and headed to the kitchen.

"I can leave after the bills are tallied," Chloe said in a thick voice behind him.

Dylan went to the restroom and splashed his face with water. No more falling under that woman's spell. All of these women who said Chloe didn't have any special abilities were wrong. She had plenty of them, and they were all aimed at making him crazy.

Crazy for her.

Tonight he had to stop it. No matter what she had done for him, he had to put an end to her involvement in the case and his life. And he was going to have to be firm about it. Maybe even a little mean. Because he couldn't have her distracting him like this. It was wrong, and it made him feel guiltier than hell.

"YOU CUT your hair," he said when they returned to her house. "You didn't really decide to go butch, did you?" Thank goodness she'd changed out of that gown and into a white top and jeans.

She led him around the side of her house to the lit courtyard. "No. I just wanted something . . . different. I don't know why I cut it, exactly. Hey, Shakespeare!" The black and white dog put its paws on Chloe's stomach and nuzzled her while she scratched his head. "How's my buddy, huh? Miss me?"

Dylan cleared his throat, and she looked up, then disengaged the dog. "We can sit here."

She sat on the stone bench in front of an enormous sea grape tree. "Thanks for coming here. I just didn't want everyone . . ."

He sat on the other end of the bench. "Watching?" he offered with a smile. Reminding himself he shouldn't be smiling.

"Exactly. So . . . what did you come to see me about? The newspaper article?"

"Yes." He stood, because it seemed too cozy sitting there on the bench with her. "Why do you have a bat hanging on your house?"

She *was* making him crazy, because that's not what he wanted to say at all.

"That's to keep the birds from hitting the glass. During the day it reflects and looks like more sky. Every time one would hit the glass, I'd feel terrible. I have a mini-graveyard of the victims of my window. Sometimes I'd find a dead bird on the ground. So I hung that ugly thing there. It was Halloween; that's all I could find."

A nut with a heart of gold. He didn't want to look at her, because he'd see all that compassion in her eyes and then he'd want to kiss her again and that was a really bad idea, considering he'd come here to tell her to butt out of his life. So he focused on those strange flower pots that circled the back half of the pond.

"I call them pot heads," she said, coming up beside him. Still smelling good and sweet and edible.

"I saw them outside the supper club. Odd things."

"Thank you." When he turned to her, she said, "I make them. In my workshop." She nodded toward a door on the ground floor. With a smile, she said, "Just because I'm an accountant doesn't mean I'm all left-brained. Except that I'm not any good at it. Grandma only puts them in the patio area because she feels sorry for me, not that she'd ever admit it."

There he was, smiling again. "Chloe, about the newspaper article . . . because of you—because you came to see me last night—people are calling with their visions and insights, and the paper is making me out to be some fruitcake who believes in all this nonsense. I want you to stay out of this whole situation. I saw the posters, and I appreciate that. But I can't have people thinking I'm buying into this crazy stuff. I'm already crazy enough with everything that's going on. Do you know what I'm saying? Can you understand?"

She stuffed her hands into the pockets of her jeans and stepped closer. "I'm sorry about the article. I didn't mean for that to happen."

"I know. But it happened because you were at my house; because you're involved. Now these nutcases are calling me and the police, sending them on wild goose chases and wasting valuable time while my son is sitting somewhere out there by himself . . ." His voice started breaking. He cleared his throat, shocked to hear the emotion in his voice. "Stay out of it, Chloe. Just stay out of it. I need to find my son, but I keep thinking about you, and that mouth, and the way the corners turn up when you're just thinking and the way your mouth feels, and jeez, Chloe, you're driving me crazy. . . ."

"Do you mean a bad kind of driving you crazy—"

He pushed her against the tree trunk and kissed her. Her surprised intake of breath quickly became deep breaths that fueled his desire even more. She had opened her mouth to his and joined him in oral lovemaking. His own breath came faster as her response ignited his body. It was crazy, it was inappropriate, and he still couldn't take his mouth off hers. Her breasts were crushed against his chest, and his pelvis was pressed against hers, pinning her to the tree. Her fingers threaded through his hair, pulling it, digging into his neck, trying to pull closer.

She made little sounds deep in her throat, whimpering, groaning sounds that were far more powerful than a whole roomful of women moaning over chocolate. He wanted her. All his primal instincts kicked in, instincts long denied. He didn't know he could want a woman with his whole body, didn't know the ache inside she both fueled and assuaged. He wanted to strip off her clothes and take her right there against the tree. He wanted to hear more of those sounds, make her breathless . . . he wanted her to scream. All the desire he'd restrained over the years came to life with a terrifying voracity.

He pulled her white cotton shirt from the waistband of her jeans and pressed his hand against the warm flesh of her stomach. And then a little higher. Her breath caught again, and his mouth slid down her throat and ravished her neck, and then the spot just beneath her ear. She shivered, head tilted back and mouth slack. Total surrender. And then she whispered his name, soft and low and throaty, and just the sound of it slithered through his body.

He unsnapped her bra in the front. His hand slid between the valley of her breasts, up to her collarbone.

She arched, responding to his teasing touch, and then he cupped her flesh, running his thumb across the raised nub.

"I think you're a witch," he whispered in her ear, making her shiver again. "And I think you've cast some kind of spell on me. I can't get you out of my head, no matter how hard I try, no matter how much I shouldn't be thinking about you."

And then he met her gaze, and she looked just as spellbound as he felt. They were both caught up in a vortex. Those blue eyes were full of desire. How could he tell her to stay away from him when he had her pinned against the tree? How could he tell her to stay away when he wanted her so damned bad?

First he heard the dog panting loudly. And then the male voice a short distance away: "I see I've come at an inopportune time."

Dylan was sure he hadn't said anything, which must mean someone *else* had said it, someone standing there watching them. He pushed back and covered Chloe so she could arrange herself. He spun around to find Detective Yochem looking smug and interested.

Chapter Ten

DYLAN SPIT OUT AN EXPLETIVE AND RAN HIS HAND through his hair. Yochem was watching them with that speculative TV-detective look. Dylan made a point to block the detective's view of Chloe as he walked toward Yochem.

What had he been thinking? He hadn't been, that's what. Nothing new when it came to Chloe.

"Do you have any news? Is that why you're here?" Dylan asked, surprised to find his voice hoarse.

"No, nothing. I spoke with your housekeeper, who told me you'd probably come out here. So I wanted to see for myself."

"See what?" Dylan hated the defensive sound in his voice.

"He was telling me to butt out of his life," Chloe said, trying to inconspicuously tuck in her shirt.

"Oh, yeah, I could tell. Listen, McKain, you gotta understand something. In child disappearance cases, the parents are always suspect until they're cleared. In so many of these cases it turns out that one or both parents killed their child. Am I saying I suspect you? Don't know yet. Have I ruled you out? No."

"You're still wasting time investigating me?"

"I have to look at all the angles. I had a case several years ago, before I came to Naples. Same kind of thing, the parents were all weepy 'cause the kid was gone, taken right out of their home. They appealed to the public, played the whole thing, and complained to me because I was looking into their stories and not looking for their kid. Their little girl was an angel, cutest thing I ever did see. . . ." He looked away for a moment, then refocused. "I spent three weeks solid, no sleep, looking for her."

"They killed their own child?" Chloe asked, obviously outraged, by the look on her face.

"He did. He was jealous of the attention the wife gave the kid."

"That's crazy!"

Yochem looked at both of them and paused. "A lot of people are crazy. Some are crazy on the outside." He looked at Chloe when he said that. "Some hide it deep inside." With those words he looked at Dylan. "I know your wife was the last person seen with Teddy, but that doesn't mean you didn't see him sometime that morning. You were chasing your wife when she lost control of the car. Maybe you wanted her out of the way too. Maybe you were both in on it, but things turned ugly. Then you don't even know your kid has autism. And from what I know about you, you're into having everything fit the norm. Everything's gotta look good. Then we got the note."

Dylan tried his best to stay calm and not to focus on the fact that they were still wasting time investigating him. "What note?"

"Wanda McKain sent us a note the day she died. I just got it; it wasn't addressed to anyone, so it got tossed around. She told us she was taking the kid because you wouldn't accept him. She was afraid you might send him away or something."

"That's crazy. I wouldn't send my own son away."

"Maybe you did something to him because he didn't fit into your scheme of things."

Hold your anger in, don't kill the man, because then even when they find Teddy you won't get to see him. "I love my son. You'll know the truth when I find him. What about the North Carolina story?"

"Probably nothing but a cover." Yochem rubbed his nose. "What I can't figure out is how the cookie fits into this whole thing. Were you two seeing each other before this happened?"

"No," she said, stepping forward. "And we're not seeing each other now."

"Yeah, right."

"Look, I was just trying to help him find Teddy."

"I know, the near-death tunnel thing." At her questioning look, he added, "Dylan had me check into you when you went to him with the story."

He hated the betrayed look on her face. And that was nothing compared to how she'd react when she saw his comments in the papers tomorrow.

"What I find strange," Yochem continued, looking at Chloe, "is that you seem to be replaying your mother's final act."

She smoothed down her hair and stepped closer. "What does my mother have to do with this?"

"I did some checking into your background. You were born in Sarasota to Amelia and Fred Samms. Your dad was a loser, never played a part in your life. Your Aunt Lena Stone was a well-known psychic, and your other aunt, Stella Maguire, talks to animals. Apparently your mother felt left out because she had no powers. After all the publicity the Martins girl produced for Lena, Amelia must have really felt left out." He recited the facts in a blasé manner, yet each word tore into Chloe so visibly, Dylan actually felt it.

"A month or so later a little boy was taken from a Tampa mall. Amelia went to the press with her so-called visions. Lena downplayed her talent or whatever you want to call it, but your mother went overboard. She had these hopeful parents running all over the place, giving them false hope. Worse, she wasted the police force's energy on false leads while the kidnapper walked right to the parents' house and left their boy's body on their doorstep. Your mother led these people to believe that their son was still alive, and they came home to find him dead."

Yochem's face suddenly looked very old and tired. "Do you know what false hope does to people? It builds them up, only to leave nothing beneath their feet when the truth comes out. People were mad, real mad. They wrote nasty letters and called her with threats. She hurt a lot of people. Even the psychics were angry at her. Maybe that's why she killed herself."

Dylan watched confusion, outrage, and hurt play across her features, but the blood drained completely on those last words.

"You're wrong, you are way wrong." Her words sounded strong, but her gesture of wrapping her arms around herself gave away her insecurity. "My mother died of breast cancer. She didn't kill herself, she didn't."

Yochem's expression softened slightly. "You didn't know, did you? Well, I'm sorry you had to find out like this. I thought you knew, and I thought you were playing at the same game."

"How? How did she die?"

"She slashed her wrists. Your Aunt Lena found her in the bathtub."

"No." The word crackled in her throat, making Dylan want to pull her against him and protect her from the truth. She looked small and fragile, as delicate as the owl pendant she wore. She rubbed her hands up and down her arms, repeating, "It isn't true." And then she walked down that long shell road toward town.

Dylan watched her go, fighting an urge to go after her. But he didn't know what he'd say. So he faced Yochem. "Good job."

"Hey, I thought she knew."

He tried to put away thoughts of Chloe and focus on his immediate problem: the man's accusations. "How much of your manpower is going into investigating me?"

"We're still looking for your son. I'm sorry, but it's the way we gotta play it. The odds always lean toward the parents. And I gotta tell you, you being involved with the cookie isn't helping your case."

"I'm not involved with her." At Yochem's raised eyebrow, he added, "It was a kiss, no big deal." But it had been, that's what his body told him. It had been a big, big deal. "And she's not a cookie." *Focus, Dylan.* "The letter Wanda sent you . . ."

Yochem shrugged. "Could be she just wanted to justify her actions. She'd have to figure that if she took the kid, the police would be all over her. She maybe didn't want the press or anyone else making her out as the bad guy. So she turned the tables on you."

That sounded like something Wanda would do. Blame everyone else. She'd gotten good at that over the years, blaming the world for everything. He wondered who she'd blamed for Teddy's autism.

"So what do you think, Detective?"

He shrugged again. "Not for me to speculate. It's my job to look at all the angles before I make a decision. And right now, the angle I'm seeing doesn't look too good for you." He nodded toward the tree where Dylan had pinned Chloe. "I'd steer clear of that one if I were you. I give you that advice for your own reputation. You don't want to lose the press's sympathy. As for me, well, if you're involved with her, and were before your son's disappearance, I'm going to find out anyway. Good night."

Dylan stood there for a while, listening to the sound of Yochem's car fade away, then to the crickets and the wind chimes. His chest hurt, and his body felt tense and stiff.

Chloe had obviously gone to confirm the story. A part of him wanted to be here when she returned. The sensible part urged him to get in his car and leave. He made himself go, fighting every step and wondering why he should even care. God knew he had enough to worry about besides her feelings.

CHLOE WISHED she could forget about it. There were times when she and her aunts had gotten into fights—arguments, really—and they'd all agreed to forget about it. But not this time.

Stella would still be working at the Blue Moon, so Chloe went directly to Lena. Shakespeare walked with her most of the way, but he eventually left to chase something behind the Pink Motel.

Warm light glowed through the cottage curtains and welcomed her. She tried to hold off the avalanche of pain that teetered above her and cast her in its shadow.

It wasn't true, it couldn't be true. That would mean that her aunts had lied to her all these years.

Then she remembered the strange conversation the day before. *What does this have to do with my mother?* Chloe had asked. Stella had looked flustered, something she rarely was. They'd talked about the press, and Chloe had thought Lena was worried about herself.

When Lena answered the door, she was still wearing

the pink fuzzy robe. Her red hair was a mess, her skin was pale, which made her vivid blue eyes stand out even more. Chloe saw the shadows and wondered if Lena already knew why she was there.

"Can we talk, please?" She walked in without waiting for an answer.

The cottage was small, and with the flowered curtains drawn in front and candles lit, it looked cozy.

"Would you like some chamomile tea? I've just brewed it. That boo-boo face tells me you need some."

Chloe walked to the window that faced the bay, arms wrapped around herself. "Say it's not true, just say it and I'll believe you. . . . Tell me about my mother."

Lena plastered on a smile. "I've told you about Amelia, a thousand times. She was a warm, loving woman, a good mother—"

"And a lousy psychic."

"Well, she didn't have any abilities, no." Lena held the teacup in her hand, stirring slowly. "But you know that."

Chloe closed her eyes. "But I didn't know about the part where she pretended to be psychic." Her voice became a whisper. "Tell me about that."

"Oh, Chloe." Lena set her cup down and went to her.

Chloe moved away, probably the first time she'd ever shunned her aunt's affection. "Tell me the truth, Lena."

"Who told you?"

"That awful detective who came to see me at the hospital. He came here tonight, probably because of the newspaper article."

Lena's face was paler than Chloe had ever seen it. "Oh, hon, I'm so sorry. I knew we should have told you, and Stella, she was always on my case to tell you. At first, we decided to wait until you were old enough to handle it. And then, well, too much time had passed. You were a happy child, content in your world. Your biggest worry was going into the water and feeling slimy things. Or saving bugs and the like. We didn't want to spoil it for you. It was all so long ago, and so far away. I thought it would be better for you not to know at all, especially since . . ."

"I'm not psychic either, and I don't fit in."

"Of course you fit in. You're one of us no matter what." Lena touched Chloe's hand. This time she didn't move away. "I didn't want to hurt you, I swear."

The tears started flowing now, for the image of the mother that was slipping away. "So you let me think she'd died of breast cancer. You let me worry that I might get it too."

"I hated that part, I really did. I wish we'd picked something else, something less hereditary. The good part is, you'll find a lump before it even starts to think about forming."

Chloe jerked her hands down to her sides. "You lied to me. For *years* you lied to me."

Lena sat down on the flowered couch. "I was afraid that you'd take it hard. And maybe that you'd take the same path. The publicity pushed her over the edge. She was always a little jealous of me and Stella. Then that case came along and made life hell for all of us. But it affected her differently. Something snapped inside her, and she had to have what we had. I don't think she lied about the visions; I think she believed they were real. And when they found that little boy . . ." She shook her head and closed her eyes for a moment. "The press really chewed her up. They weren't as hard on me, because I had really found the girl. It was too late . . . but I did find her. Amelia was an out-and-out phony."

Chloe sank down on the far end of the couch. "Is that why you won't help me find Teddy? Because you're afraid I'll do the same thing?"

"No. Yes. Both, actually. And it's been so long since I've had visions, since I've let myself have them. They try sometimes, but I don't let them come. It's taken a toll. Hon, I'm sorry. Will you forgive us?"

The hurt was too raw for forgiveness. "Does everyone in Lilithdale know?"

"A few women know, but they've been sworn—"

Chloe sprang to her feet. "So everyone knew but me. Maybe . . ." She sniffed, fighting back more tears. "Maybe if I were psychic I would have known you were lying. But I'm nothing. I don't belong anywhere."

Then she left, ignoring Lena's pleas for her to come back. Chloe walked head down, only nodding to the occasional woman who called out her name in greeting. Halfway down her dark road, she halted.

Dylan had been there. He'd heard everything. Now he'd think she was a phony too, that she'd made up or imagined her near-death experience.

Her worst fear was, maybe she had.

Shakespeare burst out of the brush, startling her heavy heart into action again. He happily pranced around her.

She wondered if Dylan was still at her house. The chilly night air wrapped around her, making her long for strong arms and a warm body to hold her close. But Dylan wasn't that kind of man. Her body strained to run the rest of the way and see if his car was still in the driveway.

It wasn't.

Everything else was dark and silent, or at least as silent as it ever was around there. Thank goodness for all the sounds of life around her. And for the family who would never betray her.

Gypsy rubbed her ankles, meowing loudly as soon as Chloe opened her door. Then Shakespeare started chasing the cat, and both were off gallivanting through the dark foliage. *Must be nice to have a dog or cat's life. Eat and play and love all day long.*

The phone startled her with its jangling ring. It was probably Lena. Or maybe a reporter wanting to know the sordid details of her mother's death.

Chloe turned, not ready to handle either. She went back downstairs and got into the canoe. The water looked ink-black where the moonlight didn't sprinkle the surface with diamonds. Her arms took over, dipping the paddle into the water with a quiet *whoosh,* speeding her canoe toward the black mounds of mangrove islands silhouetted against a starlit sky. She didn't want to think about anything, about her mother, or Dylan's kiss, or even Teddy.

She heard Shakespeare's barking in the distance. He liked going with her, but she wanted to be totally, completely alone.

She wasn't sure how long she paddled; it seemed like hours. The canoe glided to a stop, and she let the tiny ripples of water move her along. At first all she could hear was the pounding of her heart and the sound of her breathing. When she finally calmed down, she heard another sound. Water hitting the metal of the canoe . . . it brought back the dreams.

Or were they even real? Maybe she only wanted to be psychic, like her mother. Maybe she was deluding herself. And that meant she could only be headed toward the same end. Like mother, like daughter. Runs in the family.

Suddenly she realized she had no idea where she was. She could see no lights, no sign of houses nearby. Being lost in the dark didn't bother her too much, as long as she didn't tip the canoe and fall into the murky water. *That* scared her, not knowing what squirming, nibbling things were nearby.

Something else bothered her too: the old man who lived on his houseboat. At first Chloe hadn't believed her aunts, thinking they only wanted to curtail her explorations. Then she'd seen the boat, covered with years' worth of junk, newspapers covering the windows. The man sitting on the back deck. He hadn't been that old then.

"Whaddya want, kid?" he'd snarled.

"N-n-nothing, mister!"

And she'd paddled home as fast as she could. He moved his boat around so one never knew exactly where he'd be. A new twist on homelessness, she thought when she'd come across his boat years later.

She could hear water lapping against metal, but not her canoe. Sitting in the dark by herself, her imagination now created a monster of a man, gnarled with age and temperament. Though fear raged through her, she couldn't make her arms paddle backward. Her body wanted to go . . . forward. She fought it, and finally managed to control her impulse. And as darkness swirled around her, she realized she had no idea where she was.

WHEN THE sun rose the next morning, Dylan had another sleepless night to add to the rest. He hoped he was another day closer to finding his son.

In the kitchen he took the cup of coffee Camilla offered and pushed his flier across the counter to her. "Since I couldn't sleep, I put the long night to good use."

Camilla looked over the flier. "A twenty-five-thousand-dollar reward should get people interested. Good picture of him too."

Teddy looked like any regular kid. Dylan was going to do everything possible to give him a normal life so people wouldn't look at him with pity.

"You were rough on that girl," Camilla said, laying a section of the newspaper on the counter.

He winced at the headline: FATHER OF MISSING BOY DENIES WORKING WITH "NUTCASE."

"I tried to retract the nutcase part, but it was too late." He reluctantly read the article. It was all there, Chloe's mother, the fiasco in Sarasota, and him disparaging her.

"Well, you accomplished what you wanted: getting rid of her."

"You don't know Chloe. She'll help anyway, because she has to."

Camilla raised her eyebrow. "You know her that well?"

"Well enough." He subconsciously ran his hand over his mouth, remembering exactly how well he knew her. Deep in the pit of his stomach he felt uneasy.

He tried calling her, but only got her answering machine. He left a message. Where could she be this early?

He kept thinking about what Yochem said. Not the part about it being unwise to be associated with Chloe. The part about her mother being railed in the press and how it had caused her to commit suicide.

And the dire pain in Chloe's eyes when Yochem had told her about it.

"I've got to talk to her," Dylan said when Camilla walked back into the kitchen.

"If you go down there, they'll really think something's going on between you."

"If she does something stupid because of what I told those reporters . . ." He pushed the thought away, though the uneasy feeling didn't vanish. "I'll have my cell phone if anyone needs me."

After stopping at the printer, Dylan headed south on U.S. 41. He had never thought he'd go to Lilithdale once, much less twice. As he drove, he told himself he was only making sure she was all right. It was his responsibility. Were suicidal tendencies hereditary? It seemed everything was these days.

He spent most of the drive on his cell phone, selling stocks to fund the reward, contacting some of the largest businesses in Naples about distributing fliers to their employees. And he tried Chloe again.

Lilithdale looked even quainter in the light of day. One woman zipped by him in a golf cart that looked like a purple BMW. She took one look at him and nearly crashed into a hibiscus bush.

At Chloe's house a golf cart with a yellow-fringed sunshade was parked next to her T-Bird. Shakespeare came running out to greet him, all happy barks and wagging tail. Dylan rubbed the dog's head. Chloe wouldn't have a watchdog that snarled and scared away intruders. Not Chloe. Although some warning about their visitor last night would have been nice.

He followed the sound of voices through the back yard to the dock. He recognized Lena, Stella, and Marilee. Their worried looks reminded him of that day in the emergency room.

Chloe had done something stupid, and it was all his fault.

Chapter Eleven

"WHERE'S CHLOE?" DYLAN ASKED AS HE APPROACHED the women.

"Gone," Stella said.

"Missing," Lena said.

"Can't find her anywhere," Marilee added.

"The canoe's gone, we know that much," Lena said.

Dylan tried to ask, "Could she—"

"That narrows it down," Marilee said. "She could be anywhere out there!"

Stella wrung her hands. "Gypsy can't even help me; she didn't see Chloe leave. Neither did Shakespeare, who is quite upset at being left behind. Naturally he feels like he let his master down. Gypsy, how did she seem to you last night?"

"Ladies!" Dylan yelled, remembering the chaos of the emergency room all too well. "Let's think where she could have gone. Does anyone have a map of these islands?" He nodded toward the network of mangrove islands.

"We never use maps; we go by feel." Lena shook her head, causing strands of long, red hair to come loose from her hasty, upswept 'do. "This is all my fault."

"This one's my fault," he said, feeling an ache in his chest.

Stella stepped forward, holding the tortoiseshell cat he'd seen inside. "Let's not argue about whose fault it is. Our little girl's been missing all night, and we've got to find her."

"All night?" he asked.

"She hasn't seen the newspaper yet," Lena said, reading his mind. "Maybe we shouldn't let her see it."

"No." Stella waved her hand. "No more hiding things from her. That's how this all started."

"Ever since she was a little girl, she loved canoeing around the islands," Marilee said. "The last time she did this, she was looking for your son. But this time . . ."

"She's going to be all right," Stella said, nuzzling the cat. "She has to be, doesn't she, Gypsy?"

"Remember that old man, he's probably out there somewhere," Marilee said.

"What old man?" Dylan asked.

"Ah, he won't hurt anyonc," Stella said. "He's just a homeless old coot, harmless as could be. Lived on these waters for years in that old houseboat."

"We came by last night to talk to her," Marilee told Dylan. "I brought her some of my pickle soup."

"Pickle soup?" Dylan asked, trying to hold back a look of disgust.

"It's her favorite get-well soup."

Stella said, "She doesn't like that goop. She just pretends because you made it for her."

"She does so like it."

"And when you came to see her . . ." Dylan said, trying to redirect the conversation.

"She was gone. We figured she'd just taken a short paddle, to clear her head and all. None of us had any bad feelings about it. But now . . ."

"You have a bad feeling?" he asked, then realized what he was saying.

"We have no feeling about it, that's the problem," Stella said. "But we have to remember, girls, that Chloe isn't her mother. She's stronger."

"But tender, don't forget that," Lena said.

"She's always felt left out," Marilee said. "Oh, she's never actually said it, but you know she does. She never had any special ability . . ." She looked at Dylan. "Until the accident. But we're not sure . . ."

"That it was real," he offered at her reluctance to go on.

"It's not that we think she's lying," Stella said. "Maybe she conjured it up."

"Like her mother." Lena walked to the end of the dock, looking out over the sparkling water of the bay.

"We'd better round up the girls and get out the boats. I didn't want to involve everyone, but I guess we're going to have to," Stella said.

He didn't know about feelings or premonitions, but he knew worry, and it infiltrated his mind. First his son, and now Chloe. He should have stayed here last night until she returned, just to make sure she was all right.

He'd been afraid of being alone with her again. Afraid they'd really do something stupid. The way she'd come to life under his touch, the way her mouth moved beneath his . . .

He cleared his throat and focused on the islands of mangroves around him, so different from his view of the bay. His house overlooked a marina, a restaurant, and lots of boat traffic. This was peaceful and removed from everything man-made.

And then he saw a flash in the distance. He blinked, trying to clear the image from his retina. Another flash. He reached for Lena's arm and pointed to the pink canoe partially hidden in the mangroves.

"It's her canoe!" Lena said.

The other two women rushed forward, nearly knocking him into the water. "Where? Where?"

Lena jumped up and down and waved her arms. "Chloe, honey!"

Dylan didn't even think about what he was doing. He stripped off his shirt and removed his shoes, then made a shallow dive. His blood rushed through his ears as he swam through the chilly water. If she wasn't in there . . .

Don't think about that. He didn't know Chloe, not really. But he had to believe she wouldn't take her life or get careless with it. She was too special, too warm and tender—and passionate—to die.

He was out of breath by the time he reached the canoe. He grasped the edge and tipped it toward him. His heart lurched at the sight of her lying inside, motionless. She came alive instantly, arms and legs scrabbling, fighting him as he tried to balance the canoe. She twisted the wrong way, tipping too far. Her scream was drowned by the water as she plunged in.

His arms went around her waist, pulling her toward the surface and holding her against him. She pushed at him, her face full of anger and shock. Water streamed from her hair and dripped off the edge of her nose.

"Let go of me!"

He felt the most irresistible urge to kiss her, to taste her life and relish her anger. She was alive. He'd never felt anything like this before, this rush of relief and affection, of gratitude. Would he feel this way when he found Teddy?

Finally she pushed away, fury on her pretty face. "What are you doing? Are you crazy, scaring me like that? I was sound asleep! I thought he'd gotten me . . ." She shook her head, looking around for a moment to get her bearings. "Ew, get me out of this water!"

"Chloe, what the devil were you doing out here, floating around in your sleep?"

"I came out here last night and got lost. No big deal. What the devil are you doing out here?"

He didn't know what to say. All the words crowded forward, the fear that she was gone, that she'd done something to hurt herself, the relief that she was alive. So he gave in and kissed her, a wet, cool kiss that connected him with her warm mouth.

She made a sound, probably one of exasperation, but her mouth responded to his anyway. She hungrily returned his kiss, her arms going around his bare shoulders, her chest pressing against his. But a second later she pushed him away again. "D-dylan, why are you d-doing this? Are you t-trying to drive me crazy?" She was shivering, reminding his hazy brain that they were floating in the middle of a cold bay. Her aunts and grandmother were waiting on the bank, their voices calling from the distance.

"Is she all right?"

"Oh, my gosh, he had to give her CPR."

"That wasn't CPR, you dummy."

"What are you doing?" Chloe asked him again, this time in a whisper.

"I was . . . rescuing you."

"I don't need rescuing."

"Because you're the one who's always doing the rescuing. But once in a while, it's okay to let someone rescue you." Something about her touched a part of him deep inside, a part he didn't even know existed. Something that wanted to take care of her, to protect her from the world. It was crazy. He didn't need someone to protect; he had Teddy. And she didn't need a man to protect her. She was from Lilithdale, where no woman needed a man.

Then why did her dreamy blue eyes tell him that wasn't true? That she wanted a man to hold her and protect her? Whenever he'd lost his head and kissed her, her first instinct was to pull close and kiss him back.

"Come on," he said, surprised at his gruff voice. "Let's try to get you back in the canoe."

"It'll never work." She pulled her gaze from his and eyed the canoe. "I'll swim back with you. Just get me out of this water."

She reached in and grabbed a piece of rope tied to the inside bow of the canoe. He took it from her, and they swam side by side to the shore.

Stella had brought out some white towels, and she wrapped one around Chloe as soon as he'd helped her from the water. Lena wrapped the other one around him, then stepped back, not sure what to do.

"Oh, honey, we're so sorry," Stella said, hugging Chloe.

Betrayal and sadness shadowed Chloe's eyes as she moved away from her aunt. "I just went out for a late-night paddle and got lost. That's all."

While the other two women tried to reach Chloe, Lena stood and watched.

"Look, I need some time alone," Chloe said at last. "I'm not ready to talk about it."

Stella and Marilee nodded. "But you won't do anything . . ."

"I won't try to kill myself, if that's what you're worried about," she said, heading toward her house. On the way, she stopped to pull a strangling vine off a small pine tree.

"You have to tell her about the newspaper article," Stella said, talking to Dylan but watching Chloe tugging until the vine was pulled loose, then continuing on to the workshop. Stella nudged him toward the door. "Come on, girls. She needs time to heal. We've let her down; you can't expect her to turn to us now."

"Of course not. But Chloe, hon, I brought you some

pickle soup!" Marilee called as Chloe disappeared inside the workshop. "It's in the fridge!"

He grabbed up his shirt and shoes and left them by the side of the house. He stood in dappled light and looked into the dim room.

"Chloe?"

Her wet clothes were lying on the concrete floor; the same clothes she'd worn last night. The same shirt he'd unbuttoned. She was wrapped in the towel and sitting before a potter's wheel. Her shoulders and arms were bare, and he could see her legs where the towel split apart.

She closed her eyes and tilted her chin. "Please leave." Her voice was thick with unshed tears.

He should have left, but his body wouldn't allow him to. He took a step forward instead.

"You all right?"

Her hands and arms were covered in splatters of mud. "Just great."

"Chloe, I need to tell you something. It's not good."

She looked at him. "Teddy?" The pain in her voice touched him.

"No, not Teddy."

She visibly relaxed and returned to her task. Her voice was so soft, he had to lean closer to hear her. "I dreamed about him again last night. That he was out there, in a canoe like mine. I tried to reach out to him, but he kept drifting just out of my reach." She shook her head. "Except now I don't trust my dreams. Maybe I'm like my mother, who just fooled herself into thinking she had some ability." Tears slid down her cheeks, crushing his chest. She was wholly focused on the lopsided lump of clay she was working. "It was like I could feel him out there. But it isn't real. It's all in my head, just like you kept saying." She turned to him. "What? What do you have to tell me?"

He knelt down beside her bench. "When the papers came out yesterday about you working with me, being psychic . . ."

"I'm sorry. I know it was my fault, because I went to your house."

"It wasn't your fault. You didn't know they'd trace your tag." He looked around the dim room at the shelves of warped clay pots and the large kiln in the corner. "When I read the paper . . . and then the calls started coming in, psychic kooks from all over wanting to help to get credit and publicity. I got mad. And I told a reporter that you were a nutcase and I wasn't working with you. So this morning, in the paper . . ."

"You called me a nutcase," she said in a deadpan voice. "Well, thanks for warning me. Not that it matters. They'll find out about my mother and then . . ." She searched his face. "They already know, don't they?"

He nodded, wanting to wipe away those tears from her cheeks. She wiped them away herself, leaving a muddy streak behind. She stiffened her shoulders and fought to keep her expression calm. Her eyes gave her away.

"It's just like it was for my mother, isn't it? That's why you came out here, to make sure I didn't kill myself too."

He wanted to explain how he'd tried to rescind his words, but he could only say, "Yes."

"Well, you can see I'm fine. You'd better go before some reporter finds you here and causes more trouble."

She went back to her clay. But he couldn't move, even though he knew it might be true. That's when he knew he had to tell her.

"My mother was crazy."

Those words stopped her and made her look at him. "And this relates to me how?"

"I want you to understand . . . me. Maybe I want to even the score, I don't know. Nobody knows this, Chloe. Nobody but my former wife and my father. Well, and the entire town I grew up in. Now we know she was manic-depressive. All we knew then was she didn't make any sense. No one in town wanted to do anything about it. Maybe they thought pity was enough.

"She used to keep me home from school because she thought the bad guys—that's what she called them—would try to get to her through me. Then she called the governor's office to get me protection when the school protested. We spent a lot of evenings in total darkness and silence so the hidden cameras wouldn't pick up our movements. If any of my friends came over, they'd get freaked out seeing us in the dark with Mom telling them to shush, trying to pull them into our nightmare. But mostly we kept it to ourselves, hid it. My father worked all the time. He didn't have the patience to deal with it or the courage to face it. So he hid in his work and came home after we'd all gone to bed. I think he believed if he wasn't around to witness it, it didn't happen.

"But I lived with it every day. Kids would ask me questions about my crazy mother like it was some novelty. I never let anyone come to my house. Most of the parents wouldn't let me come to their houses either, because if my mother came looking for me, they'd have to deal with her. Once she went to a friend's house and accused his mother of trying to kidnap me.

"My father told me if we pretended everything was normal, then it would be normal. So I tried. I ignored the looks, answered teachers' questions the way I should, all the while trying to pretend my life was normal."

No matter what he'd done, Chloe's compassion was clear on her face and in the soft way she asked, "How did you cope?"

"I loved to build things with Legos. It was the one way I could impress people and fit in. For a while, the kids would forget about my crazy mom, and even me, and focus on my creation. I did chores to buy more and more Legos. I didn't want to ask my father for anything, not even money for that. Those Legos were my escape, and my way to fit in. I had a tenuous grip on normalcy, at least for a while."

"And then what happened?"

"It all fell apart the day my mother tried to kill my father with a butcher knife."

She looked at him in horror.

"She thought my father had a demon inside, and she wanted to cut it out. She swore she could see it peeking out between the buttons of his shirt. They finally committed her. She died two years later of heart complications. A year later I went to college in Miami. I never went back to Michigan, much less my hometown. And I swore I would never give anyone a reason to look at me like that again."

"I'm sorry," she said, working the clay again. "And now I've given people that reason. Maybe I'm as crazy as your mother."

"No, you're not. But you know what it's like to grow up having people look at you as though you're some kind of specimen, don't you?"

She met his gaze again, and he could see it in her eyes. "You know what it's like to not fit in."

"Yes. I understand. I do. I'll call the papers myself and tell them that you and I have nothing to do with each other. That I'm not helping you. Whatever you want me to tell them."

He thought it would be hard to tell her about his past. To tell anyone. Somehow telling her seemed natural.

She went back to work on the clay. "I won't interfere in your search again. I won't contact you, won't even call you." Her voice got thin. "I'll never give anyone a reason to associate your name with mine."

"Chloe . . ."

"There's nothing else to talk about."

He stood, dropping his towel on a nearby counter. She was right; he should leave now before he caused any more trouble for himself or for her. Then why weren't his feet walking—no, running—to the door?

He came up behind her. "Are you going to be all right?"

"Fine," she said on a weak breath. Her head started to lean back toward him, but she jerked away. "Go, please."

His fingers trailed down her arms, then slid around her mud-covered hands. Her foot came off the pedal, and the wheel stopped turning. He gripped her hands, palms sliding against hers. "Chloe, I need to know that you're all right."

She turned toward him, her cheek brushing his. "I'm never going to be all right if you don't stop this"—her voice got breathy and soft— "kissing me and touching me. Why are you doing this?"

"I don't know."

Her breath caught and her eyes closed. She turned around to face him then, sliding her hands free of his. Her gaze took in his bare chest and wet hair. She took a deep breath, determination in her expression. He was prepared for her to kick him out. Instead, she leaned forward and took his mouth in a hot, fiery kiss. Her hand slid over his chest, leaving a trail of wet, cool clay. He barely thought about his own hands leaving that same trail as he ran his fingers up along her neck and cradled her face.

He loosened the knot on her towel, and it fell away to reveal soft flesh and nothing else. Even her bruises looked somehow beautiful.

She pushed him back against the closed door, undid his pants, and shoved them to the floor. "We're going to do this, get it out of our systems." He guessed she had the bulldozer look on her face.

He didn't let himself think, he just let her lead him. Her gaze roamed over his body in a hungry way, but she pushed onward as though she were on some crazed mission. He understood crazed. Wasn't that why he was doing this? Wasn't that why he was getting lost in her, in the thought of burying himself in her?

She ran her mouth over his stomach, nibbling at his waistband. Which inevitably made her chin brush against the tip of him. Just that simple contact sent a wall of fire through him.

She slithered up his body, her hands roaming over his legs and up his stomach. "We're almost there," she whispered, looking as though she were anticipating . . . what?

He could feel the soft fullness of her breasts. Then she was kissing him again, devouring him like a starved woman. And even though some part of him knew this was crazy, that every time they said good-bye they ended up in each other's arms, he wanted her too much to stop.

Her eyes snapped open, and she came to an abrupt stop. "No. Oh, no!" She scrambled away, frantically searching for and grabbing up her towel and throwing it around her lush, naked body. A look of horror had replaced the dreaminess on her face. "Not you. It can't be you."

Still dazed, he started to take a step toward her, then realized his pants were down around his ankles. He yanked them up. "What are you talking about?"

"Everything's screwed up, that's all. My bad instincts have gotten worse, and it's all your fault. You have to go, right now."

"I know this is crazy, believe me. The timing's wrong, everything's wrong."

"That's my point." She was rushing around now, picking up her discarded clothes, pushing the lump of clay into a plastic pail. "Everything's wrong, so I shouldn't be having this . . . right feeling about you."

He moved close, holding her hands between them. "What are you talking about?"

She took a deep breath. "All my life I've made bad decisions where men were concerned. I mean, I've never really loved a man before, but I definitely had some intense infatuations. But I always got the feeling just in time that they were wrong. . . ." She gestured toward the door where only minutes before they'd been close to ecstasy. "So I wanted to get that feeling with you, because that kills the infatuation." She shook herself free from his grip. "And that didn't happen. It felt . . . right. And it's crazy, because you and I aren't right. Not in a million years, when hell freezes over, when the cows come home. See, I am crazy." She rolled her eyes and groaned. With the clay smeared all over her neck, her face, and her hands, she *did* fit the image. "Crazy. Which means you need to stay away from me, because you don't do crazy. Or even quirky. And I understand that, I really do. I understand not fitting in and being a specimen, like you said. So go, please."

She nudged him to the door, then opened it. "Go! Shoo! Don't come back!"

He stared at her, knowing she was right. Not about her being crazy. Well, maybe she was. But he couldn't talk. He still wanted her. Clay and craziness and all. So staying away from her was a good idea.

Still, he paused in the doorway. "Chloe?"

She clutched the towel to her chest. "Yes?"

Several sensible thoughts floated through his mind. He must be crazy, because the words that came out were, "If you ever jump me like that again, you'd better mean it."

Chapter Twelve

DYLAN'S CELL PHONE RANG ON HIS WAY BACK TO NAPLES. His heart always jumped when it rang, and he willed it to be Yochem with good news.

It was Ross Allen.

"Hey, buddy, how are you hanging in there?"

"What's up?" He wasn't in the mood to talk to Ross, the man who had seen Chloe naked, who had probably made love with her.

"First, I wanted to tell you how glad I am you disputed the whole Chloe thing. That's the last thing our theater needs to be connected with."

"I'm glad I pleased you," Dylan muttered, trying not to think about just how connected he'd almost been to Chloe.

"Second, I talked to my bud at Media Plus and got us a spot on the local news show tonight at seven. To talk about Teddy."

What else would they talk about? Dylan wondered, but said, "That's great. I'm having posters made and I'm offering a reward."

"Good, that'll get the news interested."

"*Get* them interested? They should already be interested. There's a defenseless kid out there!"

"Hate to break it to you, but they don't care unless there's something new. Believe me, I know from hearing my buddy talk about it. A kid still missing isn't news. A reward is. He was sure asking if there was something going on between you and my little Chloe."

"She's not your Chloe. Dumping her took away the privilege of calling her yours."

"Whoa, aren't you a little testy? So is it true what the papers implied? That you and Chloe are a thing?"

A thing. That would describe it. "We're not a thing. And what do you mean, the papers implied? They should be saying that I have nothing to do with her and that she's . . . a nutcase."

"They do. But there's a read-between-the-lines message. You know, cute gal, good-looking guy . . . they're always sniffing around for a scandal. If they hear something in your voice, they'll be on it like hounds."

"There was nothing in my voice that said me and Chloe were a thing." Was there? He instinctively cleared his throat.

"You could always talk about your crazy wife. People love that kind of thing, and you could come off real stoic-like, putting up with it all these years. You could even make up stuff. Heck, she can't dispute you."

Dylan would have hung up on him, but he needed this interview. "I am not going to talk about Wanda. I want to create interest in finding my son, not in my personal life."

"Chill out, buddy. Is this a good time to talk about the theater?"

"No."

"All right, we'll chat after the taping. I'll see you at the studio at six-thirty."

Dylan pounded on the steering wheel. Yochem was concentrating on Dylan's life, the media was interested in hot sex and psychic alliances between him and Chloe, and no one was looking for his son.

He dialed Yochem's number. "Yochem has been

pulled onto another case, sir. Officer Mutt is now assigned to Teddy's case. Hold a moment."

"Wait! What do you mean, Yochem's not on my case?"

"Haven't you heard? A man's got an entire toy store held hostage. Yochem's handling that. Now, if you'll hold—"

Dylan hung up. His son only rated an officer now. Five days later, and no leads, nothing tangible. Sure, a few officers were still looking. But they'd given up. He was up to ninety miles per hour without even realizing it, his knuckles white on the wheel and muscles rock-hard.

Well, dammit, he hadn't given up. And he wouldn't.

But the worst part was, Teddy probably thought he had. The man of the house and protector of his family had let his little boy down.

TEDDY WAS still sitting outside when the old woman came out. He thought he'd been out there for a day, but he wasn't sure exactly. All he knew was that he had his buttons and his clothes, and that he was cold. But now the sun was out, and he was slowly warming up.

The woman looked cold too, with her sweater pulled around her. "Ah, so that's where my buttons went."

She was looking at his buttons. Not in anger like his mom sometimes did. Before she'd try to take them away and he'd cry. Once he had them, they were his, part of his world.

The woman gestured around them. "Do you know where we are, young man?"

He didn't like to look out there. It was weird, different. He wanted his room back. One time he'd ventured a look farther out and saw a pink bird. He'd seen white birds before, walking on their skinny legs around his yard. He'd never seen a pink one, especially with a funny-looking beak.

The woman walked closer, studying him the way he sometimes studied a bug. "You're my grandson, aren't you?"

"You're my grandson," he repeated, just to give her an answer. All he knew was Mom, Dad, Camel, and other people. She was an "other" person. A bad other person.

"You mean 'grandmother,' don't you? How long we been out here?" she asked, squinting in the sun.

"How long?"

"Yes, how long? Days, weeks?"

Time wasn't important to him. It was hard to understand. He knew morning and night, but all those divisions in between weren't clear. There were minutes, and hours, which were really long. Days were forever.

"She's not coming back for us, is she?"

Those were bad words, and he tried hard to understand what they meant. "She's not coming back."

"I knew it! Your mom's left us here, abandoned us."

He worked with the words, separating them at first, then putting them together. *Mom not coming. Mom not coming*. "No!" He jumped to his feet, refusing to believe that she wasn't coming. He didn't understand the rest, but he knew *not coming*. "No!"

"She's punishing me for letting her dad put her in that hospital. I tried to tell her how it was, how you couldn't tell that man anything, and they promised it would help her. We're almost out of food and water. She's left us to starve out here in God knows where. We're going to die out here." She sank to her knees on the deck and reached for him. "Come here, boy. Give me a hug before we die. I'm scared."

"No!" He moved away from her, grabbing his buttons

and clothes tighter to his chest. She moved closer, pulling herself along the floor toward him. "No touch." He didn't like to be touched. It felt like a dull pain.

He climbed through the railing, focusing only on that gnarled hand coming at him. And then he lost his balance. Suddenly he was surrounded by cold, dark water.

And then something grabbed his ankle.

CHLOE FELT like she'd been hit by a car again—from the inside.

She kept running everything through her mind, over and over again. Waking up to Dylan tipping the canoe over, going down into that murky brown water, him pulling her up again, him kissing her. She replayed every second in slow motion.

His tenderness had been a surprise. That incredibly sexy body hadn't. She'd somehow expected that, though seeing him in the flesh had been another story altogether.

She was quite sure she'd never been knocked over with lust at the sight of any man's body, not even Ross's finely honed physique.

But Dylan . . . she made a growling noise deep in her throat. Tall and lean, muscular without bulges and veins, just enough hair . . . Chloe sighed. Perfect. Not the least bit like a poet's body. And so what did the pillar of self-control do? Jump him!

Well, there had been a reason, if reason had played any part in it. She just couldn't remember what it was at the moment and she'd never professed to being a pillar of anything anyway.

She sat in the dark room downstairs for an hour, just thinking and breathing in the scent of clay. She didn't know what was real anymore. Were her dreams about Teddy real? Her feelings for Dylan? And that awful insight about him being the right one—could she be more wrong?

None of it was real, that's what she decided after an hour. She had no special skill to find Teddy, no hints, no vibes. Time to face it: Leave it up to the police and Dylan. Put it out of her mind and chalk up the dreams to the shock of the accident and her inability to resist trying to save a lost child.

She went upstairs and showered, then lay down for a nap. Everything dragged her down. The truth about her mother, her aunts' lies, nearly making love with Dylan, and the way she still wanted him. Oh, my, the way she still wanted him, beside her, holding her, inside her. It all pulled her into an uneasy sleep, into a familiar dream. . . .

She was canoeing at dusk, gliding soundlessly through the water. She slowed when she saw the flock of pink spoonbills perched on a group of mangroves. She rarely saw spoonbills, so she took a moment to marvel at them. Their bills were flat, fashioned for sifting out morsels from the water. Their necks were long and white, flowing into their pink-feathered bodies. She loved all the birds that lived around the waterways, but these were her favorite.

The birds took sudden flight, tucking up their long legs and flapping their wings. She looked to see what had frightened them. A canoe floated in the water a short distance away. And Teddy was sitting in it. He reached out to her.

"Teddy, hold still," she said, paddling toward him. "I'm coming."

She reached out to him, trying to touch his fingers and pull him to safety. Then his canoe tipped over, and he tumbled into the brown water with a gasp.

And never came up again.

She woke with a similar gasp, hand over her pounding heart.

"It's all right, honey," a soft voice soothed as Chloe focused in on her house and then Lena sitting there reminding her a lot of her mom. Lena's red hair was loose around her shoulders. Morning sun streamed into the house, filtered by the leaves and a thin fog. Lena, smelling like chamomile tea, kept stroking Chloe's hair.

"More dreams about Teddy? I remember you used to wake up like that after your mama died. When we moved here, you started dreaming about falling in the water. You always did hate that brown water," Lena said with a soft smile. "Never could figure out why it bothered you so much."

"I don't like not seeing. It's always been about the not seeing." Chloe swallowed hard and sat up in bed. "He fell in the water out there and disappeared. But I'm sure it was only a dream." She blinked, trying to clear away the fuzzies. She felt warm and sticky. "What's wrong? Why are you here?"

"I think I know where Teddy is."

Now she came fully awake. "What?"

"I let myself go with the vision this time. Thought I owed it to you after . . . well, after everything. Maybe I did you wrong, but I was only trying to protect you."

Chloe tried to smile. "I'm not some fragile flower, Lena. I was raised by three of the strongest survivors around."

Lena placed her palm on Chloe's cheek. "But you're not like us. You're tender inside. You always have been. That's why you can't resist saving every little thing that comes your way."

"I don't want to be tender." Was that why she longed for a man in her life? Because of some silly tenderness?

"You're strong, don't get me wrong on that. But inside you're a tender flower that needs to be nurtured. We've tried to do that. It was my decision to keep the truth from you. I fought for it. And maybe you lost."

Chloe took Lena's hand and squeezed it. "I know you were only doing what you thought was right. But it hurts, hurts to be"—she cleared the tightness from her throat—"left out again." Lena's face looked more shadowed than ever. "Are you all right?"

"I'll be fine, hon."

"You said you knew where Teddy was."

"He's on a boat. I think it's a boat, but sometimes it looks more like a house. He's in the Keys, one of the less populated ones. The boat is just offshore, on the west side of the islands. I keep seeing a skull too. And the birds."

"What about the man who's with him?" Chloe asked.

"I could feel his presence, but I couldn't see him."

A real lead! "I always felt Teddy was nearby. But then, what did I know? Nothing."

"You felt he was near water."

"But it's Florida. There's water everywhere!"

Chloe leapt off the bed and hugged her tight, closing her eyes and savoring the sensation. Being separated from her family had been too scary. "Thanks." Then she started rooting through her drawers, throwing things on her bed.

"What are you doing?"

"I'm going down there. And I'm going alone. That way I won't drag anyone else into this. I can do this, Lena. I can find him."

DYLAN WENT home to shower, shave, and change. He wasn't going to do much good looking like a drowned rat.

"I'm going to pick up the posters in a while," he told

Camilla. "I'd like you to take them around the neighborhood, ask people to keep looking."

"I did that. Not with posters, but I went around and tried to get some people to search this area again. The truth is, they've already looked several times, and they're convinced he's not here. They're probably right."

Dylan rubbed his forehead, feeling a dull throb in his brain.

Camilla asked, "Do you want me to look—"

"No, you stay here. Work on the press for me. See if we can get more coverage on Teddy. Not me, not my love life, Teddy."

"I'll try, but everyone's been covering the hostage situation at the toy store." She nodded toward the television.

Cameras focused through the front window on the man clutching a frightened woman in front of him like a shield. Life was going on, bad and good. And Teddy had been forgotten.

"Maybe I'll go down there. Maybe I'll take someone hostage so I'll get some f—freaking press. I don't know what else to do." But then they'd think he was crazy like his mother.

He took a hot shower, threw on some fresh clothes, and tried to think about other ways to get press. Sane ways.

"Camilla, I—" As he walked into the family room, he realized it wasn't Camilla standing in front of the fireplace. It was his father. He looked grayer, older than when Dylan had last seen him.

"Hello, son."

Dylan's throat went tight. "What are you doing here?"

"I couldn't stay away. My grandson—"

"You've never even *met* your grandson."

"I wanted to. But I—"

"I know, you were too busy to be inconvenienced by family. Why aren't you back in Michigan now, working the markets, making those international calls?"

"Because I'm here," he said in a soft voice. "Because you need me."

"I don't need you. I needed you years ago when I was young and defenseless." Just like Teddy needed him now.

Will McKain released a long breath. "But now you're a tough guy with a big problem. Let me make up for lost time. I made mistakes."

Dylan hardened himself against his father's words. "You didn't make mistakes. You just weren't a father. And if you weren't a father, how the hell can you expect to be a grandfather? Go home. I don't need you."

Leave now, don't get started with him, Dylan told himself as he made himself walk out the door without a backward glance. He picked up the fliers from the printer and took them to the office, where he passed out stacks to every employee. "We're closing for the day and tomorrow, so get these posters out to everyone you can think of. Steve, you cover airports, bus stations, public places. Jodie, I know you can sweet-talk people into helping distribute more of them. Jake, start hitting trailer parks, particularly the ones out in the boonies."

"I'll get my wife and kids to help, too," he said, taking a stack.

Jodie touched Dylan's arm. "What made you finally decide to ask for our help?"

Dylan couldn't look at the tender expression on her face. He looked beyond her to the door. "Because no one else is looking. Because . . . I need your help."

As Dylan was locking up the office, his cell phone rang. *Please let it be Yochem with a lead.*

It was Ross again.

"Hey, buddy, bad news. Our stint got canceled."

A sick feeling twisted Dylan's stomach. "Why?"

"That situation at the Toys Unlimited. It's one of those disgruntled employee things, he went in there with a shotgun and is holding the entire place hostage. The station just arranged to interview the man's ex-wife. Sorry, but that's bigger news. Unless you've got something really juicy, like wearing women's clothing or a kinky affair with Chloe. And that's probably only going to get you thirty seconds of air time."

Dylan hung up on him. He couldn't take any more. Once again he had thoughts about taking a hostage himself. But that would be crazy. Dylan had had all the crazy he could handle in one lifetime.

BY LATE afternoon, Dylan had taken posters to Florida Power and Light, all of the post office branches, and nearly every store in Golden Gate. When his cell phone rang, he didn't harbor hope of hearing good news from the police. They were too busy saving multiple lives to worry about one little life.

It was Camilla. "Lena called. She said it was urgent."

Lena. His heart jumped. News about Chloe. "Give me the number."

Lena answered the phone saying, "I know you don't believe in visions, Dylan, and it doesn't really matter none. What matters is I told Chloe I had a vision that your son is down in the Keys on a boat. Or a house on the water, I'm not sure. Chloe's going by herself. She's determined not to drag anyone else down with her, she says. She's a smart girl, but her compassion is clouding her judgment. And she's got her bulldozer face on, which means nothing's going to change her mind. The hurricane just went through down there a few weeks ago. There's still a lot of destruction. Maybe even looters."

"And you're calling me because . . ."

"Because it's your son and because . . . I don't know what's going on with our girl. I don't want her hurt."

He tried to ignore the way the words, "our girl" tickled his stomach. "When is she planning to leave?"

"Tonight."

"But I can't leave town while my son is still missing."

"What if your wife had her mother drive the boy down to the Keys? Can you say for sure it's not possible?"

"My mother-in-law has Alzheimer's. She might not even remember how to drive."

"When has a disability ever stopped anyone, mental or otherwise?"

Those words hit home. How far would Wanda go to get what she wanted? Could he afford to ignore any lead when he'd exhausted his search of Naples? "I'll be right down."

"Don't tell her I told you. She wouldn't be happy with me, and she's already knee-deep in anger."

"What am I supposed to tell her?"

"I don't know. You're that mix of creativity and logic; you'll figure something out."

Chapter Thirteen

CHLOE WAS SITTING AT HER DINETTE TABLE BEFORE A MAP of Florida when the knock sounded on the door. It was probably Lena or Stella coming to try to talk her out of leaving tonight. Well, they could just forget it. She was her own woman. If she left tonight, she'd have the entire day to look for Teddy.

"Isn't that right, Shakespeare?"

The dog almost seemed to nod in agreement.

On the way to the door she dumped out the rest of her coffee in the sink. Any more and she'd be stopping at bathrooms the whole way down. Her mouth was open and ready to silence any and all protests from her aunts or grandmother. It stayed open as she took in Dylan wearing black jeans and a black T-shirt and looking all kinds of gorgeous.

Surprise mixed with extreme pleasure at the sight of him. Forget the pleasure part. Forget the way he looked and the way he smelled, all woodsy, and focus on why the heck he was at her door. "Five percent of one-sixty is eight," she blurted out.

"Nice to see you too," he said with a smile.

She crossed her arms over her chest. "How about, I thought I told you not to come back? Unless . . . is there any news on Teddy?"

He walked in. "No, nothing. Especially not"—anger flashed over his face—"with the hostage situation going on."

"What hostage situation?"

"You haven't heard?"

She nodded toward the tiny television set on the kitchen counter, turned off as it usually was. "I'm not much into watching TV, or listening to the radio. Too many negative vibes." Or was she too tender? Didn't she put herself in the victims' places and find herself haunted by those images?

"There's a guy holding people hostage at the Toys Unlimited store. It's all the police and the media are focusing on right now."

Outrage spiked through her. "What about Teddy?"

"I guess hostages are more interesting than a missing boy."

She could hear restrained anger in his voice. "Damn them! Double damn them!" she said. "Who do we call? What do we have to do?" Gypsy came over and rubbed her ankles, sensing her person's distress. Cats didn't like their people to be upset; it tilted the balance of their world.

Chloe caught a glint of something, admiration maybe, in his eyes. "No one. Apparently we needed to be having a kinky affair to get media attention. And the police are too busy with the hostage crisis, and too busy investigating me and you."

"I'm sorry. But why are you here?" She shuffled the papers on the table to cover the map.

"To, ah, say thank you. For the posters . . . for everything." He rubbed his chin, looking around at her house. His gaze alighted on the table. "Going somewhere?"

She turned to see what he'd been looking at. The map was hardly visible. "What, are you psychic?"

"No. Definitely not."

He seemed to wait for more explanation.

"Look, Dylan, you said you didn't want to be associated with me, that you didn't want me around at all. That was before you kissed me. And now you're back, and I don't know what to say. Are you trying to drive me crazy?"

That got a quick smile out of him. "I came down to . . . bring some posters."

"Posters?" She looked down at his empty hands.

"I, uh, must have left them in the car."

"Don't worry about it. I have enough posters of my own. Or do you want to replace my posters with yours? The vibe part bothers you, doesn't it?"

"The vibes don't bother me. Really," he added at her skeptical look. He ran his long fingers along the edge of her butcher-block counter. "So, any vibes been reported?"

She narrowed her eyes. "No, and you wouldn't care anyway. Why are you really here?"

He let out a long breath, still concentrating on the edge of the counter. "Maybe I do care. Maybe those kinds of leads are all I have."

"That's probably the only true thing you've said since you got here." She couldn't help the trill of joy that he might be open to psychic vibes.

He closed his eyes and leaned his head against the cabinet door behind him. "Dammit, Chloe, I don't know what else to do, where else to look." She could hear the pain in his voice: pain, loneliness, and desperation. "I need . . . I'd like your help."

She couldn't breathe for a moment. With those few words he'd splayed open her heart. "I'm going down to the Keys," she said. "Tonight. Lena had a vision that Teddy was down there on a boat or in a small house. She's the real thing, by the way. She confirmed what I'd been thinking all along, that he was near water. They have those ferries to Key West, and maybe Wanda put her mother and Teddy on one of those. And"—her own voice hitched—"I don't know where else to look either."

Something in her voice made him open his eyes. "You really care about Teddy, don't you?"

"Why is that so hard to believe? I care about a lot of things."

"I know you do. But this is different."

"Yes, it is different. I told you, I feel connected to him."

"I'm going with you."

"No." She folded up the map and her notes and stuffed them into her bag. "Not a good idea. Not at all."

He pushed away from the counter and walked over to her, trying to use all of his six-foot height to impose his will upon her, she guessed. "Why not?"

She looked down, trying to avoid his dark eyes, but his mouth wasn't a good place to find distraction, or his throat, or the collar of his T-shirt where a few dark hairs peeked out. She looked away from him to watch a heron stalking prey at the water's edge. "Because if he's not there, I don't want you telling me I'm crazy, or . . . turning away from me again. I don't want your disbelieving vibes around. I need to do this alone."

He touched her chin, pulling her gaze back to his. "I won't do that."

His touch filled her with liquid warmth and pulled her toward him. She moved back, shaking her head. "And . . . and we shouldn't be together alone anyway. It's sparks and fire and then cold water dousing the flames. My heart can't take it again."

"As I recall, you threw the cold water last time."

She narrowed her eyes. "You would have stopped anyway. You're too sensible, too grounded. You wouldn't make love with me because you're not the love-them-and-leave-them type. Don't ask me how I know that, but I do. And you don't want me in love with you, because I'm bad for your reputation. And . . . well, you're bad for mine. I'm not supposed to want a man in my life. I'm supposed to be strong. I am woman, hear me roar, all that kind of thing."

But she did want him, weren't those her unspoken words? He studied her while she tried to look strong and independent.

"You don't believe that, do you?" he asked. "You're going to go through life without ever getting involved with a man? You, with all that compassion and—"

"Don't say tenderness," she said, pointing at him. "I'm not tender and I'm not cute!" She instinctively ran her fingers through her hair, still surprised not to feel curls. "Maybe if I meet a poet, someone sensitive and romantic, I'll think about letting him in my life. Until then—"

"Until then, you and I are going to find Teddy."

"Why you? You just told the papers you don't believe in psychics and that you're not working with me."

"You read the paper?"

She wrapped her arms around herself, feeling the sting all over again. "You disparaged me. So fine, don't work with me. Go away and let me look on my own."

He studied her again, and she tried to put on her toughest bulldozer face. He put his hands on his hips and leaned down close. "All right, tell me this. You go down to the Keys and then what? Do you have a boat? If he's on a boat somewhere, how are you going to find him? You going to paddle your canoe everywhere?"

"You're disparaging me again."

"No, I'm making sense."

"So fine, I'll hire a boat."

He shook his head. "Get your stuff, put on your pink or yellow sneakers, and come with me. I've got a boat. We'll take it to the marina, load it on a trailer, and be on our way by dark. Don't be stubborn. We're losing time, and I can outstubborn you anytime, anywhere, sweetie-pie."

"You're disp—"

"No, I'm not. That just"—there was an interesting sparkle in his eyes—"slipped out. Come on."

She stared down, realizing he'd noticed her bare feet, and her colored Keds. She weighed her options. Being with Dylan was definitely not a good idea. He was no sensitive poet by any means, but every time she caught that glint of compassion, her heart opened a little more. And that sweetie-pie thing, oh, boy, that sounded way too nice. Then there was that instinctual thing that said he was The One, which was definitely wrong, wrong, wrong.

But he did have a boat, which meant she wouldn't have to beg and wheedle or drain her savings to hire one out. He leaned against the counter again. As if she had a choice.

"All right, but you're coming on my terms," she said.

"Yeah, okay, go pack so we can get going."

"One of those terms is that you are not the boss. I know you're used to being in charge, but we're equals in this search. You're not going to tell me what to do."

"Fine. You're in charge. You call the shots. *Now go pack.*"

"All right, as long as we have that . . ." She narrowed her eyes. "And no making fun of anything psychic. After all, you must believe a little if you're coming with me."

"I believe. Now pack."

"Seriously?"

"Yeah, seriously. Go."

"And no touching or kissing. Nothing, not even a brush of our arms."

"Chloe, touching you the first time was my biggest mistake. Now go!"

"All right," she said, turning and going up the short set of stairs to her bedroom. "As long as we have all that straight."

THE FIRST point Chloe had to concede to was about driving her car, all because of one tiny detail: no trailer hitch. So she sat in the passenger seat of Dylan's fancy Mercedes and tried not to glance over at him any more than necessary.

He spent most of the drive back to Naples on his cell phone. First he had to arrange to borrow a trailer. Then he spoke to someone named Jodie who had a sweet voice and called him "hon" once.

Not that Chloe was listening. Eavesdropping was a habit for insecure women, and you had to be *in* a relationship to be insecure.

He discussed the Kraft Theater project with Jodie, meetings that had to be rescheduled and plans that had to be delivered. Then he called Camilla asking her to pack him a suitcase.

"Where were those posters you were bringing out to me?" Chloe asked between calls.

"Posters? Oh, they're back there." He pointed to the back seat with his phone.

There were stacks of them on the black leather seat, slick color posters with both Teddy's and Wanda's pictures on them. *You and your dopey posters.*

She noticed that Dylan looked everywhere as he

drove. His eyes searched oncoming cars and people in parking lots, looking for a familiar face.

She closed her eyes and leaned back in the seat. The smell of rich leather filled her nose, and chilled air washed over her. The posters, the car, and everything in Dylan's life were perfect and polished. Including the man. He would no sooner invite her into his life than . . . well, than she could invite him into hers. And though he'd sort of admitted that he needed her during the search, he would never admit to needing her beyond that.

She tried to imagine his childhood, growing up with a crazy mother everyone in town knew about. Though she had been an outcast her whole life, both in Lilithdale and the regular world, she'd at least felt loved by the women around her. When she looked over at him, she caught him watching her as they waited at a light. For a split second she saw that tenderness in his gaze again, but he quickly masked it.

She must have drifted off for a few minutes, because the next thing she knew, Dylan spit out an expletive as they pulled into his driveway. He was looking at the Pontiac parked in the circular drive.

"What's wrong? The reporters aren't waiting to catch us."

"That's only because Teddy isn't news anymore."

She shared Dylan's frustration. If this lead didn't pan out, she was going to have to think up ways to bring Teddy back into the news. How far would she go? Anything outrageous would put her at odds with Dylan.

"Is that the detective's car?" she asked as they came to a stop in the garage.

"It's my father."

She followed him into the kitchen, where Camilla was

on the phone. Dylan lifted an eyebrow, and she shook her head and wrote "nonsense" on the pad in front of her. *They probably said the same thing about me,* Chloe thought.

An older man paced in front of the French doors, cell phone in hand. "If they drop ten more points, buy eight thousand shares. Let's hold on to GE for now. Call me if anything changes." When he saw Dylan, he hung up.

He was a good-looking man, tall like Dylan, with silver hair and dark eyes. Same long face and features. She could see pain in his eyes; apparently he hadn't mastered the masking ability like his son had.

"Dylan . . ."

"Why are you still here?"

The man shifted his gaze to her. "I'm Dylan's father, Will." He had a nervous laugh. "But you've probably heard all about me by now."

She took his outstretched hand, not sure what to say. "I'm Chloe Samms."

Dylan took hold of her shoulders and ushered her ahead of him. "We've got to get the boat ready. Excuse us."

"Do you have a lead, Dylan, sir?" Camilla asked.

"Maybe," was all he'd commit to.

They walked across the back yard to the boat dock. Dylan hit a button, and the suspended boat lowered into the water. It wasn't a big boat, maybe thirty or so feet, but it was a nice one. She watched him jump aboard and start doing things that one had to do to get a boat ready, she supposed. That's why she stuck with the canoe. She preferred the simple you-paddle, you-go technology.

Dylan walked up on the bow of the boat, then stopped. "Do me a favor and ask Camilla to get you the key for the boat."

"Sure." She walked across the spongy grass and many terraces to the house.

Camilla was just hanging up the phone when she looked up and saw Chloe. "I sure hope the press don't get word of you being here again." She held up a legal pad filled with scribbles. "We're still getting calls from people claiming to have 'seen' Teddy in everything from a rock band to a spaceship."

"I didn't mean to cause him problems. I just want to find Teddy."

"And now you got him running down to the Keys."

"It was his choice. I didn't ask him to come with me."

"I read what your mother did to those people, getting their hopes up."

"Teddy is alive," Chloe said through gritted teeth. Had her mother said the same thing with the same conviction? "Listen, I just came in to ask you . . . Dylan needs the key for the boat."

Camilla walked over to a built-in desk and searched through the drawers. When she handed Chloe the key a minute later, she said, "I hope you're right. About Teddy being alive, I mean."

Me too, Chloe wanted to say, but only nodded. Will was standing by the pool watching Dylan when she walked out onto the lanai. She had intended to walk past him, but his words stopped her.

"You're the psychic one, right?"

She shook her head. "I'm just trying to find Teddy."

"Are you my son's lover?" he asked in a soft voice.

That made her swallow back a choking sound. *Does 'almost' count?* "No. I'm . . . I don't know what I am to him."

"I'm surprised he's letting you help. He's always been

independent. I guess he had to be." He tilted his head, studying her. "Do you know about his mother?"

She nodded quickly, not wanting to hear any more. "A little. I'd better get back. . . ." She nodded toward Dylan.

She could see him moving around on the boat, focused on his task.

"How well do you know him?" Will asked. "I want to know who he is."

Me too, she thought. "I don't think he's an easy person to know. He holds in a lot, and he excels at masking his feelings."

"He learned that as a kid, a defense mechanism. I made a lot of mistakes, I can see that now. I thought he handled it well, but all he did was bury himself, the same way I did, I suppose. I kept myself insulated from the craziness at home. I worked hard, traveled a lot. In distancing myself from her, I also distanced myself from my son. I've been trying to make amends now." He looked at her, weighing what he was going to say. "I may be dying of colon cancer."

She was speechless for a moment. "Does Dylan know?"

"No, and I don't want him to. I don't want him to come to terms with me because I'm dying. I want him to love me because I'm his father. And if he can't love me"—Chloe could hear the same kind of emotion that sometimes shadowed Dylan's voice—"I at least need him to forgive me."

"Oh, I wish you hadn't told me."

He gave her a sideways look. "Bad at keeping secrets?"

She smiled. "Dylan does seem to have some kind of effect on me. I'll do my best." She turned to watch Dylan again, who was glancing over at her. "How long you going to be staying around? I mean, here in Naples."

"A few days at least. After that, it's up to God."

She swallowed hard. "Dying's not so bad. The worst is leaving our loved ones behind. But what's ahead . . . I think it makes it okay. I wish I could help, but I'm afraid I probably won't be part of his life after this is all over. After we find Teddy." She said it with casual conviction. So why was she feeling a dull pain in her chest?

"Thank you," Will said as she started walking toward the boat.

She paused. "I didn't do anything."

"You listened. It's more than my own son did."

She felt another pang inside. If only Fred Samms would ask her forgiveness. If only . . .

"Did you and my father have a nice chat?" Dylan gritted out when she handed him the key.

"Maybe that's what you should do," she said, ignoring his sarcastic tone.

"Chloe, don't lecture me. You don't know—"

"Maybe I do know, Dylan." She crouched down, level with him as he stood in the boat. To her horror, a tear sprung to her eyes. Oh, God . . . tenderness! She swiped at it, hoping he didn't notice. "Maybe I know too well."

He opened his mouth, then closed it again. "We have to get going. The marina's going to close soon. I'll meet you there. You remember where I told you it is, right?"

She nodded, then walked back to the house. She hugged his black leather bag to her chest as she walked to his car. His aftershave wafted up through the leather and reminded her of having his arms around her. It felt intimate to sit in the seat he'd sat in and to touch the leather steering wheel he'd touched.

"Ah, Chloe," she muttered. "You are a case."

IT WAS nearly dark by the time they hitched the boat trailer to the car. Chloe stayed out of sight at the marina. She didn't want anyone telling the press she was with Dylan.

When he got into the car, he smelled like engine oil and the soap he'd used to wash it off. "Ready?"

"Ready."

She wished she'd gone to the Keys alone. Then the pressure wouldn't be on her to prove Lena's vision was right. No one would have to know. But Lena had been right before.

And the child had already been dead.

"You all right?" he asked.

She started playing with her owl pendant. "Just worried."

"We don't have time to worry. We need a game plan."

"Game plan?" What did she know about games? Except that playing games meant you were either opponents or . . . "Does a *game* plan make us a team?"

"Let's not push it." He gave her a sideways smile that nearly stopped her heart. Their eyes held for a moment, and she hoped he couldn't see what she was thinking. He shifted his gaze ahead. "We'll stop along the way and distribute posters."

He turned on the CD player, and classic rhythm and blues poured out of the speakers. He started to quietly sing along with a song about lonely teardrops. She hadn't figured him for anything as soulful as R&B.

"I can't believe that you believe in Lena's vision," she said.

"A person's allowed to change his mind, isn't he?"

"I suppose. I'd like to believe that. But no matter what happens, you can't ridicule either her or me."

"I promised, didn't I?"

"Yeah," she said, sitting back with a sigh. "But men break their promises."

"Did Ross break a promise?" He looked a little surprised, as though he hadn't intended to ask that.

"You talked about me, didn't you? That day at your office. And they say women gossip!"

"We didn't gossip. He regrets letting you go."

"Yeah, I'll bet. His high-society wife is making the right connections for him, taking him to all the right parties—not that I keep up with that kind of thing. I'll bet he just misses the heck out of me." Seeing Dylan's smile, she asked, "Did he say that?"

"Do you want him to miss you?"

She wiggled to get comfortable in the seat. "I don't care. Okay, it'd be nice if he did. It would be even better if he called her by my name once in a while, particularly during those crucial moments." She gave him an impish grin, but it faded. "Nobody misses me. They wipe their hands across their foreheads and say, 'Whew!' "

He grew quiet for a moment. "Still love him?"

"No." She shook her head. "I don't think it was love anyway. More like intense infatuation. At the time . . . well, I admit to glancing at bridal magazines. I know the difference now."

"Do you?"

The way he looked at her . . . Chloe felt her insides implode. "Oh, yeah." She cleared her throat, embarrassed by the strangled sound in her voice. "What do I know about love anyway?" All she knew was that what she'd felt for Ross was nothing like the way Dylan made her feel. "I'm over him."

"Ah, so you want him pining away for you, convinced he made the wrong choice?"

"Exactly." She gave him a grin. "Hey, he's the one who broke my heart. Figuratively speaking," she added, though she'd said too much anyway.

"Men are jerks," he said.

"Really? Aren't you betraying the fraternity?"

"I'm not part of any fraternity."

"Oh, come on. You're part of that crowd. Are you including yourself in that jerk comment?"

"Definitely."

"Why do you say that?" She liked his profile, strong nose, nice chin. The beginning of five-o'clock shadow. She had an almost irresistible urge to reach out and run her finger along his jawline. To touch him, to connect. Fortunately she held herself back.

"Because I worked too much, put my firm ahead of everything in my life. My priorities were messed up."

"You say that in the past tense. Does that mean you're ready to change your ways?"

"It's going to be Teddy first, then my business, if that's what you mean."

"That all?"

"What else?"

"Oh, a small thing like a wife, like a mother for Teddy."

"No wife. I've had enough grief. And so has Teddy." His somber expression gave way to a sideways grin. "Applying for the job?"

"Heck, no. I don't belong in your life. Think what the press would say."

"I didn't mean it the way it came out."

"Sure you did. Don't worry, I have no white-lace fantasies where you're concerned." Black lace, maybe. "You're way out of my league. I want—"

"I know, a poet."

"A romantic poet. You strike me as being romantic as pea soup."

He laughed at that, and for the first time she saw what a beautiful smile he had. "I'd be insulted if it weren't true. I didn't have much of an example to follow. Unless butcher knives are considered somehow passionate."

"Er, no." She pulled her legs up and wrapped her arms around them. "You don't talk much about Wanda. Did you love her? I mean, you must have at one time."

He focused on the road again, his expression sobering. "I'm sure I was in love with her once. I married her for the wrong reasons. I wanted someone in my life. Mistake number one. I thought I needed a wife. You know, to complete the picture. Mistake number two. And she presented herself as the perfect wife for a man who wanted to be a professional and move up in society. So I married her."

"Mistake number three," Chloe added before he could.

"Right. We moved apart after Teddy was born. Neither one of us did anything to repair the gap. My heavy work schedule didn't help."

He didn't need anyone now. That's what he was saying. "I don't need anyone in my life either," she said.

"That so?" He gave her a skeptical look.

"Very so. Way so. Who has time for romance, dating . . . bridal magazines? I have my own business, friends who care about me. I have my family, my cat and dog, and my pottery, for what that's worth. What more could I need?" The thought of her frog prince betrayed that conviction. *Forget the frog.*

"If you say so," he said.

"I do."

Those two words hung in the silence, echoing in her head until they became part of a bridal fantasy with her desperately uttering those words. To her horror, she heard herself answer, "I don't, I don't, I don't!" to the imaginary Chloe saying, *I do! I do! I do!*

"What?"

"Fourteen thousand ninety-two."

"Okay." He gave her a smile. "Won't you have to move if you get married? Isn't it against some kind of law for a man to live in Lilithdale?"

"Maybe the laws of nature. There's no law that says you have to be—or think you are—psychic or extraordinary to live there either. If you're not different, you wouldn't want to live there. If I hadn't been raised there, I wouldn't live there."

"Because you're the only left-brained one in the bunch, but they love you anyway."

She smiled. "Yeah, they do." She caught him watching her and wiped the marshmallow look off her face. "And it's not because I'm tender."

"I know, I know. Or cute."

"Right."

He shook his head. "It's just too bad that you're both."

Chapter Fourteen

DESPITE DYLAN'S EARLIER WORDS, HE AND CHLOE BECAME a team, leaving fliers at every store on the way. It was well into the night when they stopped at a pizza joint for dinner.

They ate buttery rolls covered with garlic as they waited for their pizza. He watched her lick the butter from between her fingers and wished the woman didn't have such a hold on his libido. She was cute, and she was tender, neither of which he wanted in a woman. Because he didn't want a woman at all, he reminded himself. Yet, she tantalized and bewitched him. He liked the way the corners of her mouth turned up, as though she knew a secret no one else knew. A good secret. And though her hair was cropped short, the strands still looked so silky, he wanted to run his fingers through them.

"Oh, the heck with fat grams," she muttered, grabbing another roll.

"Tell me about your father," he asked, hoping to steer his mind away from licking that buttery mouth of hers.

"Only if you tell me about yours."

"I don't have anything else to say about mine."

"Then neither do I." She nibbled around the edge of her third roll. "He was a truck driver. Produce. He drove fruit and vegetables all over the state of Florida. Sometimes he'd drop off a case of oranges or beans, but he never stayed long." She kept licking the butter off her roll as she talked, running the tip of her tongue along the edge, totally oblivious to the erotic effect it had on him. Dylan lined up the bottles and jars on the table.

"He always said he loved me, but he never hugged me. Don't you hug someone if you love them? Oh, you probably don't hug either. Except for in the hospital, and I had to ask you, and you hated it."

She paused, as though remembering. He remembered that hug too, how he hadn't wanted to let her go. Had the craziness started then? "I didn't hate it."

"You didn't?"

"Go on with your story."

"Anyway, after my mom died—after she killed herself—my aunts moved me down here, and I hardly ever saw him. Sometimes he'd call, or send a card for my birthday, but that was all. Not even a green bean. He probably didn't want to be associated with the weird women of Lilithdale either."

She said it all so casually, but he could see the pain in her blue eyes. There wasn't much she could hide with expressive eyes like that. Dreamy eyes.

When the pizza came, Chloe wrestled one of the cheesy pieces from the pie. He sat back and watched her for a few minutes. She rolled her slice from the tip upward until it resembled a long roll, then started eating it from the end. Pepperoni grease and tomato sauce oozed out the back end and dripped down her pinky finger. She stopped midchew when she realized he was watching her.

"Do you miss your father?" he asked before she could ask why he was watching her. He wasn't quite sure why, or why he was enjoying it so much.

She swallowed her bite. "Yeah. But there isn't anything I can do about it. I don't even know where he is anymore. Not like you. Your father is here, and he wants to make peace. I wish my father would do that."

"Would you forgive him for deserting you?"

"I thought I was too mad at him, but now I know . . .

yes, I would. Think about this, Dylan. What if your father died before you had a chance to make things right?"

"Are you trying to tell me something?"

She blinked in surprise, then took another bite. "Theoretically. I mean, we're all dying if it comes to that." She looked at his untouched pizza. "Aren't you going to eat?"

"I haven't been hungry lately. Too much on my mind."

"You have to eat. You've got to keep yourself healthy for Teddy."

They both looked down at the pizza and laughed.

"Pizza's healthy," she said. "All four of the food groups are represented. Bread, vegetables, dairy, and protein. If pepperoni has protein, that is. Now eat."

"Bossy, aren't you?"

"I can be. Someone's got to take care of you."

Her voice had gone soft at those words, and the tenderness in her eyes snagged his heart. For a moment he forgot that he took care of himself. For a moment he wanted her to take care of him and soothe his aches and pains. Just as he understood how a man would be drawn to take care of Chloe, he also knew how magical it would be to let her take care of him. She hadn't moved as their gazes locked together, and he realized he hadn't moved either. If he didn't do something, he was going to lean across the table and kiss her. Or worse, the crazy words flying through his mind would burst out of his mouth. How beautiful she was, how lonely he'd been and hadn't even realized it, how much he needed a woman like Chloe to bring him back to life.

So he did what he had to do. He stuffed a piece of pizza in his mouth.

BEFORE THEY left, Chloe told the man working behind the counter about Teddy and asked if they could hang up a poster. He nodded toward a bulletin board at the end of the restroom hallway.

Dylan watched her take the poster to the crowded board and look for someplace to put it. He saw her body stiffen, and before he knew what he was doing, he'd joined her.

"What's wrong?" he asked.

She nodded toward another poster that was half covered with bulletins about a diving trip and a johnboat for sale. A boy's face peered out from between them, and above his picture the words: MISSING! STRANGER ABDUCTION. He'd been missing for three months.

She shivered, and he instinctively put his hands on her shoulders. She started to lean back against him, caught herself, and pulled back. Dylan walked to the end of the hall and asked the man if the boy had been found yet.

"Not that I've heard."

"Then why is his poster buried under this other garbage?"

The grizzled guy shrugged. "What do I look like, the bulletin board police? It's not my problem."

Every muscle in Dylan's body tensed. "A missing child is everyone's problem. Our society is responsible for raising the perverts who take them; it's our responsibility to make sure they don't hurt anyone's kid."

"Dylan," Chloe said softly from behind him, tugging his arm. "Let's get going."

He walked back to the cluttered board. That poster could be Teddy's, that's all he could think about, that in one, two, three months, his son's poster would be buried beneath a poster of—he ripped down a sheet of paper—a trailer park's rummage sale!

"It's only news right after they disappear," he said, tearing down the johnboat sign. "Or if there's some juicy story surrounding it." He ripped down another paper, then another, anger roaring through him. His face felt as though it were on fire. "A missing child should never fade into the background. It's not right."

A woman walked out of the restroom and stared at him with wide eyes before scooting down the hall. He kept tearing everything off the board until only the boy named Mac smiled at him from the corkboard. Then he added his own poster.

"Mister, you'd better leave," the grizzly guy said from a safe distance.

"Dylan, we should go," Chloe said, touching his arm.

He shook off her touch and stared at the board. That's how it should look, both boys center stage until they were found. Only then could he turn and leave. The man moved behind the counter as they passed.

"You're lucky that guy didn't call the police," she said the second they stepped out into the warm evening air.

He ran his fingers through his hair, realizing he was still shaking from anger. He'd lost control. He'd gone crazy for a few minutes. The reflection in his car window revealed not the together professional but a desperate man. He watched Chloe start to touch his arm, but she pulled back before making contact.

"Anger isn't the way to express your emotions," she said.

He met her gaze in the reflection. "What do you want from me, Chloe? Do you want me to break down and cry? Would that be more appropriate?"

She took a deep breath, taking in his face. "Yes. Maybe. I don't know. But anger is never the right way to handle anything. Or doing that."

"Doing what?"

"What you always do, mask your feelings. Your face

closes up. You close yourself in and everybody else out. That's why you exploded back there. You've been holding it all in, trying to be Mister Strong and Tough. Why can't you accept that you're not strong and tough all the time? That you need to reach out and share with someone?" He heard a strange thickness in her voice when she said, "Why can't you reach out to me?"

Her pained expression in the window nearly broke him down, but he held firm. "Because one day I'll reach out and you won't be there."

"I'm not your father."

He almost wanted to laugh at the absurdity of that statement. But he held it in the way he held everything in. Or almost everything. "No, you're not."

She rolled her eyes at him. "You know what I mean! I'm not going to let you down. I'm not your former wife either, hiding herself to please you. This is me, what you see is what you get. I may look . . . tender, but I'm not. I'm tough and I'm strong and I'm here. You saved my life; let me give you something back."

Those last words made him look at her. He wanted to reach out to her, or at least some crazy part of him did. Which is why he absolutely couldn't.

How shallow his marriage to Wanda had been, he realized. They'd never shared these kinds of moments. She never challenged him, or made him think, or made him need. Chloe made him look deeper. In these last five days, there were too many feelings to pad himself against. Chloe was sneaking under those layers, and he didn't like it. Those layers had kept him sane for a long time. It was going to take all of them to stay that way.

"You're doing it again," she said, pulling at his arm, trying to get him to look at her and not just her reflection.

"Just when I see a glimpse of who you really are, you put on that mask again."

He turned to her, his mask firmly in place. "This is who I am. What you see is what you get. I'm not a soft-hearted poet. And I never will be."

"Well, think about this: What do you have inside you to give your son when we do find him? I just hope you have an answer before then."

CHLOE AND Dylan had said nothing more than a curt good night before retiring to their respective rooms. When she joined him on the front porch of his bungalow the next morning, he was already looking over a map of the Keys. He pointed to Key Largo, one of the upper Keys. "We're here now. We can canvass this section today if we get a move on. Ready?"

"Good grief, I haven't even had my coffee yet!" she said, sitting down next to him.

He got up and returned with a cup of coffee. "Here you go."

"You're either more thoughtful than I suspected or you're in a huge hurry. Hmmm, let me think about that." She shot him a look that bespoke her conclusion. "You're lucky I'm not one of those women who requires an hour to prepare herself for the day." She fluffed her hair, but he wasn't amused. "Fine, let me see that map. Lena said there was something about birds. I know, there are birds everywhere down here. But maybe the name of the Key has a bird's name. She also said she saw a skull."

"I don't think we're likely to run into a pirate ship."

"I didn't think about the flag. I guess I was thinking an island that looks like a skull from the air. All right, let's look at the Keys. Look how many of them there are.

There's Eagle Key up by the Everglades National Park. Nest Key; that has something to do with birds. There's Duck Key. And Pigeon Key farther south. Cottrell, is that a bird? There's Man Key."

"And Woman Key."

Chloe met his eyes, then shifted away. "Definitely not birds."

"No." He cleared his throat. "All right, we'll launch the boat here and explore these upper Keys this morning. Let's not forget Crane Key. Then we'll head down toward Duck Key."

It was a breezy morning with lots of sunshine and minimal cloud cover. All the little islands reminded her of the Ten Thousand Islands that stretched south from Lilithdale. Maybe she should have asked Dylan to explore those clusters of mangroves, just in case. But that was her gut feeling about Teddy being nearby, and she'd obviously been wrong. She tried to concentrate on Teddy, but felt nothing.

Please don't let that mean something's wrong.

They stopped the boats they saw and showed them the poster, but no one had seen him or Anne Dodson. But, as one man explained, "People tend to mind their own business 'round here long as no one messes with their stuff. Then they shoot first and ask questions later."

"Lovely," she said with a forced smile.

Neither Nest, Eagle or Crane Key showed signs of Teddy's existence. By midafternoon, they pulled the boat back on the trailer and headed to Duck Key. That's where they started seeing wreckage from the hurricane: debris littering yards and right-of-ways and collecting in coves, crumpled homes, and splintered boats.

It was late afternoon by the time they reached their destination and relaunched the boat. Instead of being relaxed by the sea breezes, Chloe was getting edgy. She kept running her fingers through her hair, pushing the strands back out of her face. Kept catching Dylan watching her. And those looks shot an awareness through her body. *Get your mind way off him, Chloe.*

She started running calculations, this time silently. She walked to the back of the boat, then returned to her seat. A minute later, she was up again.

"Chloe, what's the matter? You're as antsy as a cat."

She pulled on pink sweatpants and the matching shirt as the breeze got cooler and the sun got lower. "Something doesn't feel right. Maybe we're not on the right track. I don't know."

Miles and miles of open water stretched out, and now only a few boats dotted the horizon. They skirted the coast for a while, covering the west side first, then venturing to the east side. They passed a marina that had been nearly devastated by the hurricane. Parts of boats and piles of broken wood spoke of lost dreams.

"We'll head farther south, hit Pigeon Key, and then call it a day."

She pulled out a bag of chips and threw some to a seagull that floated nearby. Dylan wasn't saying it, but she could feel the weight of those unspoken words. This had been a wild goose chase. Or duck chase.

"Just don't forget that you came willingly," she said, hating the defensive sound in her voice.

"What?"

She threw more chips and more birds came. "Before you say this was a waste of time, that I was crazy to put my faith in visions, and that you were even crazier to go along with me . . . just remember you insisted on coming."

He turned the boat around. "I wasn't going to say anything."

"You were thinking about saying something, though."

"Oh, brother—"

His gaze settled on the horizon, and his expression froze. He cut the engine. She followed his gaze to a small house nestled in a patch of mangroves. Not nestled, exactly. It was warped and twisted by the storm, sitting halfway in the water. Abandoned. Sort of a house, sort of a boat. It was two stories with white vinyl siding and a tiny deck in front. The front corner was tilted into the water, and it creaked as it scraped against the shattered dock.

A pirate's black skull flag hung off a broken antenna to keep the curious away.

A chill skirted down her spine. She and Dylan exchanged glances, then looked back at the house. Sitting in shadows with the drooping skull flag, the house looked ominous.

Dylan angled their boat next to the structure. Several seagulls took flight from the front deck, piercing the air with their indignant cries. Seconds later they returned to perch on the slanted deck railing.

"Birds," Chloe whispered.

"Hello!" Dylan called out.

No one answered. The house rocked and groaned with the slight wake they created. Then she heard the sound that came to her dreams, of water tapping against the side. And then another sound, a very faint one. She couldn't tell exactly what it was. Maybe a cat. Maybe not.

"Do you hear that?" she asked.

She could tell he had. His head was cocked as he tried to pick out the sound. There it was again, a mewling sound. Another chill raced down her spine.

"Should we call the Coast Guard?" she asked, searching the horizon. "Remember what that guy said about people shooting first and asking questions second."

"Take my boat out of sight and use the radio." He kicked off his shoes, stripped off his shirt, and slipped over the side.

Her heartbeat pulsed in her throat as she looked into the opaque green water. Another glance over the horizon. Nobody in sight. *Please don't let anyone shoot us,* she prayed before tearing off her sweats and boat shoes and dropping into the water.

He helped her up onto the deck first, then she gave him a hand up. The whole structure dipped lower into the water. Her heart was hammering, sending a crushing sensation through her chest. If they didn't get shot, they were going to drown—or worse, drown whoever or whatever was inside.

Newspapers and discarded food containers littered the deck. The newspapers were current, which meant the place wasn't abandoned after all. Four seagulls circled the mess, wary of the intruders. The door was bolted shut, and on it a black sign read, KEEP OUT! PRIVATE PROPERTY.

They heard the mewling sound again, and it prickled the hair on her neck. "Maybe it's a cat," she whispered. But it didn't *feel* like a cat.

"Why would someone lock a cat inside?"

Dylan tried the windows, but they were nailed shut with pieces of broken wood. He looked for something to pry the door open with while she searched the empty horizon again. Maybe they should have radioed the Coast Guard first.

He nodded toward a dangling rope where a small boat could be tied off. "Whoever lives here must be out getting groceries or something." And whoever it was would be back.

He wedged a piece of wood beneath the bolted latch and pried and twisted it. It came loose after a few minutes of struggling. Something was jammed up behind the door. Apparently whoever lived here didn't exit through this door. He shoved his whole body against it and finally the door gave in.

Beer cans littered the floor, and the place smelled like waste. It was dark inside, with the windows in the back covered with plywood. They listened for more sounds, but heard nothing. They searching the small living room area. She headed down the hall, momentarily losing her balance on the tilted floor. He grabbed hold of her arm to steady her.

The only sounds they could hear were water lapping against the side and the screech of seagulls fighting over the garbage outside. She nodded in answer to his silent question: *I've got my balance; let's keep going.*

She followed him down the dark hallway. The front room was filled with piles of junk. The right side was partially flooded. She came to a sudden halt when Dylan stopped and she didn't. His body went stiff. The door in back was bolted shut from the outside.

Chloe swallowed hard. What if they were wrong? What if—

Dylan slammed into the door shoulder first. Wood splintered as he pushed through the doorway. He stopped, and she scrambled past him into the tiny bedroom. Her chest was crushed in a grip of hope and fear. In the dim light, all she could see was a lump beneath the blankets on a bed.

And the lump was crying.

Chapter Fifteen

"TEDDY," CHLOE WHISPERED.

Small fingers pulled down a corner of the blanket. Wide, haunted eyes peered above the edge. It was a boy. But it wasn't Teddy.

This boy had tangled blond hair and blue eyes, terrified eyes, but she could understand that. After all, two strangers had just crashed through his bedroom door.

"I'm sorry," she said to him in soothing tones. "We didn't mean to frighten you."

Dylan's body had drooped, but he couldn't take his eyes off the boy.

How could anyone live in that hot, broken place? Why would they? Shouldn't the boy be in school? He was a little older than Teddy. Something wasn't right. *The door was bolted on the outside.* She looked at Dylan, who seemed to be thinking the same thing.

"What's going on here?" he asked.

Their eyes widened simultaneously. They looked at each other, then at the boy again. He watched them with eyes looking less scared and more hopeful. She knew this boy. She tried to remember the other poster at the pizza joint. He hardly looked like the same kid, but then again, he'd probably been through hell these last three months.

She walked closer and knelt down beside him. "Is . . ." She could hardly speak through her tight throat. "Is your name Mac?"

He hesitated, looking from Dylan to Chloe, before nodding. Tears filled his eyes, and his chin trembled.

A chill washed over her. "My God. This is the boy." She turned to Dylan. "It's him."

"We've got to get him out of here before whoever took him returns."

She knelt down beside the bed. "We're going to take you home, okay?"

He nodded.

She pulled the blanket back. The boy was skinny and had bruises, but he looked all right otherwise. Chloe didn't want to think about what he'd been through. She held out her hands, and after a hesitation, Mac crawled forward and into her arms, slamming into her chest and clinging to her.

Dylan watched the scene with an odd expression. She knew he must be disappointed that they hadn't found Teddy, yet he was obviously glad they'd found another child in need of saving.

They helped the boy into the water and to their boat, where Dylan radioed for the police while Chloe dried herself and Mac. She put her sweatshirt on him, resisting the urge to hold him tight.

"Are you all right, Mac? Your parents have missed you so much. Did you know they've been looking for you all this time?" He didn't know, not by the doubtful look in his eyes. He'd thought his parents had abandoned him. She looked up to find Dylan watching them, his eyes shadowed with pain, the mask gone for a moment. He turned back to his task, piloting the boat away from the house, but keeping it in sight in case the creep returned.

"They love you, Mac," she continued. "They're going to be so happy to"—her voice choked—"see you again."

She started shaking. She didn't know why; they were safe. Mac was looking at her, and she tried hard not to let him see. "It's going to be okay. Your mom and dad are going to be here soon."

His eyes filled with tears, and he moved into her arms. She stroked his hair and tried not to hold him too tight. Dylan was watching her, but this time she couldn't read his expression. He wasn't looking at her or Mac, but both of them together.

Once he got off the radio, he sat down beside them. "You all right?"

She sounded unconvincing when she said, "I'm fine. I just can't believe . . . we saw him on that old poster, and it was almost covered up, and here he is."

Dylan reached out and ran his hand over Mac's hair. The boy looked up, then buried his face deeper against Chloe. She didn't want to think about what this boy must have gone through. Once he was safe with his parents, he'd be fine. Dylan grabbed his dry sweater and draped it over Chloe's shoulders.

"Aren't you cold?" she asked.

He shook his head. He looked tired, more so with the shadow of a beard. She wondered how much sleep he'd gotten since Teddy's disappearance. She couldn't look at him without wanting to pull him close the way she did Mac. She looked at the house that had been Mac's prison.

"Lena was right. Dylan, she was right about a boy being on a boat-type house with a skull flag on it. It wasn't Teddy, but it was a boy who needs to be home with his family."

He nodded, then settled his hand on her shoulder. And together they waited in silence.

The calvary rode—or motored—in half an hour later. The police and paramedics rode shotgun on the Coast

Guard's boat. One officer and the paramedic came aboard while the other officers entered the house.

"That's the kid." The officer dialed his cell phone. "We got him, Sam. Go ahead and call his folks." He hung up and said, "I didn't want to get their hopes up until I knew for sure. I can't believe you found him."

After they had been questioned, Dylan asked, "Did you . . . suspect the parents at first? In Mac's disappearance."

"Always have to suspect the people closest to the child. Though I was pretty sure they had nothing to do with it." He surveyed the open water. "Now we have to find out who did."

"My aunt was right," Chloe whispered to herself. If Lena hadn't let herself go with the vision, if Chloe hadn't come down here, this boy wouldn't have been found tonight. Or maybe ever.

The two medics cajoled Mac away from her. "It's okay, hon," she told him as he reached for her. "I'm right here."

She caught Dylan watching, but he quickly turned away. She'd feel the same way when they found Teddy. Even though she'd never seen the boy before, she knew the elation and relief and love she'd feel for him.

She was in a daze as they followed the Coast Guard back to their home base. The press was waiting, clamoring for statements.

"How did they know?" she asked one of the officers.

"They listen to police scanners. Sometimes they're on the scene before we are. Dammit, we don't want this guy to know we have the boy."

Chloe was sitting in the small waiting area when Mac's parents came barreling in. The woman was already crying as they were ushered into one of the back rooms. Chloe smiled at the sound of happy sobbing. There was almost nothing better than tears of joy.

It was a few minutes before she tuned in to Dylan's conversation with the police officer. "Her Aunt Lena had this premonition or vision or something. She was right." He ran his fingers back through his dark hair in disbelief. "She was perfectly right. Only it wasn't my son."

She started to say, "No one's suppose to know—" when she spotted a reporter jotting down information.

"What's your aunt's last name?" he asked.

Chloe sprang to her feet. "You have to keep her name out of the papers."

"I'll find out one way or the other," the wiry man said. "Besides, psychics dig publicity. It's how they get new business. Or is there more to the story?"

"I'm not telling you anything."

He snapped his notebook closed. "That's all right. I'll find out."

She started to grab at the notebook. "Please don't print her name."

Dylan approached the man. "If you put her aunt's name in your article, I'll make your life very uncomfortable."

The man's eyes bulged. "Hey, Officer! Do you hear this man threatening me?"

"Get out of here, Schwartz!" the officer said. Then to Chloe he said, "I need your statement, and then you're free to go. We'll probably be in touch for further information later."

"Fine. Here's my card . . ." Dylan said, then patted his pants. "I think this is the first time I haven't had business cards with me."

Once they'd covered everything from why they'd been down to the Keys to the minute the Coast Guard showed up, she was able to leave.

"The parents want to thank you," the officer said. "They've gone to the hospital with their son, but they want to talk to you."

"Thanks aren't necessary," she said. "But I'd like to hear how Mac is doing."

Dylan shook his head as he ushered her back out to their boat. "You must have the biggest heart of anyone I know."

Oh, no, was she being tender again? She wiped at her eyes. Shoot. He stepped down into the boat, then helped her aboard. She stayed in front of him so he couldn't see her tears. "You say that like it's a bad thing."

"It's not a bad thing." He swung her around to face him and pushed a lock of hair from her cheek. "Wish I could be more like you."

"It's okay to wish that boy had been Teddy."

She could see a shadow of a smile on his face. And then he kissed her so tenderly, she thought her heart—however big it was—was going to break. When he finished the kiss, she whispered, "You have a bigger heart than you think."

"Don't get your hopes up," he whispered back. "Let's go."

The air was cool, and thousands of stars dotted the dark sky. She stood next to Dylan as he steered back to the dock where they'd launched the boat. She wanted to put her arms around him and snuggle up against his back. Or better yet, have him put his arms around her. But why get her hopes up?

When they reached the dock, he said, "Hold this rope while I get the car."

The black Mercedes was the only car in the small lot. He had only walked halfway there before stopping, reading a sign on the gate, and returning to the boat. "Did you happen to see the sign about the launch area closing at ten o'clock?"

"Why do you ask? And please don't tell me we're locked in."

"Let me put it this way: Would you rather sleep in the car or in the boat?"

She couldn't read the sign from there, but if she'd bothered to look just a fraction farther, she would have noticed that the gate it was posted on barred their exit. "There's got to be a way around it."

He was already walking along the length of fence. When he went back to the Mercedes, she wondered if he was going to try his crashing-through-the-door tactics. Thank goodness he only popped the trunk and pulled out their suitcases.

"Can't we call someone?" she asked. "After all, we're heroes. Someone should . . . What are you doing?"

He'd climbed back onto the boat and set down the cases. "I don't know about you, but I'm too tired to wait for someone to let us out. Car or boat?"

"Well, I'm not sleeping in a car, that's for sure."

He motored a short distance from the dock, then released the anchor. He turned off the motor and said, "Night."

"Are you nuts?"

"No, I'm not."

He looked way too serious.

"I didn't mean nuts like . . . well, nuts."

"I know. Look, I've slept on this boat before. It's not too bad, comfort-wise." At her questioning look, he added with a shrug, "When Wanda told me six months ago she didn't like sex anymore, I needed some space. More space than the guest bedroom would allow. I spent a week on this boat before I realized sex with her hadn't been that great anyway, so I moved into the guest bedroom and didn't fight it."

Her throat went thick. "I'm sorry. That must have been very hard on you. I mean . . ." Her face flushed, and he made an agonized sound. "I wasn't trying to be punny, believe me. It's just that, well, I can't believe she wouldn't . . . want you."

He met her gaze, and the corner of his mouth lifted ever so slightly. "Thanks. Just be warned that if you prance around here in nothing more than a towel, I may not be responsible for my actions."

She blinked.

"Is that all you have to say about it?" he asked.

"Fifteen percent of six thousand is nine hundred?"

"Perfect." He started down into the cabin. "Hold that thought. I'm crashing." He paused at the bottom of the stairs, looking sexy and dangerous and perhaps a little more human than he had before. "There's the head, there are two bunks down here, and enough distance between them to guarantee your virtue, whatever that may be."

She sucked in a breath, but he'd already taken that last step and disappeared into the shadowy depths of the cabin. "I'll have you know I am quite virtuous." She followed him down, pausing as she took in his bare back and luscious muscles as he removed his shirt.

"I'm sure you are." He shucked out of his pants, leaving only an image of white briefs as he threw sheets and pillows on both beds and climbed into the bed on the right.

"I've only been with two men. I'd consider that pretty virtuous in this day and age."

"I never thought I'd say this, but I'm too tired to fight with you. Let's take up the gauntlet tomorrow, shall we?"

She walked over, hands on her hips. "You question my virtue and then hide in sleep? I don't think so."

He mumbled, "I didn't question your virtue," and rolled onto his side.

"Coward!" She walked carefully in the dark to her suitcase and pulled out her toiletry bag and a nightgown, then made use of the facilities. She washed her face in the tiny sink, changed, and walked back into the cabin.

When she surveyed the beds, she said, "Uh-oh. I have to sleep on the one on the right. I always sleep on the right side at home."

"Turn around, and the bed will be on your right."

"It doesn't work that way. Look, I'll never get to sleep in that one." She walked over to him. "Out. I'm the guest, I get my pick."

He reached out his hand. "Help me up, then."

She shook her head, then tugged on his arm. Without any effort at all, he pulled her down onto the bed with him. Or, more precisely, onto him. Before she could even think to fight him, he'd slid his arms around her stomach and pulled her up against him spoon-style. His bristly chin rubbed against her shoulder, and his breath felt warm against her ear.

There was no way she was fighting him.

"I haven't had a warm, soft woman in my arms for a long time," he said in a sleepy voice. "Just for tonight, Chloe. Let me hold you."

There was no way in *hell* she was fighting him.

She settled in closer, inhaling the smell of him and soaking in his warmth. A sigh emanated from somewhere deep inside her. She was absolutely sure there was nothing better in this world than to be held by a man. Not even the purr of a cat or happy tears.

Except she wasn't the least bit sleepy. She had too much buzzing through her mind, not the least of which was being in Dylan's arms. And feeling his heartbeat against her back.

"There's only one problem with lying here like this with you," he said, breaking into her thoughts. "I'm not sleepy anymore."

A thrum of excitement washed over her body and jump-started her heart. She rolled onto her back, looking up at his shadowy face in the dark. "Dylan—"

He leaned down and kissed her, a long, languid kiss that shot heat to parts of her body that had been long neglected. She could feel his hands skim the thin fabric of her nightgown, over her breasts and stomach. She could feel sensual heaviness growing inside her. Now she could tell Dylan wasn't sleepy at all. That was quite evident.

He trailed kisses across her cheek and down her neck. She tilted her head back. His fingers teased her breasts, and one leg pinned her down to the bed, adding to the excitement. She reached out, finding his chest oh so close, the curves and planes tantalizingly warm and firm.

She wanted him so badly, it hurt. She wanted him not just for tonight, but for always. It was that feeling again, that rightness. And with the totally wrong man. She ran her fingers up into his short, soft hair, reveling in the bittersweet knowledge that she couldn't have him. Maybe she could have some parts, but not the important one: his heart.

But for now, she could have the sexy, sinful part of him. A taste to keep for always. He captured her mouth again, like a starving man finally allowed to eat. She returned the kiss with as much fervor, drowning in the sensation, fighting the crazy impulse that she wanted to cry.

She was crazy on him. Crazy to love him . . . not love, surely, but hot, deep infatuation. In love enough to get hurt again, that much she knew.

His hand slid up her leg, fingers pressing into her flesh as though he were fighting some overwhelming passion he could hardly control. She wanted to give him her love, her passion, and her body. She didn't want to think of the price she'd pay later. She just wanted to hear his heavy breathing in her ear, feel the hardness of him against her leg, and to know that he wanted her.

For this moment, only her.

"Chloe," he said in a breathless voice.

"Mmm." She loved the sound of her name on his voice, especially when it was breathless with desire.

He nibbled on her ear. "You've only been with two men?"

She nodded.

"I didn't mean what I said about your virtue. I was only being testy."

"Apology accepted. Or was that an apology? It was kind of hard to tell."

"It was."

"You know what? Let's not talk about my virtue right now."

With an agonized sound, he pushed himself up. "Chloe, I don't have to tell you that I want you."

"But you could." She couldn't see his eyes, but she felt them on her.

"I want you," he said, and she loved the agonized thread in his voice. "But I can't make any promises to you. I don't know what's going to happen in my life, and with Teddy, and . . ."

She sat up too and put her finger across his mouth. "I

know. You don't have to make any excuses. Or promises. I know I don't fit into your life, and you don't fit into mine. But right now . . ."

He leaned forward and crushed her mouth with his. After a minute, he wrenched away with a muttered curse. "I can't believe I'm doing this." He got up and dropped down on the bed across from her.

"Then why *are* you doing it?" She held her breath, wanting to hear the right reason.

"Because making love to you would be using you. You deserve more than that. Besides, I don't have any protection, and that wouldn't be fair to you either."

Bingo. She hugged herself and smiled. Not that he could see it in the dark, but she smiled anyway. "Thanks."

"You could sound a little regretful too."

Then she out-and-out laughed. "I am. Even looking at you lying there across from me . . . believe me, I am. But you gave me something more than sexual gratification. You gave me respect."

He let out a groan and rolled over. "You get respect. Not only am I not sleepy, I'm stiff as a rod."

She crept over to his bed, then reached out and ran her hand down his leg. "There might be a way to relieve you of that problem and keep my respect at the same time."

"Oh, yeah?"

"Mm-hm."

"You have my attention."

"I can see that."

"Are you sure—"

Then she found him, and he didn't say another word.

AN HOUR later, Dylan lay on his back with Chloe tucked under his arm and her cheek on his chest. He would never forget the feel of her hands on him. It reminded him of watching her with the clay, stroking, molding, shaping. Only he'd let himself close his eyes and drown in the physical sensation. Afterward she'd acted a little shy, not sure what to expect. He was too tired to think about what was appropriate, so he'd pulled her down on his bed with him. Her smile told him that's what she'd wanted. They hadn't said anything after that. He'd stared at the ceiling of the cabin, toying with her soft hair.

He felt sexually satisfied, but not wholly satisfied. Something inside him wanted more, and it wasn't his libido. Maybe because she wouldn't let him return the favor. It wasn't a completely unselfish offer. He'd wanted to touch her and watch her experience a mind-bending orgasm too. That macho part of him wanted to know he could pleasure her as well. Mostly, he felt that fair was fair. She'd told him she wanted to do this for him and wanted nothing in return.

Because he'd wanted her so badly, he took what she offered. Now she was offering him something else, even though she was asleep. She was offering him the opportunity to hold a woman through the night. He hadn't done that in a long, long time. Hadn't wanted to do it with Wanda, though she'd never given him the chance to try.

He rolled onto his side. Instinctively, Chloe rolled over too, murmuring softly as she snuggled up against him. He slid his arms around her and pulled her even closer. She was warm and soft, and fit against his body perfectly. She was completely cocooned by his body. If he could, he would have absorbed her. He closed his eyes and absorbed her with his senses instead. But he didn't go to sleep right away. In the dark, with the boat rocking from side to side, he reveled in a feeling he'd never had before.

He wanted to hold Chloe and never let her go.

* * *

IN THE light of the next morning, Chloe couldn't believe how forward she'd been. She'd kept her virtue intact, though not by her choice. Keeping it didn't resolve the ache in the pit of her stomach. He'd offered to return the favor, but accepting something like that, well, that was different than giving it. So she'd been left with an ache for more.

She'd heard Dylan get up before six o'clock. Apparently he was an early bird. She loved sleeping in late, especially when she'd been up very late in the night weighing the cost of respect versus making love to a gorgeous man. Not to mention the fact that he'd held her all night long and made her feel secure and content.

She had snuggled against his chest, felt his arms go around her, and had that same overwhelming feeling of belonging that she'd experienced in the tunnel. All she could think about was, *This is how it feels to be loved and cherished. This is how it feels to love.*

Not love, she'd told herself. Not with Dylan. She wasn't sure he could actually love and cherish someone. Now she was sure, absolutely sure, that's what she wanted.

Great.

She forced herself up and used the head. Once she changed into her pink jumpsuit and matching Keds, she came up on deck. Now the gate was open, and there were plenty of cars and boats around.

"Got locked in last night, eh?" one man said as he launched his boat. "Could be worse." He nodded toward her.

Dylan turned to find Chloe standing behind him. He gave her a lopsided grin. "Yep, could be worse."

He was wearing white pants and a dark blue T-shirt.

Now that she had touched that body, it wasn't going to be the same between them.

He caught her gawking. Instead of laughing, though, he pulled close. "Thanks for last night."

She shrugged, keeping herself from touching his clean-shaven face. "It was the least I could do. You were up early this morning."

The trace of his smile faded. "I thought it'd be a good idea. For both of us."

She wished she could stay in his arms longer, but he pulled back and got into position to pull the boat up to the dock. What did he mean by that? Would he want more than just a snuggle? Her own body came alive at the thought, but she quelled the urge.

"I'm starving," she said, not only meaning food. "We didn't get dinner last night."

"I'm hungry too. I think it's the first time since . . . well, since the accident."

The content expression left his face. He shouldn't be hungry or content, that's what he was thinking. Not until Teddy came home.

AFTER CATCHING breakfast at a roadside diner, Chloe said, "I need to call Lena. I can't wait to tell her that we found Mac, that she probably saved his life."

"You want to use my cell phone?" She'd never seen him without that phone by his side.

"I've got a calling card, thanks."

"Here, use mine. I'm going to check in at home too, see if there's any news."

Lena answered, and before Chloe could get a word out, she said, "How could you do this to me? I told you I didn't want my name mentioned. It's like Sarasota all over again, the press camped outside bothering me, people asking me to find their missing dogs, cats, and money! Chloe, you promised!"

Chloe drooped. "But you saved that boy's life."

"I know. But I was supposed to find Teddy. See, it's still not working right."

"I'm sorry, Lena. Someone overheard me telling the police. We had to explain why we suspected the boy was there. Enough to break down the door."

After a moment of silence, Lena said, "I don't want to talk to you right now. All I keep seeing is that dead little girl, and the whole mess with the press, and then your mother. I can't keep reliving this. I have to go."

Chloe listened to the tone until it got annoying. She'd messed up. Lena had helped her, and she'd messed it all up. It seemed that nothing was going right.

Dylan took in her bereft expression as he walked up. "I take it your aunt's mad at you."

She nodded. "Camilla's heard about it too?"

"Our finding Mac is the big news now that the hostage situation is over. No one was killed," he answered just as she was about to ask.

"That's scary," she said. "Don't read my mind like that."

"Reading your mind *is* scary. I also bought this." He held up the Keys newspaper, where Mac's rescue had made the front page. He pointed to Lena's name and details of the Sarasota case.

Her heart dropped down to her feet. She closed her eyes and looked away. "I don't want to read it. All right, read it to me." She grabbed the paper and scanned the article. "This is terrible. Horrible. She is never going to forgive me for this. You don't know Lena; she holds grudges, not just for weeks or months, but *years*." She shoved the paper back at him. "I don't want to read any more."

"Keep it in case you change your mind . . . again."

"Did Teddy benefit from all this?"

"A tiny mention, but not much. And, of course, more speculation about us."

"Oh. I didn't think . . ." She pinched the bridge of her nose. "I made a mess of everything."

He lifted her chin. "But we found Mac. Come on. Let's keep heading south. We'll figure out a response to the papers later. At least we can distribute some fliers. Then we'll head home, and you can make peace with Lena."

"Making peace with her isn't going to be easy."

"But she loves you. She cares about you. You'll win her over."

"How can you be so sure?"

"Because . . ." His face went blank. "Isn't it true?"

"You were going to say something. Because . . . what?"

"Nothing."

"She told you I was coming down here by myself. Didn't she?"

He put on that poker face.

"You didn't come down to Lilithdale to see how I was doing. You came because you felt obligated. Because somehow Lena convinced you to. We were never a team, were we?"

"I wouldn't say that. I thought we worked pretty well together."

"I feel like a big, dumb jerk. You didn't believe in the visions at all, did you?"

He looked as though he were trying to come up with a diplomatic response, but finally said, "No."

She started walking toward the car. "I thought . . ." She couldn't even say it.

He grabbed her by the shoulder and turned her to face him. "Thought what?"

"I thought you wanted to be with me," she pushed out. "I don't know. Maybe I am crazy. But it makes sense now." She knew how persuasive Lena could be. Dylan didn't have a chance. And now that she knew he'd just gone along to keep her out of trouble, she felt awful and embarrassed about giving in to her desires last night. "That's why you wouldn't compromise my virtue. You weren't being honest with me. Isn't that right?"

"Well, maybe."

"You're a swell guy, you know that?"

"Look, Chloe, it started out me going with you because your aunt convinced me to go. And because I thought there might be a chance that Teddy was down here. But it changed along the way."

"Changed to what? An obligation?"

"No, it wasn't that at—"

"Let's just get this obligatory trip over with. For Teddy, you understand. Only for Teddy."

"Aren't you being just a little—"

"Don't say 'tender'!" She pointed at him, daring him.

He raised his eyebrows at her. "I was going to say sensitive. But tender works."

"Augh! Maybe it's best if we're never seen together again. After we cover Key West."

"You don't want to be seen with me?" he asked.

"Exactly. You're bad for my reputation. When we get down to Key West, I want you to take me to the airport. I'm flying home."

"Fine."

"Fine."

"No, it's not fine," he muttered.

"We'll be done with our mission. We won't need to be a team anymore. Oh, but I forgot, we were never a team."

"Chloe—"

She walked to the car and waited for him to unlock the door. "You don't have to pretend you want to be with me anymore or even pretend you believe in me. The cat's out of the bag. In a couple of hours, we can go back to being strangers again. That should suit you just fine."

He leaned against the car, looking at her over the roof. "Is that what you want?"

"Absolutely."

"All right, then. Fine," he gritted out.

"And stop saying fine!"

He paused. "Fine."

And because she couldn't let him get the last word in—especially that word—she said, "I was wrong. I'm not the big, dumb jerk. You are."

Chapter Sixteen

ALL RIGHT, SO SHE WAS THE BIG, DUMB JERK. SO DUMB, Chloe could not stop crying during the short flight back to Naples. It wasn't as though she'd expected anything from Dylan. Certainly not a future. Yet, she had to admit there must be some wacky part of her heart that had hoped for just that.

She kept looking down over the water and wondering where he was on his journey home.

"Are you all right?" the man next to her asked "You're too cute to be so distressed."

Cute. She grimaced. "I'm just tender!" Fresh tears gushed as she looked out the window again. Well, she was going to have to toughen up.

Stella was waiting at the Naples airport, looking comforting and familiar in her calico hair bow and purple sundress. Rascal popped out of her bag. It would have been a nice homecoming but for the half a dozen reporters waiting with them.

"They said your aunt's psychic prediction led to the missing boy. How did she know?"

"Chloe! Tell us how you knew it was the missing boy."

"Chloe, are you and Dylan McKain romantically involved?"

With puffy eyes and a tear-stained face, she faced the bevy of reporters and realized there was only one thing she could do. Well, besides crawl into a hole. She could use the publicity for Teddy.

Stella started to pull Chloe through the crowd, but she pulled back and faced the reporters.

"My aunt had nothing to do with the prediction. It was . . . mine. Only mine."

"But the police report said—"

"They were wrong," Chloe said. "They can be wrong, you know."

"Why are you protecting your aunt?" another reporter asked. "Is it because of the girl in Sarasota?"

"I told you, Lena had nothing to do with it." She looked at Stella, who very subtly shook her head. It didn't matter what Chloe said. The press knew. And Lena probably hated her.

"I'm not romantically or otherwise linked to Dylan. He only came with me because I insisted his son was down there, and he wanted to look in the Keys anyway. He never believed in the vision or . . . in me. You all want a real news flash?" She pulled out posters from her bag and shoved one at each reporter. "Teddy McKain is still missing. Do you understand that? A little boy who has trouble communicating is still out there, and he needs our help."

Stella took charge and grabbed Chloe by the arm. "No more questions!" she said to the reporters, dragging Chloe away. She whispered, "It's been madness in Lilithdale since the news hit last night."

"Lena must hate me."

"She isn't happy, I'll tell you that. You promised not to let anyone know she was involved."

"I didn't mean to, honestly. But I had to explain why we were down there and why we broke into that house. I didn't know there was some stupid reporter standing there listening."

"Well, there's nothing to do but sit it out like any ol' hurricane." Stella ushered them into the sunny late afternoon to Chloe's T-Bird. "You sit, I'll drive. Now tell me what happened."

The whole story came out. Well, not the whole story. She did leave out some parts. "What are the Naples papers saying?"

"They're in the back seat."

All of the local papers and the *Miami Herald* had the story splashed over the front page. Mac's parents expressed their profound gratitude and said it didn't matter what means were used to find their son. Chloe silently thanked God when she read that Mac hadn't been molested. The suspect was in custody, an old man who apparently was so lonely he'd taken the boy for company.

Chloe and Dylan were hailed as heroes. Teddy only got a minor mention as being the real reason for their search. Frustration and anger surged inside her. She had to get Teddy's disappearance into the papers as a major news story again.

Yet, how could she do that without causing Dylan more trouble? The local papers brought up his involvement with her and his recent denial of same. He wasn't going to like the insinuation that he was covertly working with some fruitcake psychic.

Lena's past was detailed, along with snide speculation on her psychic abilities. They made fun of her Total Balance Women's Center and reminded everyone how her last psychic revelation ended.

"Oh," was all Chloe could say. When she looked up, she didn't see much compassion on Stella's face. Her stomach started aching. "You're mad at me too, aren't you?"

"Not mad, hon. I just hate seeing my sister go through this again. The last time . . . well, it nearly ripped her apart. You see how she gets all shadowed every time she even begins to get a vision."

"I know, but this time we found the boy alive. He's going to be all right."

"And that would have been great if you'd kept her name out of it. There's no help for it now. I'd steer clear of her for a couple of days. She's like a wounded animal, licking her wounds and keeping everyone at bay. At least wait for the press to give it up." She hesitated. "And then there's the parents."

Chloe lifted her head. "What parents?"

"The ones coming out of the wood begging Lena to find their child. That's the hardest."

Chloe had never felt so miserable in her life. She'd failed Lena, all of Lilithdale, and Dylan. Most of all, she'd failed Teddy. She'd never felt so alone in her life.

It was nearly dark when Stella dropped her off at her house. Chloe started to get out, but Stella took her arm.

"This'll blow over, hon. It might take a while, but it will."

Chloe nodded, wanting—no, needing—to give Stella a hug, but feeling too fragile to initiate one. She grabbed her bag from the back and walked into her house. Only when Shakespeare and Gypsy came running out to greet her did she let herself fall apart.

She took a cold shower, hoping to wash away all the regrets. It only left her with skin covered in goose bumps. And then she actually poured the pickle soup into a bowl and ate it. It tasted awful, but it was comfort food in Marilee's warped way. Only when Chloe had eaten every last drop was she brave enough to check her answering machine.

"Dumb jerk, Dylan's not going to be on there," she muttered, realizing that's what she was hoping.

He wasn't. Two of her clients called to say they'd be doing their own books for a while. They understood she was busy with her search for Teddy and the ensuing publicity. A reporter wanted an interview. If she talked to him, she could get Teddy's name in the news. But every time she associated herself with Teddy, she put more distance between herself and Dylan.

Despite Stella's warning, Chloe tried calling Lena. The machine picked up. Chloe curled up on her flowered pillow and listened to that soft, warm voice she'd known all her life.

"Lena? If you're there . . . or even if you're not . . . I just wanted you to know that I'm sorry. I didn't mean to tell anyone. I hadn't thought about what I'd say if we found Teddy. I wasn't prepared. Your name just slipped out, and someone happened to hear it. I'm so sorry about all the people calling you to help them. I'm sorry I brought all of this back to you." Her voice broke when she said, "I hope you'll forgive me someday. I love you."

She hung up and let more tears fall. Gypsy climbed up on the pillow and started purring against her. She held on to her, feeling as though she were her last friend on earth, and fell asleep to the lullaby of purring.

DYLAN DIDN'T get back to the house until near midnight. The drive was long and lonely, and he kept running his conversations with Chloe through his head. He had shared more with her than he had with anyone else. There was something about her that inspired sharing. A good reason to stay clear of her.

As if he needed another one.

Detective Yochem had called midway through the drive. "The officer assigned to your case said you weren't cooperative."

"I don't like being sloughed off onto some flunky."

"He's not a flunky. Well, lucky you, you got me back. Listen, I want to see you tomorrow morning. I want you to take a polygraph test. Bring a lawyer if you want."

"Am I still a suspect?"

There was a pause. "Technically, yes. There's still the question of whether you and your wife were in cahoots before something went wrong. The test is just a formality. Once we clear you, we can focus on other areas."

Dylan tried to maintain his cool, but it was hard. "Fine, I'll be there. And I don't need a lawyer."

He noticed there weren't any assurances this time. No *Don't worry, we'll find him.* Nothing. They'd given up.

Well, dammit, he hadn't. The problem was, he didn't know where else to look. He remembered standing in Chloe's kitchen admitting that. He might not have believed in Lena's vision, but searching in the Keys hadn't been a bad idea.

For the first time in his life he needed help. And he didn't know where to find it. Friends were supposed to help. But did he have any real friends? Employees didn't count. They were paid to help.

Camilla came out to greet him when he pulled into his driveway. "I was hoping you'd be bringing our boy back with you. But at least you saved someone else's life."

Dylan could only nod. Would he have traded finding Mac with finding Teddy? He felt bad for knowing that he would. Teddy might not be with some creep, but he was in just as much danger.

"Would you like a Johnny Walker?" she asked, following him into the house.

"Five of them." He eyed the legal pad full of Camilla's scribbles. "More psychics?"

"A bit of everything. Reporters asking about how you

and Chloe found that boy. Wanting all the juicy gossip." She wrinkled her nose. "That's all they care about. I felt like telling them that it didn't matter if you were an alien with an eyeball in the middle of your stomach, all that mattered was finding your son."

"You . . . didn't tell them that?"

"No, of course not."

Dylan scanned the living room. "My father?"

"At his hotel."

"If he calls, I'm not in."

When Camilla handed him a scotch, he saw the tired lines on her face. "Thanks for being here. Go home and get some rest. Take tomorrow off."

"Not if you need me." Her face pinched into a worried frown. "You haven't given up on finding him, have you?"

"No, but wearing yourself out isn't going to help him come home any faster."

"Why don't you take that advice yourself?" She grabbed up her bag and sweater and headed toward the door. "I left some tuna salad in the fridge. Eat something with that drink."

He wasn't hungry, but he remembered Chloe urging him to take care of himself. And her question about what he had to give his son. Damn her. She didn't know him. Nobody knew him. Then why was it that she could say something that ripped right to the center of him?

He stared at the amber liquid in his glass, then set it on the granite counter. He looked at all the rich finishes in his home. Not a home, but a house. A testimony to his talents and to the fact that he had it all. He provided for his family and could give them anything they wanted. But he had never given himself.

For a while he'd convinced himself he had the perfect

life. The perfect home. Then why wasn't he ever here? Because he'd never felt comfortable at home. He was the stranger who paid the bills and came home to sleep, and occasionally to take his wife to bed.

For some reason he thought about Chloe again.

She had pleasured his body, as though he were some priceless piece of art. Something to be revered. While she'd touched him, he'd wanted to let go and let himself love her. And while he'd held her in his arms, he'd felt as though he had enough inside to give her what she deserved.

But now, looking around at the world he created, he knew he'd been fooling himself. All that mattered was the facade. He'd built his whole life on it. This was all he knew.

Sometimes he felt like a boy again, trying so hard to put on the front of normalcy. It was ingrained in his soul, that need for normalcy and success. Always having to prove himself. The problem was, he wasn't sure who he was trying to prove himself to anymore.

THE NEXT morning, Dylan woke in Teddy's bed. His legs hung over the side, but he didn't care. He'd felt closer to his son.

He dressed and forced himself to eat a breakfast sandwich that Camilla made. "Anything in the paper I should see?" he asked. He hated looking anymore.

"Your friend is still campaigning for Teddy." She held up the paper. His heart jumped when he saw Chloe's tear-stained bulldozer face. But he saw pain in her eyes. It startled him that he could see her feelings. He'd never been tuned in to anyone that way before.

CHLOE SAMMS CLAIMS CREDIT FOR PREDICTION THAT FOUND MISSING BOY, the headline read. It was apparent that the writer didn't believe her. He speculated that she was protecting her aunt. There was also mention of Dylan and more speculation as to his relationship with her.

> *Then Miss Samms shoved Teddy McKain's 'missing' posters at the reporters and left with one final comment: "He never believed in the vision or . . . in me. You all want a real news flash? Teddy McKain is still missing."*

He got a funny feeling in his chest just seeing her picture and reading her words. She was the only person who'd ever had that effect on him. She was Teddy's champion, and he'd let her down.

JODIE GAVE him that sympathetic smile of hers when she brought him a cup of coffee.

"What appointments have to be rescheduled today?" he asked.

"You . . . don't have any appointments."

"You already cleared my schedule?"

"You . . . don't have a schedule."

She set a pile of pink slips on his desk, and he started to sort through them.

"They're canceled appointments, jobs taken elsewhere. Oh, they gave good excuses: financing fell through, divorce, dog died. They know you're busy and preoccupied and that you need to focus on finding Teddy."

"But?"

She let out a breath. "I think they're backing away from us. Maybe the publicity is too much. First with the psychics and that woman and . . ."

"And?"

"With the police suspecting you."

He went cold at those words. "What are you talking about?"

"It's in the paper this morning, that you're going for a polygraph."

Dylan swore, then ran his finger inside the collar of his shirt. It had shrunk in the last few seconds. "Evidently it's standard procedure to suspect the parents."

"The article said that." She brushed her curly blond hair aside. "It seems that a source close to you said you didn't like anything abnormal."

The only other thing that scared Dylan besides his son being missing was that his past would be revealed. He felt a twitch in his upper lip. His crazy genes. Everything he'd fought so hard to bury. He unbuttoned the top of his collar and loosened his tie.

"Who told them that?"

"It didn't say. But the police must be talking to everyone you know." She put her hand on his arm. "I know you had nothing to do with your son's disappearance."

"Thanks. We'll find Teddy, and everything will be cleared up."

Now he was the one spouting vague assurances, and she eagerly bought them. Perhaps as eagerly as he had once bought them.

TWO HOURS later Dylan met with Yochem about the results of the lie detector test.

"Your mother tried to kill your father with a butcher knife?" he asked.

"Yes." The interview had delved into his past, particularly instances of domestic violence. He'd tried to keep his face and responses neutral as anger had raged inside him. Maybe the lie detector had picked up on his anger, and maybe that anger looked like guilt.

Yochem nodded. "Tough life."

"I survived." *I'm not going to ask if I passed, you bastard.*

"You didn't bring a lawyer."

Dylan's fingers tightened around the metal arms of the chair. "I told you, I don't need a lawyer. Now can you start focusing your manpower on finding my son instead of on me?"

"I see you *have* been involved with the Samms woman." Yochem lifted an eyebrow at this tidbit.

"I kissed her. It was nothing more than an impulse. A bad impulse."

Yochem tapped the chart. "You haven't even asked if you passed."

"I have nothing to hide."

"That's where you're wrong. See this spike right here? That's where you told your one and only lie."

Chapter Seventeen

TEDDY WISHED AN ANGEL WOULD COME AND TAKE HIM away from there. He'd seen it on television, a beautiful angel who came down from Heaven and took people away. He didn't like this place anymore. He was cold and wet and alone.

There were things in the water, things he couldn't see. Something like a snake had grabbed his foot as he'd tried to swim. But he'd gotten away and reached the trees. These trees grew right out of that brown water, without even having dirt to grow out of. He could walk on the branches that came out of the water like funny-looking legs. He could sit on some of the bigger ones, but it was hard to sleep on them.

The old woman had called him, but he kept climbing through the branches until he couldn't hear or see her anymore. Only then did he feel safe. Except he'd left his buttons behind. He missed them.

The worst was the night. He could hear sounds, but he couldn't see anything. Sometimes he heard a loud sound that made birds fly away. It scared him, so he'd crouch down and hide.

The birds made him feel better. The pink ones came back and watched him. He'd focus on them and not move a single muscle. They would forget about him after a while and go on looking for things in the water. They weren't afraid of the water. He saw them put their faces into the water and sometimes they pulled out a wiggly little fish.

It reminded him of something. That hole feeling in his

tummy, that's what. But he didn't know how to ask for things. Sometimes he tried, but no one seemed to understand him. So he got it himself. Mommy didn't always like that. What he wouldn't give for some Cocoa Puffs.

He wrapped his arms around himself and whispered, "Are you hungry?"

The birds flew away.

He watched the boat where the old woman was. He was going to wait until he hadn't heard her in a while, until she took a nap. Maybe if he was really, really quiet, he could swim over and climb up on the engine and steal the box of cereal. And maybe his buttons too.

ANNE DODSON hated days like these. She knew she was supposed to be doing something—something important. But she couldn't remember what. Dammit, why couldn't she remember?

She wished she were back in her room at the home. The nurses there reminded her if she forgot to do something. *Anne, have you brushed your teeth yet?* Or *Anne, it's time for dinner. Come on, I'll walk with you to the dining room.*

Now there was no one. Wanda had done this, taken her from the safety of her home. Anne just couldn't remember why. It seemed like a good reason at the time, but that reason remained elusive in her few remaining memory cells. It was so very frustrating.

She hated days like these.

She closed her eyes and tried to remember. Wanda had been a young child. She did remember that much, the child running away, falling overboard. Her eyes opened. My gosh, her child had fallen overboard!

She started calling Wanda's name, but there wasn't

any response. And no one around to help look either. How had she ended up here, in the middle of nowhere on a boat? Maybe she could call someone. She searched for the phone, trying to remember who she could call. Tried to remember a phone number, any number. Used to be she could remember the phone number for every place she'd lived.

What was she looking for, anyway?

She couldn't remember, but she knew she had to get out of there and get some help. There had to be keys somewhere. Maybe that's what she'd been looking for. Yes, that made sense.

Stay focused, Annie. We have to find Wanda. Keys first, then Wanda. Keys, Wanda, keys, Wanda.

There was so much junk everywhere. Why had she kept all this stuff?

Keys. Keys.

She found them in an old bait bucket. They were on an orange and white float key ring. *Remember how to drive, Annie. Key in the ignition, turn. We can do this.*

It was almost dark when she put the boat into gear. It went backward, ramming into some mangroves, the propeller making a horrible sound as it hit the roots. Anne pushed the lever forward, and the boat jerked forward. Finally she got it turned around and headed . . . somewhere. Neither way looked right, but she had to choose. She couldn't just sit there waiting anymore, waiting for something she couldn't remember.

It was almost dark. She was usually in her bed by now watching television. One of the nurses always came to bring her to her room in the evenings. Anne often got involved in a game of Parcheesi and lost track of the time. Sometimes she lost track of the game too.

But she couldn't lose track of her mission. Her mission. She held on to the steering wheel and tried to remember: What was her mission?

She hated days like these.

LATER IN the afternoon Chloe ventured into town. Although the temperature was in the eighties that day, the social temperature had cooled considerably. She'd hurt one of Lilithdale's own, and never had she felt so out of place before. Margo made a snide comment to her friend about keeping secrets. Gerri gave her a sympathetic look, but ducked into the hotel office without saying anything. That huge hole inside her grew larger.

"Hey, hon," Nita said. "How you doing?"

Chloe could only shrug. At least Nita had smiled at her. Just that seed of kindness had tears nearly bursting out of Chloe's eyes. She handed Nita the stack of balanced accounting books and started to leave.

"I just want you to know that I'm not taking sides. I know you didn't mean to hurt Lena. This'll all die down and everything will go back to normal again."

"I hope so," Chloe managed to say in a thick voice. Would it be normal again? Would she ever feel even marginally part of Lilithdale?

She stopped by Tabitha's Goods and picked up some milk and eggs. And, curiously enough, a box of Cocoa Puffs. For reasons she couldn't begin to fathom, she had a sudden taste for the chocolate cereal. Afterward she found herself outside the Total Balance Women's Center. Marilee was talking to some outsider. *Another* outsider, Chloe thought miserably.

"She ain't interested in talking to anybody," Marilee was saying. "Go make up some story about someone else, would you?"

"I'm the one you want to talk to. I'm Chloe Samms."

The woman glanced down at her notepad. "You're the one who actually found the boy, right?"

"Yes. We were looking for another boy. Teddy McKain's been missing since—"

"That story's already been covered. What I'm after is Lena Stone's story. Why she disappeared years ago, if she's had any other visions over the years. I'm after the human interest angle. I'll bet you can help me, though."

Chloe glanced over at Marilee, who was waiting to see what she'd say. "Teddy McKain's three years old, with brown curly hair. He has autism—"

"No, no, I'm here to get Lena's story."

"Teddy is the story."

The reporter slipped her recorder into her pocket and walked away. Marilee gave her an approving nod before disappearing inside the center. Chloe looked at the stained-glass doors and for the first time didn't feel welcome to go inside as the sign implied.

She returned to her refuge, had a bowl of Cocoa Puffs, and headed out in her canoe with Shakespeare. She paddled in the other direction this time, but found nothing. Why did the nagging feeling that Teddy was nearby persist?

Seeing the occasional coconut floating like a head in the water gave her heart a jump. So did the sweater. She fished it out, hoping it might be a little boy's. It was too big, though. It had someone's name written on the tag, but it was too faded to read. There weren't any buttons on it so it was probably a discarded piece of clothing. She tossed it on the floor of her canoe.

It felt as though she'd searched the entire area. Were the dreams and feelings that he was nearby only her imagination? Heck, maybe the whole near-death experience had been in her head.

That kind of thing seemed to run in the family.

Just before dark she spotted the old houseboat heading to a new location. It was covered with junk the owner obviously considered personal treasures. He moved around occasionally to keep the marine patrol from hassling him. She figured he was harmless, though he gave her the creeps anyway. Still, she waved her paddles and hollered, "Yoo hoo!" Maybe he'd seen something suspicious. Most likely he hadn't even heard about Teddy's disappearance.

The boat was only putzing along with its small engine. She put all her energy into paddling as fast as she could to catch up to him. The windows in the back part of the cabin were covered with old newspapers for privacy. From the side she could barely make out the old man at the wheel. He didn't even glance her way, and finally even his little motor outpaced her.

Still drifting with her momentum, she leaned back and yelled, "Teddy! Please come home!"

DYLAN SPENT the rest of the morning distributing fliers. Doing it alone wasn't as productive as it had been when he and Chloe had been a team. He couldn't help smiling at the memory of her asking if they were a team. Like it meant something.

His smile faded. It had meant something to her.

A lot of things meant something to her. She was passionate, involved. She always took a moment to savor things, like a sunset or a great blue heron stalking prey. Even when they'd been focused on finding Teddy, she'd taken a moment to appreciate things.

It wasn't something he'd been good at, taking time to

notice and enjoy things. Now, as he drove around town, he found himself doing just that. If he hadn't been looking, he probably wouldn't have noticed the eagle soaring just above a busy intersection. He sat at the light and watched it gracefully dip and soar, tilting from side to side. Until some idiot behind him slammed on the horn.

Camilla called on the cell phone. "How did the lie detector test go?"

"Fine." Well, almost fine. Dylan had swallowed what felt like a cotton ball and waited for Yochem to elaborate on what lie the machine thought it had picked up.

"You told the operator you weren't romantically involved with Chloe Samms. It looks like you're more involved than you want to admit. Maybe even to yourself."

"I'm glad to hear that," Camilla said, bringing him out of his thoughts. "I knew the test would be okay, of course, but you never can tell with those things. Jackie Gardener from your mother-in-law's nursing home just called."

Dylan took the number. "Thanks. I'm not far from there, so I'll stop by."

"I thought you might be interested in this," Jackie said fifteen minutes later. "Anne doesn't get mail, ever, which is why I thought it strange that she received this out of the blue."

The envelope was postmarked from Vermont. Dylan ripped it open, figuring it was probably from one of her girlhood pals. It wasn't. It was the title for a 1980 houseboat, along with a letter from a Margie Grace apologizing for taking so long to send the title for her father's boat.

"Does it mean anything?" she asked.

"Patients aren't allowed to make large purchases, are they? Such as a boat?"

"No, sir. Not that they couldn't, if they did it on an outing. But most don't have access to money."

But Wanda did. He gripped the grimy title that was signed over to Anne. And then, to his surprise, he touched her arm. "Thanks for calling me about this."

He ran out to his car and nearly fishtailed out of the parking lot in his hurry to leave. Anne might not have a reason to buy a boat. But Wanda had a reason to buy one and put it in her mother's name. She'd taken Teddy and Anne somewhere on that boat. To an island, maybe. Perhaps one of those vacation cottages that dotted Keewaydeen Island. Maybe Wanda had broken into one and stashed Anne and Teddy there.

When he had Margie Grace on the phone, he asked if she'd sold her boat to his wife.

"Let's see. I think her name was Wanda, yes. But we made the sale to a . . . what was it? Oh, Anne Dodson."

Dylan felt his heart fall right out of his chest.

"I never personally met either woman. You see, my father had been living on his ramshackle houseboat for God knows how long. He's always been a bit . . . eccentric, shall we say? I haven't talked to him in years, so I didn't realize he'd actually been living on that old boat. When he got ill, I went down. He told me where the boat was and that I could have it. Whoopie-do, a piece of junk. He died a few days later. I cleared out his personal effects, found a place that would let me dock it until someone bought it, and advertised it in the paper. I guess your wife saw something in it, because she bought it. She sent me cash, and once I found the title in all of his junk, I sent it to her. Is there a problem with the boat? I did sell it to her as is."

"Where was the boat docked?"

"An empty lot near Bayshore Drive. They'd built a dock and never did build the house, I guess." She gave him the East Naples address.

"Can you describe the boat?"

"It's old and junky, that's all I can remember. And blue. My father said he'd been living around the backwater ways for years, moving around every once in a while so no one hassled him. Sad way to live, don't you think? . . . Hey, you there?"

Old and junky . . . he knew that boat! "That's great. Thanks."

He'd seen it around. Most everyone had over the years. No one probably even knew the guy was dead. Dylan called his friend Joe at London Helicopters and secured the use of his services.

And then he called Chloe. He didn't even think about it, just dialed her number. Her answering machine picked up. "Hello, you know the drill. Leave your name and number, and puh-leeze speak clearly. Have a nice day!"

"Chloe, it's me . . . Dylan. I know where they are. And you were right, he probably has been nearby all this time. I'll let you know when I find him. I'm bringing Teddy home."

Chapter Eighteen

FIRST CHLOE HEARD THE HAPPY YIP OF HER DOG. SHAKEspeare jumped up, and Chloe's head hit the bottom of the canoe. *Oh, no, not again.* Groggily she pulled herself up and peered through the trees. A man was walking along the flagstone steps. Her eyes catalogued him as her heart began its dance. Man, tall, Dylan's eyes, not Dylan, go back to sleep.

Wait! It was his father. She told herself she wasn't disappointed. She wasn't. She scrambled out of the canoe and made her unsteady way across the back yard. If there was news about Teddy, she sure wasn't expecting it from Will.

"Hello!" she called out.

He turned. "Out for an morning walk?"

"You could say that." What were the neighbors going to think? Three men in one week!

"I'm Will, Dylan's father. We met—"

"Yes, I know who you are. Has Teddy been found?"

"Not that I know of. I'm not exactly in the loop. I bought some commercial time on a local station, but I don't think Dylan even knows. I'd like to talk to you, if you have a minute."

She glanced down at her wrinkled clothes. "Sure, come in. Let me put on some coffee and change."

A few minutes later, she poured them both a cup. Will was looking at her flower-face lamps. Before he could make a disparaging comment, she said, "We can sit outside if you'd like."

He nodded, then followed her to the small table out on

the deck. Wind chimes stirred in the cool breeze, accented by the chirping of the cardinals breakfasting at the birdfeeder. She always thought of Teddy when she came out here. Especially when she saw a bird soar by. But the bird connection was to Mac. Wasn't it?

She took a sip of her coffee while scratching Shakespeare with her bare foot. "You wanted to talk to me?"

He stared out over the bay. "Did you . . . mention to my son that I was dying?"

"No. Absolutely not. I mean, you said not to."

He nodded, looking somewhat relieved. When he met her gaze, though, his face had a sheepish expression. "It's not true. I just . . . said it. I didn't mean to say it, hadn't thought about using something like that to get my son back."

"Oh," was all Chloe could manage. All of the empathy she'd felt for him dissipated. "You thought I'd tell him?"

"Maybe. I mean, I didn't think about it at all until the words came out of my mouth. But later, yes, I hoped you'd tell him. I'm glad you didn't. The more I thought about it, the more unwise it seemed. If he found out the truth, he'd hate me even more. I *did* have cancer, by the way. Prostate. They think they got it all, so it's no longer a threat. That's what got me thinking about dying without making peace with my son."

Some of that empathy returned at the pain she saw in his eyes. "I don't think he hates you. He felt betrayed because you weren't around. He feels a lot of bitterness."

Will leaned forward and rubbed his forehead, a gesture she'd seen Dylan make. "How do I bridge the gap? You probably know him better than I do. Is there a way to reach him?"

Chloe couldn't help the strangled laugh. "I don't know him that well. As far as reaching him, well, that's a tough one. He has a wall around his heart." She would never forget the passion he'd displayed at that bulletin board in the Keys. For a few moments that wall had come down.

"I remember listening to 'Cat's in the Cradle' and realizing that song was about me. I buried myself in my work and ignored my son. I made promises I didn't keep. Years later, he was too involved in his own life to take time for me. And I had the terrible feeling that he might have turned out the same way."

Gypsy jumped up on Chloe's lap and started nuzzling her. Chloe had to talk around her. "How long have you been trying to . . . reach him?"

"A few months. It took me a long time to get up my courage for even that." He gave her a wan smile. "I'm a shark in the investment world. I've never backed down from a fight, never gave away anything. But the thought of approaching my own son scared me to death."

Warmed by his admission, she smiled. "That wall he puts up can be pretty intimidating." Oddly enough, the thought filling her mind was Dylan holding her through the night. And sometimes squeezing her against him, as though he were afraid to lose her.

Gypsy became interested in a tiny green inchworm inching across the table. Chloe rescued it and watched it inch across her finger.

"But he likes you," Will said.

This time her strangled laugh was even louder. "You definitely have that wrong."

"Maybe he doesn't want to like you, but he does. Years after Dylan and I went our separate ways, I met a woman. She meant everything to me. She was the woman I wanted in my life forever. I know the way I looked at her. That's the way Dylan looked at you the day we first met. Just for a second, but I saw that look."

Don't believe it, don't even go there. "Must have been a trick of the light." She let the inchworm travel from one finger to another, then asked, "What happened with your lady?"

"There was a fire in the building where she worked. She never made it out."

Chloe could feel the pain in Will's voice and caught herself placing her hand on his.

His brown eyes met hers. "I want Dylan to have that kind of love. But because of what I did, he may not be able to. And . . ." His voice broke. He looked away and ran his hand down his jaw the way Dylan often did. Just that stupid little gesture made her long for him. "I don't know how to"—he took a deep breath, and his eyes filled with tears—"fix it."

She had no idea how to respond to a man who cried. She merely squeezed his hand while he composed himself. "Loving Dylan isn't going to change him. He has to learn that giving love is much more important than getting it. Loving is what counts. Maybe Teddy will help him to learn that. And maybe Teddy will teach him to accept someone who doesn't fit the normal parameters. Teddy is the only one who can do it."

"You've given up on him, haven't you?"

Gypsy had given up on the worm and jumped down to chase a leaf skittering across the grass. Chloe thought about his question as she transferred the inchworm to a nearby potted tree. "I never harbored any hopes of him loving me." *Liar.* She cleared away the thickness in her voice. "Dylan epitomizes the boy in school I could never have. The popular, good-looking one who, if he did look my way, hardly gave me notice. And I understand, I really do, about his need to look normal."

"Because of his mother."

She nodded. "Image is important to Dylan in a far deeper way than it is to other people. It drives him. I'll never fit into that normal image. Especially not now that my story's been in all the papers."

Will pushed his empty coffee cup aside and stood. "Thanks for listening and not judging."

"I learned long ago not to judge people."

He gave her a watery smile. "I'll bet you have."

She stood too. "Don't give up hope. Maybe he'll come around. He's going to need help when Teddy comes home."

Will shook his head. "Dylan won't ask for help. He's been that way since he was a kid. My fault too. I was never there when he did ask, so he stopped asking and started fending for himself. And what you said is so true. Loving is so much better than being loved."

When they reached her door, he said, "I've got to leave in a few days, wrap up a deal I've been working on for over a year. But I'll be back." He smiled. "Don't give up on him. He may not know it, but he needs a champion."

In some ways Chloe felt better after Will's visit. At least Will wanted to try, even if Dylan didn't. Somebody needed to touch Dylan's heart. She wanted to believe what Will had said about seeing something in Dylan's eyes. That something had probably been annoyance. That's what she had to believe to protect her heart. Because she already knew her heart was long gone to the man.

She loved him.

Oh, no, it was far worse than she thought. She wanted to nurture him and hold him and give him all of the love she had inside. And she knew he wouldn't accept it.

She thought about her words to Will too. She wasn't sure where those words had come from, but when she'd said them, her heart had filled with the sudden knowledge that they were true. Now she knew it didn't matter who loved whom most. The winner loved the most.

So where Dylan was concerned, she was the winner.

She dropped down onto one of her large pillows and closed her eyes. Then why did she feel so lost?

As she lay there, a scene replayed through her mind. She saw the houseboat again, the old man driving, herself paddling to catch up to him. She could see him there at the steering wheel. He looked over at her. And then he morphed into a woman. Chloe blinked, sitting up straight. That hadn't been part of the scene. And the guy who owned the boat . . . well, it was a guy. But the image persisted. No, it couldn't have been Wanda's mother.

She tried to push it out of her mind, but the nagging feeling was pounding through her head, insisting that Teddy was nearby.

"All right, all right," she muttered, putting on her Keds, calling Shakespeare, and heading out the door. "If I have to find that old man and ask if he's seen Teddy, I will." She shook arms already achy from paddling. "And I'm going to borrow Lena's little boat."

She watched Shakespeare's expression to see if he understood. Nothing. He bounded happily beside her, oblivious to her stress. How the heck did Stella do it?

Three hours later, she was motoring through the back waterways looking for the old houseboat. The guy never went far. Was this another wild bird chase?

After a prolonged choking sound, her engine petered out and wouldn't even think about turning over again. "Great." Half an hour later she caught the attention of a passing boat. "Hi! I need a tow, please. And do you happen to have a cell phone I could use?"

As the kindly guy tinkered with the engine, she dialed Dylan's house. Camilla didn't know where Dylan was. Worse, the woman wouldn't give Chloe his cell phone number. "But it's important," she insisted.

"Sure, it is. You give me the message, I'll get it to him."

"Have him call—shoot, I'm not home. Tell him the old man isn't a man at all, it's a woman, and . . . oh, forget it!" She knew how crazy it would sound.

"You're out of luck," he said, voicing her thoughts. "There's something seriously wrong with this engine. Let's get you towed back."

An hour later, her savior delivered her and the boat to Stella and Lena's boat dock. She tied up the boat and ran the whole way home, with Shakespeare at her side. She was almost afraid to check the answering machine when she saw the blinking light.

She closed her eyes when she heard Dylan's voice, and then she jumped up and screamed when she heard the message.

JOE FLEW the little Robinson helicopter over the Ten Thousand Islands while Dylan hung out of the opening and searched the maze of mangroves. He spotted Chloe's house, the Marco Island bridge, and then . . . the old blue houseboat crammed into the mangroves.

"Joe! Down there. Am I really seeing what I think I'm seeing?"

Joe pushed back his sunglasses and took the helicopter down closer. "You're seeing it, all right."

Dylan mapped out how to get there from the bridge. "Take me back."

All the way back he couldn't even speak. All he could think about was finding Teddy at last.

It felt like hours before he inched his boat close to the houseboat. His boat's engine ground up sand in the shallow depths.

"Oh, my God. That's it."

Breathe, breathe, it's really the boat.

He dropped the anchor and jumped overboard before even thinking of taking his shoes off. A chill scattered down his spine when he heard a plaintive voice ask, "Wanda, is that you? Where have you gone? What have you gone and done now?"

Not Teddy . . . but Anne. He hoisted himself up over the edge. "Teddy!"

The little door was open, but it was too dim to see inside. The windows were covered with faded newspapers. It reminded him of the house down in the Keys. Anne stood inside, fear in her eyes while she waited for the intruder. No recognition passed over her expression when she saw him.

"Anne, it's Dylan. Wanda's husband." She didn't know about the horrible accident that had taken her daughter's life yet. His gaze scanned the tiny living area.

"I was supposed to remember something," she said as he pushed past her to check the back bedroom. Teddy's toys were scattered around, but there was no sign of his son. He returned to Anne and put his hands on her shoulders. "Where's Teddy?"

Her eyes were blank. "Who's Teddy?"

He gave her a shake. "This is important, Anne. Focus. The little boy who was here. Where is he?"

Slowly the blank expression changed to the pain of trying to remember. "It wasn't a boy. It was Wanda."

"All right, where's Wanda?"

Anguish transformed her features. "She jumped."

"What?"

"Out there. She jumped. I don't remember why. I was scared, so scared, and I couldn't see her. I kept calling, calling . . ."

He rushed out onto the back deck and searched the surrounding area. "Teddy!" He knew Teddy might not respond, but he couldn't keep from calling him. "Teddy!"

"So I left," she said from behind him. "I remembered the keys, I remembered." She smiled, proud of herself. "I found them and knew I had to get help."

"You left?" His heart went cold. "From where Teddy—Wanda—jumped?"

"We were lost there, no one around, and I couldn't find her by myself."

He grabbed her shoulders again. "Where? Do you—oh, God, please say yes—do you remember where you were?"

She started to say something, but her mouth stayed open and silent.

"Anne?" She was way too thin. She probably hadn't remembered to feed herself, much less Teddy. "Anne, you've got to remember. Where were you?"

"So many trees, on and on, everything looked the same. . . ." Her voice was fading, and she walked to the couch and sank down. "Is it tea time yet? I can't remember the last time I ate. It feels like forever."

Had Teddy jumped? Or was she remembering it wrong? "Teddy!" He started tearing the place apart, opening every cabinet, looking under the bed, climbing on the roof. He stopped when he saw the curls of brown hair scattered on the floor. His fingers sifted through the silky strands, then gathered up a lock. He felt them slide against his palm as he continued searching. Wanda had stocked the boat with canned food and cereal. He stopped when he saw the box of Cocoa Puffs, Teddy's favorite. He found cash tucked under the sink. Why couldn't she have taken the damn money, all of it, and left Teddy?

He saw buttons spread across the deck, and then clothes scattered over the back of the deck. He picked up one of Teddy's shirts. All the buttons were missing. Was his son really that small? He bit his lip and forced back the emotions as he stared at the mangrove islands around him. He wadded the shirt in his hand and pressed it to his mouth. He kept it squeezed in his hand as he continued to search the mangroves.

When he leaned over the back and looked down, his heart jumped into his throat. "Oh, God. No."

His face burned and his eyes stung, but he blinked away the haze and forced himself to look at the house-boat's propeller.

There was a shirt wrapped around the blades.

"THEY CAN'T tell whether Teddy was hit by the prop or not," Yochem said forty minutes later. "The fact that his shirt was caught on it. . . . well, it doesn't look good. In fact, none of it looks good. A three-year-old with autism who's been out there" he nodded toward the islands of mangroves—"for who knows how long . . ."

Dylan kicked the side of the marine patrol boat, his body tense with anger and frustration. He couldn't believe this. No matter what, no matter that his son had been gone for over a week, that he might have autism, or that he was only three, he believed his son would come home alive.

"I know this is hard on you," Yochem said, softening his voice. "We never suspected he was on a boat."

"But Chloe did."

"What?"

"Chloe said he was in a boat. She kept dreaming about it."

"Look, everyone knows that woman has no psychic abilities. And I doubt her aunt does either. I think the two of you got lucky finding that other kid."

And unlucky with Teddy. He opened his hand and looked at the locks of brown curls. Anne, or Teddy himself, had cut his hair.

Just like Chloe had cut her hair.

"I've got to go. My son is out there somewhere."

"But it's dark. How are you going to—"

Dylan had already jumped overboard and was swimming toward his own boat. The chances of finding Teddy in the dark were minuscule, he knew that. The chances that he was still alive . . . probably the same. If Teddy had been injured, he wouldn't have made it very long. Did sharks come in this far from the Gulf?

"Dammit!" *Don't think about that, don't picture it, don't imagine it.* But he did, and he'd do anything to put himself in his son's place.

Breathless, he pulled himself onto his boat and started the engine. A towing company was maneuvering the houseboat out of the mangroves. Margie had been right: The boat was a junker. He hated the thought that his son's last days were spent here wondering why his mother or father weren't coming for him. Agony crushed his chest and made it impossible to breathe.

He started looking through the mangrove islands. He circled each one, calling Teddy's name, searching in the shadows of the roots that grew over the water's surface.

His boat startled a group of white egrets that took graceful flight into the air. They reminded him of Chloe.

He had to tell her. Why did that prospect seem so hard? Why did his stomach churn?

He kept searching, trying not to think about her. But as the chance of finding Teddy lessened, she became an ache in his soul, and the need to see her became a gnawing hunger in his heart. The sky was a cobalt blue as he made his way toward Lilithdale. Chloe's house wasn't far from where they'd found the houseboat. She'd kept saying he was nearby.

It was nearly dark when he arrived. The lights were on inside, warm and welcoming. She was waiting on the small dock behind her house. As though she were waiting for him. She came to her feet when she recognized him, her eyes wide with concern.

He maneuvered next to the dock, and she caught the lines he threw and tied them to the cleats. As soon as he climbed onto the dock and saw her standing there in the moonlight, all in white, he knew this was where he had to be.

He didn't have the fight left to deny it.

"Dylan?" she whispered, walking closer. "I got your message. You found him, right?" Her eyes searched his face. "He was on that old houseboat, wasn't he?"

"How . . . how did you know? About the boat, I mean. I didn't mention it in the message."

She shrugged, still studying his face. "What about Teddy? He was there, wasn't he?"

"He had been there. But he jumped off. I don't know when, and I don't know where." He wondered if she could hear the crack in his voice. He had a feeling she could, because she went very still.

"Then he's probably just on one of—"

He reached out and put a finger against her mouth.

"They think he might have been hit by the propeller. They're pretty sure he's dead."

She sucked in a breath. "Oh, my God."

She looked like she needed to be held, and dammit, he needed to hold her. But he held back, fighting the need like he always did.

"Dylan . . ." Her lower lip trembled as her watery eyes met his. "Hold me. Please."

How much could one man take? He gave in and pulled her hard against him.

"He can't be gone," she said in a teary voice, shaking her head against him. "He can't be."

He closed his eyes as he held her even tighter. She moved closer against him, hands splayed against his back. He felt like a drowning man holding on to a life preserver. He could feel her tremble, and then he heard her sniffle. He pulled back just enough to lift her face to his. Tears sparkled across her eyelashes and cheeks.

"I'm sorry," she said in a thick voice. "I'm sorry I couldn't do anything to find him."

"It's not your fault, Chloe."

"It's not your fault either."

He circled her face with his hands and ran his thumbs down over the tracks of her tears. He wanted to bury himself in her, to get lost in her. He wanted to touch and be touched. He needed to connect to another human being, and Chloe was the only human he'd ever felt close to connecting to.

He kissed her. It started out soft and tender, mouths touching, rubbing against one another. He moved closer, hands still holding her face. Her breasts brushed against his chest, filling him with heat. With life. That's what he needed too, was life.

Her mouth went slack beneath his, and he deepened

the kiss. She tasted like red wine, and he somehow felt her loneliness. And he felt it inside him, pulling them together, twining their souls. The tightness in his chest dissipated, becoming liquid warmth that flowed through his body.

He unbuttoned her blouse and pushed it back over her shoulders. Then he unfastened her bra and let it drop to the dock. His hands flowed over her flesh, cool in the night air. It quickly heated beneath his touch. She looked beautiful in the moonlight, all shadows and curves. Like an angel who could ease the pain. He needed to touch her, to keep that connection and feel her against him.

It wasn't real, more like a dream, with time flowing like a river. *Don't think, just be lost and connect,* he told himself. He did connect with her, and then they were naked, and he drank in the feel of her skin against his, life and warmth, and they stumbled to the chaise lounge, never stopping, just reaching and kissing, and then he was drowning, surrounded by her, going under again, coming up for a breath, sliding down again, unable to think or breathe, not caring, seeing waves of bloodred before his closed eyes as he sank for the last time.

Chapter Nineteen

DYLAN OPENED HIS EYES AND STARED AT THE PEAK OF A ceiling far above him. Chimes sounded nearby, a gentle sound, and something fuzzy brushed against his leg. He felt hazy and heavy inside, as though something were crushing his chest. For a few moments he kept the feeling at bay, an ominous monster hovering just out of reach. He focused on his immediate environment, on the mattress beneath him that was so soft he sank into it. On the dim morning light filtering in from a window. A drape of pastel fabric hanging from the ceiling moved in an air current. On the warm body laying half on his and the thin layer of sweat where their skin touched. The warmth of the room and the scent of lovemaking.

He let himself remember in small pieces. She'd been shivering outside on the dock, and in his groggy sleep he'd tried to cover her with his body. He'd realized his skin was chilled too, that he needed to get her inside. And they'd made love again on this bed, without words or thought, just a blind reaching out, a burning need.

The monster loomed closer as he remembered docking the boat and Chloe coming into his arms. The gaping ache in his chest that she'd temporarily filled.

The reason for the ache.

Teddy. He squeezed his eyes shut. His son was probably dead, and he'd made love with Chloe. Guilt stripped away his numbness, and red-hot pain ripped through his chest. What kind of cold animal was he?

He sat up, and she opened her eyes. She touched his arm, a tender look on her face.

"Don't . . ." he said, pushing her hand away. He got out of bed, found his pants, and pulled them on. Gypsy, the fuzzy thing he'd felt, stretched and jumped off the bed.

"Dylan, don't shut me out," Chloe said, wrapping her nakedness in a sheet and getting to her feet. "Talk to me. I'm here for you." She looked like a waif with mussed hair and flushed cheeks.

"My son is probably dead, and what did I do? I had sex with a woman." She winced at the generic statement. He looked at her, then away. "With you. If that doesn't prove how cold I am . . ." He ran his hand over his face. "You were right. I don't have enough to give my son—or anyone.

She grabbed both arms and gripped them hard. "It proves I was wrong. You're human after all. You have a heart."

He looked into those fiery blue eyes. "It proves I don't have the capacity to love anyone, not even my own son. That in the worst moment of my life, I thought about sex."

She winced at the last word. "It proves you needed me last night. That you needed to connect with me, needed the comfort I could give you."

He stared at her for a moment, denying that need. "Sex isn't comfort; it's sex. I don't need anyone, Chloe." She held on to him as he tried to move away. "Let go of me."

She let go. "It wasn't sex, and you know it. When you came here, when you reached for me, it wasn't because you were . . . horny."

Her eyes implored him to admit what part of him knew to be true. No, it wasn't true. He had to remind himself that anyone he'd ever needed let him down.

"Let me be here for you," she whispered. "Believe in me, Dylan."

He shook his head. "I have to look for my son. I have

to . . ." He drank in the desperate look on her face before wrenching away from her.

"Let me help you. We've worked together before—"

"We're not a team, Chloe. We never were, and we never will be."

And then he left. What he needed was to put distance between them, to separate himself from her and forget the devastated look on her face and the way she'd caved in as though he'd punched her in the stomach. Somehow she'd become entwined in his soul; somehow she'd become a part of him. He couldn't let that happen.

He heard her footsteps pounding down the stairs. "Don't go!"

Don't look at her. If you don't look, you won't see the pain, and you won't want to reach for her again. His shoes and socks were still on the dock. An old sweater was draped on the railing. He threw his shoes on the boat and jumped aboard.

"Dylan, wait!"

He stopped for a moment, but didn't look at her. "I know your compulsion to save things. I can't be saved, Chloe."

The sound of the boat's engine tore through the quiet morning air, sending a flock of egrets into the pink sky. Her next-door neighbor watched him with curiosity as she watered potted plants. He must look a sight, bearded, disheveled, turning his back on Chloe's pleas. He knew what he looked like: a monster.

WEARING THE yellow robe she'd thrown on, Chloe shivered in the chill morning air. *Way to totally humiliate yourself, Chloe.* If she could have persuaded Dylan to stay and hear her out, she could have gotten through that thick head of his.

He didn't even look back. She'd hoped for at least a backward glance, one more chance to give him a meaningful look. A look that meant what?

Love?

Please, anything but that. She sighed as she watched him head out, single-minded in his actions. That's when she saw the flash of black and white, and the beloved face in the cabin window. Shakespeare! He must have jumped aboard after they'd fallen asleep. The boat cut through the water and disappeared out of sight.

Just to make sure she wasn't hallucinating, she called him. Only Gypsy appeared, meowing for breakfast. Chloe knelt down and scratched her chin. "What are you saying? If only I could understand you the way Stella does."

Well, at least she'd see Dylan one more time.

"You all right, Chloe?" her next-door neighbor Belle asked, oblivious to the stream of water hitting the dock piling.

"Just a little . . . misunderstanding." She forced a smile, knowing damn well she wasn't convincing anyone.

She went inside and started to prepare Gypsy's food. Tuna and the other ingredients went into the blender, but her mind was elsewhere. She looked at the posters sitting on her counter. Teddy smiled back, and she felt the first tear fall. Last night she'd been in too much shock to think about him. She'd been too numb to do anything but soothe Dylan's pain. Now she let that pain wash over her.

The pain increased when she remembered reaching up to brush Dylan's hair back and feeling the wetness of a tear. The bottom had fallen out of her heart. She'd vowed to take away his pain, if just for a little while.

Forget his pain. You have enough of your own to deal with. She'd never met the boy, but he'd been part of her soul for the last week. Whether it was real or not, he'd been connected to her. Now he was gone. And no matter how Dylan felt about her, she would always be connected in his mind to his son. She'd lost both Dylan and Teddy, and she felt incredibly empty.

Even though Chloe hated listening to the news, she turned on the radio and soon heard about Teddy. She held her breath as Yochem spoke. He believed Teddy was dead, but they were going to look for him as long as they had resources to do so. He said the body would probably come to the surface in a day or so, if nothing else got to it.

"You cold bastard," she said, feeling her insides cave in. Still holding on to the blender, she rocked her head back and let herself go. The pain was so intense, she thought she might shatter into a hundred pieces. Her body went weak, and she sank to the floor. Gypsy climbed onto her lap, anxious to make things right. But nothing would be right again. Chloe held on to her cat and buried her face in the soft fur. She was crying so hard, she hardly heard the phone ring.

She pulled herself to her wobbly legs and picked it up. The dial tone surprised her, especially when it was followed by another ring coming from her bedroom. She followed the sound until she uncovered Dylan's cell phone under the blanket on the floor.

"Hello?" she answered in a barely audible voice, dropping down onto the unmade bed.

"I'm looking for Dylan McKain. Do I have the wrong number?" a man asked.

She cleared her throat, reaching for a corner of the sheet to wipe her nose on. "No, this is his phone. He's . . . not here right now, but he'll be back later. Can I get a message to him?"

"Is this Chloe Samms?"

Another surprise. "Yes."

"This is Dr. Jacobs. We—"

"Teddy's doctor." She sniffled. "You know, then? About . . ."

"I heard on the morning news. I called to tell Dylan how very sorry I am."

"We just kept hoping," she said, her voice still thick and squeaky.

"Hope is a double-edged sword." He paused for a moment. "There's something else I need to tell Dylan. I asked him to donate blood, just in case. We routinely test donated blood to make sure there are no contaminants and to type it. That's when I discovered it."

"What?" Her heart seized. Was something wrong with Dylan?

The doctor paused. "I shouldn't be telling you this. Will you have Dylan call me as soon as he returns?"

"Yes, of course." What she wanted to say was, *How can you leave me hanging like this?*

For half an hour she paced and wondered and worried. She told herself it wasn't going to do any good, but half an hour later she was still pacing and wondering and worrying.

When her phone rang, she lunged for it.

"Is this Chloe Samms?" a man's voice said. Not Dylan.

"Yes."

A woman said, "We're Mac's parents."

"Oh, yes, hello." Chloe leaned against the counter and tried to picture them. "How is he?"

"He's . . . okay. It's going to take some therapy, but it looks good. We wanted to thank you and Mr. McKain for what you did. I know you weren't looking for our son, but . . . you saved his life."

Chloe smiled. "I'm glad we did."

"Have you found your boy yet?" the man asked.

Your boy. Chloe's voice went thick again. "It looks like he . . . drowned."

"I'm so sorry," the woman said. "What horrible timing we have."

"No, it's all right. At least something good came out of all this." She cleared her throat. "I'm so glad Mac's going to be all right."

"He wants to see you. He said you held him and cried with him. We want to do something for you. And the reward . . . we offered forty thousand dollars—"

"Keep it," she said. "I know I speak for Dylan, too. It was enough to return him to you. And I would love to see Mac. But not right now."

"Sure, we understand," he said. "We'll let you go for now. But we want to give you our number. In case you change your mind about the money."

"And when you're ready to see Mac," she said.

Chloe wrote it all down, hung up, and sank into the nearest chair. They were so happy. She wished she could be happy too. But Teddy's story wasn't going to have the same kind of ending.

During the day some of the ladies of Lilithdale called with condolences. Gisella offered to take down the posters. Chloe was in tears again by the end of that call.

When she finally got control of the grief, she spotted a piece of paper on the carpet. Whenever Gypsy killed something, she always covered it. Let it be a roach or a spider, Chloe thought, removing the paper.

The shattered remains of a butterfly lay on the peach carpet. Gypsy meowed and came over, probably proud of her kill. Chloe tried to fight the new wave of tears, but her lower lip trembled, and out they came.

"Why does everything have to die? Why?"

Gypsy climbed on her lap and nuzzled her chin.

"Don't die, okay?"

A short while later Chloe dragged herself up to answer her door. Stella and Marilee stood there with worried expressions on their faces. Without Lena. Chloe found herself falling into their offered embrace, wallowing in their warmth and familiar herbal scents, clinging like a little girl who'd just lost her mom.

"Hon, we're so sorry," Stella said when they finally parted. "We saw the paper this morning. We thought you might need some company."

Marilee held up a purple container. "Brought you some more pickle soup."

"Oh, goodie."

"And something else." She pulled out a silk ribbon with a red stone wheel. "A jasper necklace. Earth's energy stone for inner strength." Chloe bowed her head and Marilee slid it over her head.

"Thanks. I could use some inner strength," Chloe said in a raspy voice. She felt as fragile as that butterfly on the carpet.

Chloe put on some coffee and a Sarah McLachlan CD. Soulful, plaintive music fit the mood. The three women sat on the cushions in her living room and drank Sweet Dreams coffee. Chloe blew bubbles and Gypsy jumped up to catch them. For a while no one talked. The only sounds were the thump of paws on carpet and the melodious tinkle of wind chimes outside. Stella sat behind Chloe, rubbing her shoulders with a woodsy-smelling patchouli oil.

"Lula said she saw a man leave this morning on his boat," Stella ventured after a while. She was wearing a green caftan and matching hair bow, and Rascal was nestled in the length of fabric.

"Lula?"

"Well, and Belle."

"Oh, brother. It was Dylan. Well, you probably knew that. He came by last night to tell me . . . about Teddy."

"Sex is great comfort," Marilee said with a knowing nod, poised in a yoga position. "It renews the soul, signifies life. What, you didn't think I got to be this age and not know everything there is to know about sex, did you?" she asked at Chloe's surprised look.

Chloe found herself smiling. "No, it's not that. I just didn't think you thought about it anymore."

"A woman never forgets the glory of sex," Stella confirmed with a nod.

"Let's not talk about sex," Marilee said. "We're here to talk about you. Are you all right?"

Chloe nodded, then shook her head. "I feel dead inside. I feel like I let everyone down. Especially Lena."

"She couldn't come. She wanted to, but she just couldn't. You understand, don't you? It's too close. Her chakras are a mess, let me tell you."

"I do understand the way she feels. Because most of all I let Teddy down. I keep thinking, was there something I could have done? Why couldn't I have sensed earlier that he was on that boat?"

"You did more than most people would have done. And you and Dylan did save that poor kid who'd been kidnapped."

"Yeah. His parents called to thank me."

Stella looked over at Marilee, then back at Chloe. "Hon, we're worried about you. You've been through a lot lately. First the accident, then this boy you're obviously connected to, and falling head over with his father—"

"I'm not head over," Chloe said. She looked at their

doubtful expressions. "I'm . . . attracted to him. Who wouldn't be?"

"You might fool yourself, but you're not fooling us," Marilee said. "We know that face. What would you call it? A la-la face, maybe."

"It's a marshmallow face," Chloe muttered.

"We're not here to give you a hard time over it. There's a lot of emotional turmoil swirling around you. We thought we'd balance your chakras, see if that'll help."

"You think I'm head over Dylan because my chakras are off?" Chloe asked, then realized what she'd said. "Okay, balance me." She looked from one to the other. "Go ahead, I dare you."

Marilee got to her feet and walked over to where Chloe sat on her cushion. She rubbed her hands together, then let them hover over Chloe's head. "Let's concentrate on your sixth chakra—the third eye. The chakra that governs your imagination, your ideas, and your awareness. Focus on the area between your eyes and visualize a spinning blue orb. Imagine it filling your mind with beauty and healing. And repeat after me: I am receptive to the Higher Self's direction and insight."

Chloe closed her eyes and repeated the words.

"Now picture yourself as a child, running through a field of dandelions, sending the seeds floating into the summer breeze. Let the image flow through your mind. Feel the sun shining down on you, filling you with love."

"I can see the field," Chloe said, smiling. She was running and laughing. And there was Teddy, absorbed in one of the dandelion puffs. Dylan was watching them.

"Better?" Marilee asked after Chloe opened her eyes.

There was no use lying to them. "I think I'm beyond balancing. I'm still head over him. But you don't have to worry about me. Dylan's not my soul mate or anything. He isn't. We're so incompatible it's almost funny. And with . . . now that we're not looking for Teddy, there's no reason for me to see him again. Well, except for Shakespeare."

"Shakespeare?"

"He stowed away on Dylan's boat. I imagine he'll come back for his cell phone too. Dylan, not Shakespeare. And that'll be that. Everything will go back to normal, the press will forget about us again, and life will go on." She didn't believe that for a second, but she hoped wishing would count for something. "I plan to go back to work tomorrow. Some of the women in town"—she fidgeted with the hem of her pajamas—"have taken away their accounts."

Stella waved that away. "They've got their panties in a twist. They'll get over it and come back, you'll see. You're right, it'll all die down, Lena will come around, and we'll be just like normal."

"One normal, happy family," Marilee chimed in.

"Well, as normal as we ever were," Stella said.

"Sure," Chloe said, forcing a smile.

It obviously wasn't a very good smile, because Stella and Marilee both frowned. "We're sorry you had to go through all this. Sorry about the boy."

"Sorry you're head over," Marilee put in.

Chloe had to laugh at that one. "Yeah, me too. But that too will pass."

They shared another cup of coffee in comfortable silence, looking out at the bay. Chloe tried to pretend she was watching the way the wind rippled across the surface of the water. She gave up and stared in the direction Dylan would be returning from.

Stella was the first to get to her feet. "I'd better get

going. I have a dachshund at four who needs to learn some manners where a cat is concerned."

"And I have to get things rolling for the six o'clock show," Marilee said.

"Thanks for coming over. It means a lot to me."

"We didn't want you to think you were all alone, hon," Stella said.

Chloe clung to each of them as they gave her a hug good-bye.

They were right. She had to get back to work and get on with her life. Since the accident, her world had revolved around Dylan and Teddy.

It was almost dark before she heard the boat engine. Well, she'd heard them all afternoon, running to the windows each time to see if it was Dylan. This time it was.

She couldn't help the speeded heartbeat, but she attributed it to finding out what Dr. Jacobs was going to tell him. She was also anxious to see if he'd found anything.

Don't run down to the dock, that's good, walk very fast, and great, now he'll think you couldn't even take a second to put on shoes. No matter that he looked sunburned, tired, and windblown, with a face shadowed with stubble, he was still gorgeous. And still locked away. The drained look on his face told her he hadn't found anything. She secured the lines, hoping it would be a while before they were untied. Setting herself up for disappointment.

Shakespeare hopped off, looking happier than either human. She knelt down and hugged him. "I missed you, buddy." She looked up at Dylan, wishing she could hug him too. He looked like he needed a hug.

"Nothing?" she asked, though she already knew the answer.

He shook his head. "Some of the marine patrol were

out there looking, but they can't keep expending resources for the search. It's time I accepted it too."

She didn't want to give up, but she remembered the doctor's words about hope being a two-edged sword.

He nodded toward the dog. "I didn't know he was on the boat when I left."

"I kinda figured that. He looks like he had a good time."

Shakespeare gave himself a shake, then wandered off to chase a blue jay.

"I gave him a hamburger from Snook Inn," he said. "He wouldn't eat it unless I held it for him."

"That's my Shakespeare. Thanks for feeding him. You left your phone here."

"I realized that too."

Had he tried to call her? She wished she could ask. That sword again. "You want to come in for a cup of coffee or something to eat?"

"I'd better just get my phone and go."

When she started up the stairs to her house, she realized he intended to wait in the yard. She hated the pain inside, but it was time to accept that she didn't belong in his life.

The shadows of the courtyard nearly swallowed him up. She turned on the light when she returned with the phone. As soon as he took it from her, he started to leave. Had he even noticed how their fingers had brushed?

"You had a call today," she said softly. "From Dr. Jacobs."

"He'd heard?"

He sounded so weary that she wanted to hold him close the same way she'd held Mac. She stiffened her body against the impulse.

"Yes. He sends his condolences."

He nodded, and she could see that condolences didn't mean anything right then. "There was something else he needed to tell you. About your blood."

"What?"

"I don't know. Call him." She handed him the paper with the number and waited. No way was he leaving before making that call.

He looked at the paper for a moment, then dialed. Chloe caught herself leaning toward him.

The weary expression on his face turned pale with disbelief. "What are you talking about? That can't be right. Uh-huh. Well, a test isn't going to make any difference. If the test is even right." He listened for a moment. "Good news? No, that's not good news to me." His gaze shifted to her. "The last thing I ever intend to do is have more children. No, I understand, it was your obligation to tell me. Good-bye."

Dylan crushed the paper and tossed it to the ground. She saw the same fire in his eyes she'd seen that day at the pizza joint.

"What's wrong?" she asked. His whole body seethed with angry energy. She took hold of his arm and made him face her. "Tell me."

He hesitated, searching her eyes for a moment. "Teddy's not my son."

He may as well have punched her in the stomach. "What?"

Dylan had put on his mask again. "I donated blood just in case Teddy needed it. They typed it, and there's no way he could be my son."

"Is he sure?"

"Positive."

She was trying to piece the conversation together. "Did he say it was good news because he thought it would ease the pain?"

Dylan shook his head. "Because I wouldn't have to worry about the autism gene affecting future children."

That's when he'd looked at her and said he would never have children again.

"Are you all right?" she asked.

He realized her hand was still on his arm and pulled away. "It's all wrong. Everything is wrong."

He turned and walked toward the dock. Shakespeare followed him, but Chloe called him back. This time Dylan looked back once, just before he started the boat's engine. She knew everything she felt for him was in her eyes, but there was nothing she could do about it. He turned the boat around and headed out of the bay.

Feeling as though she carried five hundred pounds on her shoulders, she trudged back up the stairs to her house. She looked at the pale colors, the soft fabrics of the curtains, the flowered coffee cups in the sink. No wonder everyone thought she was tender and fragile. She fingered the strands of hair that used to be curls. Everything about her looked tender.

She sank down on the cushions, hugging one to her chest. Maybe she *was* tender. She surely felt like a fragile piece of blown glass that was just about to hit the floor. With a meow, Gypsy curled up next to her.

When she really felt vulnerable, she always thought of God. She closed her eyes. *God, help me to be strong. Help me to accept Teddy's death. And please, help Dylan too.*

She drifted into an uneasy sleep and dreamed about Teddy.

Chapter Twenty

CHLOE DREAMED SHE WAS LYING IN THE BACK YARD IN A patch of sunshine. The light was all shimmery and swirly like in the tunnel. A touch to her cheek woke her. Teddy was standing over her, his finger poised to touch her cheek again. He smiled, but he didn't say anything, nor did he meet her eyes.

She sat up, and he sat down in front of her. She held out her hand, and he mirrored the movement. Their palms touched, and he smiled again. He was beautiful, though he didn't have curly hair like he did in the pictures. He stared at their joined hands as though it were some mystical event. His hand was so small. Then he raised his other hand and held it out toward her. She placed her palm against his, and they sat like that for a long time.

Contentment glowed on his face, a face that looked nothing like Dylan. She tried to reach out to him, but he moved back. *Let him advance,* a voice said. She pulled her hand back and left it poised in the air. He placed his against hers.

When she watched their hands, she could see him looking at her. As soon as she turned, he shifted his gaze away. She tried to remember what the doctor had said about autism. Communication was the problem. Connecting to other people. But Teddy was connecting to her at his own pace.

She leaned forward so that her face was between their hands. After a few moments, he did the same. Their noses were nearly touching. She leaned just a fraction of an inch closer and grazed her nose against his, then moved back before he could object.

He did the same. When he smiled, she felt her heart fill with joy.

Then he got to his feet and started walking toward the dock. He turned to see if she was following.

All right, then, she'd follow. He teetered at the edge of the dock. He stumbled backward. She tried to grab him, but he plunged into the murky brown water.

Suddenly everyone was around her, even Dylan, saying how sorry they were, how sad that Teddy was gone. She could see Teddy beneath the water holding out his hand to her. She kept pointing to him, saying, "But he's still alive. Don't give up yet!" But no one could hear her.

Chloe came awake to find that she was standing on the dock. She couldn't see beneath the water because of the moon's bright luminescence on the surface. Her heart was pounding from the dream. What did it mean?

Was Teddy in that inky water? Is that what the dream was telling her? Was God trying to tell her something?

She and Shakespeare climbed into her canoe, and she paddled as though her life depended on it. But it wasn't her life; it was Teddy's.

That's when she knew Teddy was still alive. It was just like before, the way she felt him. Teddy was out there somewhere. The police would never believe her, but maybe others would. She was going to have to do whatever she could to energize people to join her cause.

"Teddy, can you hear me? I'm going to find you."

"CHLOE, THIS has got to stop."

She blinked awake to find Stella hovering over her. Shakespeare jumped up, and her head banged down on the canoe seat.

"Gypsy came over to tell me you'd fallen asleep in the canoe again. She's worried. Rascal's worried. We're all worried!"

Her cat sat at Stella's feet, head tilted as though to confirm it. Chloe climbed out, feeling a bit groggy. It had to be early; the sun was fresh off the horizon. Then she remembered her dream, and the grogginess evaporated.

"Teddy's alive!"

"What? I didn't hear anything on the news."

"It's not on the news." She put a fist to her heart. "It's here."

"Oh, no, Chloe."

She was halfway up the stairs when the tone of Stella's voice stopped her. "What do you mean, 'Oh, no'?"

Stella put her palms to her chest. "Don't you see? It's your mother all over again. This is what Amelia did."

Chloe went cold for a moment. "But this is real."

Stella hesitated. "That's what Amelia thought too. She believed it."

"But this really is real. I'm not jealous of Lena's psychic talents. I don't even want to be psychic. There's a little boy out there who needs my help. I met his mother in that place, and God let me come back to save him. Don't *you* see? I'm the only one who's still looking for him. But that's going to change." She ran up the remaining steps.

Stella followed her up to Chloe's bedroom. "What are you talking about?"

Chloe turned on her shower and started rummaging through her clothes. Something respectable, no pastels and nothing tender. "I'm going to get people involved again. Anyone with a boat and a heart. We can find him if we've got enough people looking. That's all we've ever needed, but no one thought he'd be on a boat." Her eyes widened. "No one but me. I knew he was nearby, but I didn't trust myself. I would never forgive myself if months later they find Teddy's body, only to discover that he was alive now."

"But Chloe, he's been out there for over a week. Who knows when he fell off the boat? And they think the propeller hit him. If he was injured and in the water, there's no way he could have survived. They said on the news—"

"I don't care what they said. He's alive" Chloe stripped off her clothes and gave Stella her best bulldozer face. "And I'm going to find him."

When Chloe came downstairs twenty minutes later, she was surprised to find Lena sitting on the couch. Her red hair was loose around her shoulders, making her look so much like those old photographs of her mother.

Chloe felt a bittersweet ache in her heart, and a small sense of hope. She knelt at Lena's feet, took some of the fabric of her long, gauzy dress, and wrapped it around her.

"Lena," Chloe said. "How are you?"

For a moment, a wistful smile came over her face as she looked down at Chloe's position. "You've done that since you were a little girl."

"It's always made me feel . . . I don't know. Secure, I guess."

Lena looked away. "It's nice to have security. We all take it on our own terms."

Chloe tilted her head, not sure if she understood. "Have you come to help me? Did you have a vision?"

"No." Lena didn't have a helping expression on her face. It was more troubled than ever. "Stella told me about your bulldozer face." She studied Chloe's expression, then shook her head. "I can't let you do this. It's your mother all over again, and I won't sit by and watch you destroy yourself."

"Then don't sit by. Help me."

"No. I cannot get involved, I can't."

"What about Mac? You saw the skull. You were right about that."

Lena wasn't looking at Chloe now, but out the windows. "You don't know what I went through to suppress the visions. That one slipped through, and I let it because I felt I owed you. For concealing the truth about your mother and all," she added. "But I couldn't even get that right. There are no more visions. Ever again."

"Forget the visions." Chloe stood. "You have eyes, don't you? All I'm asking is that you look for him."

"Chloe, don't do this to yourself."

"Who are you trying to protect? Me? Or yourself?"

Lena stood too, her face pink with anger. "Destroy yourself if you want. But you're going to destroy us as well. Look what you've already done. The press is all over the place, poking fun at us, asking questions. Do you want to alienate everyone in Lilithdale? The poor boy's dead, Chloe. You just don't want to believe it. It's become an obsession, the boy and his father."

Chloe felt a stabbing pain at Lena's words. Did she know that Teddy was dead? No, Chloe wouldn't believe it. "If saving someone's life is an unhealthy obsession, then I admit it. Yes, I'm guilty." *You are only talking about Teddy, aren't you?* She gathered up her canvas purse and her keys, then turned back to Lena. "A little boy's life is at stake. If I have to lose everything to save him, I'll do it. I'm sorry you don't believe in me. I'm sorry that I've brought you unwanted attention. But I can't let this go until I find him."

Lena's fingers squeezed Chloe's arm. "It's not just Lilithdale or myself I'm worried about."

Chloe wished she could hug Lena. It hurt to hold back the need. "I know. You're worried that I'm too fragile to handle this. But I'm not my mother. I've learned to be strong, just like you and Stella."

A shadow crossed Lena's eyes. "I'm not strong. I thought I was, and that's what fooled me."

Chloe's heart tightened as she watched pain cross her aunt's expression and shadow her blue eyes. "You *are* strong."

Lena shook her head. "Even if I'd found the girl in time, your mother . . . she would have still done what she'd done. She caused a lot of pain for those parents and everyone involved in the search. Then she couldn't live with herself. And I . . . I couldn't either. I couldn't live with failing that girl's family, and then failing Amelia."

Chloe's throat tightened now. "What are you saying?"

Lena took a deep breath and let it out slowly. "I tried to take my life too."

"Oh, my God," Chloe said, giving in to her impulse to put her arms around Lena.

Lena returned the hug briefly, then pulled away. "I thought I was strong, Chloe. I was stronger than you are. No matter what you say—what you want to believe—you're not strong enough to handle this. Some people think suicidal tendencies run in families. You could be genetically predisposed to take your life. I know well, all it takes is one event to tip the balance. You're tender, and there's nothing wrong with that. Let this go."

"I can't," Chloe whispered. "Thank you for trying to protect me. But I couldn't live with myself if I let it go. I'm going into this with my eyes wide open. There's something deep inside driving me to look for Teddy. I'm connected to him somehow. I have to find him."

Chloe couldn't take the pain in Lena's eyes any longer. The warning loomed on the horizon, the threat of a despair so deep it might consume her. But she had no choice. She turned and walked out the door.

Everything around her took on a new clarity. She noticed the sway of the palms, the patches of sunshine on the flagstones, and the green moss that grew between those. The roses that were finally flourishing, and the briny scent of the bay. It all seemed so crystal clear.

As though she weren't going to be seeing it much longer.

She felt the ache in her heart at that thought. She also knew that ache would be even bigger if she went on with her life and put Teddy out of her mind.

Chloe got into her T-Bird and pulled out of her driveway. First she had to see Dylan. If she could spare him, she would. Hope, that double-edged sword. But if her plan worked, he was going to find out anyway. Better that he heard it from her. And maybe, just maybe, he would join her. Of his own volition this time.

She could already feel the sting of the sword.

DYLAN TRIED to bury himself in the Kraft Theater plans. He tried to remember the triumph of outbidding Wahlberg for the project and the excitement of reaching a pinnacle in his career. All he felt was empty. The board was only interested in having the "top gun" work on the project, but Dylan's heart was no longer in it. Out of fairness to the Kraft family and the board, he called Ross.

"I'm off the Kraft project. I'll work with Dave Wahlberg to assure a smooth transition."

"What? Are you nuts? Do you remember how hard you worked to win it away from him? And now you can actually work on it."

"What are you talking about?"

"Well, you don't have the search to occupy your attention anymore. I mean, I'm sorry it didn't work out, but—"

"Ross, *buddy,* there is no way in hell I will ever work with you on any project again. I just hope you become human before you have children of your own." Dylan hung up, muttering calculations before realizing what he was doing. He had to get out of there.

He found himself at the hospital looking for Anne. She was in for observation before they released her back to the nursing home. She looked tiny and frail in the white bed. Her blue eyes showed recognition when he walked into her room.

"Is she really gone?" his mother-in-law asked.

Thank God she was lucid. He pulled a chair beside her bed. "They told you?"

She gave him a wan smile. "They had to. I kept asking for her, and I guess I got a little . . . hysterical. I'd been waiting so long on that boat, and she didn't come. Sometimes . . . I wondered. The boy on the boat, he was my grandson, wasn't he?"

He nodded, gripping the sides of the chair to keep the pain from showing. "Teddy." His voice was hoarse and thick.

She surprised him by reaching over and touching his arm with her bony fingers. "I'm sorry." Her eyes were watering, her mouth trembling. "It was my fault. I can remember bits and pieces of those days on the boat. Sometimes I was in the past, when Wanda was a little girl. And I thought Teddy was Wanda. I tried to hug him.

He ran away from me and jumped over the side. I kept calling him, but he wouldn't answer. Then I knew I had to get help. Even when I thought it was Wanda, I knew I had to. . . ." She choked back a sob. "But I forgot. It's so frustrating, being 'there' and then losing it. Knowing there's something you must do and not knowing what it is." She fisted her hand, then brought it to her mouth.

His hand hovered over hers, then slowly settled. "It wasn't your fault. Can you remember where he jumped?"

Her mouth looked like a starburst of wrinkles as it twisted in agony. "The police asked me that too. It all looked the same, water and trees and more water and trees. I don't even know how long it took to get where I did. I just kept thinking I had to get help."

He focused on the side of the bed for a moment, burying his own frustration. It wasn't Anne's fault. It was only Wanda's fault, and she couldn't be confronted. "Anne, why didn't Wanda tell me about her mental problems?"

"Because I told her to hide it. Not just from you. It started with her father. He tried his best, but he was a hard man. No tolerance. Always threatening to put her away if she didn't stop talking to the imaginary people. He would spend hours in her room with her trying to make her stop. It only got worse."

Dylan didn't want to delve deeper. "So she learned to hide it."

"Yes. She was so afraid you'd find out. And then one day she decided she couldn't pretend anymore. She just wanted to live her life . . . with her son."

"Was she . . . seeing someone? Having an affair?"

Anne blinked. "No, she'd never do that. But she talked about people, always talked about different people. There was Larry and Bill and . . . Brian or something. But I figured they were her imaginary people. Why?"

He shook his head. He tried to attach names to the people they'd known four years ago. *It doesn't matter who Teddy's real father was. Not now, not ever. He'll always be your son.* "I just wondered. Anne, I want you to think. When you started the boat . . . did you feel . . . anything?"

She looked up. "Feel anything . . . feel . . ." She looked at him again and smiled. "I feel tired and hungry. A little light-headed if I move too fast. When can I eat, Doctor?"

"Anne?"

"Do you starve your patients in here?"

He'd lost her. He stood, feeling more sad than frustrated. Then again, losing memories might not be such a bad thing. Then he could forget his past, his wife, the pain of losing his son . . . and Chloe.

DYLAN HAD given Camilla the week off. The dark, quiet house suited him better anyway, and Camilla's valiant effort to hold back her tears wasn't helping his nerves.

The day before, reporters had clamored to get his reaction. Teddy had been news again, but it wasn't going to help him. Dylan had declined all interviews and locked himself away. Now all he wanted to do was sink into anonymity again. And he wanted to do it alone.

What about Chloe? a voice in his head whispered. Great. Now *he* was hearing voices.

The phone rang again. At first he'd listened to the messages, people calling to give their condolences. Then he couldn't take their words anymore. He turned down the machine and ringer.

A knock on the door startled him. His first thought was Chloe. He felt a pang in his chest at the thought of her being there. An image of holding her in his arms filled his mind. *Forget it. No holding Chloe.* He looked through the peephole and saw his father. He closed his eyes for a moment, contemplating ignoring him. Then he unlocked the door and stepped aside.

"I've been trying to talk to you since . . . well, since the news," Will said, walking into the dark foyer. His expression held both sympathy and pain. "I know what losing a son is like. Now I've lost the chance to know my grandson too."

Dylan didn't know what to say. He supposed he could shock the man and tell him that Teddy wasn't his grandson. But Dylan had made a promise to himself that he would never tell anyone. Not to protect his image, he realized, but Teddy's. Teddy had been his son in the way that mattered.

"What do you want?"

Will shifted from foot to foot, loosening the collar of his shirt. Dylan couldn't remember his father ever looking uneasy. Then again, he hadn't seen his father much.

"I've come to say good-bye. I have to return. . . ." He gave a feeble smile. "Work. Deals."

"I remember." *You're the same way,* that blasted voice whispered again.

Will wrung his hands. "I came to say I'm sorry. About everything. I can't make it up to you now. I wasn't there as a father, I know that. I hid my head in the sand that I called work. I pretended that everything was all right, that I was doing my part by paying the bills, giving you a nice home and lots of toys. Pretending is a lot easier than facing the truth."

Those words struck Dylan in the heart. *That's you. You're staring at yourself, hearing your own words.*

"I know it's too late to make amends," Will continued. "I just want you to know how sorry I am. I thought I could come down here and be a hero, find Teddy, connect with you again. Now I know that isn't possible. I don't blame you for not wanting me around. I . . . well, I want you to know that. Maybe you don't care if I blame you or not. But I don't." He started to turn, but stopped. "Chloe said something that really hit home to me."

"Chloe?" Dylan blinked, at both the surprise of hearing her name on his father's lips and just the jolt of hearing her name, period.

Dylan swore Will had an almost sheepish expression on his face. "I went to see her Tuesday. Before they found the boat. I had to clear up a, er, misunderstanding. She's a terrific lady, in case you didn't notice."

"I noticed," Dylan said.

"The most kindhearted—"

"I noticed."

"Then why aren't you with her now, helping each other, comforting each other?"

"You're giving me advice on my love life?"

"This has nothing to do with your love life. It's about friendship. No wonder she's about given up on you. She cares a great deal about you. Did you notice that too?"

She'd given up on him? Good. She should give up on him. "Why are you telling me about Chloe?"

"Because I don't want you to push her away like I suspect you push everyone away. She said loving you wasn't going to change you. She was right. Oh, maybe if I had shown you love when you were young, that would have made a difference. But now, no."

Dylan felt warmth touch the edges of his frozen heart. "She said she loved me?" Instantly he wished he could take back the words. She didn't love him.

"Not in so many words, but judging from the look on her face, yes."

"I'm sure you were mistaken." Still, Dylan felt that warmth grow a little brighter.

Will's laugh was bittersweet. "She said the same thing when I told her what I saw in your eyes when you looked at her. What did she say it was? Oh, a trick of the light. Look in the mirror and think of her, then tell yourself that's what it is. If you can, then you're too far gone for anyone to reach." He paused. "Much as that would be a great exit line, I have more to say and probably only this chance to say it.

"You probably hate the fact that Chloe comes from that oddball community. Being with her would make you look bad. She won't like that I told you this, but she described you as the boy in high school she could never have, the one who never noticed her. She understands your need to look normal to the outside world, and I think she's prepared to gracefully back away. I say it's your loss if you let that gem go. She's pretty, more grounded than most women I know, and she's smart. Which is what I was getting to. She's right about loving you making no difference. You have to love. Giving love is more important than receiving it. I did learn that . . . once."

Dylan saw grief flow across his father's face. He held back the questions about a love that was obviously special. And lost. "Is that all?" he forced out through a tight throat.

Will lifted a shoulder. "I guess it is. I know . . . I know you probably won't ever let yourself love me as a father. Or even like me. But don't close yourself off from love completely. When everything looks bleak and hopeless, you want to shut everyone out. I know, because that's how I felt when I lost the love of my life. That's how I always was. But she changed me. Because she loved me, but mostly because I loved her. I reached out, and you know what I felt? Friendship. People who cared about me and who were willing to help me through the bad times."

Dylan knew the truth of those words. He just didn't have the energy, or the heart, to reach out to anyone. Particularly his father.

"Let someone come in, Dylan. Chloe's your best bet. In the end, it only matters that you let someone in. Here's my card. I wrote down my home number in case . . . well, just in case. Good-bye."

Dylan watched his father leave. He didn't know what to say. He was too shattered to reach out to him now. He remembered too many times when he'd reached and no one had been there.

Dad, can't you come home for dinner tonight? Mom's in one of her moods. I don't want to be alone with her again.

Tough up, kid. Can't you even handle your own mother? Look, I've got meetings until seven, and then some new stocks to run down. All right, I'll see what I can do.

He never lived up to his word.

Dylan never made promises to Teddy that he couldn't keep. But then, Teddy hadn't begged him to come home early. Dylan had once been grateful that his son wasn't needy so he could focus on his business, just for a couple more years, and build it to a point where it could be run by his senior architect. Only Dylan had a hard time letting go.

He'd only broken that promise to himself.

DYLAN'S LEGO structure was three stories high when the scream interrupted him. It sounded like Chloe, though it couldn't be. Still, he opened the door to find Chloe shooing a cat away from the fountain. She was wearing a pale blue suit that set off her eyes, and pumps instead of matching sneakers. She saw him standing at the door and straightened up.

"A cat was about to pounce on a cardinal taking a bath." She self-consciously smoothed down stray wisps of her blond hair as she made her way up the steps. The scrapes on her cheek and lip were nearly healed, the bruises faded. Her embarrassment at being caught saving the bird turned to concern. "You look terrible."

"Thanks."

He rubbed his hand over his face, feeling a day's worth of bristle. She looked so beautiful, he wanted to pull her into his arms and hold her. He stiffened his body against the urge. She had been watching his face, and when he'd put a mask of indifference on his face, she followed suit.

"I need to talk to you," she said in a businesslike tone of voice. Well, as businesslike as Chloe could get.

"Come in," he said.

A glance in the mirror revealed just how bad he did look. His eyes were bloodshot, his hair mussed. And there was something else, something he'd never seen before. He turned away from the mirror.

"I hope I didn't disturb you," she said, pausing near the living room.

You always disturb me, Chloe. "Would you like something to drink?"

"No, thanks. I won't be staying long."

Those words pricked at him. He didn't want her to stay long, not even a minute. She was already making him want things he shouldn't want. He caught himself trying to see the love in her eyes that his father had mentioned. All he could see was worry and, worse, that bulldozer face.

"Where's Camilla?" she asked. Her pumps clicked on the tile, and he realized Chloe usually walked silently in either her sneakers or bare feet.

"Off," he said, pulling his gaze from her small feet that shouldn't be crammed into pumps.

She clutched at her big canvas bag. "Are you all right? I mean, not all right. Of course you're not all right. That's a dumb question." She looked away for a moment. "But are you . . . okay?"

"I haven't pulled out the rope yet."

She smiled nervously, but even that smile faded fast. "After you left—"

He ducked his head. "Look, I'm . . . sorry about leaving like that. I came to you, and then I stormed off. I didn't blame you. It was my fault." She didn't look comforted by his apology. Damn, what did he know about comforting a woman?

"I don't suppose there's much to say about that until you realize what you came to me for was comfort and not . . . sex. But I didn't come here to talk about that. I . . ." She saw the structure he'd been working on. "You've been busy." When she touched the wall of yellow Legos, it felt as though she were touching him. He'd told her too much.

"I couldn't sleep," he said.

"Well, what I'm about to say isn't going to help." She took a breath. "Not that I think you'll believe me. In fact, I'm sure you won't." She clutched her bag even tighter. "Ever since the accident, I've felt connected to Teddy. I have these dreams about him, only they're not really dreams. I always felt that Teddy was nearby, and it turns out that he was. And now . . ."

"And now?" he prompted when she stalled.

"I still feel him. Dylan, he's alive. I had a dream last

night, and I know—*know*—that child is alive. It's like God's telling me not to give up."

"Chloe . . ."

"Don't 'Chloe' me. I've already heard enough 'Chloes' from my aunts."

"Even they don't believe you?"

She looked away, her mouth tightening. "No. They think I'm re-creating my mother's drama."

"That's what it looks like to me."

Her eyes got that bulldozer gleam again. "I'm not giving up on this. I don't expect you to support me. I know it's going to dredge up more pain for you. And it's going to create havoc in my life, and I'll probably lose everyone I care about and maybe I'll even have to move out of Lilithdale. I don't care. I'm going to do everything I can to get people out there looking for Teddy. I just heard on the radio that there's a cold front moving in with rain and temperatures dropping down to the fifties. That makes it even more important that I find him now."

He didn't want to open himself to hope. "You're just setting yourself up for a fall. He's been out there for well over a week, and the propeller—"

"Don't even say it." She held out her hand.

"I can't let myself believe he's still alive."

"Then don't. I don't care what I have to do to get attention, and that includes sounding crazy. I'm not asking for your permission. I'm just warning you." She started to turn away.

"Chloe, why are you doing this?"

"I have to. Don't you understand? It's not a matter of choice. If I ignore this, I'll never live with myself. Maybe this is how my mom felt. But I'm not wrong. My mistake was not believing in myself before. If I had, maybe I would have realized Teddy was on that boat."

"Don't do this. Let it go."

"Don't you care? Is it because he's not really your son?"

He tried to hold in the anger, but this time he couldn't. He smashed the Legos creation, sending pieces skittering over the tile floor. "Of course I care! I'm not some unfeeling monster. Teddy *is* my son. I want to find him and bring him home, but I can't keep letting myself believe he's alive when he's not."

"The double-edged sword," Chloe said softly.

"What?"

"I promise I won't bring your name into this. I'll swear you're not involved. But know that I'm prepared to go all the way with this. I just want you to understand that. And know that I understand this severs all ties between us." Her chin trembled, and her bulldozer look melted for a moment. "If there *were* ties between us, that is. But I know you can't be associated with me once I go public with my . . . feeling about Teddy."

"Chloe, you're not going to get people to look for a child everyone knows is . . . dead. They're not going to believe you."

"I'll make them believe."

"They already think you're a flake."

"Is that what you think, Dylan?"

"I don't know what I think. I try not to think about you."

He saw the shadow cross her face, but she shuttered it the way he did. And he hated it. He didn't want her to be like him.

"I'd better go. Good-bye, Dylan."

Had he imagined the strain of emotion when she'd said his name? He watched her leave. He both feared for her and admired her. She was wrong, of course. He might have a little more regard for psychic visions since finding Mac, but Chloe was no psychic. Even she had admitted that. And her connection to Teddy? The same compassion that had her saving lizards and birds.

Now she was going to throw herself to the media hounds, and everyone would think she was crazy. No one believed her when she'd claimed Lena's psychic vision. She would lose all credibility now.

And so would he, if he went with her.

She'd relieved him of the choice. She'd also relieved him of choosing whether to reach out to her or not. All he had left in his life was his business, and even that was suffering. If he was to have a chance at resurrecting it, he had to cut ties with her, as she'd said.

He had to let Teddy go. And he had to let Chloe go too. He closed his eyes at the sharp pain that accompanied both thoughts. Walking away was going to be the hardest thing he'd ever done.

Chapter Twenty-one

CHLOE TOOK SEVERAL DEEP BREATHS ONCE SHE REACHED her car. She'd stayed tough. Well, as tough as a tender woman could be. On the way to the police station, she stopped at a phone booth and called three of the reporters who'd covered Teddy's disappearance.

"I have information that Chloe Samms had a vision about Teddy McKain not being dead after all," she told them in a deep voice. "She's going to the police right now to force them to keep looking. Hey, you never know. They might even throw her in jail."

She hoped not. But for Teddy, she'd endure anything. Maybe even a hunger strike. Nah, she was rather fond of food. Something else, then. She hoped it would come to her, a brilliant idea that would rock Naples.

Chloe pulled into the police parking lot and took another deep breath. *Don't stop now. Remember, this is for Teddy.*

"DETECTIVE YOCHEM, please," she told the woman behind the glass. "Chloe Samms. He'll know what it's about."

Ten minutes later, the detective came out from the back offices. He had a slightly annoyed expression on his face as he approached.

"Miss Samms, what can I do for you?"

Chloe smoothed down her blazer. "Hi, Detective. I have some information about Teddy McKain's case."

"That case is closed."

"It isn't closed until you find Teddy. Can we talk?"

She hoped the reporters would come in about then, but apparently this wasn't hot news. "I know that Teddy is still alive."

"You do, huh? Is this one of your aunt's visions?"

"No. Absolutely not. This one is mine."

"Yours. Yeah."

She started to reach for his arm, but stopped herself before making contact. She didn't want assault on the list of charges. "That little boy is out there, and he needs to be found. All I'm asking is that you put more effort into finding him. He's somewhere in the Ten Thousand Islands."

"Look, Miss Samms, we've put considerable effort into this case."

"It's not a case. It's a boy! A little boy who doesn't understand why no one's come for him."

"I understand your emotional involvement in this . . . case, but we're ninety-eight percent sure that boy is dead. We do have the marine patrol on the lookout for him, but it won't be a tearful reunion when he's found. If he's found."

"Ninety-eight percent sure? What about that two percent?"

"We only have so many resources."

A skinny man her age walked in wearing a baggy shirt and pants.

"Can I help you?" Yochem asked the man.

"I'm Wes Sherman from the *Naples Daily News* here to talk to Detective Marshall about a domestic abuse case he's working on."

"No! You're here to talk to me," she said. "I'm Chloe Samms, and I know Teddy McKain is alive. The police refuse to keep looking! Are we going to let this travesty of justice slip by?"

The man looked disconcerted for a moment, but then he narrowed his eyes. "Chloe Samms. You're the one who helped find that missing boy in the Keys."

"Yes! And I'm still trying to find the missing boy here in Naples. I've had another vision about him, and he's still alive."

"Wasn't that vision your Aunt Lena Stone's?"

"No, it was mine. Only mine." She let out a breath of exasperation. Couldn't anyone focus on the real problem? "Teddy is the issue here. I'm connected to him. I met his mother when I had a near-death experience. You know, the light at the end of the tunnel, seeing loved ones who have passed on. His mother was in that tunnel, and she begged me to find her son."

The guy finally took out a notepad and started writing. She let out a sigh of relief. Finally! "Near-death experience, you say?"

He took notes as she told him about the accident that had changed her life. "And I'm going to hold the police responsible if Teddy is found dead," she finished, turning to Yochem. "I'm talking lawsuits, Court TV, Judge Judy—"

Yochem crossed his arms over his chest. "Miss Samms, you're overreacting. We've done everything possible to find that boy."

"Not everything. He's not here, is he?"

"Our business is finished," he said, turning to leave.

"Did you write that down?" she asked the reporter. "He turned his back on me. And he turned his back on Teddy. We need to get people together, anyone who has a boat, and get them to look."

The man closed his notepad. "Look, I'm sorry, but this isn't a story. It's interesting, yeah. I'll try to get it in the paper, but there's no real hook here."

"Hook?" She grabbed him by his shirt. "Hook? A boy's life is on the line! How much more of a hook do you need?"

He tried to gently remove her hand. "I said I'd do what I can."

She narrowed her eyes. "All right, you want a hook? You've got one. Come with me."

Now would be a really good time for that brilliant idea. As she drove, she searched her mind for stories that had grabbed her attention. *What about that guy who swam over an old mine in the Keys for twelve hours to protest dolphin abuse?* A little crazy, a lot brave. That's what she needed. Unfortunately, she couldn't think of one mine nearby. But there was water. Water where you couldn't see the bottom. Deep water. Everyone was so fascinated by Lilithdale's annual New Year's Eve swim. The brilliant—but crazy—idea began to form.

She drove to the city dock, the reporter right behind her. She gathered up her homemade posters of Teddy and her heavy-duty stapler. He followed her from the car to the entrance of the docks. She stapled two posters to each post and handed another one to the reporter.

"You want your hook? Here it is. I'm swimming in the bay until the police, or the public, get out there and look for Teddy. And . . . and I'm going to do it naked."

At that, she swiveled, tossed off her pumps, and started walking to the end of the dock—taking off clothing as she went. First her jacket, then her scarf, then her pants. She could hear the camera whirring behind her. Just what she wanted, her backside splashed across the front page.

It wasn't quite the way she'd intended to get attention, but then again, she hadn't had a game plan anyway. At the end of the dock, she turned back to the reporter.

"Remember, I don't leave until somebody takes some action. Better yet, until a *hundred* people take action!" She set the remaining posters on the dock, anchored by the stapler.

Then she shimmied out of her panties and bra, keeping her back to the reporter—no need to show him anything more than her big white butt—and dove into the water. The dark, deep water. The cold water that took her breath away. *Oh, God, what am I doing? Are you sure you really want to do this?* When she surfaced, the man was laughing.

"Lady, you've got your hook." He snapped several rounds of photographs. "And you've got style. I'll turn this story in for tomorrow's edition. Let me ask you some questions."

Chloe answered his questions through chattering teeth. Damn, she hadn't thought about the water being cold. Not icy, but still cold. Well, she'd have to get used to it. If she'd already wimped out by the time the story hit, no one would give her any credence at all.

As it turned out, she didn't have to wait until the story broke. A crowd started gathering immediately, followed by two more reporters. She treaded water as she talked to anyone and everyone who would listen. What better place to motivate people to search for Teddy than at the docks?

After a while the water felt warmer. Or maybe she was as chilled as she could get. Between talking to people and treading water, she was maintaining some warmth. Not to mention decency. She had to remember not to lift her arms too high. Not only did she want to keep this from being a peep show, she wasn't sure how long ago she'd shaved under her arms.

The dock manager had collected her clothing for her.

The guy in the mini-store sent down a hot cocoa once in a while.

"How long do you think you can actually stay in the water?" one woman asked, taking notes for her paper.

"As l-long as it takes, or until I drown, I suppose."

Then the television crews arrived. Chloe couldn't help but smile. Pay dirt.

"Why protest naked?" the reporter asked.

"I n-needed a hook," she said. "N-no one would listen to me standing there with my clothes on."

"Chloe, what if they find Teddy dead?"

"They won't. N-not if they start loo-looking for him now."

"What about the boy's father? There were rumors that you were romantically involved with him."

"I'm not." She glanced across the bay. His house was over there somewhere. "He has nothing to do with this. Or me."

"What do you think his reaction will be to what you're doing?" another television reporter asked.

Oh, he'd probably want to throttle her. "This isn't about his reaction. Or about him at all. It's about finding Teddy. That's all I care about."

"What about the women who live in Lilithdale with you? Why aren't they here supporting you?"

Ouch. That question stung. "There's n-no need to drag them into this."

The crowd behind the reporters shifted, and Detective Yochem pushed his way through. He shot her a disapproving look. "I figured it was you. This woman is nuts," he told the reporters. "She's only looking for attention, just like her mother. This is a waste of all our time."

"So you believe the child is dead, then?" the reporter asked him.

"Yes, I do. We are searching for his body, but we have no hope of finding him alive at this point."

"But she does," a man called out. "Maybe she is nuts, but I'm willing to look. What if the kid is still alive?"

"Yeah, you haven't found a body," another man said.

"I'll look," another man offered.

A dive boat named the *Bimini Twist* that had come in paused to catch the story. The captain exchanged glances with his divers and shrugged. "I'm game if you all are."

"Sure," the two couples on board said simultaneously. "Let's go!"

"What fun!"

Before the boat left, they pulled up to her. "Here's a BC," the captain said, handing her a vest.

"A what?"

"It's a buoyancy compensator, used for scuba diving. Slide it over your shoulders and blow in that tube. It'll inflate. I'm Stacy Mullendore. Just give me a call later, and I'll come get it."

She wrangled herself into the thing and blew it up. Buoyancy! "Thanks, Stacy!" she called as they headed out.

Within a few minutes, five boats had departed. Chloe watched with satisfaction.

"The marine patrol is coming to get you, Miss Samms," Yochem said. "I suggest you cooperate."

"Not until I know there's a full-scale effort under way to search for Teddy. That means eighty-nine more people."

He had a smug look on his face. "What are you going to do when it gets dark?"

The dock manager stepped forward. "We'll shine lights on her, so no one will run her down."

"And we'll supply her with food and water," another

man said. "I work at the Dock Restaurant. You like lobster, Chloe?"

"Sure," she said, glancing around at the water. "I j-just hope they don't like me."

More laughter filled the air with sweet hope.

And all the while, the cameras rolled. She'd never taken a chance, never put herself on the line. Maybe she'd never had a reason before. But now she did. She glanced across the bay again, wondering what Dylan would think. It saddened her to think she'd sealed her fate with him by doing this. He would never let himself be associated with her now. And she didn't blame him.

The marine patrol sidled up next to her a few minutes later. "Listen, lady, just let us help you into the boat. You don't want to be arrested, do you?"

"How can you arrest me? I'm n-not doing anything illegal. Am I? It's p-public water, I believe. I'm not drunk or disorderly."

The younger officer laughed. "You're disorderly, that's for sure."

"I'm n-not coming out. You can j-just put a warrant out for my arrest. You know where I'll be. When I know Teddy's being searched for, then I'll t-turn myself in."

He shook his head, then said in a low voice to his partner, "We can't just strong-arm her into the boat with the cameras rolling. Especially considering she doesn't have any clothes on."

"What a nut," the other one said.

They both looked up at Yochem, who shook his head with resignation.

"You gotta admire a woman who goes the length for what she believes in," the younger officer said. "I guess it wouldn't hurt to take another look."

Chloe smiled, until she felt a fish slide by her thigh. She nearly jumped out of the water. "Are there sharks in these w-waters?" she asked, hoping she didn't sound as scared as she thought she did.

"Yep," Yochem said.

"We'll keep an eye out for any," one man said. "Turn on your fish finders, guys!"

"Gee, th-thanks," she said, forcing a smile. "I feel so much better."

Was she nuts? Without a doubt. All she knew was she couldn't give up until they'd found Teddy.

"Is SHE *nuts*?"

Dylan had been rebuilding his Lego creation when Camilla had called and said, "You'd better put WINK news on. Jim McLaughlan just announced a whopper of a story coming up next."

He'd turned it on to find Chloe's face looking up at him. Her wet face, surrounded by water! She looked small, wearing what looked like a life vest. Spotlights lit up the area where she was treading water and talking to reporters.

The camera panned to the female reporter crouched on the end of a dock. "Jim, Chloe has a point to make. After going to the police and finding no help there, she's turning to us. She believes that Teddy McKain is still alive. And she's willing to make that point in a most unique way to get our attention."

They panned in on Chloe again, blond hair plastered to her head and cheeks. "I'm not leaving the water unt-til I know a h-hundred people are out th-there looking for T-Teddy."

"Why a hundred specifically?" the reporter asked, oblivious to Chloe's chill.

Dylan's heart lurched. She was somewhere out there in the cold water.

"Where is she?" he asked the television.

"I n-needed a goal, something to sh-sh-shoot for. With a hundred p-people, we have a g-good chance of finding him. I'm hoping for more th-than that, though. There's a cold front coming in tonight."

"How many people are looking now?"

"Eighty-one," a man to her left said, consulting a notepad.

"Chloe's been in the water for ten hours now. Food and hot chocolate are being brought to her via boat. But she won't leave the water." She turned back to Chloe. "And tell us, why did you choose to stage this protest naked?"

"*Naked!*" That shot Dylan right out of his chair. He started walking away from the television to find a phone, but turned right back to it.

"I n-needed a h-hook," she said with a quivery smile.

She wasn't kidding about this, was she? No matter how crazy it sounded, she was committed to finding his son. She looked tired and cold, and he'd never seen such a beautiful sight in his life. The heart he thought was dead came to life again. She believed in her vision, or whatever it was. He didn't want to get his hopes up, but she had pinned everything on her own hopes that Teddy was alive.

"You've denied any romantic involvement with Dylan McKain, Teddy's father."

"Right. N-nothing romantic. This has n-nothing to do with Dyl—Mr. McKain."

"Then why are you doing this?"

"B-because I have to. T-Teddy's out there, and I h-have to find him."

She was protecting him, just as she'd promised.

"Something's working," the reporter continued. "People are taking out their boats and looking for the lost boy. There must be something about a naked woman in distress."

Despite the fact that she looked cold, her face glowed. "They're looking—that's all I c-care about."

Dylan tore his gaze off Chloe and studied the docks and surroundings. He was pretty sure he knew where she was. He walked out back and looked across the bay. His hand came up to cover his mouth. Lights and boats and people. Chloe.

If he showed up, everyone would know he was involved with her. It would be the death knell to what was left of his respectability. Wasn't that all he had left now, that and his career? Salvaging his business's reputation meant steering clear of Chloe.

He forced himself back into his chair. The news had gone on to other stories, but Dylan kept seeing Chloe in that water. Nothing would happen to her with all those people around. Give her an hour or two and she'd give up. His fingers gripped the arms of the chair.

"Leave her be. Remember the look on her face when you walked away from her. You blew it then."

He searched the channels and caught the final seconds of another spot on Chloe. He felt his body strain to get to his feet. He forced himself back. "Teddy's gone and none of her crazy antics are going to bring him back."

In the end, it didn't matter what he told himself or what made sense. He grabbed up towels and a pair of his sweats. Then he walked to his boat and jumped in. No way was he going to let Chloe spend the night in the bay, especially with a front moving in. She might be nuts, but she was trying to find his son. That was reason enough to love her.

Love her?

No, he'd meant reason enough to pull her nutty tush out of the water.

He pulled on a jacket and headed across the bay toward the lights. Boats were anchored around her as a shield. A crowd of people huddled at the end of the dock. The reporter he'd just been watching was kneeling down talking to Chloe. The cameras were off now. He spotted Stella trying to get through the crowd, but the police had the far end of the pier roped off.

Dylan maneuvered through the tangle of boats surrounding her. He asked one man to move his small boat so he could talk to Chloe, and the man obliged.

All the while, she hadn't even looked in his direction. That was probably good. A surprise attack. If only he could pull her into the boat before she realized what was happening.

Chloe's teeth were chattering even more. All he wanted was to get her warm and dry. Only then might he throttle her for endangering herself.

"Chloe, I'm one hundred," he said from behind her. He wasn't sure he was the one-hundredth person, but he had to convince her he was.

She swiveled around in the water. "D-Dylan! You're not s-supposed to be h-here. We-we-we're not associated!"

"I'm the one hundredth boat to search for Teddy. Now come on."

"Look! It's the kid's father!" someone yelled.

The camera lights came to life again, and the reporter jumped to her feet and grabbed her microphone. "Are we on? Good. Dylan McKain just arrived on the scene. Mr. McKain," she yelled. "Do you believe Chloe's vision?"

He was about to hedge, but suddenly it all clicked together. She'd cut her curls, she'd known Teddy was nearby and on a boat . . . and something else slipped into place. He'd seen a box of Cocoa Puffs at Chloe's house. Teddy's favorite cereal, what he'd been eating on the boat. "Yes," he said. He was looking at Chloe as he spoke the words in his heart. "I believe her. And I want her to get into this boat right now."

Chloe was looking at him, her face filled with both question and elation. "You believe me?"

"Yes. The Cocoa Puffs convinced me."

"Huh?"

"I'll explain later. Just get in the boat. Now." He held out his hand to her.

"Do we have a h-hundred b-boats l-looking?" she asked the man with the notepad.

Dylan coached him, nodding his head. *Say yes so I can get her out of here.*

"With him, I believe we do," he said. "Yes, we definitely do."

She turned back to Dylan. "All r-right." She swam over to his boat with stiff movements.

"Cut the lights!" Dylan yelled. "If you're really naked," he said to her.

"As a b-blue jay," she said with a grin.

"You are crazy, you know that?"

"I p-probably am."

Her hands were ice cold when he reached for her, her fingers stiff. The lights went down, and Chloe came up. He grabbed a towel and wrapped it around her, but not before glimpsing her nice white bottom. His own body went around her too, trying to infuse her with his warmth.

The lights came back on, and the reporter started asking more questions. He held up his hand and squinted in the glare. "I've got to look for my son."

As soon as they reached the open bay, he said, "What the hell were you thinking of?"

"I wasn't th-thinking, if you m-must know. I tried t-to get a rep-porter to d-do the story, and he couldn't m-make any promises. He s-said he had to h-have a h-hook. So I gave him one."

He shook his head, but couldn't help smiling. "Go down to the cabin and change. I brought some sweats for you."

A few minutes later, she came back up again, lost in the oversize sweats. Her hair was still wet and sticking out all over, and her cheeks were pink. Before he could think any better of it, he pulled her in front of him. She was shivering, and her nose felt like an ice cube. She burrowed against him, and he held her with one arm and steered with the other.

"I have a couple of lights in the back. When we get near your house, we'll pull them out and start looking."

She nodded, face buried inside his jacket. He squeezed her tighter. *This is better. She's not in the water anymore.*

After a few minutes, she looked up at him. "Why did you come get me?"

"I didn't want you in the water anymore."

"Is th-that the only reason?"

"Chloe . . ." He pushed wet strands of her hair away from her forehead. "I just couldn't let you stay there anymore." *Don't think about what drove you to get her. Don't think about how good she feels, how right she feels.*

She nodded, then looked ahead. He squeezed her closer against him and closed his eyes for a moment. He didn't want to let her go. It was crazy to have this kind of feeling about her. *She* was crazy.

"I saw Stella there. At the dock," he said a few minutes later.

"She was there?"

"We could go back and get her. If you want to face everyone again."

"She was p-probably just there to tell me I'm nuts. Or to tell me they've voted me out of t-town." She sighed. "No." He liked the way she leaned into him. "I've already blown it anyway. With my aunts, with everyone in Lilithdale. For the first time in my life, I really, truly don't belong anywhere."

She belonged in his arms, he felt like telling her. But she didn't. He didn't want anyone in his arms.

As thcy neared the Ten Thousand Islands a short while later, he pulled out the lights and put the engine on coast. They'd seen other boats searching along the way. No matter how crazy it had been, Chloe had convinced people to look for a boy who was considered a lost cause. He could love her for that alone. If he could love her at all.

Every time he passed a boat that was obviously searching for Teddy, Dylan would get on the radio and thank them. Soon that channel became the Teddy channel, with people occasionally reporting what they'd seen. Or more appropriately, what they hadn't. Each person checked out a certain area, and Dylan marked it on his map. It became a real system. But there were far too many personal messages for Chloe. "Tell Chloe she's a sweetheart." "Tell Chloe she's got real guts."

She was too focused on finding Teddy to pay much notice. She took one of the jumbo lights, climbed up on the bow of the boat, and shined it through the mangroves.

"I'll shine low, you shine high," he said. "We can cover more territory that way."

He didn't want to hope that his son was still alive, only to find it wasn't true. But hoping, he realized, was better than feeling dead inside.

"Are you warm enough?" he asked, watching her curl up on the bow with the light propped on her knees.

"I'm fine."

"Here." He handed her his jacket, and she slipped into it.

"Thanks."

He felt colder now that she wasn't standing beside him. It was odd how she'd made him warmer, hotter, more of anything than he'd ever felt. And tonight, he'd felt afraid for her. Pretty amazing for a man who didn't feel much.

They stayed silent for the next hour, working as a team, searching the shadowy mangrove islands. They were a team, he had to admit. Maybe later he'd admit that to her too. The only sounds were the occasional crackling report on the radio and the hum of the engine. In front of them stretched a sea of blackness.

An hour later, they pulled into the area south of Chloe's house. The wind was picking up, carrying the damp forewarning of rain.

"I kept feeling he was nearby," she called out. "I kept taking canoe rides looking for him."

"I'm beginning to think you're Teddy's guardian angel."

She smiled at him, looking more than angelic in the lights. Her smile faded and she looked into the darkness. "If I were his real guardian angel, I would have already found him."

But she hadn't given up when everyone else had. Just the thought made his throat feel thick.

"Dylan, stop! Go back! Put this thing in reverse."

"What'd you see?"

She'd sprung to her feet and her light bounced against the trees. Her voice was a heavy whisper. "Maybe I was imagining it. But I thought I saw Teddy."

Chapter Twenty-two

DESPITE HER HOURS IN THE COLD WATER, CHLOE FELT AS though a Mexican mariachi band had taken up residence inside her. Her heartbeat was the rapid shake of the maracas, so loud she could hear them in her ears.

Don't get your hopes up. It was probably a raccoon.

Dylan reversed the boat, and she held her light high.

"There!"

He cut the engine and climbed up on the bow with her. Her face felt hot, and she could already feel tears forming in her eyes. A little boy's face caught the light just before he ducked out of the glare.

"Oh, my God, it's him!" she said, turning to Dylan and nearly knocking him off the deck.

He was still staring at where the boy had been, as though he couldn't believe it. Then he took the light from her and played it over the area. His shaking hands made the light wobble. Until he spotlighted the boy again.

He shoved the light back at her, dropped the anchor, and jumped over the side. She kept the light aimed at the boy. Dylan swam to the edge of the mangroves, then started picking his way into the tangle of roots and branches that grew over the water's surface. She alternated the light now, helping Dylan to see his way and keeping the light on his goal.

"Seventeen times seventeen equals two eighty-nine. Forty-nine times five equals two forty-five," she said.

She could hear Dylan talking softly, coaxing the boy, who was moving away.

"It's him, isn't it?" she asked.

"It's him, Chloe." She hardly recognized his voice, it was so filled with emotion. "And he looks all right. No cuts, no blood that I can see. He can sure move."

She put her hand to her mouth and bit her knuckles, also biting back a sob of relief.

"Teddy," she could hear him say. "Teddy, it's your dad. It's going to be all right."

But Teddy kept moving away from him. Chloe could hear his puffing little breaths as he maneuvered deftly through the branches. The boy had gotten accustomed to living among the mangroves and not having ground beneath his feet. It amazed her that he still had the strength.

"Chloe, call for help. All I'm doing is scaring him."

"Let me try. I want him on our boat before the other boats arrive. They'll only frighten him more. I've been here before. I know what I'm doing."

"What?"

"My dreams. I know exactly what to do."

This time the murky water didn't bother her. She grabbed the battery-powered flashlight Dylan had been using and dropped over the side of the boat.

Dylan was moving toward her, but she said, "Stay there and keep him in your sight. I'll make it all right."

The soaked sweatshirt weighed her down. She awkwardly climbed into the mangrove forest holding the flashlight in one hand.

As soon as she neared Dylan, he took the light and helped her climb the remaining way to where Teddy sat clinging to the branches. Just the sight of him, so near, so alive, shot adrenaline through her veins and filled her heart. There were smudges of dirt on his face and hands, and he huddled against the chill, damp wind that filtered through the leaves.

"Don't aim the light at us," she said, maneuvering closer to him. "Just enough so I can see him and he can see me."

She remembered the dream and slowed down. It was hard not to reach out and grab his arm. But she held back, remembering the gentle ways she and Teddy had touched hand to hand. She stopped two feet away from him, and for a moment all she could do was soak him in.

He didn't look like his picture. His blue eyes were wide with uncertainty. His cheeks looked gaunt. His hair was messy and without curls. Just like in the dream. She ran her hand down over her own hair. He watched her. And then he did the same thing.

She smiled. "Teddy? Are you all right, Teddy?"

He opened his mouth, but no sound came out.

One of the roots below her right foot started buckling, and she had to find a new one to support her weight. He watched her intently.

"Chloe," Dylan said from behind her. "What are you doing?"

"Trust me," she whispered.

After a moment, he said, "Like no one else."

She bit her lip as those words warmed her from the inside. She wasn't looking directly at Teddy. It was hard not to look at him, but she remembered the doctor saying he wasn't comfortable meeting anyone's eyes. So she started plucking first one leaf, then another, off the tree.

Teddy watched her, and she watched him from the corner of her eye. Then he plucked a leaf from the tree. While he did that, she inched closer. He was absorbed in the leaf for a minute, and she moved closer yet, until she was precariously balanced on the roots a foot away.

She mimicked him now, looking at the thick, leathery leaves in her hand, pretending not to pay attention to him.

The only sounds she could hear was the water splashing around the roots of the mangroves and a distant boat engine.

That's why his voice startled her, even though it was soft. "One. Two. Three."

She shifted her gaze a bit and found him counting the leaves in his hand.

He dropped one leaf. "Two." Then another. "One."

Hey, she could relate to counting. "Three," she said, holding up her leaves. She tugged another leaf free of a branch. "Four."

He pulled another leaf to add to his. "Two. Two. Two."

Chloe dropped two of her leaves. "Two, two, two."

Teddy giggled. It was the most wonderful sound she had ever heard. She giggled too, because her joy was overwhelming. She couldn't believe that he was still functioning after days without food and water. But he was, and that's all that mattered.

Then he handed her his two leaves. She stared at that little hand for a moment, stunned.

"Grab him," Dylan whispered.

She merely shook her head, then took the proffered leaves. "Three, four."

"Three, four. Three, four."

"Chloe, do you know how much I want to touch my son? To see if he's all right? To get him to the hospital?"

She nodded, but didn't look at him.

"And you're perched in a tree counting leaves."

She could hear the edge of his impatience. "You said you trusted me."

"I do, but—"

"Then shhhh!" She knew, absolutely knew, this was

the way to reach Teddy. She wasn't sure how she knew, but she was trusting her instincts from now on.

That's when she felt a touch on her cheek. Her first reaction was to give in to the joy in her heart and turn to him. She resisted the impulse, remembering the dream. Instead she held out her palm. He held out his hand and touched hers, and Chloe drew in a breath. She couldn't hold out her other hand, like in the dream, because she had to hang on to the branch. She smiled, though, and she could see him smiling back.

"Hi, Teddy," she whispered, feeling giddy.

"Teddy," he said.

She squeezed his hand very gently, then let go. "Come with me, Teddy. Home. Do you want to go home?"

He tilted his head, as though trying to understand her. "Home," he repeated.

"Yes, home."

"My room?"

"Yes, your room." She could hardly contain the excitement in her voice. She pulled her hand back, nodded toward the boat, and then started climbing away from him. Every few minutes she turned to see if he was following. At first he was just watching her, and then he plucked a leaf from the tree and stared at it.

She let out an exasperated breath, catching Dylan's gaze. Or at least what she thought was his gaze in the dark behind the light. "He'll come. Just wait and see."

Dylan kept the light between Teddy and Chloe, so both could see. She looked at the water below her and saw a cache of food containers. "Dylan, he's been catching discarded pop bottles and drinking them. Eating other people's leftovers."

"Smart kid," Dylan said, and she could hear the pride in his voice.

"Teddy," she said in a singsong voice.

He looked up at her, smiling. She repeated his name, and he smiled wider. And then he took a step across the roots toward her.

A gust of cold wind shuddered through the mangroves, stilling Teddy. She heard raindrops plopping against the leaves. The process took time, but getting him toward the boat without his fighting or being terrified was worth it. At the water's edge, she slipped into the cold water and splashed. Teddy crept to the edge and watched her for a few minutes. She was already wet and cold. A few more minutes in the water wouldn't kill her.

"Stay there," Dylan told her. "I'm going to radio for help and get a flotation device."

She could hear the cheering on the radio once Dylan had announced that he'd found Teddy. He asked that everyone but the Coast Guard stay clear of the area so as not to frighten his son.

Teddy didn't seem afraid of the dark water. He jumped in, creating a big splash. Dylan tossed her the orange life jacket, and she held it out to Teddy. As she suspected, he was fascinated by it. She was surprised when Dylan tossed her one too, since she was able to stand up. He dropped back into the water again. The night was getting darker, with clouds obliterating the stars. Thunder rumbled in the distance.

"Instead of trying to put it on him, show him how to hold on to it," he said, drifting up behind her.

"Good idea." She pulled it up to her chest and held on.

It didn't take Teddy long to follow suit. Dylan ducked beneath the water as Chloe sang Teddy's name again and again. He looked just the way he had in her dreams. She couldn't believe he was real. She wanted to touch him, but she remembered autistic children didn't like to be touched. But Teddy had reached for her. She let her hand float in front of her, and Teddy watched it in fascination. She splashed a little, and he mimicked her. Raindrops hit the water, not a downpour yet, just a warning.

Dylan surfaced right behind Teddy. Chloe kept him occupied and Dylan gently pushed him closer to the boat. Teddy was so involved with Chloe's hand, he didn't even notice.

She went to the stern of the boat and started climbing up the ladder. Then she reached down for Teddy. It took a few minutes, but he finally reached one hand out to her. Then another. Dylan lifted him up, and Chloe helped him onto the boat.

A spotlight slashed over the water as the Coast Guard drew up. "Is the boy all right?" one man asked.

Dylan was kneeling in front of Teddy now, taking him in with eyes that showed love.

"Yes," she answered. "As far as we can tell."

"Everybody in the boat?"

"Yes."

Two men came aboard, one with a medical kit. Chloe kept Teddy occupied while one of the men checked his blood pressure and other vitals. "How long has he been out here?" he asked.

"We don't know for sure," Dylan answered. "He's been missing for more than a week, but he's probably only been out here for a few days." He ran his hand over his face, looking at Teddy. "It feels like it's been a year."

"You're a lucky man," the man checking Teddy said. "He looks like fine. Heck, my kid wouldn't eat nothing but canned mac and cheese for three weeks. Kids are pretty tough. You'll need to have him checked out at the hospital to be sure."

"My car's at the city dock," Chloe said. "My house isn't far from here, but I'd have to borrow a car . . . from someone."

"Follow us," one of the Coast Guard men said. "We'll get you back to your car. I can have an ambulance waiting there too if you want."

Dylan looked at Teddy, who was now trying to wrestle out of the towel someone had put around him. "We'll take him."

Once again, the press was already waiting at the emergency room entrance to catch the drama. Dylan carried Teddy into the hospital while flashes went off everywhere.

"Was it Ms. Samms's brave antics that got your boy found?"

"Exactly who did find your son?"

"Is he all right?"

"He's going to be all right," Dylan told them as he walked through the doors. "And Chloe found him. Only Chloe."

"You found him too," she said. "If you hadn't come out—"

He stopped for a moment and looked down at her. "You found him, Chloe. You're my hero. Don't take that away from yourself."

Then he walked up to the desk and told the nurse who he was. Chloe basked in his words for a moment before watching Dylan retreat into the emergency room. Less than two weeks ago she had been there. And Dylan had gone in to talk to her. It did feel like a year ago.

With all the excitement and drama of the last few hours, everything seemed to come to a screeching stop. She was standing in the waiting area alone, wet and cold.

She knew she didn't belong with Dylan and Teddy, but she wanted to be with them anyway.

The other people in the waiting room looked either anxious or somber. Chloe could only celebrate. Teddy was alive. Alive! She hugged herself. When she dropped down into one of the seats, the shivering began. The shock was wearing off, and reality was setting in.

The good reality was that Teddy was okay. The rest wasn't as good. She'd alienated the people who meant the most to her. She'd made a spectacle of herself, and even though it was for a good cause, who would want to be associated with her?

And then there was Dylan. He was going to have his hands full, though he might not admit he needed help. Or her. And probably he didn't. She was in love with the man, and now she wouldn't have a reason to see him again.

At the peak of the shivering, the tears starting coming. She wasn't sure what they were for, exactly. Loss and gain, she guessed. Finding Teddy was worth any loss, including that of her heart. She hardly knew Teddy, yet he'd stolen her heart as surely as his father had.

TWO HOURS later, Dylan and Teddy emerged. They didn't look much alike, other than both being tired, and gaunt.

Dylan's face had taken on a calm she'd never seen before. Chloe pushed herself out of the chair and walked over.

"He's fine," Dylan said, looking down at Teddy. Teddy was looking at Chloe's dirty sweatpants. "They did a complete exam, took some blood. So far he looks great, considering what he's been through. I've got to keep an eye on him over the next few days. They wanted to keep him overnight for observation, but I want him to sleep in his own bed tonight. I'll make an appointment with Dr. Jacobs in the morning." He nodded toward the emergency treatment area. "I thought you'd come back with us."

"I didn't know if I was . . . if I should."

"I figured you were getting a change of clothes."

She looked down at her bedraggled clothes. "And give up this glamour look? No way."

They shared a laugh, and for a moment she imagined that in his eyes, she did look glamorous.

He turned away and knelt down to Teddy's level. "Hungry?"

Teddy didn't seem to understand. "Hungry?" he repeated, tilting his head.

"I've got so much to learn about him," Dylan said on a sigh, coming to his feet. "For now, I just want to get him to bed. Are you ready?"

"My, yes." She looked down at the little boy who had been her obsession. He was real. She wanted to hug him, but settled for just saying his name.

"Teddy," he repeated in the same soft tone of voice.

Reporters were still outside when they emerged. Dylan had a hold on Teddy's hand. When Teddy shrank back from the lights and noise, Chloe reached down and took his other hand. The boy looked at their joined hands and became intent on them.

Dylan ignored the questions as he faced one of the cameras. "My son is going to be all right. I want to thank everyone who helped search for him. I want to thank everyone who prayed for him." He reached over and slid his arm around Chloe's neck. "Mostly I want to thank Chloe. She saved my son's life." He looked at her as though he were going to say more, then swallowed the words.

She relished the warmth of his arm around her shoulder as he guided them through the crowd and the rain to her car.

They were quiet on the drive back to his house. Chloe helped get Teddy out of the car. He was drooping fast, though he struggled to look at the house. She saw recognition, and maybe even a shadow of a smile before his eyes drifted shut. Dylan pulled him up into his arms. She felt just as tired and wished she could snuggle into his arms too.

"Why don't you crash here tonight?" he said. "If you think you should," he added with a tired smile, probably remembering how she wasn't sure about going into the emergency room with them. "We've got an extra guest bedroom and I'm sure you can fit into Wanda's clothes."

Chloe figured she probably shouldn't, but she was too tired to resist. "Thanks, I will. I'd probably fall asleep on the drive home. Unless you think it's a bad idea, what with the publicity and all."

He paused for a moment. "I want you to stay."

The decision was made, and she didn't have the willpower to walk away from that.

Teddy lay slack in Dylan's arms, and all she could think about was that he could be dead. If they'd given up, he might have been. If they hadn't found him tonight, he would have been out in the cold, pouring rain. She pulled back the blanket, and Dylan set his son down on the bed. Working together, they stripped off his dirty clothes and tucked him under the blankets.

The only light in the room was a Snoopy night-light. Even in the dim glow, she could see the sheen of moisture in Dylan's eyes as he gazed down at his son. Chloe knew that it really didn't matter that their blood didn't match, that some other man had fathered Teddy. Just seeing that look of awe and gratitude in his eyes made tears spring to her own. What a sap she was.

"It's a miracle," he said.

"God brought me back for a reason. I just knew it."

Dylan looked at her. "Yeah, He did."

Thinking she ought to give them a few minutes alone, she said, "I'll go get him a glass of water in case he wakes up thirsty."

"Good idea," he said in a thick voice, his gaze on Teddy again.

She gave him ten minutes, wandering through the house, watching the rain coat the windows and obliterate the pool and terrace area. Dylan was still sitting beside the bed, but he looked up when she entered.

"I can't believe he's really back," he said in a soft voice, running a finger down the boy's arm. "I forgot how small he is."

"He's beautiful," she said. He looked like an angel, long brown lashes grazing his cheeks, mouth pink and relaxed.

"I've missed out on a lot of his life. I worked a lot, and because Wanda didn't want me to know that something was wrong with him, she kept him from me even when I was home. She always made excuses why I couldn't see him. And I believed her."

"Why wouldn't you? She was his mother."

"It's still my fault. It was easier to stay at work than to come home to a place that never felt like home. It only looked like a home, and that's all I thought I cared about." After a moment, he said, "Come on. I'll get you some clothes and show you to the shower. Then I've got some calls to make."

Chloe took a shower in the master bathroom. She noticed that none of Dylan's things were in the bathroom, then remembered he'd moved into the guest bedroom. The bedroom was huge, with a sitting area and windows overlooking the bay. The bed was king-size, with a large built-in headboard. She sat down on the edge of the bed to finish towel-drying her hair, but ended up lying back for a moment. She imagined what it would be like to wake up next to Dylan in this room every morning. She wasn't sure if she'd fallen asleep or not, but she sensed that something had changed. She opened her eyes to find Dylan standing beside her, a soft smile on his face. "Thought you'd fallen asleep."

"Nearly." She quickly got up and smoothed out the wrinkles she'd created. "It's a nice room," she said, trying to cover her embarrassment.

He shrugged. "I haven't slept in here for months. I miss waking up to the view."

"Is that all you miss?" she asked, instantly wishing she could take back the words.

He traced a drop of water from her cheek down her collarbone to the top of the towel she had wrapped around her. "I miss sex, of course, but not sex with Wanda, if that's what you're asking. I'm not sure she ever liked it. I think she endured it because she thought she had to fit protocol."

How awful, how terrible, she thought, but she held back any expression of sympathy. "But there must have been . . . others, then. A man wouldn't . . . couldn't . . ."

He was already shaking his head. "Cheating wasn't an option. But to be honest, I never met anyone who tempted me. Or tempted me enough, anyway. And I didn't have time to cheat. I didn't want to develop a reputation for messing around with my clients either."

"I'll bet you were a lady killer in school, though."

His mouth tilted in a half smile. "Yeah, all the girls

loved the son of the crazy woman in town." At her expression, he added, "I did okay in college."

"Okay, no details, please."

His gaze swept slowly down her towel-clad body. "You'd better get dressed. I'm going to take a shower now, if you'll keep an eye on Teddy."

"Did you make your calls?"

"Some of them. I called Yochem and Camilla. I told my assistant Jodie that I wouldn't be in for a few days. Do you want to call your aunts?"

"I probably should."

Dylan handed her the portable phone and left. A few minutes later she heard his shower start. She changed into one of Wanda's flannel nightgowns and a pair of socks. She wished she had her yellow silk jammies. The gown made her look like a tent sale, and wearing Dylan's dead wife's clothing wasn't exactly on her top ten wardrobe fashion list.

She headed back to Teddy's room but paused outside the door to Dylan's. Placing her hand against the wood door, she caught herself picturing that magnificent body beneath the hot water. If only she knew where she stood with him. He probably didn't know either. She had to keep in mind that he'd be grateful to her and not to mix that up with anything else.

She continued down the hall and peeked in on Teddy. He'd turned on his side and curled up in the fetal position. She was still leaning in the doorway when Dylan returned. He was wearing white cotton pants and had a towel slung over his shoulders. He smelled like shampoo and freshly washed male, and Chloe had to stop herself from inhaling. He winced when he took in the nightgown.

"Bring back bad memories?" she ventured.

"Yes. She wore those things to bed from the day we got married."

She whispered, "I can take it off if you want."

His eyes got dark and liquid, and he tugged on the string tied at her neck. He trailed his finger from the hollow of her throat to her chin, tilting her head up. His hand cradled her face with one hand, and he rubbed his thumb up and down her cheek. All the while he looked at her as though savoring the sight of her. Like a blind man, he touched every curve on her face and then ran his fingers softly over her mouth. She could hardly breathe. All of her energy went into absorbing each touch. The chill vanished, leaving behind a misty heat.

"Thank you, Chloe," he whispered. "For not giving up. I don't know what I could ever do to repay you."

"You don't have to repay me." *Just love me,* a voice urged. But she didn't want his love as repayment. "You don't owe me anything."

He took a step back and tugged on her gown. She followed his lead, moving toward him again. He very gently kissed her, and then his mouth parted, and he deepened the kiss. His breathing quickened, but he pulled away to undo the ribbons. He paused to kiss her again, as though he couldn't go for more than a few seconds without his mouth on hers.

They did this through the doorway of the room next to Teddy's, all the way to the bed. This was where Dylan slept, Chloe thought. Maybe Wanda had never slept with him in here.

The cascading sound of thunder matched the booming of her heartbeat. The light spilled in from the adjacent bathroom, which still smelled of soap. The bed wasn't as large as the one in his master bedroom, but it was big enough.

He undid the tiny buttons down the front of her maidenly gown, building the anticipation with each one. Then he slid it off her shoulders, leaving his hands on her bare skin as the gown slid to the floor. She wore nothing beneath it, and he took in her body as a hungry man takes in food.

She knew hungry. She felt it down to her core. Only this man stirred her so. She pulled the towel from his shoulders and dropped it on the floor. Then she untied the string at his waist and pulled down his cotton pants.

He kissed her as though he were savoring her. Her body was alive with fire, and she arched to feel his skin against hers and the slight fuzz of his hair. He made a growling sound deep in his throat before nibbling her throat and ear. She shivered, feeling the impact of that nibbling right down to her curled toes. His fingers slid up into her hair, and his other hand roamed down the sides of her breasts.

He touched her everywhere. Not like some men, who only touched the parts that they thought mattered. His palm skimmed down her ribs and over her stomach. It didn't seem to matter that it wasn't hard and flat. His fingers swirled over the soft flesh as though she were perfect. He trailed down to the ridge between her thigh and pubic area, and then grazed the soft skin of her inner thighs.

She touched him, when she wasn't too distracted by his touches. He *was* perfect, hard and firm. Even if he was the man she could never have, he felt so right. Her hands hungrily roamed over his shoulders and across his chest. Smooth skin, defined muscles. She ran her fingers over his ridged stomach, brushing against his maleness. He sucked in a breath and slid his hands up into her wet hair, tilting her head back and sating some of his hunger with her mouth.

He inched them backward until the back of her knees touched the bed. With his arms around her, he lowered her to the plum bedspread. And then he started kissing her all over. Not just the erotic zones, but odd places that sent a jolt of electricity through her, like beneath her breast, her belly button, and the inside of her elbow. Then he concentrated on the erotic zones, and oh, boy, she couldn't think about anything. All it took was a touch of his finger, and she was gone. She tangled her fingers in his hair and arched her body toward him. But he didn't stop. He kept teasing her until, to her amazement, she went over the edge again.

When she came back down to earth, he was leaving a trail of moist kisses across her stomach. When she could breathe again, she whispered, "Oh, my. . . ."

He leaned to the side and opened one of the nightstand drawers. "I apologize for forgetting my manners last time," he said with a sheepish expression on his face, holding up a condom package. "I wasn't in my right mind. This time I want everything to be right."

Her heart leapt at that. Last time he needed her, though he wouldn't admit that. This time he wanted her. To celebrate Teddy's return.

"Everything is right," she whispered. "It's perfect. Here, let me," she said, taking it from him. She hadn't done this often, but she tore open the packet with her teeth and pulled out the condom. She rather liked the way he sucked in a breath every time she ran her finger over that sensitive ridge at the top.

"I'll never make it if you keep doing that," he said on a ragged breath, taking the condom from her and rolling it down over the length of him.

In one quick move, he was hovering over her again, kissing her mouth crazy. She slid her legs up and around him, then guided him inside. When he filled her, she felt complete for the first time in her life. More confirmation that this was where she belonged.

She held on tight, feeling his muscles moving as he slid back and forth. He was large enough to fill her completely, sending little shock waves every time he pressed against her center. Those shock waves built until she was sure she would explode from the pressure.

And then she did.

She felt herself shoot right up into the stars. She saw the rings of Saturn and the moons of Jupiter. She touched Orion's Belt as she flew by. Then she rode a shooting star back down to earth . . . just in time to catch his ascent. His mouth came down hard on hers. And because he kept moving inside her, she went with him.

Chapter Twenty-three

IT TOOK CHLOE A LONG TIME TO GO TO SLEEP, DESPITE THE fact that she was dead tired, satisfied, and snuggled into Dylan's arms. And completely happy. Every once in a while he'd squeeze her a little tighter. She wanted to believe he was doing it because he wanted her even closer. But he was asleep, and probably dreaming.

She hated this insecurity. Sure, she'd felt insecure with Ross sometimes, but he didn't matter. Dylan was totally different. She was sure she would die if he didn't love her.

So much for the strong, independent female theory.

She was so wrong for him, and this was the wrong time of his life for her to even think about being part of it. He was now a single father with a special-needs son. The last thing he needed was a woman in his life. *But if he can accept Teddy,* a hopeful voice added, *he can accept you.*

Lying in the darkness, the other fear crowded in too. That he'd only made love with her out of gratitude. *No, don't go there, don't think about that.* Hadn't he thanked her just before making love to her? How could she be so physically close to a man and feel so far away from him at the same time?

All that matters is that Teddy is home safe and sound. Let the rest take care of itself.

She was also chilled. Even with all the heat Dylan put off, she was still fighting the shivers.

Early in the morning she wandered down the hall to check on Teddy. Still safe and sound, though he'd thrown the covers off sometime during the night. She rearranged them, then leaned down and kissed his cheek. He smelled like sweat and salt. She smoothed his hair back and returned to bed. Later, she thought she felt Dylan get up and check on Teddy too. And finally, she sank into a deep, dark sleep.

When she woke, she felt drugged. She was still cold and shivering. Dylan wasn't in bed, and she wondered if he'd ever come back after looking in on his son.

Sunlight poured through a crack between the designer curtains, and she struggled to turn and look at the clock on the headboard. Ten-thirty! She shoved out of bed and went to the bathroom, grimacing at her reflection. Her hair was sticking up all over from sleeping on it wet. Her skin was pale, her eyes red.

After brushing her teeth with Dylan's toothbrush, washing her face, and taming her hair, she realized she had no clothes to change into. She started to put on the nightgown that was rumpled on the floor, then smiled. Dylan had left three outfits on the dresser. She chose the pink dress, naturally, happy to find it was loose on her.

You're not competing against Wanda. You're competing against the kind of woman who fits into his life. A woman who comes from a normal family and a normal town and isn't connected with supernatural visions.

She peered into Teddy's room, but he wasn't there. Voices floated out from the living area.

"There's our hero," a woman said as Chloe walked into the family room.

A smattering of applause filled the room, and Chloe stopped to take it in. The lush blonde was Jodie from Dylan's office. She was sitting on the floor near Teddy, who was eating an egg sandwich. Dylan was sitting on the couch next to her, and Camilla was in the kitchen. Two other men were sitting on the other couch.

Jodie got up, walked over, and gave Chloe a hug. "You did a great thing. Wish I would have thought of it. Though I wouldn't have been as brave as to swim in the bay naked."

Chloe could only say, "Thanks. I wouldn't call it brave. Crazy, maybe."

"Crazy and brave."

Teddy smiled up at her, though he wasn't quite looking at her. At least he looked happy and content. Dylan led her over to the couch.

"This is Chloe, the woman who saved my son. Chloe, this is my senior architect, Steve Ritter."

More of that gratitude.

Steve stood and took her hand. "A real honor to meet you." He was an attractive man in his fifties with thin brown hair.

"And this is Dave Wahlberg, an, er—"

"I'm his archenemy," he cut in, standing to shake her hand. He was a well-built blond about Dylan's age with a nice smile. "We've been rivals since our University of Miami days. He won the mayor's house from me, but I won Gloria Estefan's Miami mansion from him. Though I ended up with Kraft Theater on the rebound. Now that Dylan's going to be a busy father, I'm trying to convince him to join forces with me. We could rule Naples." He squeezed Chloe's hand before letting go. "You're one wild lady, but you get things done. I like that."

She turned to Dylan. "You gave up Kraft Theater?"

"That was the first shift in my priorities. I have a few other in mind too."

He caught her gaze for a moment, his brown eyes shining at . . . could she believe a future? She dared not hope.

Jodie, oblivious to the silent exchange, said, "I hear

the Krafts are asking that Ross be removed from the project. Some question about his ethics."

"Really?" Dylan asked.

Her eyes twinkled. "Could be they heard about what a jerk Ross was, trying to use Teddy's disappearance to make himself look good. Could be it kind of slipped when I was talking to Andy Kraft. His computer maintenance company does, after all, handle our network."

Camilla brought Teddy a plate of Cheez Whiz after he'd finished his egg sandwich. No crackers, just the coils of cheese. She shrugged, giving Chloe a smile. "He likes it, what can I say?"

Chloe sat down beside him and watched him poke his finger into the orange goo. He scooped some up and stuck it in his mouth. "Yum," Chloe said.

"Yum," he parroted.

"I've got an appointment with Dr. Jacobs later today," Dylan told her. "We're going to set up a visit with the Dan Marino Center in Weston for a full diagnosis and treatment plan." He looked at his son. "I'm going to make sure no one looks at him with pity. He's going to fit in."

An ache started in her chest, but she ignored it. *Nothing's wrong. Nothing.*

As they talked, Camilla fielded calls from acquaintances and well-wishers. Yochem had already been by. She realized she was sitting near Dylan's feet and remembered Lena's comment about Chloe always having done that.

Crazy, isn't that what Dave had called her? No, he'd called her wild.

Dave stood and stretched. "Well, I'd better get going, leave you time alone with your son."

Steve took the cue. "Me too. Someone's gotta run the place," he added with a wink.

Dylan was looking at Teddy. "Some things are more important than work."

Chloe got a chill at those words. If only they were meant for her as well. *They're not, so don't even think it, don't go there at all.*

"I never thought I'd hear you say that," Dave said.

"Talk about a wake-up call on priorities. It's not going to be easy, but I've got to change. Teddy needs me."

And who do you need, Dylan McKain?

No one. No way, nohow. The ache was spreading. The flu, maybe. No, something Dylan had said.

"Think about merging. That would solve some of the problem. You'd have more time at home," Dave said.

"I will."

Chloe stayed with Teddy while the four walked to the front door. She heard another woman's voice outside greeting Dylan warmly. "I'm Susan Carter. You probably don't know me, but I live three streets over. My husband—excuse me, ex-husband—borrowed your boat last year to tow his back."

"Oh, yeah, I remember."

The rest of the group departed, leaving Dylan alone with the woman.

"I came by to tell you how glad I am that Teddy's home. I've been following the story, praying, lighting candles. I have a little girl, and I know how it would feel to have her lost like that. The reason I came over is because I'd know exactly how you feel. My Emily is autistic too. If you have a little time, I'd like to talk to you about it. I've been there, and I've fought the system to get autistic programs in place at the schools. I wanted to tell you what's available for Teddy. Emily's six now, and she's in the Vineyards Elementary School autism program. I can't begin to tell you how much progress she's made."

Dylan led her into the family room. Susan was in her early thirties, attractive—no, downright beautiful—and well dressed. Her tiny waist was emphasized by a wide belt. She had blond shoulder-length hair that swished when she walked.

"I know you too," she said, extending her hand. "You were something else." She turned to Dylan. "I know I couldn't have swam in that cold, yucky water."

Chloe took her limp hand and tried her best to smile. "I did what I had to do. I didn't think about the yucky water." Well, she had, but not much.

Susan gave her a smile that was a bit too sweet. "Well, you're from Lilithdale. You people probably swim naked in that water all the time." She sat down on the floor on the other side of Teddy as comfortably as though she lived there.

"Does he greet?" she asked Dylan.

"Greet?"

"Does he say hello or acknowledge you when he first sees you?" She studied Teddy, though he was interested in Chloe's butterfly ring. "Yes, I recognize that look in his eyes. Wait until I tell you how much progress these kids can make. It is so exciting."

Dylan took a seat between the women. "Tell me."

Susan launched into a long explanation of what autism was and what it could be. "What's hard to get used to is how they sometimes act up in public. When Emily throws a temper, as we call it, the best thing to do is ignore her. The looks people give you, like you're a bad parent. The problem with autistic children is they don't look handicapped. It's not like you can educate everyone or put a sign on them."

She told him how she'd gone from doctor to doctor, each telling her she was overreacting. At every other sentence, she touched Dylan's arm. "So then I met with the mayor—"

"You know McCormick?" Dylan asked.

"Corky's an old friend of the family's. You know him?"

"I designed his house."

"Oh, it's beautiful! I'd love a house like that. Well, anyway, I didn't jump in water." She gave Chloe another artificial smile. "But I did nag Corky until he dug into the problem. I'm kind of a hero in my own right."

Blah, blah, blah. Chloe couldn't blame Dylan for listening intently to Susan. He wanted to learn more about his son's disorder. She really couldn't blame Susan either. She'd found someone to teach, someone to share her pain and triumphs. That he happened to be successful, gorgeous, great in bed—Chloe blinked at that thought. Not that Susan knew that.

The real problem was that Susan fit into Dylan's world. They ran in the same circles, lived only a few blocks away from each other, and they each had an autistic child. The ache now vibrated through her chest. Not that she had any claim on Dylan. He'd made love to her, yes, but once out of grief, and once to thank her.

Chloe's sniffle caught his attention. "I think I may have caught a cold from my little adventure last night."

Susan held out her hand as though Chloe had just crawled out of the yucky water. "Don't come near me! I've just gotten over the worst cold of my life after catching it from Emily. If I go through that again, I swear I'll die. Having a cold is no fun without someone there to baby you through it." She cleared her throat. "Emily has had marvelous success with music therapy. It's based on the theory that music connects everyone. The kids learn to communicate through the songs."

Chloe walked to the bathroom to blow her nose, feeling heavier with each step. And frumpier. So what if she didn't have dainty feet with polished toenails? And a size-two figure? One look in the mirror, and Chloe knew why Susan had held out her hand. Further, she was surprised Susan hadn't done that at first sight of her. She imagined the heroine in a Frankenstein movie screaming to ward off the monster. That's what Susan should have done.

"What am I doing here?" she asked her bedraggled reflection.

She walked to the master bedroom, where she grabbed her bag after a long, wistful look at that wondrous bed.

Susan's voice wafted from the living room before Chloe even walked back in. "We can help each other out. If you need to get out, I can watch Teddy. And vice versa. It's so hard to find help that understands our kind of children. I think the kids'll play well together too. I'll bet Emily could teach Teddy a lot. And they'd understand each other because they're in the same boat," she said, emphasizing that with another touch to his arm.

Was she talking about the kids or the parents? By the twinkle in the woman's eyes, probably both.

Dylan looked up when Chloe entered the room. He came to his feet when he saw her bag slung over her shoulder.

"Where are you going?"

"I . . ." She looked away for a moment, not wanting him to see the pain. Damned tenderness. "I'd better go. I never did call my aunts, and they'll probably want to hear all the details. And I need to feed the animals, you know how Shakespeare is." She tried to inject some humor into that.

Before Dylan could respond, she walked over to Teddy and held out her palm. He pressed his palm against it. That simple touch filled her with such joy, she had to blink away the tears.

"Wow," Susan said. "He likes to touch. Maybe getting him to hug won't be too hard."

Chloe quickly circumvented the couch and headed to the door.

"Good-bye, Chloe," Camilla said, surprising her with the warmth in her voice. And the sympathy in her expression.

Dylan was suddenly beside her, holding on to her arm. "You don't have to leave," he said in a low voice that shivered up her spine.

"Yeah . . . I do. I'll check in from time to time, see how Teddy's doing." Again she had to look away. The ache was throbbing . . . and now she knew why.

"Chloe, don't leave."

"Dylan, I know you want what's best for Teddy. But do him a favor. Don't try to make him fit your idea of a normal kid and then tell yourself it's for his sake. Some people . . . can't be fit into that mold. Accept him for what he is. That's what's important. Good-bye, Dylan," she said in a thick voice. Then she turned and left. She might be tender and quirky—and that was all right, she realized. But she'd never change who she was, not for Dylan or for Lilithdale.

With every step to her car, she felt her insides break apart. It was better this way, that she leave before he could tell her there simply wasn't a place in his life for her. Better that, for once, she be the one to walk away.

DYLAN WATCHED her leave, a feeling of helplessness shadowing him. There was something final about that good-bye. He wasn't sure what he was going to do with her—he had too much going on to think about that. But he wasn't ready to let her go yet.

"Something wrong?" Susan asked from behind him.

He could follow Chloe, but she obviously wanted to be alone. He turned to Susan. "Will Teddy ever be . . . normal?"

"He'll probably be able to function independently in society, but he'll always be different. When you realize your child is autistic, you give up one set of dreams and build another. Chloe's right. You can't make him fit 'normal.' "

He nodded. "I appreciate you stopping over, but I think Teddy needs a little quiet time. I haven't been alone with him since . . . well, for a long time."

"Sure, I understand." She took his hand in her cool, manicured one. "I'm here if you need me. Only a few streets away. Here's a card with my phone number on it. I know it's a tough time for you. I can be an ear to listen, a shoulder to cry on . . . or anything else you might need."

She gave him a meaningful look and walked to the front door. One last look, a toss of that obnoxious dyed hair, and out she went.

"Brother, what a come-on," Camilla said, bringing Teddy another plate of Cheez Whiz. "You're going to get a lot of that, I bet."

"What do you mean?"

"You're available, good-looking, successful . . . why not?"

Dylan made a face. He didn't want to be a list of statistics on a find-a-date application. He wasn't even sure he wanted a relationship. But if he did . . .

Chloe's beautiful face flashed through his mind.

"Susan's not my type."

"Really? I thought she'd be perfectly your type. Got her own money, probably, chock-full'a charm, pretty . . ." Her lip went up. "Thin."

Another list for the find-a-date application. "Too thin, too pretty, too charming." But he realized that's what Wanda had been. On the outside, anyway. "I don't want to think about that right now."

"Or maybe you like another type of woman now," Camilla said with a mischievous twinkle in her eye.

This time the memory was of holding Chloe in his arms. Waking up to find she was real and not a dream, squeezing her just to make sure.

"Chloe's not my type either."

"She might not be," Camilla said, leaning on the counter. "But she's no nutcase. I'm afraid I misjudged her. She's one tough lady."

Chloe, a tough lady? That was the paradox of her. She was tender . . . and she was strong.

He sat down next to Teddy, who had found some stray Legos and was constructing something that looked vaguely like a building. Teddy didn't look up at him the way he'd looked at Chloe. Dylan put out his palm, but Teddy ignored it, standing up and saying, "She she."

"What's she she?"

Teddy climbed up on the table next to the fish tank and plucked out a goldfish. Before Dylan could make a move, Teddy popped it into his mouth.

"Told you he liked to do that," Camilla said at Dylan's grimace.

"Wait a minute. That's how he survived out there. He caught fish."

Teddy tried to snag another one, but Dylan grabbed

him around the waist and brought him back to the Legos. He brought out the rest of the set too.

"I'm going to do some laundry," Camilla said. "I'll catch the phone if it rings, but I won't hear the door."

She was being discreet, he supposed, giving him time alone with his son.

His son.

Teddy looked enough like him that no one would ever guess he wasn't his biological son. Dark hair, anyway. Curls like Chloe's, though for some reason they'd been cut.

"Do you know who I am?" he asked Teddy.

Teddy didn't look up at him. Remembering how Chloe had communicated with him, he started picking up Lego blocks.

"One, two, three."

Teddy didn't repeat them as he'd done with Chloe. For some reason, he'd connected with her.

"I'm your dad," he said. "Daddy."

Nothing.

He and Teddy sat on the floor for an hour, making their separate Lego creations.

Building new dreams.

CHLOE DROVE directly to her aunts' cottage. Marilee was there too, toying with a glass of green liquid. They were sitting out on the screened-in back porch playing cards, though the cards looked abandoned, since none of the ladies were actually facing the table.

"There you are!" Stella said, coming to her feet when Chloe walked around the corner. "We thought you'd died or something."

"Or something," Chloe affirmed, stepping inside but remaining by the door. She wrapped her arms around herself, hating the awkwardness she felt. "I meant to call you last night, but I was too exhausted."

"Sure, we understand," Stella said. What their eyes said was, *We know you were too busy making love to call.*

Lena sat there looking dignified in her upswept hair. The blank look on her aunt's face, neither love nor anger, sent a sharp jab through Chloe's stomach.

Chloe dropped down to the floor. "I'm sorry about everything. I know I've caused you a lot of pain and aggravation. But it's over." She forced finality into that word. "Totally over."

"Even with the fella?" Marilee asked.

"Yes, even with him. Hey, I don't need a man in my life, right?" *Hadn't you decided no more trying to fit in? Yes, but I'm not ready yet.*

Stella crossed her arms in front of her chest and shook her head. Her zebra-striped hair bow shimmied with the movement. "Maybe *we* don't, but who do you think you're fooling?"

Chloe winced. "What are you talking about?"

"The frog prince, for one thing," Marilee said. "Yeah, we seen it. You think you can hide anything from us?"

Chloe felt her cheeks flush. "Silly me."

"We seen a green leg sticking out of your chaise lounge once," Marilee said. "Wondered what the heck it was."

Chloe uttered a sheepish, "Oh."

"Plus," Stella said, "you are so head over that man, it hurts to look at you."

"Head over," Marilee agreed.

Chloe dipped her chin. "Because I'm tender?"

"Because you're you," Stella said, taking Chloe's hands.

"Tender," Marilee agreed.

"All right. I'm head over him so bad, it hurts to look at myself. And I do want him in my life—but he . . . he doesn't fit in my life, and I don't fit in his. So there. Now I'm a total pariah in Lilithdale. Maybe I shouldn't have stayed here so long. I certainly never belonged here."

"Why not?" Marilee asked, looking genuinely perplexed.

"Because I'm not strong like you all are. I want a man in my life. And I'm disabled. And tender. Isn't that enough? Look, I don't need to stand here and alienate myself even more. I'm drained."

"But we want to hear about the boy," Marilee said as Chloe turned to leave.

"He's going to be okay. I'll tell you all about it later. I need to be alone now."

"Want some pickle soup to take back with you?" Marilee asked. "I've got a whole batch in the fridge."

Chloe tried to make her grimace a smile. "Marilee, I . . . I don't like pickle soup. I'm sorry, but I never did."

"Told you," Stella said.

"I only made it because you said you liked it."

"I only said I liked it because you made it for me."

"Told you," Stella said again.

"Well, good night," Chloe said, backing out the door.

"That's it?" Stella said, coming to her feet. "You're going to give up, just like that?"

"Yeah, you're a fighter," Marilee said.

Chloe paused on the step going down. "I'm tired of fighting. For once, I want someone to fight for me."

THAT NIGHT Dylan gave in to his urge and called Chloe. There was no answer, but he felt better just hearing her voice on the message. "Hey, it's Dylan. I just called to say . . . hi. Dr. Jacobs ran a full battery of tests today, and Teddy's in good shape. I thought you'd want to know. You looked a little, I don't know . . . something, when you left. I wanted to make sure you were all right. Call me."

He thought about what Susan had said. Teddy would always be special, different. A man who wanted to blend into the woodwork might consider an autistic son a curse. But it didn't bother him. It really didn't. He loved that kid, so he'd accept it.

He felt a decided emptiness lying in bed without Chloe in his arms. *Face it: You need that woman. You need her in your arms and in your life and to hold her through the night and never let her go.* He ran his hands over his face. It was true. His soul ached for her the same way it had that night he'd thought Teddy was dead. Not for sex. For her. What an idiot he'd been. To punish himself, he replayed the scene through his mind when he'd walked away from her. She'd been telling him the truth, and he'd been too dense to see it.

But he saw it now.

She'd taught him to believe in miracles. Taught him to believe again. God hadn't only brought her back for Teddy. Chloe's mission was to teach Dylan to love, to know what was important.

Then why had she walked away and said good-bye like it meant forever? He let out a groan as he replayed the conversation with Susan. The woman had waltzed in and fit into his world. That's when Chloe had crumbled. He could see it now, in her expression, in the way she'd retreated. He'd been too dense to realize it at the time.

All Chloe wanted was to be accepted, and when he'd said he wanted Teddy to fit in, she thought he'd make her change too. But he didn't want her to change. He loved her just the way she was.

He loved her.

And he was going to bring her back where she belonged: in his arms.

Chapter Twenty-four

THE PLAN HAD HATCHED IN DYLAN'S MIND DURING THE long, restless night. He wanted to throw a big bash in honor of everyone who had helped search for Teddy. He would invite the police, the Coast Guard, all the boaters who supported Chloe that night, and even the press.

Wanda had tried to hide their son from everyone. Dylan wanted everyone to see him, the good and the bad.

First thing the next morning, he called Chloe. She still didn't answer, but he left a message for her to call him right away. The next call went to one of his friends who owned a piece of vacant property on the beach—the perfect spot for a party. As soon as Camilla arrived, he put her to work making arrangements for the food and tent while he called and invited everyone he could think of.

The party would take place Sunday afternoon. He was sure it was the fastest-assembled party of its size, but because of the occasion, everyone cooperated.

Well, not everyone. He still hadn't heard from the guest of honor. He called her again, and this time she answered.

"Chloe, I've been worried about you," he said before he could think about it. "And then you didn't return my calls. Are you all right?"

"I've got a bit of a cold, but I'll live." She sniffled, reminding him of the doleful look she'd had on her face when Susan had shunned her at the mention of a cold. Just the thought of it made him want to pull Chloe into his arms.

Which was rather difficult, since she wasn't there.

I don't just want you or love you, Chloe. I need you. In my home and my life. I want to see all your faces and I want to make up names for new ones. The words wanted to burst out, but he couldn't tell her over the phone.

"Are you there?" she asked.

"Mm? Yeah, I'm here."

"How's Teddy?"

"He's doing okay. But he misses you." *And I miss you.* The ache of need wasn't terrifying; it was sweet and warm. She hadn't let him down; he'd let her down.

"How do you know that?"

He had to clear the hoarseness from his voice. "Because he keeps pointing at your picture in the paper."

"Oh." He could clearly imagine the smile on her face at that because he heard it in her voice. "I miss him too."

"Good, because you're going to see him tomorrow."

"I really can't—"

"You have to. I'm throwing a party, and you're the guest of honor."

"Me?" she croaked.

"Yes. I'm celebrating Teddy's return and having a little get-together in appreciation of everyone who helped search for him. Since you found him, that makes you the guest of honor."

"No, I really can't."

"Do I have to come down there—"

"No, don't do that! I'm not feeling up to it, that's all. You have your get-together. Have a drink for me."

"Chloe . . ."

"Look, I don't belong in that crowd."

"Of course you belong." He remembered her words about the tunnel being the first place she really belonged. But she was wrong. Where she really belonged was with him. But he wasn't about to say that over the phone. He was going to have to prove it to her in a big way.

"Just come tomorrow."

"No, I'm not putting myself through that. Look, I appreciate your appreciation. You've already shown me how grateful you are, believe me. But I think the best thing for both of us is to end this here. I can't give you what you want and you can't give me what I want, and frankly, it would hurt too much to just be friends. I'm being honest with myself these days and with everyone else. I need a man in my life who will accept me for who I am, a man who needs me and isn't afraid to express it. I won't settle for anything less."

He started to spill it all out, but held his tongue. He tried another tactic. "What about Teddy?"

Chloe paused, but held strong. "He'll get attached to Susan. I'm sure . . . you'll all be very happy. It's a perfect situation. She's perfect."

He couldn't believe how stubborn she was being. Didn't she want to see him? Or Teddy?

A realization slapped him hard. *She* was putting up a wall. He should have recognized that wall; hadn't he erected the same one over and over? And didn't that make him the expert on breaking it down?

"All right. If that's what you want—"

"It is," she said too quickly. "But thanks for the invitation. Tell everyone I said thanks. Good-bye, Dylan."

Her voice had gotten oddly pitched at the end of her speech, and he could have sworn he heard tears in her throat. Why was she crying if she was the one saying good-bye? And this time he couldn't be mistaken. That's exactly what it was. Final, forever.

He dropped down on the couch and looked at his son.

The article was tucked beneath Teddy's knee as he sat on the floor and dipped Goldfish crackers into his Cheez Whiz. The ache of relief at having his son back was shadowed by an ache of loss. Something was missing.

Chloe.

He laughed. He wasn't grateful. Well, he was, but that wasn't the only reason he wanted to see her. He wanted . . . wanted . . . just wanted her. If he could hold her in his arms, everything else would fit into place.

He sobered, realizing what she meant. She thought he'd made love to her out of gratitude.

"Oh, jeez," he muttered, running his fingers through his hair. That's what he'd told her just before he'd started last night's lovemaking.

He needed her in his arms and in his life. For the first time, he'd held a woman and not wanted to let her go. Ever. Holding her through the night meant something. He didn't want to be Ross a year from now, lamenting how he'd lost the one woman who had touched his soul because she didn't fit the image. It was true, Chloe didn't fit the image he'd created for his life. Neither did Teddy. So he'd re-create the image. He was an architect. If anyone could rebuild a dream, he could.

"All right, Chloe. You want to play tough, we'll play tough."

And then he picked up the phone to call in one last favor.

CHLOE WAS still in bed when Stella and Marilee knocked on the door the next day at eleven. If she ignored them, maybe they'd go away.

They didn't.

"Isn't it illegal to break into someone's house when they're asleep?" Chloe said as Stella tugged off the sheets and blankets and Marilee pulled her across the bed by her feet.

"Not when you have a key," Stella said, holding up the blasted key she'd given her.

"And if you're related. I'm pretty sure that's an exception," Marilee added. Her lime-green pantsuit was enough to wake Chloe up without the benefit of coffee.

Chloe rolled her eyes. "All right, what do you want? You both look way too cheery for this early on a Sunday morning."

"It's not early, in case you hadn't noticed," Stella said.

"I'm moping. I'm entitled to sleep in."

"Hogwash. You're coming with us. You can't mope around the house all day."

Once Stella got her out of bed, Marilee pushed her toward the shower.

"Where are we going?"

"We're taking you to the Day Spa of Naples," Marilee said. "Nice massage to get the blood flowing. I even scheduled you with Eduardo. You know, the one with the fingers."

"They all have fingers, Gram," Chloe said as the cold shower blasted her fully awake.

"Yeah, but he's got magic fingers."

"Then we're going to take you to lunch someplace special."

"Does this mean you forgive me for being such a bitch yesterday, and all the days before that?" Chloe asked when she got out a few minutes later.

"Nothing to forgive," Marilee said, holding out a towel. "You did what you had to do to save that boy's life. How can we fault you that?"

"I didn't have to fall in love with his father, though," she said sheepishly.

"Yeah, you did. It was fate."

Stella grabbed the hair dryer and fluffed Chloe's hair as she got dressed in shorts and a tank top. "Fate? Hah!"

"Listen, there's something you got wrong," Stella said. "We never said *you* couldn't want a man in your life. That's *our* philosophy; we don't push it on anyone else."

"I figured it was one more thing that made me not fit in."

"First of all, you do need a man in your life. It's your fate. I could have told you that years ago." At Chloe's surprised expression, she said, "I didn't know you were hiding it."

"Oh. And second?"

"*You* were the only one who thought you didn't fit in. Nobody cares if you don't have any abilities. We love you anyway. You're the one who always stayed at the outer edge, excluding yourself."

Chloe's eyes widened. "Why didn't you tell me?"

"I figured you'd realize it when you were ready. Now, are you ready?"

"Well, now that you've told me—"

"No, I mean to go to Naples. Our appointments are in forty minutes. We've got to hustle."

"What about my being tender?"

"Nothing wrong with that. Heck, we're all tender; we just have tougher hides," Marilee said.

Chloe dabbed on a bit of makeup, then remembered her face would be fitted into that padded donut thing and it would all come off anyway.

Because her aunts only had a golf cart for transportation, Chloe drove. "Lena's not coming, is she?"

Stella and Marilee got silent for a moment. "No, she had things to do."

"Is that why we're going to Naples instead of her place?"

"Nah, we just need a change of scenery. And besides, she don't have any men," Stella added with a raised eyebrow.

"She's never going to forgive me, is she?"

"It might take a while," Marilee conceded. "You know how stubborn she can get. When we were kids, I dyed her hair with food coloring. Experimenting, you see, for a school dance. Came out fluorescent orange. Took her years to forgive me. Ah, don't you worry. You've got us until she comes 'round."

Chloe gave them each a hug, so grateful to have them back.

"Oh, I've got one quick stop to make," Stella said. "It'll only take a minute. There's a woman I've got to see, lives down near the beach."

"Is that the one with the incontinent poodle?" Marilee asked.

"The very. Sheila something-or-another. I met the woman once, a real gem, that one. Spoiled, bitter, thinks-the-world-revolves-around-her type. She sent her son to bring the dog to me. That dog told me every time it does anything wrong, Sheila kicks it. I'm going to tell her so and that I don't work with brutes."

"You tell her, Stella," Chloe said.

Chloe followed Stella's directions down to the old-money side of Naples. Huge mansions lined the street to the right with the beach as their back yards. The sun shone brilliantly, and she began to feel a tiny bit better. Until Dylan crept into her mind.

"Something's going on up there," Chloe said, slowing down with the traffic. Cars were lined up and down the street. "Must be a huge party. Look, they have valet parking! How ridiculous. There's even a television crew here. Someone famous must be there. Or someone infamous."

As she neared the man directing traffic, he slowed her to a stop and opened her door. "Have a good time."

Chloe laughed. "No, you've got it all wrong. I don't belong there."

She was more confused when Stella and Marilee hopped out of the car and came around to her side. "Oh, yes, you do." They pulled her out before she could even think to protest.

"Dylan's party! Is this the party for Teddy?" she said as they ushered her to a vacant lot that had been set up for a no-holds-barred party. "I can't believe I didn't see this coming."

"You didn't want to stop us, that's why you didn't see it," Marilee explained. "Your Higher Self knew all about it, but it also knew you wanted to be here."

People were laughing and drinking and eating. Slabs of ribs smoked on huge grills and filled the air with delectable aromas. A couple people she recognized from her naked protest waved at her or patted her shoulder. Will McKain lifted a plate of food to her in salute. Her heart was already beating faster at just the prospect of seeing Dylan, and her eyes were already seeking him out.

"Did he do this? Orchestrate my kidnapping, I mean?" Her heart sang at the prospect, but she hushed it with the fact that this party was only more of his gratitude.

"Yep. He called Lena last night, and she put me on the phone. He said since he went down to the Keys with you at her request, he was calling in the favor."

"We would have dragged you out of bed anyway," Marilee threw in. "But he gave us a better reason."

"It's your party, Chloe. You can't not be here."

"I wish I'd dressed better. And put more makeup on!" she said, slapping her cheek. Spotting Susan didn't help matters any.

"You look great, hon. Besides, I don't think it matters to Dylan."

She followed Stella's gaze to the man who put the beat in her heart. He wore white shorts and a blue shirt, and his eyes fairly sparkled as he met her gaze. The tallest, most handsome man there walked over to her. He nodded to his right, and a television crew carried their equipment over and aimed it at him. She started to move away, but he caught her arm and pulled her against him.

"This is our guest of honor, Chloe Samms." He turned her toward the camera. "She also happens to be the woman I want to marry." He turned to her then, not seeming to mind that her mouth was hanging open. It was a good thing he was holding on so tight, because she'd probably have crumpled to the sand. "The woman I want in my life. More importantly, the woman I need in my life. She not only saved my son's life, she taught me to believe in miracles . . . and in love." His fingers caressed her face as though he couldn't believe she was there. "You taught me that my priorities were all wrong, that love comes first." She could see that love in his eyes as he looked at her. Not a trick of the light this time. "I want to teach you that you belong wherever you are. That mostly, you belong with me." Then he kissed her, with everyone watching and the camera rolling. For a few minutes she forgot about all that, until he broke the kiss. "The open mouth—is that a yes?"

She clamped it shut, then muttered, "Are you crazy?"

"Certifiably. About you."

She whispered, "What will people think, you marrying the strange Lilithdale woman?"

He moved back a bit, head tilted. "What will people think, you marrying that idiot who didn't see love right in front of his eyes? Who almost lost it? You taught me something else too. That it's okay to be different. Promise me you'll never do anything just because you think I want you to. Don't be anything other than who you are." He gave her a pained expression. "Are you trying to make me suffer? I know I deserve it, but I'm a little too tender to be kept in suspense."

She felt shell-shocked. "What do you mean?"

"You haven't answered me yet."

She put her hands on his face the way he had with her. "You think I'm crazy? Of course I'll marry you!"

He squeezed her tight, and she'd never felt so loved in her life. After a minute, he pulled back. "You'll be marrying Teddy too, of course."

She grinned. "I already love that kid."

He turned to the crowd surrounding them. "She said yes!" Then he picked her up and spun her around until she was dizzy and giddy and totally free. She was laughing when he finally set her down again. After squeezing her against him, he turned her to the right.

First she saw Teddy, spinning around too. And beside him . . . Lena, with a tender expression on her serene face. She came forward and hugged Chloe.

"I'm so happy for you. I hope you'll forgive me for being so horrible to you. You have made me, Stella, Marilee, and everyone in Lilithdale so proud. And if you want to live in your house, you and Teddy and Dylan, we'll welcome you all with open arms."

She turned to Dylan, who squeezed her hand. "Happy?" he asked.

"I don't know how I could be any happier. I'm afraid I'm already illegal as it is."

"Don't lose your head," he whispered in her ear. "I want to finish a particular scene that involves you in a towel and wet clay."

She tilted her head back and smiled. "Oh, I believe I can arrange that."